MISERERE

AN AUTUMN TALE

Miserere

An Autumn Tale

Teresa Frohock

NIGHT SHADE BOOKS
SAN FRANCISCO

Cover art by Michael C. Hayes
Cover design by Rebecca Silvers
Interior layout and design by Amy Popovich

Edited by Jeremy Lassen

First Edition

Printed in Canada

ISBN: 978-1-59780-289-5

Night Shade Books
Please visit us on the web at
http://www.nightshadebooks.com

*Dedicated to my husband
and best friend
Dick Frohock*

PART I

Haunted by ill angels only…

—Edgar Allan Poe
"Dream-Land"

CHAPTER ONE

woerld in the sabbatical year 5873

Night shadows deepened when Lucian extinguished the candle beside his bed. The cry from beyond his chamber ended too soon for him to determine its source. He sat on the edge of his mattress and listened for the noise to repeat itself. The hearth fire crackled. The blaze saturated the room with heat, but Catarina forbade open windows. His twin sister was always cold.

Sweat crawled through his hair. He dared not move; he had no desire to draw attention to himself. The seconds ticked into minutes, but Lucian remained still.

Listening.

Sounds drifted upward from the room beneath his chamber. A man laughed too loudly with a thin note of hysteria edging his mirth. The sound gave Lucian goose bumps.

Something—perhaps a vase or a mirror—shattered. Another peal of laughter clipped the air before indistinct voices murmured in approval.

Reaching for his cane in the half-light, Lucian stood and limped across the room. His knee was stiff with the premature arthritis afflicting his old wound, and when he first rose, he moved more like a man of eighty than one of forty. He despised his crippling infirmity, and in his agitation, he turned the key with more violence than was necessary. It was a futile gesture; if his twin and her company wanted access to him, nothing so flimsy as a lock would stop them.

As he went to his chamber's sole window, he kept to the carpeted areas so the rugs would muffle the sound of his cane against the floor. Elaborate tapestries covered the marble walls with his sister's favorite hunt scene. Firelight distorted the images woven into the cloth, elongating the faces of the hunters and hounds into freakish mutations. The stag's eyes were almost human with their pleading, but there would be no mercy. The hunt was over. All that remained was death.

Lucian averted his gaze from the wall hangings as he passed his desk, piled with papers full of endless calculations. Books littered every flat surface, including the ottoman that squatted between two cushioned chairs by the hearth. He had only to ask and his every request was filled, but all the gifts in Woerld couldn't replace the life Catarina had stolen from him.

A prison, no matter how finely furnished, was still a prison. He reviled her house and all she stood for, but he had not tried to escape again. He had learned to fear his sister after his first failed attempt to leave her.

In spite of her edict, he went to the casement and pushed aside the heavy drapes to open the window over her sprawling gardens. The wide window-seat accommodated him comfortably, but his humor didn't improve with the cold breeze. Years of helpless rage slow-burned through his chest to rise like bile at the back of his throat.

On the opposite side of the city, the construction of the sprawling bastion for the Fallen Angel Mastema continued unabated. Dozens of fires illuminated the black stone turrets rising to meet the night. Girders stretched upward to the overcast sky, forming an open claw as if stone and steel could snatch the paradise the Celestial Court had denied the Fallen.

Lucian had no doubt Mastema would win a foothold in Woerld if Catarina's plans succeeded. Instead of searching for a site of power to hold back the Fallen, she perverted the teachings of the Citadel to calculate the appropriate longitude and latitude to find a weak Hell Gate in the city of Hadra.

The harsh northern provinces of Golan were isolated from the lower lands. Lucian was certain that Woerld's other religious fortresses were unaware of Mastema's temple; otherwise, they would have sent emissaries to assess the situation. Once they were assured of Catarina's goals, the various bastions would send their armies to stop her. Yet no word came from any of the three closest bastions: the Citadel, the Rabbinate, or the Mosque. The Hindu bastion of the Mandir, at the heart of Woerld, remained silent as well.

Of course, they had no way to know. Catarina was careful to mask her bastion's true intent from the general populace, and the city of Hadra, nestled deep within the Aldilan Mountains, was especially secluded from the rest of Woerld. His twin sat in the center of her intrigues like a great dark spider, spinning her web of deceit and growing her army.

Downstairs someone shrieked; one voice rose above the others in pleasure and pain. Catarina no longer hid her perversions but reveled in them and dared him to admonish her. She ignored his efforts to guide her from her chosen path. He had failed to keep her safe. He had failed them all.

Lucian swallowed his misery as the sky lightened with dawn. Doors slammed below him; Catarina's guests were taking their leave to sleep through the morning. He wished he could flee with them. He had to get out of the house, even for an hour, to some place undefiled by her corruption.

Lucian closed the window, careful to secure the latch. He had to calm himself before he went downstairs. If she sensed even the slightest resentment in his attitude, she would slam the doors shut on him. Today he feared he would go insane if he couldn't leave.

Rather than call his servant, who would no doubt bring the usual array of light indoor clothing, Lucian dressed himself. Although it was only autumn, Golan's northern winds had started to blow cold, so he chose his heaviest clothing and his boots. The merchants and priests knew him too well. Should he step inside a teahouse or church for too long, the proprietors would ask him to leave rather than risk Catarina's rage.

At his bedside table, he opened the drawer and removed his Psalter, wrapped in a silk scarf with faded crimson flowers. Other than his father's signet ring, the scarf and book were the only possessions he maintained from his life before Hadra. He placed the scarf and Psalter in his breast pocket close to his heart.

With any luck, his sister would be in bed, exhausted from her night of debauchery, and he might slip out unnoticed. He opened the door to find a frightened manservant, who had been prepared to knock. The servant lowered his hand.

Lucian tightened his grip on his cane. "What does she want?"

Relieved, the man bowed twice before blurting, "She wants to see you. She's in the dining room." He hesitated, glancing up and down the hall. "If you please, sir," he whispered.

No, it doesn't please me. Not at all. He wouldn't send the trembling servant back to her with that message. She would have the old man beaten to death. Lucian gestured brusquely, and the man scurried ahead of him.

It took him several painful minutes to navigate the wide, marble staircase, and he made no attempt to hurry. As he reached the main floor, one of the maids stepped into the corridor beside the dining room door. Tears streaked the livid bruise forming on her cheek, and she wiped her nose with her apron. In spite of her distress, she lifted her long skirts and curtsied as he passed.

He entered the room to find his sister seated at the head of the table wearing nothing but a loosely tied dressing gown. The deep frown that pulled her full lips downward marred her beauty. A gold filigree pendant that depicted two ravens, their beaks locked in an obscene kiss, hung between her breasts, which were partially exposed by her open robe. Without acknowledging him, she pushed aside the report she had been reading and violently rang a small golden bell.

Three of her guards were in the room, each wearing a pendant with her raven seal, each guarding a different door. They didn't acknowledge Lucian and he ignored them.

Catarina's obsidian eyes locked on him. The bruised circles beneath her dark lashes deepened her gaze. She looked like a cadaver. "What took you so long?"

Her sharp tone reignited his anger. "I was delayed." He twirled his cane and thumped it on the floor, indicating his leg. "*Darling.*" A cobra couldn't have spat more venom into his endearment.

"Don't mock me today, Lucian. I'm not in the mood."

When are you ever? He clamped his teeth against the words. Antagonizing her was pointless. He wanted out, and he knew the game he had to play.

A shadow slid by on his left as his sister's demon familiar, Cerberus, entered the room. The creature disguised itself as a large hound but fooled no one. His pallid flesh sported no fur; the large bat-like ears carried no canine resemblance. His talons clicked on the tiles as he moved to Catarina's side. He appraised Lucian with cold, silver eyes and rolled his thick tongue over multiple rows of teeth to grin lewdly. Mercifully, he did not speak.

Now our little ménage à trois is complete, Lucian thought desperately.

His sister slammed the bell down and shrieked for her coffee. Lucian was gratified to see Cerberus and one of the guards recoil at her outburst. The door leading to the kitchens slammed open, and a young woman almost tripped over her skirts to get the tray to her mistress. There was only one cup alongside the urn. Lucian said nothing.

Catarina waved the girl away and served herself. Appeased, she sipped her drink with imperious calm, then said, "Close the door, Lucian. We need to talk."

He pushed the door shut with his cane and took a seat at the foot of the table directly opposite her. She was beginning her assault early this morning. He had no doubt she intended to dole out his pain in slow increments today.

Cerberus went to his mistress and tugged the sash of her robe. She pushed him away and tightened her belt. At least Lucian wouldn't be treated to one of their displays of affection this morning.

"Captain Speight tells me he has had some difficulty with you." She shifted the pages and read from the report. "According to Speight, you've been warning priests, rabbis, and imams to move their congregations out of the city by mid-winter. You've also advised a bhikkhu and a brahmin to do the same." She met his gaze evenly and tapped the report with a manicured nail. "Is this true?"

He presented no defense; he was guilty. The cities' religious houses usually stood immune to Woerld's political instabilities, but Catarina's intercourse with the Fallen brought the churches and temples into the direct line of battle. Once Mastema's temple was complete, she would force the people of Hadra to worship the Fallen Angel and sacrifice those who refused on his altar.

"What are you trying to do?" Catarina asked. "Commit suicide by proxy?"

Better than dying by inches. To his left, a log popped against the hearth and sent a blaze of light up the chimney. The hissing fires were the only sound as they played their demented game to see who would break first.

"Answer me!" Her spittle flew across the captain's report.

"Yes," he said.

Whether she was shocked at his honesty or that he wanted to die, he had no idea, but she made no retort. Instead she sipped her coffee, and her hand shook slightly as she rattled the cup back to its saucer. Shunning Golan's nasal dialect, she spoke to him in their native Walachian so the guards wouldn't understand her next words. "*Good God, Lucian. Are you serious?*"

She must have seen the answer in his face, because she held her hand out to him, and he could have sworn the tears glittering in her eyes were heartfelt. "*Why do you wound me like this? You know I don't want you hurt. If you were dead, I would be cut in half. You tear out my heart when you talk like this.*"

The cadence of her speech resurrected his nostalgia for the days when they had loved one another and lived in harmony. In the past she had coddled him back to her graces with promises of familial love spoken in words remembered from their youth.

This morning was different. Whether it was his bad night or his worse morning, he felt nothing for her platitudes, not even regret for the love they had lost. Sometime in the night he had died, and he wasn't sure he would ever live again. His misery complete, he was numb to her pleas.

"*I love you,*" she crooned, oblivious to his disregard for her manipulation. "*I don't want to see you hurt again. You misunderstand—*"

"There's been no misunderstanding, Cate. You've made your position clear," he replied, speaking in Golanian. "You expect obedience from me. Absolute obedience."

Her head rocked as if he had slapped her, and her eyes grew cold again. She leaned back in her chair. "Mastema has named me Seraph of his fortress."

Now Lucian felt the blow of her words settle in his stomach as icy fear. If the Fallen Angel had claimed her as the high priestess of their warrior-prophets, her political influence in Hadra was assured. The ever-present fire roared, and a rivulet of sweat tickled his collar. "When?"

"Last night. And what is my first order of business as Seraph?" She clenched the pages of Speight's report and threw them in Lucian's direction. "My recalcitrant brother." The paper wafted to the center of the table as ineffectual against him as her rage. "Let me be clear, Lucian. The only reason you're still alive is because of me. If you continue your flagrant disobedience, even I won't be able to plead your usefulness to our cause."

"Are we finished, Cate?"

Cerberus pushed his head under Catarina's hand, and she shoved him away. "Have I dismissed you?"

Lucian didn't answer, but neither did he leave.

Another servant brought a tray laden with breakfast for his sister. The odor of the food nauseated Lucian.

"I've appointed Malachi Grusow as my Inquisitor. He assures me that our Katharoi will be prepared to march on the Citadel in the spring."

Lucian looked down and picked an imaginary piece of lint from his pants so she would not see his scowl. *Katharoi.* She and Grusow demeaned the honorable title of the bastions' warrior-priests by bestowing it on their ragtag army of mercenaries and cut-throats. A true Katharoi spent years training in martial and spiritual arts while the men in Catarina's army were little more than ruffians who owned armor and sword.

"Grusow believes our spies within the Citadel are close to creating a schism within their ranks." Catarina raked the tines of her fork across the slab of meat, and when blood rose to the surface, she smiled. "And Rachael is dying."

A terrible pain filled Lucian's chest, and his numbness fled before the familiar guilt that destroyed his nights. He'd betrayed Rachael with an act that could never be undone, but surely she wasn't dying. The Citadel had other exorcists just as skilled as Lucian, and Rachael would have submitted herself to an exorcism; she had no choice. As the Seraph's last heir, Rachael was all that stood between anarchy and unity within the Christian bastion's ranks.

Catarina's smile broadened. "When she's gone, there will be none to stand against you, and the Citadel will be defenseless against Mastema's legions."

She lies, he warned himself. *Half-truths and lies.*

Catarina buttered her bread. "Rachael never allowed anyone to cast out the Wyrm, and the demon has started to take her mind. She is lost in her prophecies. They say she dreams awake." Her glare held him until he lowered his eyes in shame.

"You're lying." He called her bluff, surprised at his even tone. "The Wyrm should have been adjured years ago."

"She allows no one to heal her, no one to touch her." Catarina picked through her food. "Someone she loved must have abused her trust."

Horror settled over his body, stealing his breath. Rachael could be stubborn and she would believe herself able to handle such a minor demon, but she was not an exorcist. If she had fought the creature for this long, it was entirely possible she had grown weary, and the Wyrm was most dangerous to those who dreamed. Lucian bowed his head and pinched the bridge of his nose between forefinger and thumb to stop his tears. Not now, not here.

"Oh, please, Lucian, don't tell me you're still pining for your little whore. Your benevolent God left her in Hell to become a one-eyed, drooling monster lost in her dreams. The least you could do for yourself is bed someone who will recognize you in the morning."

"I left her there, not God."

"And you were right to do so." She slipped a bloody piece of meat to Cerberus. "She was in the way, an obstacle."

You were jealous of her. "I left her there in exchange for your freedom."

She shrugged, dismissing his sacrifices for her with that one banal movement.

"I left her there because of your lies!" The strength of his baritone rattled one of the guards. The man stepped forward.

Startled, Catarina almost dropped the sliver of flesh in her hand. "Never raise your voice to me."

Lucian rose so fast that he unbalanced his chair. The air around him darkened and crackled. He was rewarded by the fear in his sister's eyes.

Cerberus' muzzle snapped as he jerked his head in Lucian's direction. "Have a care, Lucian," the demon said, his silver eyes narrowing.

"Don't make us subdue you, brother." His twin reached over to rest her hand on Cerberus' broad forehead.

Her guards waited on Catarina's word. Everyone knew the eventual outcome of the tableau; it had been enacted enough times in this house. Lucian might be more powerful, but she held the tactical advantage with the demon and her guards. When he had fought them in the past, she'd called on her followers to restrain him. She wouldn't hesitate to do so again.

They both knew it.

Lucian simply didn't care anymore.

"You're strong, Lucian, but you're not invincible. Now stop your tantrum and sit down. We have more to discuss."

In his agitation, he gripped his cane until his hand ached. He examined the woman before him and felt nothing but revulsion.

"Damn it, Lucian, I said sit down."

For this callous bitch, he had sacrificed Rachael, only to remain locked in battle against his twin until there was nothing left inside him but ice and apathy. His heart lay quiet now, cold as sorrow, dry as hate. Lucian turned and walked away from her.

"Where are you going?"

He heard her chair scrape the floor as she stood. He jerked the door open. The maid he had passed earlier fled down the corridor.

"Lucian? Answer me!"

Cerberus spoke in the background. Lucian neither heard nor cared what the demon directed. He slammed the heavy dining room door hard enough to shake the frame.

She was still calling his name as he grabbed his mantle from the hook in the foyer. He emerged into a day as gray as his mood. Another of her guards attempted to impede his way. Lucian shoved past him and reached the wide avenue before the soldier recovered himself. A note of panic edged his twin's voice as she called after him. Lucian didn't stop. If she wanted to make him pay later then let her; he would lie down and take it because he had purchased his pain.

And the price had been dear.

Lucian stepped off the residential avenue catering to Hadra's elite and followed a shortcut the servants used. Smoke from the construction fires hazed the skyline and curled around the battlements of the city's walls. Ash coated the streets and the populace, shrouding their prosaic lives in gray. Mastema's fortress sucked the life from Hadra and its inhabitants, turning the city into an open crypt.

At the next street, he hurried across during a gap in the traffic and stepped into a narrow alley. From the shadows, he watched a line of draft horses pull wagons filled with slabs of marble in a cumbersome procession, their hooves pounding the cobblestones in a solemn dirge.

Two of his sister's soldiers emerged on the other side of the street. They looked over the crowds and temple traffic then apparently decided to search their side of the road first. One man jogged off to the left and the other went right. Lucian turned and waded through the alley's muck; he'd evaded them. For now.

He soon reached the commercial district where vendors hawked their wares and customers haggled over prices beneath ragged awnings. The walkways were congested to avoid wagons. The market crowd raised a cloud of dust and noise rivaled only by the clamor of the temple construction.

A cold wind gusted into his face as he left the alley and shouldered his way into the mass of bodies. Far ahead, he glimpsed a woman with hair the hue of sunlit autumn fields, and he almost cried out Rachael's name. The woman turned; she wasn't Rachael, but a pale replica. A sparrow imitating a phoenix. He passed her without a second look, chiding himself for a fool.

He stepped into another alley to lose himself in the winding paths between the stone buildings. Entrapped by the city's walls, he had explored every garret and undercroft of Hadra in hopes of finding an escape route. The days had dragged into years; his dreams of leaving faded to nightmares of captivity. His only recompense was learning to evade his twin's guards by disappearing into the labyrinth of alleys leading deep into Hadra's decaying heart.

The buildings became more dilapidated, the streets dirtier, and the people more furtive as he moved east toward the slums. His fine, ermine-lined mantle and sturdy clothes marked him as an outsider, but none dared to impede his journey. Lepers were greeted with more enthusiasm than Lucian Negru, because where he walked, his sister's soldiers were soon to follow.

Lucian stopped in front of a small church nestled between two leaning tenements. He'd walked this route many times, but he couldn't recall ever seeing the simple crosses on the doors. Now that she was Seraph, Catarina would waste no time in shutting down the various houses of worship to force them into her cult for Mastema. This lonely church would burn with the rest.

His leg was on fire from his walk, and he needed to sit. Perhaps he could warn the priest to take his congregation from the city. If he could save one of them, he might be able to justify the pain of the last sixteen years.

The street was strangely empty. Only a dirty yellow dog rooted amongst the trash three buildings down. Even the animal didn't mark Lucian's presence. It was as if he had died and become a ghost in his sister's city.

He was a corpse in need of a grave.

The chapel door was unlocked and he entered the sanctuary where only eight rows of pews stood between the entrance and the pulpit. After he genuflected to the humble wooden cross at the altar, he took a seat on the back row. He closed his eyes and leaned his head back, resting in the silence.

His thoughts drifted and for one mad moment, he half-expected to feel Rachael's hair touch his cheek. If he was very still, he was sure he could summon her memory and breathe life into her shadow, making her real and whole again. She had always known where to find him when he was troubled. It was her habit to lean over his shoulder and press her lips against his ear. *Come away*, she would whisper. *Come away with me.*

Lucian was so lost in his reverie he didn't hear anyone enter the room, so he was startled when a hand clasped his shoulder. Terrified one of Catarina's guards had found him, he jerked upright only to see knuckles gnarled with arthritis.

The old priest's smile faltered momentarily. "I've seen a dead man's eyes that looked like yours. What makes you so weary, son?"

Lucian dropped his gaze; there weren't enough days before them to spin his tale.

"Aren't you Lucian Negru?"

The old man's voice exhibited no condemnation, but Lucian didn't want to hear the contempt that would follow his answer. "I'm sorry. I just needed to rest. I'll leave."

Genuine alarm passed across the man's features. "No, no, you shall not. All are welcome in God's house, especially those who are called prophet. You are Katharos, are you not?" The old man imbued the title of Woerld's warrior-prophets with a reverence Lucian hadn't heard in years.

"Was. I was once a Katharos."

The priest patted him on the shoulder. "Did God rescind His calling and send you home to Earth?" The old man's lively green eyes shined with compassion. "You *are* Katharos; that power can never be taken from you."

"I was banned from the Citadel many years ago. I've lost my power."

The priest shook his head. "Your power comes from God, not the Citadel. So long as God's throne stands, then so does your power. You've just lost your way. We all get a little lost from time to time." The priest sat sideways on the pew in front of Lucian, turning so they could talk face to face. "What troubles you that you wear your misery for Woerld to see?"

Tears burned Lucian's eyes and he forced them down; why should he weep for a woman already lost to him? When he felt he could trust his voice, he said, "What if I told you about... an evil man who betrayed the woman he loved to save his sister's soul?"

"Is this man truly evil or does he just think himself so?"

"Once upon a time, he was selfish and wicked."

"And now?"

"He's sorry for the suffering he brought to her."

Minutes passed with the priest considering Lucian's sincerity as if it was a jewel to be bartered. Not since he had lived at the Citadel had he watched someone so thoroughly study his words for their truth.

The priest asked, "What if this selfish, wicked man, who is now sorry, was presented with an opportunity to amend his grievous act? Would this man take such an opportunity?"

"Please don't mock me."

"I'm not mocking you, son. I'm asking you a question. Would you take the opportunity?"

Lucian searched the old man's face and found only kindness. He had not been the recipient of benevolence in so long he wasn't sure how to respond. "An opportunity?"

"Nothing more. Nothing more can be promised, just the chance to see if she'll forgive you. Would you take that opportunity?"

He didn't hesitate. "With both hands." He waited for the priest to render a proverb about good intentions being the first step toward redemption.

Instead, the chapel door opened and one of the slum's dirty waifs slid inside to scurry to the priest. "The soldiers have come, Father Matt."

"Good boy, Jamie." He reached inside the folds of his cassock to find a coin and tossed it to the child. "Go out the back way. Be careful not to be seen."

The boy vanished with the same ease with which he had appeared. The priest pulled himself to his feet and patted Lucian's hand absently.

The sound of horses in the street choked Lucian with terror. He had been a fool, and now he'd endangered everyone who had seen him here, including the kind priest. "Do you have a side entrance?" He couldn't be sure, but he thought the old man winked at him.

"I thought you wanted an opportunity." Without another word, the priest turned and walked toward the altar.

"I don't think you understand." Lucian rose and followed him as quickly as he could, trying desperately to keep the telltale thump of his cane quiet against the rough wood floor. "I only need for them to find me on the street so they don't connect me to this church."

"They're going to burn it anyway, son. You have no control over them." He went behind the altar and opened a low door, which was all but invisible against the dark paneling. "I dream, you know."

And those that dream, prophesy. Lucian had once desired those dreams simply because they denoted power, but that talent had been denied to him. He did not dream; he did not prophesy; he could not see the truth in another's words. Those were Rachael's talents.

Stunned, Lucian stared at the old man. "You were Katharos?"

"Am, son. I am Katharos, just as you are Katharos. It's not a coat you can take on and off at will. God remains on His throne so we are Katharoi. Mastema might win the battle, but that dark angel has yet to win the war." Father Matt stooped to pass through the low doorway and disappear into the darkness. The priest's face reappeared suddenly. "Don't dawdle, Lucian."

Lucian followed and found himself on a wooden stairwell where he could almost stand straight. Father Matt was waiting three steps below.

"Pull it closed and latch it." The priest mimed pulling the door shut. When Lucian obeyed, they were plunged into suffocating blackness.

Father Matt grunted softly. "Well, isn't that the wickedness of it? It's the first trick they teach us and it's the first one we forget." The priest stopped talking abruptly as a small yellow globe formed in the palm of his hand. The ball of light strengthened until it acquired the soft luminosity of several candles revealing Father Matt's delighted features. "There we are!" He held his soul-light before him. "You've thrown the bolt on the door? Good. Come on, we haven't much time."

Lucian followed him down the stairs into the sepulcher beneath the church. "If you are Katharos, then why are you not at the Citadel?"

"Not all of God's warriors in Woerld fight with magic and sword. Some of us have more traditional callings. Now hush or they'll hear us." He led Lucian past alcoves lined with bones, skulls staring wide-eyed into the shadows. Rats scattered before Father Matt's soul-light and then closed over the men's wake like a rippling brown pool.

They wound their way deep into the vault until Lucian was so lost he doubted he could find his way out alone. The priest slowed, examining the floor as he kicked aside the slower rats. The beasts squealed like old women vying for vegetable scraps at the city's waste heap.

Father Matt grunted in victory. He went to the wall, unceremoniously shoving skulls, femurs, and finger bones aside. Opening a trunk that had been hidden by the bones, the priest removed an iron bar and leather sack with a thick strap. He handed the heavy pack to Lucian before he rammed the heel of the bar into a slot in the floor. His face reddened with effort as he slid a metal panel aside to reveal a ladder descending into darkness.

He gauged Lucian's bad leg and shook his head. "I'm sorry for you, son. You'll have to find it in yourself to get down there."

Lucian took one look before he stepped back from the rank odor of rust and mold flowing out of the darkness. He had no chance of escaping his sister's guards on foot, especially through damp caverns. This was a cruel joke. "Are you mad? You expect me to crawl into that hole and go where?"

"I thought you wanted an opportunity, or are you still looking for an easier way?" The priest's voice turned as frigid as the air flowing out of the pit. "Perhaps you would rather crawl back to your sister and throw yourself to her mercy."

A pit of ice opened in his stomach at the thought of Catarina's rage. Suffering upon suffering would result from his walking out on her this morning.

"I thought so." The priest held the little ball of light up before Lucian's fearful eyes. "The light comes from our souls, Lucian, and you know by my light that I am Katharos, because the Fallen can't make light—"

"They only steal it," Lucian whispered.

"Yes! You're remembering, son. I dream and the Lord has spoken to me. I have done everything that's been commanded. You have enough food in your pack to get you through the caverns and deep into the Wasteland if you're frugal. In the caverns, follow the right-hand path at all times. No matter how they twist and turn, never deviate from the right-hand tunnels. You'll find your way out."

Father Matt took Lucian's free hand and passed his soul-light to hover over the younger man's palm. "They might find you if you use your own magic. Go with as much speed as you can, because once my light dies, you'll know they've wrung the truth from me."

Chilled, Lucian looked into the old man's steady gaze where there was no fear, only cold resolve. "I don't have your courage."

"You lost it when your heart turned to stone." The priest leaned forward and tapped Lucian's chest twice. "Find the heart of flesh that still beats within you. There lies your courage."

Another draft of air blew out of the hole. All his life, Lucian had calculated his every decision, factored every coefficient, every possible outcome, but now there was no time. Did exchanging one black hole for another really matter? At least this way, his dying was in his own hands, and there was a slim chance that he could right a terrible wrong. Before he could change his mind, Lucian lowered himself to the edge of the hole and released Father Matt's light down into the darkness. The rusting ladder ended about twenty feet down.

"Come with me." He threw the pack over his shoulder.

"I'm eighty-six, boy. I'll only slow you down, and you'll be slow enough on your own." He blessed the younger man quickly. "God goes with you. He's a much stronger ally."

Lucian took a long time descending the damp ladder, but eventually found his feet on solid ground. He looked up when the priest called his name one more time.

A long slender object fell toward him, and he thought perhaps it was another cane. Unprepared for the weight of it, he almost dropped it. It was a Citadel sword; the hilt bore the Greek letter Omega embracing the Alpha, and though he didn't draw the blade, he was sure the inscription, *Ut unum sint*, was etched in the steel.

That they may be one.

"John Shea remains as the Citadel's Seraph," Matthew called down. "Take the blade to him, and you tell John Shea that Matthew Kellogg did what was right in the end."

At the mention of John's name, the sword felt heavier. Lucian tried to imagine facing John again after all these years. The only image he could summon was the look of John's grief when he had discovered Lucian's treason sixteen years ago.

Lucian shoved his anxiety aside; he would have to face them all eventually. He looked up. "I will, Matthew, I swear it." Lucian couldn't see the priest's face, but the silhouette of Matthew's head nodded before he disappeared. "I won't forget you," he whispered.

Lucian rubbed the rust from his palms onto his pants and took up his cane. Above him, the sound of metal screamed against stone, and then silence. His way back was sealed from him forever.

†

Judging by the growth of his new beard, he had been in the darkness for five, maybe six days when Father Matt's light flickered. Lucian had known something was wrong with the old man hours ago when Matthew's soul-light deepened to the color of urine. Now it went out briefly before glowing back to life only to darken again like a dying firefly.

"Oh, God, please take him quickly. Don't let him suffer." His whisper echoed down the branching tunnels as he stood mesmerized by the flickering soul-light before him. Automatically he touched his heart and drew comfort from the presence of his Psalter.

And please don't let me be next, he prayed selfishly.

The priest's light faded before it burst into a shower of sparks. When the last ember faded, Lucian was immersed in blackness.

In the eternal night of those caverns, the steady drip of water resumed, filling the quiet. From somewhere behind him, he heard the hesitant click of claws against the stone floor. The rats were returning with the darkness.

He held his palm up, but hesitated to say the prayer that would bring his own soul-light into existence. He had no idea how far he had come, and as he walked through the long hours in the dark, he often felt he was moving in a large circle. If he used a small magic, then his sister and her council might not sense his presence, but there were no guarantees.

More rats joined the first few, their squeaks multiplying as they sensed their prey's vulnerability. Before his panic could overwhelm him, he prayed and was rewarded with a spark that burned brighter as he charged it with his life-fire.

He turned on the rats and they fell back, tumbling over one another in a black-brown sea of fur, teeth, and tails. He backed away from them; when they continued to retreat from his soul-light, Lucian turned and began walking again.

With the death of the priest behind him, he moved faster. If Matthew had talked, then Catarina's guards would soon be on his heels, and he had no desire to be dragged back to his sister. She had already promised that if he tried to escape her again she would give him a chance to experience Christ's Passion in excruciating detail.

Though his pace quickened and he rested only when he couldn't walk another step, he guessed it was still three more days before pale sunlight began to push against the darkness. He found himself steadily moving uphill, and the rats fell back to the caverns behind him. Craving daylight more than food or water, Lucian didn't sleep and rested little as his eyes gradually adjusted to the ever-increasing brightness. The air became fresher and dryer as he emerged from the depths of Woerld to find himself on a ledge where he could look out over the Wasteland.

The tunnels had spiraled and he had indeed followed a circular path. Approximately thirteen leagues away, Hadra lay to his left, belching smoke and death into the air. Stretching out before him were thousands of acres of blighted wood and sour magic left over from the War of the Great Schism.

The War between the Katharoi and the Fallen had lasted six years and involved every religious bastion on Woerld. The Zoroastrian bastion had been destroyed along with the country of Norbeh, and the reverberations had carried over into Earth's time to create a devastating conflict there. John claimed the very Gates of Heaven had shuddered when the Katharoi's forces summoned their magic to clash with the Fallen's hoards.

Both sides left nothing but destruction in their wakes. Trees bleached of color reached for the sunlight with their bare limbs creaking against one another, dry as bones. Soil blackened with long burns of desolate ground flowed like stretch marks between the forests and abandoned towns.

But the sky was blue.

A clear crystalline blue.

The sun glowed, and he realized it was rising.

The sun was rising.

Lucian leaned on his cane and wept.

He had an opportunity.

Nothing more.

But for now, that was enough.

CHAPTER TWO

earth—present day

The bright lights of Ferrell's Dance Studio faded when twelve-year-old Lindsay Richardson turned the corner to step into the shadows of Watlington Street. Shaggy trees, thick with kudzu and poison ivy, deepened the twilight where the forest ran adjacent to the road. The woods crept toward the asphalt to eclipse the three neat brick homes across the road. Leaves whispered to the ground when a mild breeze rattled limbs heavy with vines.

Normally, the sound of cars speeding less than a block away were loud, but tonight the swampy woods muffled the drone of engines. Even the mouth-watering smells from the neighboring restaurants were strangely subdued. Lindsay's sneakers jarred against the odd silence as she stomped home. She didn't notice the lack of sound; she only heard the pounding of her older brother Peter's tennis shoes hitting the pavement behind her.

When Peter called her name again, she set her jaw and walked faster until her ponytail swung violently and her gym bag rapped her hip. *Jerk.* She hated the tears stinging her eyes; she had never been so humiliated. It just wasn't fair. She'd practiced all week on her second position. In spite of her efforts, Mrs. Ferrell accused Lindsay of looking like a dead bird. Again.

The mirror behind the ballet barre had reflected the other girls' glee when Mrs. Ferrell allowed her outstretched arm to sag comically. She chastised Lindsay for her lack of practice in front of the entire group. It wouldn't take long for that to get around, not with Melissa Kent watching Lindsay's downfall with hungry eyes. Half the school probably knew by now. Melissa yapped on her cell phone as she walked out of class, and Lindsay heard her name followed by a giggle.

Yet the worst part had been her older brother sitting in a chair by the wall, watching the entire demonstration. Her pride in having a family member stay and watch her practice had crumbled into horror when Peter laughed out loud.

Lindsay kicked a can into the ditch and swiped a tear from her burning cheek. Her dad already said dance classes were a waste of time and money on a klutz like her. This just proved his point. Lindsay hoped he was drunk when she got home, even though his jibes were more vicious; at least then, she could pretend it was the booze talking and not her dad.

"Come on, Lyn, hold up!" Peter's hand touched her shoulder, and Lindsay whirled on him.

"Thanks. A lot." Lindsay shoved him; he barely moved. Why did she have to be so small? "I didn't laugh at you when you fumbled at Tuesday's game and cost the team a point."

"Seven points," he said.

Another renegade tear slipped past her defenses and she bit her lip. God, couldn't she get anything right? Her dad was right, she was stupid.

Peter sighed and brushed the tear from her chin. "Lyn, it wasn't that big of a deal."

Lindsay's left eye narrowed as she glared at him. How could he say such a thing?

Peter said, "I wasn't laughing at you. It was Mrs. Ferrell that was so funny. When she flopped into that weird position, she looked just like a dead bird with her bug eyes and pointy nose." Peter snickered at the memory then sobered when Lindsay didn't smile back. "Jeez, Lyn, you're twelve going on twenty. You really take yourself too seriously."

She was not going to let him put this back on her. "Everybody thought you were laughing at me. That's how it looked, Pete."

He sighed and raked his hand through his hair. "I'm sorry, okay? I really didn't mean to hurt your feelings."

Lindsay slid the purple band away from her cornsilk white hair, then gathered her hair and pulled it back into a ponytail. In the past, when Peter's laughter had been aimed at her, he wouldn't stop teasing her. He wasn't ragging her now. His eyes, the same pale blue as hers, were earnest and no smile turned the corner of his lips.

"Hey, listen," he said as he straightened and raised his right hand, "I swear I will never laugh at you in front of your friends again. Even when faced with fowl old ladies. No pun intended." He winked at her. "Well, maybe a little one."

"Don't make fun, Pete. It's going to be all over school. And you know Dad is going to find out. He plays golf with Melissa's dad, and oh, shit." She couldn't do anything right for him as it was and now the teasing would never end. She looked for another can to kick.

"Come on, Lyn, you're tougher than that! Don't let that bitch Melissa screw with your head. You're better than her." Pete's eyes lit up. "Hey, I got an idea. We'll tell Dad that it was really her that did the funky bird."

She sighed and answered her brother. "We're not going to do that." She could just imagine the hurt in her mother's eyes if she found out Lindsay had lied about someone else. No, maybe Peter was right. She was tough enough to deal with Melissa, but she'd do it on her own terms.

"So." He shrugged. "Are we good, Lyn?"

She scuffed the asphalt with her shoe and looked up at him. She never could stay mad at Pete for long. "Yeah, we're good."

He held out his fist and she touched knuckles with him, their private sign of peace. Peter put his arm around her and turned her toward home. As she fell into step beside him, she glanced into the woods where an odd red glow pulsed in the twilight.

At first, she thought someone was playing with a laser, but the light didn't waver or move erratically. The illumination widened to the size and shape of a door. She stopped walking and Peter halted beside her. He frowned at the light.

"What do you think it is?" Lindsay asked.

"Aliens?"

"Jeez, Pete, be real." She would have given him one of her most withering looks if only she could have taken her eyes off the hypnotic light.

Entranced, Lindsay watched the beam expand until it ascended from the ground to the sky. The glow shimmered like heat waves rising from summer roads, but the October evening carried a chill that promised an early frost. Her mom had even made her pack her winter coat and gloves for the walk home.

Lindsay examined the Veil. *And where did that word come from?* It did look like a veil, though... a red veil...

The eerie quiet prevailed.

The Veil shimmered and the swampy woods of Watlington Street disappeared. On the other side of the red haze was a forest with old trees. She saw a huge gray rock covered in lichen, and a man who dozed with his head tilted back against the stone. His sword lay across his lap and shone with a pale luminance. She made out a cane and a pack beside him.

She thought the moonlight enabled her to see him so clearly. When she looked harder, she saw that the radiance didn't descend to him from above but rose up from within him. Though his appearance was rough, his face was serene in sleep, and rather than fear, she felt drawn to him.

Peter murmured, "Wow, it's like another world."

"Yeah," Lindsay said, but Peter was saying it wrong. It was really 'Woerld.' She shivered in the cool air.

"Oh, man, that's one cool looking horse."

Lindsay had no idea what her brother was talking about. "What horse?"

"The gray, Lyn. Can't you see it? It's dappled gray with a black mane and tail. It has one blue eye and one brown eye and it's looking at somebody walking in the dark."

How could he know all that about a horse in the night? Stepping closer to the red curtain...

...*Crimson Veil*, her mind whispered...

Lindsay peered into the darkness; she saw no horse, no one walking.

The supernatural silence drained the life from their surroundings.

She reached out and gripped Peter's hand. Neither of them noticed the Veil inch closer to them in the deepening gloom until it was too late.

Pete dragged Lindsay's hand backward, but her terror overwhelmed her and she stood rooted to the spot. The light rushed forward and the Veil swept over them. It was like getting sucked under a wave. She gasped for air. Peter's hand clenched hers until she thought her fingers would break.

The street faded to black then burst into a blinding white brilliance before the world she knew vanished. A deep whine filled her head, soft and changing in pitch like tractor-trailers zooming on an interstate, but nothing as metallic as machinery. This noise erupted from things alive.

Alive but best not seen.

Peter looked over his shoulder with wide eyes and held on to her. Both Watlington Street and the forest where the man slept were shaded red. She and Peter were carried deep into the Veil. She had no control over her destination; she couldn't go back, only forward.

She'd felt sick like this when her mom lost control of their car in an ice storm. The world became a blur. All she could do was hold on and hope for the best. She and Peter stood in the eye of a hurricane where, instead of thunder and rain, another world eddied around them. Yet she never lost sight of the sleeping man. Somehow she knew if she could get to him, he'd know what to do.

Shadows deepened in the Veil. Out of the corner of her eye, Lindsay caught flashes of movement. The shadows turned into dark canine shapes running beside them. She tried to turn. Peter jerked her closer to him and held her tight. More of the dogs flitted by them and Peter paled. Pushing her backward as hard as he could, his mouth formed a word: *Run.*

What was he thinking? She couldn't run; she was at the mercy of whatever force pulled her. Unable to focus on the danger he saw, she reached for him. He didn't wait. Peter disappeared into the red mist. The dogs ran past her to pursue her brother deeper into the Veil.

Sick with dread, she screamed his name only to have her voice swallowed by a rising wind. Then she was whirling through the Veil. Her gym bag slipped off her shoulder to land near the sleeping man. He stirred but didn't wake.

Subtle changes in the air pressure signaled her exit from the Veil and her ears popped painfully. Another force wrenched her past the man. Reality frayed, threads pulled from a tapestry. The dead, white trees faded into a wraithlike mist. Lindsay stumbled through the cold fog to trip and land in a pile of ash.

She choked from the acidic dust flying into her nose and throat. Coughing, she scrambled to her feet and looked around. The man and the forest were gone. Stifling her fear, she tried to calm herself enough to think. Less than a minute had passed from the time the Veil swept over her and Peter. Even if the man was gone, Peter couldn't be far.

"Peter?" she whispered. A cold wind lifted the loose grit and swirled dust clouds in the semi-dark. The land surrounding her was flat with rock formations jutting out of the darkness. In the distance, mountains lined the horizon, and a volcano belched smoke and fire into the sky. Rivulets of lava poured like bloody tears down the mountainside. Lindsay's mouth went dry. God, what was this place? She raised her voice. "Hey, Pete!"

He didn't answer.

Her heart beat so fast she wondered if she was having a heart attack. *Okay, don't panic. Everything is going to be all right.* Panic set in nevertheless. She should look for Peter, but she couldn't make her legs move.

The ground beneath her feet gave a low, ugly rumble. Moans vibrated in the dank air and a group of people emerged from the dusk. A hidden force seemed to tether the lumbering mass of bodies together, prodding them onward, their joints twisted and bowed beneath its pull. As they neared, light erupted overhead and the group was illuminated in a photoflash moment.

Their heads twisted in her direction as if the weight of their skulls were too great for their necks. Parchment flesh clung to their bones and their vacant stares chilled her to her bones.

One of the men stopped walking to retch violently. "Water," he croaked through cracked lips.

She thought she saw the vomit wiggle as she backed away from him. "I'm sorry," she managed to whisper.

"Stupid girl." He swayed unsteadily.

A sob, such a small sound in that great expanse of misery, scratched her already sore throat. She stepped just out of his reach. Oh, God, she just had to find Peter and get home. Please, God. "Please? What is this place?"

He opened his mouth but could only gurgle as he doubled over in a spasm. Another flash of light punctuated the semi-darkness and he lifted his head. In his gaping maw she saw worms chew the back of his throat.

A nasty squeak burped through her lips, gaining momentum, growing to a wail. Pressing her fists to her mouth did nothing to stop the sound and Lindsay's screams ravaged the night.

✝

Heart punching against his ribs, Lucian awakened with a child's shrieks echoing in his ears. He drew Matthew's sword with his left hand and stood to survey the low mist hanging over the forest. Deep, rocky gullies sheared away on either side of the hill where he camped. The terrain made good cover for both the hunters and the hunted.

It was only a matter of time before Catarina's guards located him. Last night, he could have sworn he heard soldiers and horses. Whether it was his sister's men or a haunting from the dissonant magic of the Wasteland, he did not know.

The War of the Great Schism had turned the country of Norbeh into a wilderness unfit for habitation, and the Wasteland's fractured spells confused his senses. Four days had passed since his emergence from the caverns; instead of relief, he felt more exposed. During his long nights he realized his terror of the unknown would break him long before Catarina had her opportunity.

A flicker of light caught his eye and he turned. This was no haunting from the Wasteland's fractured spells but illumination from the Crimson Veil. On the other side of the Veil, he saw an asphalt street and three brick houses standing in a row, each with neatly maintained yards. He didn't have time to wonder about the purpose of the poles connected with heavy cables before the Veil closed. The houses wavered and dissipated from sight, and Lucian forgot everything when he saw a bright blue and green bag on the ground.

A foundling.

Lucian stared at the bag in disbelief. It couldn't be a foundling, not for someone like him. Only those with the highest integrity were selected by God to foster the Citadel's next generation of warriors. He wouldn't be so blessed as to draw a foundling through the Veil.

She is here. He had heard her voice, and he knew without a doubt it was a girl. Those weren't things he would know about another Katharos's foundling.

He used his cane to snag the bag's straps and lifted it within easy reach. Inside he found a skirt made of stiff lace, slippers, a heavy coat, and a pink cell phone. He replaced everything except the phone, which he held with all the reverence of a holy relic. He had once seen such a device when another Katharos's foundling passed through the Veil; John showed him how to use the phone and the dangers that accompanied it.

Dangerous or not, the phone in his hand could be his only clue to his foundling's whereabouts. The girl might be pictured in the display, or he might find one of Hell's denizens struggling for a way out of Hell and into Woerld through the tiny screen. Only the most minor demons would seek escape through a device such as this, and Lucian had once been the finest exorcist at the Citadel. He wouldn't be cowed by such a trivial foe.

On Earth the foundling would use the device for remote communication, but on Woerld the qualities of ownership and communication manifested differently. The machine should still be bound closely enough to his foundling to show her physical location. He flipped the phone open with a flick of his wrist and narrowed his eyes to better see the tiny screen.

Static filled the display before solidifying to show the image of a girl standing in Hell. Her fists were pressed to her face and her eyes were wide with terror at the soul before her. The soul reached out to grab her. The girl twisted and stumbled out of his reach. She turned to do the most dangerous thing she could by running blindly into the shadows.

Lucian closed the phone; his breath quickened. He concentrated on the resonance of magic around him. After several seconds, a buzzing sensation traveled up his arms. The weak reverberation of a broken Hell Gate grew stronger then faded again.

Had she passed through the Veil anywhere but within the

Wasteland, her journey would have ended beside him. The child must have slipped through the nearby Hell Gate where evil waited to take the unwary or inexperienced, especially those foundlings new to Woerld.

Lucian could save her, but it would mean opening the Hell Gate. To use so much force would automatically inform Catarina of his approximate location. Even someone as dense as Speight would feel the surge of power and the parting of worlds. Everything he had sacrificed, everything Father Matt had sacrificed, would be for nothing.

Don't dawdle.

Startled by the sound of the old priest's words, Lucian looked over his shoulder, half-expecting to see Father Matt standing beside him. He was alone.

"You don't understand—" He stopped talking. Good God, he was going insane.

To open the Hell Gate would be a breach of his covenant with the Citadel to never manipulate the Gates again. Taking the pledge was the lone reason he had left the Citadel alive and, until this day, he had never considered breaking his oath. If he violated his covenant, he would have to stand trial to answer for his recidivism. His exile would be revoked, and he would face a death sentence.

A foundling, Lucian, drawn to your light and allowed through the Veil by God's hand, Matthew's voice chided. *Will you let her become like Rachael? A one-eyed, drooling monster lost in dreams?*

His sister's mocking words sounded no gentler in the old priest's voice. Lucian pressed the phone to his lips. Real or imagined, Matthew's words were true. Lucian couldn't let the child die, even if it meant giving himself over to the Citadel courts. He had squandered his life, but the foundling deserved her chance to live. Perhaps this was the opportunity Matthew had offered, for what better way to make restitution to Rachael than to save another from the fate she had suffered?

He pocketed the cell phone, closed his eyes, and tried to remember the Psalm to open the way between Woerld and Hell. Yet all he could recall was standing with Rachael the last time he held her. When he'd stroked her cheek to soothe her, she turned her face to press her lips against his palm. He almost stopped, almost took her back to the Citadel on some pretense, but his pride and his sister had set his course.

Lucian snapped free of the memory and opened his eyes. The words wouldn't come. Panicked, he tried to clear his mind. If he delayed too long, the time could slip, extending the girl's torment in Hell without a second passing in Woerld.

While inhaling the rotted air of the Wasteland, he caught the faintest whiff of clover. Rachael always smelled of sunshine, clover, and some sweet musky scent all her own. He touched his Psalter, wrapped in the scarf she had once wound through her hair.

Lucian had not prayed since his exile, but this request wasn't for him. He hoped God would hear him for the child's sake. "Please, God, help me remember."

The only words he recalled belonged to Rachael: *John doesn't think I'm ready for the Gates.* She had been breathless and impatient. Always impatient was his Rachael and it would prove her undoing.

The memories he'd evaded for the last sixteen years floated to the surface, and this time, Lucian didn't stop the recollections. Let them come. Let him remember. If he intended to face Rachael, he must stop running from his past.

His fingers tightened around his cane. "Psalm 20," Lucian whispered to the dawn. That was it. They had used Psalm 20 to open the Gate, and Rachael never lost her focus. Neither of them ever lost their focus. It would be their triumph; it would be their ruin.

"'The Lord answer me in the day of trouble. The Lord...'" He couldn't recall the rest of the Psalm. What if he could no longer command the Gates? What if God no longer answered his call? He, who had once guided her so confidently, couldn't remember the next words in his anxiety. Clearing his throat, he stilled his nerves and began again, recalling once more the musky scent of her skin.

"'The Lord answer me in the day of trouble! The name of the god of Jacob protect me!'" *Yes! Yes! That was it!* He was no longer sure to whom he prayed, the God of Jacob or Rachael. "'May he send me help from the sanctuary, and give me support from Zion. May he remember all my offerings and regard with favor my sacrifices.'"

The hesitancy fled his voice and peace filled him. He felt for the spatial ripple in time as he chanted. "'May he grant me my heart's desire, and fulfill all my plans. May the Lord fulfill all my petitions.'"

The words flowed back into his mind as easily as the unseen strength allowing him to channel this greater power. Humbled by the force filling him, he sensed a give in the air and knew the Gate was close to obeying his command.

His baritone thundered through the Wasteland, and he spread his arms wide, feeling Woerld give. "'I shall rise and stand upright. O Lord; answer me when I call.'" On the final word, he rapped his cane against the earth, a rush of air rippled around him, Woerld fell away, and he was alive again.

CHAPTER THREE

cross creek

A flame swelled and receded behind the dirty hurricane glass surrounding a thick gray candle. Its light illuminated a dusty dresser and black cobwebs wafting from the ceiling. On a rickety nightstand, another candle cast shadows around the dying boy and the scarred, one-eyed woman occupying the austere room.

Rachael pulled her rocking chair closer to the bed and peeled back the blood-soaked quilt. She narrowed her left eye as she frowned at the youth. Pink bubbles formed at the corner of his lips where his skin had been ripped. She'd stitched him up as best as she could, but there were too many wounds, too much lost blood. The boy's eyes were open slits, dull with death. She was sure he didn't see her. Perhaps that was just as well.

She wiped her fingers on the tail of her filthy shirt and picked up the stack of cards she'd found in his wallet. An identification card contained his name and address—Peter Richardson, 909 Country Club Drive, Taylorsville, North Carolina—and a fingerprint beside his smiling picture. The boy's library card was next then his social security card.

A thin headache threaded its way into her brain. She rubbed the black patch over her right eye. This was her fault. It didn't matter whether he was attacked within the Veil or in Woerld. He was her foundling, and she should have sensed his coming so she could be there to help him.

She was slipping. A tendril of fear burrowed into her heart; she killed it before it could take root. Fools whined.

Peter closed his eyes and his chest rose and fell as he slept. She placed the cards on the table and settled back in her rocker, the creak of wood against wood the only sound above the wind. Rachael remembered her own pain when Caleb had brought her out of Hell. Sleep had been her only escape; deep, dreamless sleep where her agony couldn't touch her. Lulled by the rocker's smooth motion and the warmth of the room, Rachael's thoughts drifted in the semi-dark. Her mind wandered into a dream where she dreamed herself back on Earth.

She was eleven years old again and running through the field behind her father's house. A rusty pick-up truck obscured by kudzu and weeds loomed out of the twilight. Her hip bumped the fender before she could swerve. Rachael caught her scream before it fled her lips. She left a bloody handprint on the hood as she passed.

A quick glimpse showed her father following her at a dead run. He was only a few yards behind her. Pale blonde hair stood in stark contrast to his red, furious face, but Rachael only saw the bloodied ax that he carried. From the open windows of their farmhouse, the radio blared. Her father grinned and Mick Jagger growled a song about a man with railroad spike driven through his head.

Rachael ran toward a strange crimson fog. She cringed when her tennis shoes hit the boards that covered the old well, but the wood held. For her. Seconds later, her father crossed the same boards. A resounding crack drowned the chorus of the song.

She heard the crash and looked back, but the field was blurred by the red haze so like the blood that covered her. Suddenly someone grabbed her and she screamed. She stumbled into John's arms hard enough to drag them both to their knees.

Her father's cries rang through the Veil. *Rae-baby, you come on over here and help your daddy now.* From the depths of the well where he'd fallen, his voice echoed strangely into Woerld. *Rae? Get daddy a rope. Baby? I know you're there.* There was a splash and a panicked groan.

Goddamnit, Rae, you quit fucking around and get your ass over here! Right now!

Rachael turned to John, but he was gone, and she was in Lucian's arms. He spoke her name with a voice like thunder and silenced her father's pleas. With a touch, he drove her demons into the night and made her safe. She reached for him; he slipped away, swallowed by a mist.

A mighty wind dispersed the fog to reveal a city of death where the gale shrieked through empty buildings. Lucian stood before her, his dark eyes ruined with grief, a blaze of white marring the black of his hair. He leaned upon a cane and called her name. She was drenched in blood, only now it was her own. She thrust her crimson hands forward, her life pooling at her feet.

I can't make it stop, she said as a fly whined past her face.

Peter's final whistling breath woke her with a start, and her dream dissipated into the night with a little boy's soul.

Rachael leaned forward. "Peter?" She rubbed his hand between her palms. "Come on, Peter." She pulled the blanket off his body and listened for his heartbeat. Silence. The room blurred and her throat burned. She choked her tears down. Weeping wouldn't bring him back. The dead never came back.

"Hey, you tried. You really tried." Rachael smoothed his hair and kissed his cheeks. "I'm sorry." Sorry for him and for herself. "I'm so sorry." Her first foundling and he'd died before they could know one another. She reached over the headboard and took down the rosary hanging on the wall then wound the beads around his broken hands.

The quiet house echoed her loneliness as she knelt beside him. After rummaging through her exhausted brain, she settled on the Lord's Prayer and recited the verses by rote. She remained still for a few minutes after she finished, resting her head against the mattress.

On the floor beside the nightstand leg, a piece of paper caught her eye, and she reached down to pick it up. The photograph must have slid out of Peter's wallet. Rachael stood and carried the picture to the candlelight. Two young people posed on a beach, laughing at the camera. The boy was Peter in the not-so-distant past; the girl was obviously a very close relation, possibly a sister.

How happy they looked. Rachael tried to remember if she'd ever laughed with such wild abandon but no memory would come. A tear wept through the stone of her heart; she swept it away before it could weaken her.

A fresh drop of blood splashed across the photo, landing on Peter's face. Rachael examined the red blotch in wonder. When she dabbed her nose, blood smeared across the back of her hand. The headache returned and rammed into her skull with the riveting agony of a spike through her temple. She screamed in surprise and anger. Fire snarled her synapses, driving her thoughts like quicksilver before the beast in her head.

Somewhere a Katharos opened a Gate between Woerld and Hell.

Her brain burned with cold as the Wyrm surged from the abyss of her soul. The demon seized her distraction and scratched against the back of her mind, a cadaverous fingernail scraping against a tomb. She started her Psalm of protection: '*I cry aloud to God, aloud to God, that he may hear me…*'

The Wyrm flinched back.

This was nothing. She could control it.

The body on the bed sat up.

"Rigor mortis," she murmured, but she knew the corpse was too warm for rigor.

Peter's head turned toward her and his eyes shot open.

Or not. She continued the Psalm through parched lips. "'In the day of my trouble I seek the Lord.'"

The temperature in the room dropped until her breath misted before her in a cloud of white. Her fear raised beads of sweat to her upper lip. The air was oppressive in spite of the cold, a dark heaviness settled on the room, and the Wyrm uncoiled in her brain. The creature sought a vein, an artery, a canal to its birth; the Psalm held the demon back. For now.

"Save her," Peter croaked, the stitches on his cheek ripping open his flesh again. The air in front of his mouth did not turn white. No warmth in his lungs; the dead didn't breathe.

She glanced at the rosary. Peter's skin didn't burn so the boy's spirit had returned, nothing more. Had there been another foundling with him? The girl in the picture?

"'…in the night my hand is stretched out without wearying,'" her hoarse whisper broke the stillness.

"Lyn… Lyn." The remnant of Peter's hand started to jerk within the rosary. "Save—" The corpse gagged horribly.

A thin stream of smoke began to smolder where the rosary touched his flesh. There was a sudden change in the pitch of Peter's voice as the minor Possessors surged forward, seeking a body to command. The boy's mouth worked. A shrill cacophony erupted from his throat, each voice striving to be heard one over the other through his dead lips.

Certain her head would explode, she shut her eye. Her hands shook as the Wyrm fought for control of the body they shared. "'…my soul refuses to be comforted…'"

The Gate closed against the shadows rushing out.

"Leave us alone!" The hellish chorus vomited from Peter's lips. His flesh burned.

The Possessors receded, clawing to remain in Woerld before they were sucked back into Hell. Shadows dry as October spiders skittered into the corners of the room. The Wyrm withdrew to the recesses of her soul where the demon would await its next opportunity. Peter's body flopped back to the bed and twitched before it resumed the illusion of sleep that was death.

Half blind from the sweat pouring into her good eye, Rachael staggered to the window and threw it open. Cool night air washed her face. Vomit slipped through her lips before she could lean over the sill where she retched until she thought she would see her lungs. She took deep breaths, glancing once to the inert Peter, now a shadowy husk.

Lucian had commanded that Hell Gate. The residue of his magic tingled through her veins, and she raked her nails across her forearm. Not even pain drove the warmth of his prayers from her soul. Ever since his exile, she'd starved her heart of his love and purged her flesh of his touch. Until tonight, he'd been dead to her.

She slammed her hand against the wall and strangled her angry cry. The dead don't come back. She prayed mindlessly, *I think of God, think of God, oh, God, please God, God, God,* forcing down the despair that threatened to engulf her. *Lucian. Oh God, oh damn, not Lucian.*

CHAPTER FOUR

the citadel

T he sun rose over the trees before the pungent tang of wood-smoke aroused Rachael. Someone had lit a fire in her stove. She lifted her head and rested her chin on her arm as the yard crept into focus. Her head pounded; she felt hung-over.

Her dog Caesar barked and Rachael thought her scalp would peel from her skull. She sat up to see a black mare and a small roan tethered to her hitching post. The roan's saddle displayed the Citadel's black and red colors. The mare also wore the Citadel's alpha/omega emblem on her bridle, but the rest of her tack was nondescript.

That was not a good omen because the plain saddle meant someone was going on a directive. Around her throbbing headache, she recalled the previous evening. The shock of feeling Lucian's magic had receded to become the silent rage she'd learned to live with.

Half the Citadel must have experienced Lucian opening the Gate, and John wasn't going to let Lucian slide again. The Seraph had obviously sent the judge and constable for an extra horse.

A door slammed from the direction of the kitchen, and she winced. "Rae?"

She recognized Caleb's voice and frowned. He was one of the few constables who didn't fear the Wyrm and frequently dropped by to check on her. He was also John's primary choice to accompany her on directives. Her heart quickened to send throbs of agony into her head. Surely John didn't intend to send her after Lucian.

"Rae, you up?"

Peter's wallet was cool in her hand, and she realized she still held the photograph. She licked the tip of her finger and managed to rub her blood off the image before she returned it to the inside flap.

Caleb came into the room and leaned against the doorjamb, surveying the mess. Instead of his cassock and collar, he wore a brown shirt and pants to blend in with the locals of the surrounding countryside. Caleb was definitely going on a directive. "Rae?" He assessed her condition with a critical eye, and she knew he watched to see whether she was connected to reality or immersed in her dreams.

"I'm all right." She tried to stand and slipped in her vomit. That couldn't look good. The sour stench gagged her and she choked down her bile, willing her body into control.

Caleb came to her side and took her arm, helping her balance herself on numb legs. Very few Katharoi bothered to touch her; they all complained the resonance of her magic was as tainted as the Wyrm. It was just as well; she didn't like being touched anymore. She shook the constable's hand off her arm.

She smelled coffee and tobacco on his breath when he said, "Take it easy, Rae. What happened?"

"Foundling." The bed was empty. God, had she dreamed it? She touched Peter's wallet for reassurance. "Where is he?"

"Outside. We cleaned him up and gave him a shroud so we can get him to the Citadel." Caleb reached out to her, but she stepped away from him. "Why didn't you send for me?" he asked.

Rachael plucked at the bloody sheets, pulling them off the mattress. A strand of Peter's hair drifted through a shaft of sunlight. Even Lucian with all his healing skills couldn't have brought the boy through those injuries. "There was nothing you could have done, Lucian."

"Caleb," he said.

"Caleb," she dutifully replied, looking away from him.

He took the sheets from her and tossed them to the mattress. "Come on, Rae. Get yourself together."

He had no business patronizing her. Even debilitated with the

Wyrm, she stood above him in rank. When Caleb had first brought her out of Hell after Lucian's betrayal, she'd been grateful to him, but over the years, he'd misinterpreted her gratitude for something deeper. She refused to foster his hope for any relationship other than a professional one and discouraged his attempts at familiarity.

Before she could answer him, the front door closed. Rachael snuffed the candle on the nightstand with her fingertips, pinching the wick and not letting go. The pain oriented her mind.

"Master Caleb, I've fed the animals." The soft voice announced Caleb's oldest foundling Victor.

Caleb went to the hurricane glass to blow out the flame. "Okay. Victor, go down and saddle Ignatius for Judge Boucher; she'll be riding back with us."

"Yes, sir." The youth left the house, and Rachael glimpsed him on his way to the stables. He was a tall, handsome young man with auburn hair and olive skin, about the same age as Peter. Caesar trotted at Victor's heels and the youth bent down to scratch the dog's shaggy ears.

"Rae? Are you paying attention?"

She focused on Caleb and frowned. The Wyrm had yet to blind her soul's eye. To anyone else Caleb would appear to be the epitome of calm, but she sensed apprehension hunkering beneath his facade. "What?"

"The Seraph wants you at the Citadel."

She barked a short, nasty laugh, unable to remember the last time anyone wanted her at the Citadel. She kept her apartments there and attended the quarterly Council meetings but that was all. More and more she felt like the discarded piece of a puzzle, swept into a corner away from all the other joined pieces. "It's Lucian."

He wouldn't meet her gaze. "You know it is."

God, she had escaped him never to escape him. "And John is issuing a directive for you and me?"

"Yes." He sighed and gestured at her filthy clothes. "You can't go like that. You look awful. And you'll need to pack. Looks like we're going on a long trip. Lucian is northwest of us in the Wasteland."

"All right, all right," she murmured, but it wasn't all right. It would never be all right again. Lucian Negru had seen to that. "Give me a few minutes."

"Sure, I'll make you some coffee."

Caleb had thoughtfully placed two large buckets of water in her room. She must have been in a coma for him and Victor to move around her for so long, but when was the last time she'd slept? The unmade bed gave her no clue as she closed the door to her bedroom and pulled the curtains across her window. She tugged her shirt off and tossed it into the corner.

On her right arm her flesh suddenly rose as if there was a pebble just beneath the surface of her skin. The pigmentation around the blemish became discolored. Before she could clamp her hand over the bump, it moved up her arm to disappear into one of the raised scars mapping her body. The disfigurements became more pronounced as the Wyrm gained another inch of her with every passing year.

Hands shaking, Rachael made certain to choose a shirt with loose sleeves. She pulled on the gloves she'd made to hide the joining of her pinky and ring fingers on her left hand. The physical deformities were not readily noticeable, but nothing hid the pall of the Wyrm's resonance, which hovered over her like a shroud.

She finished dressing and packed. When she opened the curtains again, she caught a quick glimpse of herself in the glass. The scars on the right side of her face and neck undulated where the Wyrm crawled beneath her skin. The movements were barely perceptible unless someone looked very close. Rachael never allowed anyone to get too close.

Her long hair looked like she had cut it in the dark with a dull knife. She reached up and dragged the ragged layers over to shadow the right side of her face. Maybe she couldn't hide the Wyrm's resonance, but she obscured the demon's physical presence.

Satisfied, she left her reflection and went to collect her sword. She loosened the strap of the scabbard and slung the blade over her shoulder, then grabbed Peter's wallet and pushed it into her pack. Whether his death was her fault or not, he was the first foundling she had ever drawn through the Veil. Since he had no other family on Woerld, she'd hold on to his personal possessions. The wallet might give her some small comfort in the night.

In the kitchen, Caleb poured her a cup of coffee, and she could tell by his appraisal that she looked presentable. She would have to rely on him because she removed all the mirrors from her house years ago.

She paused by the table where the account book for Cross Creek was open. She set her pack down, unable to recall leaving the book there. Her eye was drawn to the heavy slashes of ink scarring the paper. The pages that had once held neatly spaced columns of handwritten numbers were now filled with nightmare sketches of incomprehensible violence. She turned the leaves slowly, marveling at the detail of familiar faces pulled in agony. Sickened, she slammed the book shut and took it to the stove where she shoved it into the fire.

Without a word, Caleb took the poker and mashed the curling paper deep into the flames, making certain they burned. "Blackout?" he asked. He likened her episodes of dreaming to alcoholic blackouts. A fitting enough description of the times when she dreamed and the Wyrm took her for its own.

She nodded. "Did Victor see that?"

"No. It was on the table, but it was closed. While Victor fed the animals, I flipped through it and saw, well, you know." He shrugged.

She took her cup and steadied her hand to drink.

Caleb looked at her.

She shuddered. "You know it's worse when I'm alone. I fell to dreaming. That's all. It's nothing. A minor fugue. I'll be all right."

"Is there anything else here that might be like that?"

She felt sure there was nothing. "No."

"Good, because John's sending Sara and Stephan to steward Cross Creek while you're gone." He closed the stove.

Rachael grabbed her pack and went outside with Caleb following her. She lashed her saddlebags to Ignatius' saddle as the dapple gray fixed his one brown eye on her. The constable mounted his black mare, and Victor turned the buckboard carrying Peter's body. The youth was obviously eager to be away from Cross Creek and the sour stench of the Wyrm's magic.

Caleb said to Victor, "Judge Boucher and I are going to ride ahead. You take your time."

"Yes, sir."

They soon left Victor and the plodding wagon behind. They rode in silence, keeping a steady pace. As they neared the Citadel, the congestion on the road became thicker with merchants and local farmers coming and going either to the Citadel or the Semah River with their wares. Most of them remained on the central road to the Citadel to enter the main eastern gate. A few followed another narrow side-road to the village of Banias, a dirty river village that snuggled up to the Citadel's western wall like a tick.

Rachael and Caleb followed a less traveled road to enter the Citadel's northern gate. Not one of the better-maintained thoroughfares, the road boasted less traffic but became a mud-hole during the heavy autumn rains. Rachael didn't care; she was glad to be out of the crowds.

They crested a small hill and on the plain below rested the Citadel, high on a manmade mound. In spite of her years on Woerld, the sight of the bastion never failed to take her breath away. The Semah River sparkled, a jeweled necklace that curved behind the Citadel. A fortified outer wall gave the Citadel its first line of defense, and a second inner wall encompassed the cathedral and grounds.

The cathedral faced the east where the basilica rose to form a dome between two towers. At the top of the dome, the lesser spires of adjacent buildings surrounded a great resurrection cross. The towers contiguous to the cathedral housed the apartments and offices of those Katharoi who resided at the Citadel.

Most of the Katharoi lived on their holdings and only reported to the Citadel for council meetings or in times of war. The supplies from the holdings kept the Citadel functioning so that in Woerld, the Katharoi stood outside of Ra'anan's local government. They supported themselves and rarely interceded in Woerld's political arena. To keep Ra'anan's King Phillip happy, the Seraph sent an annual tribute and helped in years of famine or plague.

In return, King Phillip never interceded in the Citadel's business and trusted the Seraph to keep the Fallen from corrupting his lands. The War of the Great Schism had made a deep and abiding impression on all of Woerld's kings, and none wanted to see their countries turned into a barren wasteland like Norbeh. They left the bastions to their own devices so long as taxes were paid and the Fallen remained in Hell.

The Citadel and the Katharoi who lived there formed a splendid machine that never seemed to lose its way. *Even when a piece falls from the cogs, the wheels continue to turn*, Rachael thought as she and Caleb approached the postern gate to the outer wall.

She bit down on her self-pity and nodded to the guard who motioned them through the open portcullis. The sun disappeared as the long, dim tunnel swallowed the light. They emerged back into the brightness of the middle ward and passed through the second gate into the crowded courtyard.

The alley between the summer kitchen and the bake-house was congested with a few Katharoi and staff on their way out of the Citadel. The crowd parted reluctantly for Rachael and Caleb. Rachael ignored the three Katharoi who made the sign of the cross as she passed.

They hated her, and those that didn't hate her feared her. She carried the stench of the Wyrm on her like a vile perfume, and they sensed it the same way they sensed one another's magic. Rachael turned her face away from them and guided Ignatius to the right, toward the cathedral.

The courtyard was busy with Katharoi and staff members who served the Katharoi going about their daily business. Katharoi from other bastions moved amongst the Citadel's members. Emissaries from the Mosque and the Rabbinate laughed together as they walked toward the Citadel's great library to the left of the cathedral. The blue robes of an Avalonian priestess contrasted with the red clothing worn by a Deg Long from the Tibetan temple as they wound their way through the crowd, heads bent close to converse over the racket.

Members of other bastions came from all over Woerld to visit the Citadel's famed library like they traveled to the Mosque to learn astronomy. In her youth, Rachael had journeyed to the bastion of the Hindus, the Mandir. There she had studied the Dharmacakra and the confluence of energy that created the spokes of the Dharmacakra's wheel. Under the guidance of the Mandir's Seraph, Rachael had come to understand how the realms of existence—Heaven, Earth, Woerld, and Hell—interrelated with one another. The four realms were like four lakes joined by tiny streams; toss a pebble into Hell and the ripples would extend to the farthermost reaches of Heaven.

Rachael scanned the crowd to see if any of the Citadel's visitors were disturbed by Lucian's opening of the Gate, but the only tension she sensed came from the Citadel's Katharoi. Everything else seemed normal. The steady ring of metal against metal announced the blacksmith was well into his day. Four women wearing cooks' aprons whispered amongst themselves as they sauntered to the gardens swinging empty baskets. Rachael ignored their stares, wishing she didn't have to undergo this indignity every time John needed her.

When she and Caleb stopped at the western entrance to the cathedral, grooms came forward to take their mounts. Caleb ordered a third horse be saddled and brought to them, and one young man took the animals to the shade while the second ran to the stables.

Over the doors of the cathedral's entrance was a relief carved in stone. With his great wings outstretched and his sword drawn, Saint Michael pressed his foot against the fallen Satan's throat. Satan's eyes were defiant, in spite of his crushed wings and Michael's obvious rage, the fallen angel exuded confidence. His gaze promised he would rise again.

Rachael instinctively crossed herself as she approached the steps. The doors were open to take any breeze up to the highest floors. They stepped into the coolness of the atrium where tall arched windows allowed natural light to spill into the cathedral. Approximately twenty feet ahead, another set of doors opened into the nave, an area almost as busy as the atrium.

The nave extended for several yards before an ornate wooden screen interrupted it. Through the latticework of the screen, Rachael glimpsed the quire and high altar where the Katharoi held both Mass and court.

She turned away from the nave and looked beyond the carved colonnades to the arcades that melted into the shadows. With Caleb on her heels, Rachael slipped around a small group of protégés.

Rather than take the straight path to the Seraph's formal entrance where emissaries from other bastions might be waiting, she veered right toward an arcade that led to a dim passageway. Tapestries depicted battles from the War of the Great Schism when the Fallen had almost destroyed the Zoroastrians by dividing their ranks over theological differences.

The Fallen's adherents had infiltrated the Zoroastrian bastion and convinced the Seraph that the unity of Woerld's religions betrayed their beliefs. The Zoroastrian council voted to separate from the

Council of Seraphs and their respective bastions. Not even the most passionate pleas from the Mandir's Seraph had swayed their hearts. From the moment the Zoroastrian bastion divorced itself from the Council, it had only been a matter of time before the Fallen attacked, and without being able to rely on the other bastions, the Zoroastrian fortress fell to the powers of chaos.

By the time the surviving Zoroastrian Katharoi reached the other bastions with news of the breach, the Fallen had secured their defenses in the city of Melasur. John was a foundling during the last years of the War, and he recounted how the ripples from the War of the Great Schism had extended into Earth's realm in the form of World War II. John never wanted his Katharoi to forget how close they'd come to losing Woerld and Earth to the Fallen.

Rachael and Caleb passed the last of the tapestries and the chattering crowd thinned as they reached a plain door that connected the cathedral to the adjoining tower. The next corridor ended at a narrow stairwell used by the Katharoi and serving staff to access the Seraph's chambers. The less she was seen, the better.

The ride to the Citadel along with the climb to the fourth floor cleared her head. Once John heard about her latest blackout combined with the loss of her foundling, he would surely rescind his directive. Then she could go back to Cross Creek, raise warhorses, and drown herself in forgetfulness again.

Rachael stepped into a passageway lit with a few scattered sconces. No ornamentation lined the stone walls. The only occupants of the hall were the two guards who flanked the side-door to John's office and a line of three empty chairs. The guards came to attention as Rachael neared them.

She said, "The Seraph has summoned me."

The soldier bowed and knocked before he opened the door. He returned and gestured for Rachael to enter. "Judge Boucher. Constable Aldridge, you may wait there." He gestured to one of the empty chairs.

Into the abyss, Rachael thought, steadying herself for the interview to come.

In the expansive office, she inhaled the scent of leather and tobacco tinged with the faintest odor of incense. It was a smell she had long associated with John's book-lined shelves in the well-lit room. When she was young, this chamber had been her sanctuary. With the coming of the Wyrm, she had sought comfort from her Elder's presence less and less.

Parallel to the door she had entered was another entrance, which led to a comfortable antechamber where formal guests awaited their private audiences with the Citadel's Seraph. Flanking the door were two large globes atop brass stands. The globe on the left was of Earth and the one on the right represented Woerld. The thirty-one spokes of the Dharmacakra's Gates crisscrossed both globes and reflected what John believed were the corresponding sites of power between Earth and Woerld.

To her left, natural light from three tall, arched windows flooded the room. The rest of the chamber was given to bookshelves except for the one wall farthest from the door, which sheltered the hearth. Cushioned chairs surrounded the open fireplace where John often entertained the visiting emissaries of other Seraphs. Seated in one of the chairs was Reynard Bartell, the Citadel's Inquisitor, and he rose when she entered.

At the center of the chamber was John's desk, as ornate as any throne, the wood burnished to a deep cherry. As soon as she shut the door, John said, "You took your bloody time getting here."

John Shea's voice had been the first Rachael heard in Woerld, and as her Elder, she had come to know his moods better than her own. He wasn't angry with her for her tardiness, but he intended to know the reason.

He was seated behind his desk, looking up from the paper he held. He wasn't a large man physically, yet he commanded the room nonetheless. Though he was well in his seventies, he could still put one of the younger Katharoi in place with either sword or argument.

Reynard Bartell clasped his hands before him as he moved into the light. His cassock and crimson scapular were immaculate. In spite of her recent washing and clean clothes, Rachael felt dingy.

As if sensing her discomfort, Reynard smiled benevolently. Her gut constricted. A master courtier, Reynard had been a judge when he'd used Lucian's trial to secure his position of Inquisitor, chief Citadel judge.

She ignored Reynard and went to John's side. She took his hand as she knelt to kiss his ring of office. "Forgive me, your Eminence."

His hand lingered on top of her head. Though he tried to keep his face impassive, she saw his revulsion at what she'd become. Worse than his disgust was the disappointment in his eyes over her failure to master the Wyrm. John released her and gave her leave to rise with a wave of his hand. "Don't let it happen again."

Taking a deep breath, she pasted a smile on her face and turned to greet Reynard.

"Judge Boucher." He reached out to her. "We were becoming concerned."

Rachael braced herself for the contact and didn't resist him when Reynard took her shoulders and kissed her left cheek, then her right. He cupped her face, his hands remaining a second too long, and the Wyrm rose briefly, whether to feed on her hate or Reynard's, she didn't know. The demon fell back to the recesses of her mind when Reynard released her. He said, "The Lord be with you, Judge Boucher."

"And with your spirit, my Lord Inquisitor." She responded with a slight tilt of her head. She didn't take his proffered hand. As John's heir, she wasn't required to submit herself to Reynard's authority. She bent her knee before the Inquisitor only during the most formal ceremonies when John allowed no breach of etiquette.

Reynard's fingers curled but didn't close.

"Sit down, Rachael." John indicated the chair across from his desk. "I'm sure Constable Aldridge has briefed you."

"He has." She didn't like the way Reynard positioned himself just behind John's right shoulder. The entire scene was reminiscent of when she had to answer for her actions in Lucian's crime. John spared her a public trial, but the inquisition by John and Reynard had been intense nonetheless.

"What kept you?" John asked.

"There was a foundling."

"Was?" Reynard raised an eyebrow.

Rachael stilled her nervous fingers and met John's gaze. "He was dying when I found him. His name was Peter Richardson, he was fourteen and from the early twenty-first century. He died this morning just before dawn. Victor is bringing him."

"What killed him?" When she didn't answer, John prompted, "Jackals?"

"I believe so."

"You believe?" Reynard shook his head.

"I never saw the Veil," she said to her boots.

John leaned forward. "So you don't know if he was attacked within the Veil?"

"No."

"Did the jackals cross over and attack him in Woerld?" Reynard snapped.

"I don't know."

John threw his pen into the stack of papers, and the nib spurted ink across several pages in defiance of its mistreatment. Rachael felt sorry for the novice who would have to laboriously re-copy the marred pages.

John asked, "What do you know, Rachael?"

"I was lost in dreams. I don't even remember the last two days." She pressed her fingers against the patch covering her missing eye and stopped talking. Shakier than a foundling, she took a deep breath and tried to pull herself together; it wasn't working. This was going very badly, but maybe this was the wake-up call John needed to remove her from service. Let him name Reynard as the Seraph's heir; she was nothing more than a figurehead anyway.

"Rachael. Look at me." John's tone broached no disobedience.

She swallowed against the burning in her throat and forced herself to meet his gaze. With a slight turn of her head, Reynard disappeared from her sight, and she pretended it was just her and John in the room.

"Show me," John commanded.

A hoarfrost nip of fear bit her heart. He didn't need to elaborate for her to know he wanted to see her soul-light, and while it was the simplest of tricks, it was the most revealing. John wanted to see if the Wyrm had taken her, if she had become complicit with the creature she harbored. If her light didn't burn true, then being the Seraph's only remaining heir wouldn't save her from a formal inquisition.

"We're waiting, Judge Boucher." Reynard moved into her line of sight.

Rachael clenched her jaw and held out her right hand. She summoned her soul-light and almost wept with relief when the white globe appeared to hover inches above her palm. Her reprieve was brief. Shadows formed within the sphere, streaks of black lightning—

signs of the Wyrm's progress. Rachael concentrated harder and the dark spots faded to the background. Sweat prickled across her brow as she focused on the light, and the shadows fled. Her light burned true.

"That's enough," John said.

Rachael extinguished the illumination.

"It's progressed, your Eminence." Reynard stepped from behind John so he could face the Seraph. "I strongly suggest we attempt another exorcism before you send her into the Wasteland."

"You've had sixteen years, Reynard." John sounded as tired as the argument Rachael had heard a thousand times. "If you haven't divined the demon's true name by now, another week isn't going to make a difference."

"We can't afford to lose her, my Lord, even as a symbolic heir." Reynard twisted his ring of office. The Inquisitor wasted no opportunity to point out her uselessness, and John no longer defended her. Rachael's coffee soured in her stomach.

"I've got Lucian Negru opening Hell Gates in the Wasteland and drawing God knows what back through with him. No. There's no time for another exorcism." John sorted through the mounds of papers on his desk to unerringly retrieve the one he sought from the stack. He shoved the paper at her like an accusation. "And sending you is against my better judgment, but I've dreamed and the Lord has spoken to me."

Rachael's fear turned glacial and spread over her heart. Once John dreamed, no one changed his course. A prophecy would not be denied, no matter how much commonsense stood in the way. She took the document and scanned it. Her head began to hurt, distorting her vision.

"I'm issuing a directive for you to bring Lucian Negru back to the Citadel to be tried for violating the terms of his Ban. If the Council finds him guilty of desecrating his covenant, he will hang."

She swallowed the bitter taste of her regret, keeping her eye on the document so she wouldn't have to look at John or Reynard. The sorrow gripping her heart took her off guard. *It's the foundling*, she reasoned, pressing her finger to her eye to squelch a tear. She hadn't adequate time to mourn the loss of Peter. This was not about Lucian.

John went on as if he didn't notice, but she knew he did. Nothing escaped her Elder. "Lucian will surrender himself to your authority. I will determine the retribution when he arrives, which means I'm expecting him to arrive here alive. Do you understand, Rachael?"

"I do." Feeling more in control, she folded the document and held it loosely.

"Caleb has received his directive and he will serve as your constable." John sighed and lowered his voice. "Rachael, this can't be botched."

Reynard made a derisive noise. Rachael's fingers crumpled the directive before she willed herself to loosen her grip on the document.

"Go," John said. "God watch over you while you're out of my sight." He made the sign of the cross over her and turned back to his papers.

Reynard smiled as she rose and turned away.

She was almost at the door when John spoke again. "Rachael, be on your guard. I want you here, where you belong. Come back to me safe."

Rachael nodded and opened the door to step into the hall. Caleb stood a few feet away, speaking to the Citadel's Commissioner Charles Dubois. The two men were the same height, but Dubois was broader in the chest than Caleb. Life at the Citadel's court had softened the Commissioner's once athletic body, but nothing dulled the man's vigilant gaze. Rachael remained as wary of Dubois as she was of Reynard. They were vultures hanging over her deathbed.

Dubois bowed in her direction; she gave him only a cursory nod in return. Rather than wait for the men to finish their conversation, Rachael went to the stairs.

Within minutes, Caleb was rushing down behind her. "Is everything okay, Rae?"

"Everything's fine." She lifted the paper without turning. "We have our directive."

Outside, she paused so her sight could adjust to the sunlight. Caleb passed her and went to the horses where the groom now held the reins of a chestnut gelding that stood alongside Ignatius and Caleb's mare. Rachael assessed the gelding and complimented the groom on his choice before she moved to take Ignatius' reins from him.

"Rachael."

Rachael shoved the directive into her pocket like it was a dirty secret and turned. John's wife Tanith stood within arm's reach. Still a priestess in the Goddess' service, her pale blue gown reflected the colors of an Avalonian. Like John, she was small in stature, but her poise and self-confidence gave her the illusion of height. Usually a smile teased the corners of her eyes, but not this morning. Today sorrow dragged the corners of her mouth down, and Rachael's heart twisted with guilt. She was no less responsible for Tanith's grief than Lucian.

Tanith held her hands out to Rachael. "Will you leave without seeing me?"

"Of course not." Rachael forced her false smile back to her face and touched Tanith's fingers.

Other than the slightest twitch of her lips, Tanith showed no sign of revulsion at the Wyrm's taint. "Walk with me to the gate so I may see you off." She took Rachael's hand in her own.

Rachael loved her for that one small gesture.

Caleb cleared his throat and bowed to Tanith. "My Lady, we're on a directive from the Seraph. It's of the utmost importance."

Her dark eyes flashed from Caleb back to Rachael. "Then wait for her at the gate."

Caleb's protest withered under Tanith's glare. He gave Rachael a look of appeal, but she didn't acknowledge him. If Tanith wanted him gone, then she had a reason. Without another word, he mounted and took the gelding's reins from Rachael before he disappeared into the crowd.

Tanith lowered her voice as she fell into step beside Rachael. With the clamor of noise around them, no one would hear her words. "It's grown worse, hasn't it?"

Rachael kept her pace slow to accommodate Tanith's shorter stride. "It comes and goes."

"The truth," Tanith whispered, barely moving her lips. She nodded to Ganak, the emissary from the Mandir.

Rachael ducked her head in a move that could be interpreted as a slight bow so her hair shadowed her face. She hoped Ganak didn't recognize her.

"Rachael." A note of warning changed the pitch of Tanith's voice.

"I can control it." Ignatius nuzzled her shoulder and she shrugged him off.

Tanith stopped walking and faced Rachael. People flowed around the women and horse like they were stones in a stream. Other than an occasional nod to Tanith, no one spoke or approached them. They could have been alone.

Tanith took both of Rachael's hands in hers and squeezed. "Adam Zimmer wrote to me recently. He's very worried for you."

Rachael bit the inside of her cheek and nodded. She had first met the Rabbinate's Inquisitor a few years after Lucian's betrayal. Adam had looked past her scars and often brought a smile to her face through his witty observations. They had grown close over the years through their correspondences, but last year, no matter how she tried, she could no longer read Adam's letters. The words swam before her eye to become senseless shapes that fed her headaches.

Too proud to admit she could no longer read Rachael had stopped writing to him. In spite of her lack of correspondence, Adam continued to write to her once a month with what she assumed was news from people they knew at the Rabbinate.

"Adam asked me to give you his regards. He tells me he prays a Mi Sheberakh—a prayer of healing—for you every day. He wants to hear from you."

Rachael blinked against a burning in her eye and lowered her head.

"You are loved, Rachael. More than you know." Tanith brought Rachael's face close to hers to kiss her cheek. Her breath tickled Rachael's ear as she whispered. "Make no sign you've heard. Trust no one."

Rachael's blood chilled as Tanith repeated the gesture and kissed her other cheek. "We are infiltrated," she whispered.

"Who?" Rachael hissed the question into Tanith's ear.

Tanith gripped Rachael's fingers tightly and stepped back. She raised her voice to a normal tone. "I wish I knew, but the ways of the Goddess are hidden from my eyes. I will write to Adam for you and give him your gratitude for his prayers. If you like."

"Yes." Rachael never had to ask; Tanith always knew exactly what to do. "Please. I would like that very much."

"Good. You'll not be long, I hope."

Rachael forced a smile to her numb lips and looked down into Tanith's worried gaze. She wished she had some reassurance for her, but they could share only the most banal pleasantries in the courtyard. "I'll return as quickly as I can."

"Good." The older woman smiled. "I came to give you my blessing. May the Goddess ride with you all the days of your journey, and may She bring you home to us safe. Here. Where you belong."

The hair on her arms rose at Tanith's eerie echo of John's parting words. Tanith stepped back and melted into the crowd before Rachael could whisper goodbye. Alone again, she mounted Ignatius and turned his head toward the gate. She rode away without looking back.

We are infiltrated.

Rachael found her flask and took a quick drink to drive the taste of fear from her mouth. If Tanith suspected members were complicit, then surely John did too, and neither of them would warn someone they thought complicit. No, John trusted her, Rachael was sure of it. She never would have walked out of his office if he believed her corrupt, but that didn't mitigate her danger.

With the Wyrm, she would be a prime suspect if accusations were made. No wonder Reynard had been so eager to see her soul-light fail to burn true. He rooted out the complicit with savage zeal and was not known for advocating mercy for the condemned. With Rachael gone, no one would stand in his way as heir. Whether he could prove she was complicit or not, Reynard would use any opportunity to further his advance to Seraph.

Ahead, Caleb stood talking to one of the guards. When he saw her, he mounted his mare and was ready to ride by the time she reached him. "Everything all right?" he asked.

"Fine." It would have to be for now. She couldn't do anything about complicit members until she finished with Lucian. She led the way beneath the portcullis and tucked Tanith's words close to her heart.

She steered Ignatius back toward the farm. "We need to go back to Cross Creek. I want to backtrack Peter's trail. I need to know where that child was attacked."

"Sure," Caleb said. "It shouldn't take us long."

Rachael didn't care how long it took. Now more than ever she needed to know if she was at fault for the boy's death. Reynard could easily claim she murdered Peter through her neglect, or worse still, that she summoned the jackals to cheat the Citadel of another warrior. She had to have a plan of action in place, and she couldn't do that until she knew the truth.

She set Ignatius to a trot, and Caleb covered her blind side. The sunlight burned the Wyrm to the recesses of her soul. By the time they reached the field where she had first seen Peter, her head felt clear.

Caleb dismounted and checked the foliage for blood before following Peter's tracks. As they moved between the trees, her home slipped away in the background. She was already sick with longing for her familiar routines, meaningless though they were.

They followed a slight incline, then up another hill where Peter's blood trail ended. The only disruption of the earth came from a young boy's feet. No paw prints marred the ground. Rachael released the breath she had been unaware of holding and dismounted to search the leaves with her own eye.

Caleb validated her conclusion. "I can't find any jackal tracks. They took him inside the Veil. There wasn't anything you could have done, Rae."

Rachael relaxed. If Caleb bore witness and affirmed she wasn't at fault for Peter's death, Reynard couldn't claim otherwise. Caleb reached down and picked something up.

"What did you find?" she asked.

"Cell phone."

Of course, twenty-first century parents tethered themselves to their children with their electronics. The devices usually worked while the Veil between Earth and Woerld was thin; sometimes as much as forty-eight hours, sometimes as little as five minutes.

Rachael held her hand out, and Caleb gave it to her. She flipped it open and punched the power switch. The little screen lit up, but it didn't show Peter or his last moments as she had expected. Instead, she saw the smiling girl from Peter's photograph.

Lyn. Save her.

Shadows and darkness set the background like some macabre wallpaper. Rachael recognized all too well both Hell's landscape and the young woman from the photograph. Only her summer beach smiles had vanished beneath tears and terror. There was no doubt she was Peter's sibling, and Rachael suspected Peter had given himself to save her.

Rachael gave Lyn only the most cursory examination. She focused on the man who held and comforted the distraught child. Lucian.

The ragged figure stood, favoring his lame leg. Good God, was her dream this morning a prophecy? Rachael frowned at the screen and remembered his dark gaze ruined by grief. A doubt crept soulfully into the back of her mind, a tiny seed of disquiet that the man she loathed was not the man before her. She silenced the misgiving for fear it would unravel her heart.

The picture distorted momentarily, breaking her reverie; if she was lucky, the Veil remained thin enough for the phones to connect. She pressed the menu button and examined the list of numbers; there were two possible Lyns, Marilyn Anderson and Lindsay. Rachael pressed the number for Marilyn and received silence. She touched a button then chose Lindsay's number and was rewarded with a ring.

CHAPTER FIVE

hell

The cold sank into Lucian's bones as he entered Hell and closed the Gate. The Possessors slammed against his consciousness. Cheated of their opportunity in Woerld, they sought entry into his mind. He drove them off as he would gnats and surveyed Hell's landscape. Steel would be useless here so he slipped the strap of Matthew's sword over his shoulder to free his left hand.

He noted with some dread an open pit behind him. He had no way of knowing the hole's depth, nor did he hazard a guess as to what might lie in wait at the bottom. He had no desire to find out.

Light flashed overhead and he glimpsed the girl running toward him, her blind stare glazed with fear. As fast as she was moving, she wouldn't be long in reaching him. There had to be a way to stop her without injuring her. His dark clothing shadowed him in the twilight and calling out might startle her into changing direction. If she switched course, he'd never catch her.

A minor tremor shook the ground, and Lucian glanced over his shoulder. Dust and gravel rolled into the pit. The vibration ceased almost as soon as it began.

When Lucian turned again, the girl was upon him. He barely had time to throw his arm around her waist as she shot past. With her shriek in his ear, he caught the pivot on his good leg and they spun. The speed of her forward motion caused them to slide. He dug his cane deep into the loose grit, finding purchase at the last second to jerk them to a stop. Her feet hung over the emptiness of the hole. She must have realized her predicament, because rather than fight him, she clenched his arm in a death grip and whimpered.

Their hearts pounded in time with their panic as he maneuvered them by slow, steady inches away from the pit until he felt safe enough to set her down. The child trembled so violently her teeth chattered. She refused to release his arm. He knelt beside her and set his cane down so he could gently rub her back. Her fingers dug through his layers of sleeves to pinch his forearm.

Her eyes were glazed and he feared she would withdraw into herself to become catatonic. Without thinking, Lucian cupped the back of her head with his palm and lowered his head until their brows touched. He paused. What if by calming the girl, he caused her to become like Catarina, so that she relied on him to soothe her every anxiety?

Lucian pulled away from her. No. This child's mind couldn't comprehend what she'd seen. She needed help or she would be lost to the Katharoi forever. This was a necessary healing. He pressed his brow against hers and concentrated on her mind until he felt his soul connect with hers.

A jolt went through him, and he knew her name. Lindsay Richardson. The only other time he had felt like this was when John first touched him and he had immediately known John's name. Lucian remembered how John had given him the knowledge necessary to communicate in Woerld through their initial contact. How he had bound their souls together and offered Lucian his love while shielding him from the harsher realities of Woerld.

Lucian couldn't overwhelm the girl, but she needed to know Golanian and Ra'ananian in order to communicate with him. Nor could he open his heart and soul to her as a true Elder would. The Citadel Council would never allow an outcast such as him to be her Elder. For Lucian to bind their souls too closely at the beginning would only bring the child great pain later so he shielded his heart from her and didn't offer her his love, only his protection.

In her terror, Lindsay didn't try to shield her emotions from him, nor was she conscious of his presence in her mind. As he had so often done with Catarina, Lucian took Lindsay's fear into his heart for his own. His heartbeat accelerated until he thought his chest would burst. Her anxiety coupled with his and almost disrupted his focus, but after several moments, he was able to dispel Lindsay's fear from his soul.

When her fear dissipated, Lucian gave her the two languages of Woerld that he knew and guarded his thoughts from her. Then he gently withdrew from her mind and soul. The glassiness left the child's sight, and though she still trembled, her teeth no longer chattered.

He returned his hand to her back and spoke to her in a soothing rumble, "You can let go now. It's all right." Just the same words over and over until she started to relax little by little.

It would take a few minutes before she would fully understand the languages he had given her. In every foundling's beginning, comfort initially came with soft sounds and a gentle touch until the child found the words to communicate. Lucian stifled his impatience, swallowed his fear, and murmured to the distraught child one quiet lie after another. "Everything is going to be all right. You're all right now."

He used the time to examine her delicate features. Her long hair was the color of cornsilk and she wore it pulled back into a ponytail with a band that matched her purple sweater. Wisps of her bangs fell into almond shaped eyes that were the palest blue he'd ever seen.

Her shuddering eased and she loosened her grip on his arm but didn't let go. She looked at him as if seeing him for the first time. Wonder replaced the wariness in her gaze. "I know your name." She mixed Golanian with Ra'ananian, using words from both languages in a jumbled patois. He didn't correct her; it would be a few hours before she would separate the two into distinct languages.

She clapped her hand over her mouth.

"It's all right." Lucian spoke to her using Ra'ananian. She needed to be proficient by the time they reached the Citadel, and he prayed she would never set foot in Golan. "It's all right," he said. "You know two new languages and my name."

She nodded and moved her hand away from her lips.

"Good. That's supposed to happen." She would eventually lose her native language unless she met another foundling at the Citadel from her homeland on Earth. The only reason he and Catarina retained their knowledge of Walachian was because Catarina had insisted they use it between them as their private twin-speak. The memory of his sister reminded him of their danger. "Can you say my name?"

"Lucian." She frowned.

After a moment of watching her struggle with his last name, he helped her. "Negru. You may call me Lucian."

"Okay." She released his arm and stepped back but not too far. "Lucian. Can you help me find Pete?"

"Who is Pete?"

"My brother."

"Was he with you when you saw the Veil?"

"Yeah," she whispered. She bit her quivering lower lip and took a long shuddering breath before she continued. "We got separated when we were coming through the Veil." Unable to stop her tears, she used her palms to wipe them away and only succeeded in smearing ashes across her cheeks.

Lucian didn't interrupt her as she recounted her adventure through the Veil. He gauged her reactions and though she was still upset, she could function. Relieved he'd done the right thing by alleviating her terror, he relaxed somewhat.

He promised himself that would be the last time he would take her emotions from her. From this point forward, Lindsay would have to learn to deal with Woerld's shocks on her own. He wouldn't cripple this child as he had his sister.

Lindsay's voice disrupted his thoughts. "Pete got pulled one way and I went another and he said to run, but I didn't know how, because everything was moving really fast. This doesn't make any sense, does it?"

"It makes perfect sense. You saw a red glow and it grew, and somehow, you knew it was called the Crimson Veil."

"That's right." She tilted her head to scrutinize him and her left eye narrowed. "That's exactly what happened. I saw you sleeping. Did you see me?"

He shook his head. "I heard you scream. Where were you and Pete separated? Inside the Veil or here?"

"Inside."

Lucian felt better knowing there wasn't another foundling wandering Hell's landscape. "Then he was drawn to another Elder, that's all. We'll go back to Woerld and we'll find your brother."

She looked over her shoulder to the line of the damned that shuffled deeper into the shadows then back to him. "My mom said I'm never supposed to go anywhere with strangers. I really just need to find Pete. That's all. Just help me find Pete, and he'll take care of me." Her anxiety grew with every word.

"Your mother is correct: you shouldn't trust everyone," he said. "You said you saw me sleeping. What did you feel when you saw me?"

She stared at the ground and pressed her fingertips to her lips. Precious minutes passed before she answered. "I wanted to come to you, because I felt like we belonged together." She looked up at him. "I knew you'd know what to do. That doesn't make any sense, does it?"

"Yes, it does. When you looked into my eyes just now what did you see?"

"That you want to help me." Yet her caution didn't dissipate.

"That's how I felt when I saw my Elder. I knew John would keep me safe even though I didn't understand what was happening to me. If you'll allow me, I'll keep you safe until we find your brother." He stood clumsily and held his hand out to her.

Her eyes followed his every move, and now she assessed him in much the same manner as he'd examined her earlier. It was evident she still wasn't comfortable with the situation and he could hardly blame her. His ragged appearance couldn't be very reassuring, and she had no guarantee he was taking her to a better place, much less to her brother. Lucian sighed but didn't give up. "We'll find Pete, Lindsay, if you will just trust me for a little while." Lucian forced himself to be patient while she scanned the landscape.

"Okay," she said. "But you better be what you say you are. My brother is going to be looking for me. He's big, you know. He plays football." She crossed her arms and thrust her chin at him defiantly.

Lucian raised an eyebrow at her, but his retort was cut off by a jaunty tune that tingled in the air. He had quite forgotten the cell phone until it started to ring, bringing hope to Lindsay's eyes.

"Peter! That's Pete's ring tone! Where's my phone?" Her defiance left her and she quivered in anticipation of something familiar, some rational event in this surreal world.

He reached into his pocket for the device. "Lindsay, think about what you are doing. Think. What's making your phone ring?"

Her anticipation died and her lips parted, but she made no sound.

"I'm going to answer and if it's Pete, I'll hand it to you."

"Okay, but do it quick before it goes to voicemail."

He flipped the device open and the voice on the other end opened his heart.

"Lucian." It was Rachael. He thought of smoke and honey and the memory of a summer night when she pressed her lips against his ear to moan his name.

He shook his head. The hope in Lindsay's eyes died and her shoulders slumped.

He turned so the child wouldn't see his face. "Rachael," he said before his shame choked him silent.

The static screeched between them, then her next words rang through loud and clear. "I'm coming for you, Lucian." Yet where he expected her magnificent rage, she sounded cautious, as if reassessing her position.

That slight hesitation on her part was all he needed to feed his hope. Perhaps his chance to make restitution to her wasn't as slim as he first thought. Rachael Boucher was never easily parted from her hate, but her doubts could work as his key to her heart. Everything he wanted to say to her scattered before his panicked thoughts. "I'm so sorry," he whispered.

She didn't hear him, or if she did, she ignored the feeble apology. "I have a directive from the Seraph that you are to surrender yourself to my authority."

"I will."

"What did you say?"

"I will surrender myself to your authority," he said more clearly. Lindsay edged into his line of vision; she mouthed her brother's name. Lucian put his finger to his lips. She crossed her thin arms over her chest, thrust her hip out, and frowned at him. He didn't have time to address the girl's frustration before Rachael spoke again.

"Where were you in the Wasteland before you opened the Gate?" she asked.

Acutely aware that in Hell he was on his sister's undisputed territory, he tried to think of a way to let Rachael know his route. Three days ago, he had passed a sign that had not been consumed by rot; although the letters were faded, he had made out the name of the destroyed city: Ierusal. When they were young, Rachael had called Ierusal the Forbidden City because John forbade them from patrolling north of the town.

"A few days northwest of the Forbidden City. We should reach it before you. We'll wait for you there."

She was silent for so long, he thought they had lost the connection. After an interminable wait, she asked, "Where?"

"Where you always knew to find me when I was troubled." *Where you always came to me when I needed you the most.*

"I know the place."

Keenly aware that if the Citadel already had a Judge moving because of his manipulation of the Gate, it must be later in the day than he thought. "Rachael, the time. What time is it?"

"Just after noon."

"Merciful God." The time had slipped, moving faster in Woerld than in Hell. He'd lost five hours from Woerld in the hour he'd been in Hell, and his sister's guards knew his location.

Her patience gone, Lindsay grabbed for the phone. "Ask about Peter!"

Lucian lifted his arm so she couldn't snatch the device from his hand. White noise distorted the connection. When the reception cleared, he heard someone speaking behind Rachael. Of course, she would have a constable with her; they always investigated in pairs.

Uncertain how much longer the connection would last, he spoke quickly, "There is a foundling here. Her name is Lindsay. Her brother came through the Veil with her. His name—"

"Peter." Feedback squealed through the earpiece. "I'm sorry." He heard her grief in those two words and wanted to reach out to her sadness, ease her pain. The static roared between them like a feral wind. He thought he heard her say something about jackals then the line went dead.

He dropped the phone to the dirt.

"Has she seen him?" Lindsay snatched the phone up before he

could destroy it. She flipped it open and stared at the blank screen.

"Yes, but he may be hurt. She said she was sorry." If there were jackals involved, he feared the boy dead. Yet this was neither the time nor the place to guide the child through grief. An obscene rumble shuddered through the ground, and Lucian turned to look at the pit behind them. Large chunks of gravel rattled to the edge of the hole and fell into the cavity.

"Lindsay, we have got to go. Now." He returned his attention to her. "And you're going to have to leave the phone behind."

She ignored him and punched the buttons savagely, trying to make the phone work. Her lip quivered. A fat, pallid spider crawled through the display, and Lindsay flung the phone down like it was on fire. "Gross! What did you do to it?"

"It doesn't work anymore." He brought his cane down on the phone, shattering it and killing the spider. "The Veil has closed, and your phone is merely a doorway for the damned."

From the direction of the pit, a high-pitched keening rent the air, and the girl's eyes widened. "What's that noise?"

Lucian had no idea. Despite his experience, he didn't know all the horrors Hell contained nor was he in any mood to further his education. "We have to go. Are you coming with me?" He held out his hand.

The phone forgotten, she ran to him. "Don't leave me!"

He remembered Rachael's panic when he'd abandoned her at the Gate so long ago. She'd screamed his name and he'd left her anyway. Never again. Lucian put his arm around Lindsay and waited until she grabbed his forearm. "I won't. I won't leave you. Close your eyes."

Light flashed overhead and for one nightmare instant, he saw a tentacle shoot upward from the pit. He focused his mind on the Psalm and started his chant. Hell's landscape danced in his retinas. The threads of time frayed the landscape before them like a worn tapestry. For a split second, the two worlds overlapped with Lucian's encampment in Woerld shining through Hell's barren landscape. As he finished the Psalm, Hell gave way in a blaze of light to allow them to pass through the Gate into Woerld.

Although the overcast sky clouded the hour, he was sure that Rachael's calculation of noon wasn't far from the mark. Their packs were undisturbed. Catarina's guards may not have felt the surge of his magic when he opened the Gate. If they did, they were too far away to respond immediately.

Lindsay snatched her bag off the ground and rummaged through the contents. After a thorough inspection, she seemed satisfied that her possessions were undisturbed.

"Put your coat on," he said.

She fished her coat out of her bag. "Jeez, can you do that anytime you want to?"

"Do what?"

She waved her hand. "You know—that whoosh-thing you just did."

The Gate. She wanted to know about the Gate. "No. I'll explain how that works later."

"Is Pete around here?"

He shook his head. "This is the Wasteland. Peter is farther south at the Citadel with Rachael." He helped her into her deep green coat and noted with some relief that her pants and shoes appeared sturdy enough for the terrain. At least he didn't have to worry about clothing for her. He shouldered his pack. "Now, listen: we must go very quietly. There are some bad people here, and we must be careful to avoid them."

A horse nickered in the distance. He held his finger over his lips. She tried to peer around him and started to ask another question. He put his hand over her mouth and her eyes went wide.

"Hush and listen," he whispered.

She tensed against him and nodded. He released her.

The woods and hills sheltered them and their enemy from one another's sight. Though Lucian saw no one, he heard the jingle of tack. This was no haunting.

"You've got to hide." He gestured for her to follow him and when she lingered by the road, he grabbed her wrist.

"Hey!" She glared at him and tried to pull away, but he jerked her close and clapped his hand over her mouth again.

"If you give us away, we're both dead," he whispered and was gratified to see fear in her eyes. He didn't release her until she nodded.

The wariness that crept back across her face stung him, but he had no choice. She would inadvertently give them away if she wasn't careful. She needed to be afraid. Her words were barely audible.

"You're hurting me."

He let her go and glanced down; an angry red mark encircled her wrist from where he had gripped her. His cheeks flushed with shame, but he didn't drop his gaze. "Do you understand, Lindsay? We must be quiet."

Lindsay rubbed her wrist and nodded.

"Good, now move quickly." He guided her behind the huge rock where it jutted over the ground to form a ledge. The bright gym bag went in first, and he shoved it deep into the crevice. He motioned for Lindsay to hide beneath the stone.

She scooted into the crevice. "What about you?"

He put his pack beside her. "You said you would trust me."

The horse snorted, and Lucian looked toward the trail, then back to the girl. Lindsay's anxiety became palpable. A special bond formed between foundlings and their Elders and already Lindsay was becoming sensitive to his emotions. He wished he could say something to wash the fear from her eyes. "Don't move until I come and get you."

Her head moved up and down once.

A talisman, he thought, *something for her to hold and believe in.* He had nothing to give her.

Only he did.

He reached into his breast pocket and removed his Psalter. He pressed it into her small hands. "I need your help, Lindsay."

Surprised at the sudden gift, she gripped the small book and opened her mouth.

He shook his head. "Listen. This is something very old and very magical. Close your eyes, hold the book tight, and pray to whatever god you worship that we get away safely. Can you do that?"

She nodded and held the Psalter close to her chest.

Satisfied a small portion of her fear had diminished, he left her. He went to the side of the rock where he could see the road without being seen. Only when he was out of her sight did he unsheathe Matthew's sword.

Several minutes passed before the soldier's mount ambled into view. The man wore Catarina's livery and her raven seal. Lucian didn't recognize him. The soldier rode with the sloppy abandon of someone on an afternoon jaunt rather than a hunt.

Why not? In their minds, Lucian was nothing more than Catarina's crippled brother, a ghost. They believed they had only to show themselves and he would fall subservient at their feet. They forgot that he was once Katharos.

Are Katharos, Matthew's voice whispered. *You are Katharos; God remains on his throne.* The memory of the priest's words poured courage into Lucian's heart. He would teach them to taste the fear that had soured his palate for the last ten years.

The horse would be a boon if he could take the man and leave the mount, but he needed a distraction. He bent and picked up a rock big enough to fit in the palm of his hand. Several feet away, the ground dropped to form a deep ravine. The soldier would be forced to dismount in order to investigate.

Not believing the plan would work, Lucian nonetheless threw the stone into the gully. The rock snapped a dead branch from a tree.

Horse and rider perked up at the sound. The guard drew his blade as he rode past Lucian's hiding spot. Surely no one was so stupid as to fall for that trick. To Lucian's amazement, the man dismounted and lashed the reins to a strong limb. He didn't raise the alarm to any cohorts as he gazed down into the foliage.

In his sister's house, Lucian had learned to move silently to avoid notice. Now, quiet as the specter he once was, he crept forward until only a few feet separated him from the guard. He had no choice but to thrust his blade into the man's back. He struck below the soldier's left shoulder blade and drove the steel upward into the man's heart before he withdrew the sword. For one terrifying moment, Lucian was afraid the man would scream. Instead, the soldier dropped to the ground without a cry.

Lucian crossed himself. There would be no absolution for this cold murder, and though it wasn't his first, he despised the slaughter. This killing would cling to him no less for being necessary.

Careful as he was, he still had blood on his hands when he finished cleaning his sword on the man's cloak. Lucian rolled the soldier's body to the bottom of the ravine where it stopped, mercifully face down. A short prayer and a wave of his hand brought forward a small breeze to blow fluttering leaves over the corpse. Within minutes, the soldier was covered in a shallow grave.

The horse snorted and pulled against its reins before Lucian gentled the beast with a touch. He gave the mare soothing images of the herd and a fertile field. Whether it was from opening the Gate or his newfound confidence, he felt God's Spirit return to his limbs. Acts that had once taken the greatest deliberation to accomplish were returning to him as second nature. The animal calmed, and he led it to the rock where he had left Lindsay.

Face gray with fear, Lindsay huddled beneath the outcropping. Her eyes were squeezed shut and her mouth moved silently while she hugged his Psalter.

"Lindsay."

She jumped and bumped her head on the rock. "Are they gone?"

"He's gone, but keep your voice low. There may be others nearby. Come out and don't forget your bag."

She scrambled out from beneath the rock and gave him his Psalter, then stepped back out of his reach. Without getting too close to him, she snagged the strap of her bag. Her guarded actions made Lucian wonder if she saw him kill the soldier. How would he explain the need for such a murder to her? She rubbed her wrist again, and he remembered grabbing her.

"I'm sorry," he said as he returned the Psalter to his pocket. "I didn't mean to hurt you."

"Yeah, well," she glanced down at his pack, which still rested by the ledge. She leaned over, snatched it off the ground, and handed it to him. "You scared me. Okay?"

"No, it's not okay. I shouldn't have hurt you."

She gazed into his eyes and he was sure she examined his words and intent with the same deliberation as any Citadel judge. She sighed and pulled her hair band free, twisted her long hair back into a ponytail and secured it once more. "It's okay, I guess." Her eyes lit up and she pointed over his shoulder. "How'd we get a horse?"

"God is with us."

She forgot her fear of him and went to the mare, stroking the horse's nose and murmuring to her. "My friend Cindy has a horse."

"Have you ridden before?" He secured his pack to the saddle, then held his hand out to her.

"Dad let me ride in the Cindy's corral but that's all. Are we both going to ride?"

"Two people, one horse." He shrugged and patted the mare's neck. "She is a strong mare; she'll carry us. We really need to get moving, though. In case there are more soldiers."

Lindsay went to the side of the horse and allowed him to lift her until she could get her foot in the stirrup.

Lucian mounted behind her and indicated that she should grasp the pommel. "Hold tight in case we have to go fast."

He felt her nod through her hood as he wrapped his mantle around her, more to obscure her from prying eyes than to keep her warm. He listened and thought he heard someone call out. Lindsay went rigid in front of him, but after several moments, no other sound penetrated the Wasteland's silence.

She tensed against him again when he guided the horse onto the deer path that had once been called the Great Road. When he kept the beast to a slow walk, Lindsay relaxed. Each hoof-strike against the earth sounded like thunder to him. Walking gave them the advantage of stealth, but Lucian couldn't move quickly on foot, and Lindsay's presence changed everything. The girl needed to be away from him as soon as possible.

The Council wouldn't allow him to foster this child. It would be better for them both if he remained emotionally detached and turned her over to Rachael before Lindsay's powers started to develop. With the horse and good weather, they would meet Rachael within four or five days; soon enough for Rachael to form a fostering bond with the youngster.

Lucian rode for the better part of an hour without seeing or hearing anyone else; he hoped the man had been a forward scout. He kicked the horse to a trot. His confidence rose until they reached a clearly defined crossroad. He reined the horse to a stop.

"Why are we stopping?" Lindsay whispered, and her pulse fluttered bird-like beneath her wrist.

"I'm not sure of the way." The trees and clouds obscured the sun so he couldn't easily tell the direction; the signposts had long ago deteriorated. Lucian had never approached Ierusal from this route. Examining the dull sunlight again, he guessed the southeasterly road would go left. He reined the horse in that direction, but the beast became skittish and danced back to the center of the crossroad.

Examining the road and the woods beyond, he didn't see anything that should have caused their mount anxiety. He tried the road to the right, and the horse exhibited an even more violent reaction.

"What's the matter with her?" Lindsay's knuckles were white from her grip on the pommel.

"I don't know." Once more he calmed the animal with a touch and guided the beast to the road before them. The horse plodded along docilely.

Lucian looked over his shoulder and caught a glimpse of a ghostly figure with a halo of white hair and mischievous eyes. He wheeled their mount in time to see a man's image fade into the early afternoon mist. He could have sworn the ghost winked at him with the same knowing wink Matthew Kellogg had given him in the church.

Lindsay twisted to look up at him. "Is everything okay?" Her hood fell back to reveal her white-gold hair.

"Fine. We're fine now." He guided the horse back to their original route. "I'm sure of it." Twice more, he looked over his shoulder before they rounded a bend and the crossroad was out of sight.

"Can we talk now?" Lindsay asked.

"Of course, but softly."

"Where were we, you know, in that place where you found me?"

"You mean Hell?"

"No shit? That was Hell?" She twisted again, her eyes wide.

"Don't swear, Lindsay. And yes, that was Hell."

She blushed and faced forward. "Wow."

"You're in Woerld now." They passed an open field on their right where a lone hut hunkered at the edge of the wood. The door hung askew and vines wrapped the frame. It was the first physical evidence he had seen that humans once lived here.

Lindsay leaned over his arm to examine the abandoned home. "Are we the only people here?"

"No. There was great war here many years ago and it made the country uninhabitable. We call it the War of the Great Schism, because the Seraph of the Zoroastrian bastion withdrew from the Council of Seraphs." The same type of schism that his sister hoped to promote within the Citadel, but Lucian didn't see the point in telling the child. She was too young to understand the delicate balancing act that the Seraphs maintained to keep the peace between their various religions so they could focus on their common enemy, the Fallen. "There are a lot people in Ra'anan. That's where we're going."

"Pete's there, right?"

"Yes." He hoped the boy was all right.

"Pete and I were just walking home. How did we get here?"

"You and your brother passed through the Crimson Veil."

"I remember that—Crimson Veil—but I don't know what it means." She sighed as she turned her head to take in the forest around them. "I don't understand any of this."

"It will become easier. We'll take it in small steps and start with the Veil. The Crimson Veil shields Earth from Woerld. It's like a curtain that only becomes visible at certain times."

"Why?"

"Did you ever go to church, Lindsay?"

She took the band from her hair. "Dad always called us C and E Episcopalians."

"Church of England?"

She gathered her hair back into a ponytail and popped the band in place. "Christmas and Easter."

He smiled, and the expression felt strange on his face. He couldn't remember the last time he'd smiled or even laughed. "Did you ever hear about the war in Heaven between God and Satan?"

"Yeah, God won and put Satan and all the angels that followed him into Hell. My dad said it was bullshit the preachers used to scare everybody into giving them money."

Lucian winced. He could tell from Lindsay's tone that she probably believed her father's worldview on religion. "I'm afraid your father is wrong."

She narrowed her eyes and gave him a distrustful glance.

"There really was a war in Heaven, and here in Woerld, we call those evil angels the Fallen. The Fallen Angels want to take over Woerld so they can move through the Veil to conquer Earth. Then they intend to storm Heaven's Gates. It's a matter of strategy. They consolidate their forces and solidify their positions on one level, then move to the next, invariably cornering Heaven's host."

Lindsay was silent for several minutes before she said, "That's insane."

"It makes perfect sense. I'll show you." He reined the horse to a halt and dismounted, grinding his teeth against the pain in his leg when he put his weight on it. He leaned on his cane until he could walk the stiffness from his knee. "Come down."

"What for?" She tightened her legs around the horse's sides and narrowed her left eye at him.

"I want to show you something." When she still didn't move, he sighed and looked off into the woods. This was his fault; if he hadn't hurt her back at the rock, she wouldn't be so cautious of him. Yet every second he wasted trying to explain Woerld to her was another second Speight and his men drew closer to them.

Lucian kneaded the head of his cane and tried to still his anxiety. With or without Speight hunting him, he had to teach Lindsay the rudiments of Woerld. Otherwise, she would be ill prepared when her talents started to emerge, and that could make her as dangerous to him as Catarina. "Lindsay, please."

"All right, all right." She slipped off the horse gracefully and stood just out of his reach. "Now what?"

"Watch." He used his cane to draw four circles in the dirt and connected them with lines. "Now." He pointed to the bottom circle. "Pretend this is Hell."

She glanced at him and edged closer to better see his crude outline.

He pointed to the next ring. "This is Woerld. Woerld stands between Hell and Earth." He pointed to the fourth ring. "Heaven encircles us all. Each dimension exists parallel to the other." He glanced at her, but she seemed absorbed in the diagram. "The Fallen Angels are trapped in their prison behind the Hell Gates, which are another form of—"

She shook her head. "I'm not getting any of this."

Lucian examined his diagram; he didn't know how he could possibly simplify the matter. All he had given her so far were the bare essentials. He hadn't begun to explain how the chaos of Hell could shift time to run faster or slower. Nor would Lindsay understand the Celestial Court's ability to create rifts in the timespace continuum to link Elders and foundlings who were perfectly suited for one another. How could he when even Woerld's greatest mathematicians failed to find the calculations to explain how time worked?

Lucian stifled his irritation and listened for Catarina's soldiers. The mare nosed the ground and found a rare patch of grass to nibble; otherwise, the Wasteland was quiet. All Lindsay needed to know was how she came to Woerld. He pointed the tip of his cane to the circle that represented Earth. "You started out here. And you passed through what we call the Crimson Veil." He dragged the tip of his cane along the line connecting Earth to Woerld. "Into Woerld. The Veil closed behind you." He closed the blurred line between Earth and Woerld. "You passed through a weakened Hell Gate and into Hell." He pushed the tip of his cane into the circle representing Hell. "I went in and brought you back into Woerld." He moved his cane to represent their journey.

"This is closed now?" She pointed to the line symbolizing the Veil.

"That's correct. The Veil only opens for a brief amount of time. It never allows anyone or anything from Woerld to pass through to Earth. It's like a great fence that keeps the Fallen from their objective."

"You're saying I can't go back to Earth?" Lindsay's lower lip trembled, but she didn't lose her composure.

He nodded. "I'm afraid that's so. We can never go back."

"But my mom," she whispered and her voice trailed off. Lindsay twisted her fingers in her ponytail as she contemplated the meaning of his words. "Oh, shit, this is bad."

"Lindsay, I'm sorry." Lucian reached out to her.

She stepped away from him; her distrust was back. "Nevermind. Pete's good at this stuff. He'll find a way home."

"You can't go back, Lindsay. I wanted to go home. I still haven't found a way."

"Yeah, well, Pete's smarter than you." She crossed her arms and thrust her chin at him, daring him to contradict her.

Lucian relinquished the argument to her for the time being. Very few foundlings initially believed they would never go home. Perhaps that hope sustained them in their early years in Woerld. Lucian knew his dream of finding a way back through the Veil had nourished him through his first days. Whether Lindsay believed him or not was irrelevant at this point. Time would teach her the truth.

She studied the diagram for several minutes. "So what made the Veil open? And why did Pete and I pass through it? Why not a cat or a dog that was walking by?"

"It has to do with the Fallen."

"You keep going back to those fallen angels."

"Exactly. You see the Hell Gates are sealed, but seals can be broken. The Fallen want to break free from Hell so they can overrun Woerld. Some of the Fallen were once archangels. Once free of the chains that hold them in Hell, these fallen archangels believe they can force their way into Woerld. Here in Woerld, the various bastions that represent Earth's religions work together. Each religion has very special talents and the Katharoi of these religions understand the spells to keep the Fallen out of Woerld. But we must work together. Otherwise, the Fallen will take over Woerld and once they solidify their position in Woerld, their next goal is Earth.

"Earth guards Heaven's Gates, but Earth's religions are fragmented and at war with one another. They have lost their ability to hear the Celestial Court, because they have entrenched themselves in politics and temporal matters. They have forgotten the spiritual and cannot pull together to defeat the Fallen. So we must hold the Fallen back in Woerld. Otherwise, Heaven falls and chaos will reign forever."

When she looked up at him, her left eye was almost shut. She gauged him as carefully as she had back at the rock. "Are you kidding me?"

"Did you find Hell amusing?"

Her lips parted, then she shut her mouth and without a word, she walked several paces down the road. Lucian gripped the reins and debated riding after her, but Lindsay halted, her back rigid, her hands clenched at her side. When he was sure she wasn't going anywhere, he relaxed and used the time to scan the forest. They were alone, but for how long? He wanted to move, but he couldn't rush her.

Obviously raised in a secular society, Lindsay couldn't possibly grasp everything he wanted to tell her. Religion had been an everyday part of his life before Woerld, so John's talk of Heaven and Hell had been natural to Lucian. However, he remembered how Rachael had struggled like Lindsay when she'd first come to Woerld. Lucian racked his memories to recall how John handled her disbelief, but he drew one blank after another.

Lindsay returned to him. This time, she came close to him. "You still haven't told me why Pete and I are here."

"The Crimson Veil only opens for children who have special talents."

"Talents?"

"Yes. We are drawn through the Veil to defend Woerld from the Fallen. When the Celestial Court decides a child is worthy, the Veil between Earth and Woerld parts to draw the child into Woerld." He wiped the diagram out of the dirt and pushed some leaves over the ground. "Let's talk while we ride." He couldn't still his anxiousness another minute. "We need to get moving." He held out his hand and to his astonishment, she allowed him to help her back onto the horse without protest.

He mounted behind her, relieved to put more distance between himself and Catarina's soldiers. "There is something special about you and Peter or neither of you would be here. We'll just have to wait for your talents to manifest before we know for sure." A fallen tree obstructed the road, and Lucian guided the horse off the trail to bypass the obstacle.

"What do you mean by talents?" She picked up the ends of the reins and passed them through her busy fingers.

He tried to think of a way to make her understand. "Talents are your ability to channel God's spirit."

"That's the magic you were talking about? The magic the Katharoi work to hold the Fallen back?"

"Yes. My job as your Elder is to teach you how to control the power that comes from inside you." He ducked under a low hanging branch as they skirted the log and regained the road. "The Katharoi will always manifest their light from within, and the servants of the Fallen must rely on amulets and incantations to work their magic. That's how you know the Katharoi from those who serve the Fallen."

"Are you a Katharos?"

Father Matt's words came back to him, and Lucian whispered, "Yes."

"And you're my Elder."

"For now." He felt her twist her torso so she could look up at him, but he kept his eyes on the road ahead. "The Citadel council will decide whether or not you will remain with me or if you should have another Elder to teach you our ways."

She was quiet for a while, watching the dead trees. The road wound down a steep hill, and the horse balked. Lucian coaxed the mare down the hill.

Lindsay shifted her weight in the saddle. "Did you get to stay with your Elder?"

"I did. My Elder is the Citadel's Seraph John Shea." He kept a tight rein on the horse as they ascended the knoll. Lindsay held on. When they reached the top, he said, "He is also my sister's Elder."

"Wow." She stroked the horse's neck. "Your sister is in Woerld too?"

"My sister lives in Hadra." His words suddenly hung in his throat and speaking became an effort. "Hadra is a city. In the north." He hesitated, unsure how much to say. For the time being, her fate was tied to his, she had every right to know the danger she was in, but he couldn't bring himself to tell her. He felt her gaze on his face, but he didn't look down. "Catarina. That's her name, Catarina. She is very angry with me." He paused again, and when she didn't ask why, he continued. "She wants me to return to her house in Hadra."

"But you don't want to go back."

Surprised at her perception, he shook his head. "No, I do not, and that has made my sister very angry." *And when she becomes angry, she becomes violent.*

Lindsay nodded as if she understood his reluctance to speak. "And that soldier we stole our horse from? He works for her, right?"

Lucian winced. *The soldier I killed.* "Yes."

Lindsay shifted until she faced forward and they rode in silence, Lucian listening and watching the wood around them, Lindsay deep in her own contemplations. As the day faded, he started looking for a good place to camp, and just before dusk, he reined the horse to a stop.

He led the animal off the trail and behind a large bush that would give them some cover from the road. Several feet from the bush, a stream burbled through a gully, and Lucian took the horse to the water. Lindsay dismounted and washed Hell's ashes from her face while he took care of the horse. Soon they settled down to a small dinner of the guard's rations. The shadows lengthened as the sun dipped behind the mountains.

Lindsay picked at the hard biscuit. Strands of her hair escaped her hair bow and wisped around her delicate features, creating a halo in the fading light. "Hey, Lucian?"

"Yes?"

"If we can do magic, why don't you just whoosh us?"

He raised an eyebrow at her. "Whoosh?"

"Yeah, you know, like when we were in Hell, when you did whatever it was you did: chanted, wiggled your nose, whatever, then *whoosh*!" She threw her arms wide. "We were in Woerld. Why don't you just whoosh us to the Citadel?"

Laughter burst from him like a rainbow.

"I'm being serious." A lop-sided grin teased the corner of her mouth at his infectious laughter. "What's so funny?"

The image was too ludicrous. "I'm not sure that I can."

"Whoosh us?"

He shook his head. "Wiggle my nose."

She toed the dirt with her tennis shoe and giggled. "Come on, Lucian, I'm being serious."

"So am I. Oh, Lord." He wiped his eyes. "Oh, child, it simply doesn't work like that."

She blushed. "Well, how does it work?"

"The Gates only open to certain places and knowing which ones are safe to pass through takes many years of study. And magic, well…" He carefully wrapped half of his ration for tomorrow.

"Yeah? What about magic?" Her eyes were bright with interest and she leaned forward, her elbows on her knees.

"We have major and minor talents. For example, I'm a healer and an exorcist. I can also command several Hell Gates simultaneously. Those are my major talents. I can't use those powers for anything other than healing and exorcism. And the Gates, well, the Gates will take you to Hell, no place else." He smiled at her. "I have to rely on regular modes of transportation and live by my wits like everyone else."

"Oh." Her face sagged with disappointment. "So how do the talents work?"

"Do you remember I told you that the Katharoi use the power within us?"

"Yeah."

He brushed his hands off and recalled John teaching him how to bring his soul-light into existence. "All right. I'll teach you a trick so you can understand."

"Cool." She wrapped her biscuit and put it in her pack, then gave him her undivided attention.

"Close your eyes and take a deep breath." He waited for her to comply and when she did, he smiled. "You have a light in your soul, and that light comes from a divine presence—God, Allah, Providence. Whatever you choose to call this presence, it is a part of you. Do you see it, Lindsay?"

She started to shake her head, then her whole face brightened with her smile. "I see it," she whispered as if any greater sound would chase the light away.

"Hold your hand out, palm up. Good. Now open your eyes and I want you to envision a small portion of that light floating above your palm."

Lindsay watched her palm, her eyebrows almost touching with her concentration.

"See it, Lindsay. Make it real." He watched her struggle with her concentration, then her soul-light burst over her outstretched hand to illuminate her triumphant grin.

"I did it!"

"You did indeed. We call that your soul-light. It's a minor trick, but important. You pulled the divine from within yourself and made it manifest. That is how your talents will work."

"And the Fallen can't do this."

Aware of how bright her light was in the encroaching darkness, his nervousness returned and Lucian said, "Let it go out now. We don't want to be seen."

She looked disappointed but extinguished her light.

Lucian felt better with the dusk cloaking them. "The Fallen cannot make light. They can only steal it."

"So that's why they have to use charms?" She wiggled her fingers and stifled a yawn.

Impressed that she remembered that detail, he grinned at her. "Precisely! You're very smart, Lindsay."

She blushed at the compliment. After a moment, she frowned and sat straighter. "Wait a minute. Wasn't using that magic book like using a charm?"

The book. It took him a moment to realize she meant the Psalter that he'd given her to hold this morning. "There's no magic in the Psalter. You were channeling God's power through yourself. A Katharos's power comes from within."

"You said the book was magic."

He flinched at her accusation and promised himself he wouldn't lie to her again. "You were frightened, and I thought if you had something to hold, you would find comfort. You merely used the book to focus your mind. Any power you channeled came from within you, not the Psalter."

"What's a Psalter?"

He withdrew the book from his breast pocket and she came close to see the pages. "It's a book of Psalms, but that's not what makes it special. It was gift to me from my mother. She gave one to me and a matching Psalter to my sister. These are highly prized and cost a great deal of money."

Lindsay tried to suppress her next yawn. "Does your sister still have her book?"

He settled against his pack, easing some of the pain in his leg. "No, she gave hers to a man when she left the Citadel."

Her eyes brightened and she rested her chin on her palm. "She must have really liked him."

She did it to mock him because she hated him. Lucian looked at Lindsay's expectant face and realized she anticipated a love story. Such a tale would be a lie, so he relied instead on the flat truth. "I don't think she liked him very much at all. She just wanted him to think she did."

"Oh." The word turned into a yawn she couldn't resist and she covered her mouth daintily.

"Here." Lucian took off his mantle and spread it on the ground for her. "We need to get some rest. We've got a long way to go tomorrow." He gestured to the soft ermine fur that glowed in the last of the day's light. "Lie down." When she was comfortable, he wrapped the heavy wool around her so she was shrouded in darkness and hidden from prying eyes. He gave her the gym bag to use as a pillow. "Are you warm?"

"Yeah, but what about you?"

"I'll be fine; I'm used to the weather." He went to his pack a few feet away and sat down. He didn't dare recline for fear he would sleep too deeply; instead, he sat with his back against a tree and stretched his leg out.

"Lucian?" Lindsay's voice drifted out of the darkness. "Do you think Pete's okay?"

"I don't know." He feared the boy was dead, but Lindsay's hope of finding her brother would anchor her until she learned Woerld's ways. Lucian refused to kill her expectations based on a suspicion. "I don't believe speculation in either direction will do you any good. You need to concentrate on your own survival for now."

"You don't have any magic way to, you know, see if he's okay? Do you?"

"I'm sorry, Lindsay, I don't have the Sight. It's not one of my talents."

"Oh." Just that one word, pregnant with her disappointment.

Lucian rested his head against the rough bark and listened to Lindsay's breathing even to the slow measured pace of sleep. He kept most of his promise to her by watching into the night. Dozing intermittently, he monitored the subtle shifts of the Wasteland's spells so that nothing bled through to take them in their sleep.

CHAPTER SIX

trinity

At the second floor landing, Catarina stopped with one bejeweled hand resting on the banister. The diamond clips wound into her elaborate coif reflected the firelight from the sconces and bathed the walls with stars. Flames danced along the golden threads woven into her burgundy gown to give the illusion of fire burning the seams. No woman at the mayor's dinner had rivaled her in beauty or wit this evening, yet they had all retired to their houses with their families.

To her left, Lucian's empty room taunted her. Silence upon silence was all he gave her these last few years as he'd withdrawn into himself. She could no longer penetrate his languor; it was as if he had become a phantom limb. By his own admission, he chose to walk the city day after day, seeking the suicide he couldn't bring himself to commit.

She had not thought she would feel his absence so keenly.

But she did.

Rather than go to her room, she went to Lucian's chamber. The new lock she had commanded to be installed on his door was in place, and she admired the intricate face carved into the dark metal. Part gargoyle, part demon, the lock glowered at her with blind eyes.

Lucian would find some startling changes to his living arrangements when he returned.

"Will you enter, Lady?" the lock whispered.

"I will." She turned the latch and the lock allowed her to pass.

The fire burned in the hearth and Lucian's bed was turned down for the night as if he would arrive any minute. Everything was just as he left it. His desk remained piled with papers, and books accumulated on every flat surface the room offered. Everything she had found and purchased for his happiness was here, yet he took nothing from her house but the clothes on his back.

From his desk she picked up a prism and held it to the light. Once, when they sat in the garden, he showed her how to capture the sun. They had laughed like children when the light burst forth in a rainbow against the garden wall. The sight of the colors magically filling the space took her breath away, and he had smiled at her wonder. They sat perfectly still, his hand around hers, and in that multihued moment, they had been one.

"We are never the same without you at my side," she murmured, echoing the words her twin had spoken to her when they were children. There was no he, no she, only we. Childhood pledges rendered to heartbreak by his latest treachery.

"You're home early."

She placed the prism on Lucian's desk and turned to find Cerberus sitting on the threshold, his long tail curled cat-like around his paws. His canine form filled the lower half of the doorway.

"They bore me," she said as she went to Lucian's chair and ran her fingers over the soft upholstery. She caught a faint whiff of his cologne and longed to feel his flesh beneath her hands.

The demon entered the chamber and caressed her with his silver gaze. "They're here to counsel you, not entertain you."

"They're sycophants." She kicked off her slippers and went to Lucian's bed where she relaxed, her head on her brother's pillow.

"Did they ask for him?" Cerberus stopped at the hearth to luxuriate in the heat.

"Of course they did. He's like a talisman to them; they see Lucian and all their worries disappear. The king of Golan's northern provinces—Abelard is his name—has agreed to attend our next council. The Council wants Lucian there so he can swear fealty to me before Abelard." She had until the next new moon to find her brother and wring his loyalty from him. "I don't know why they believe having Lucian there will make any difference."

"They are mortal and need reassurance of their victory. You have seen the face of our lord and master, darkling. They have not. Their faith is weak. They must be nurtured." The demon sauntered to the bed and leapt to the coverlet beside her. "Deep in their souls, they still fear John and the Citadel. Lucian is their insurance. They have confidence in his ability to open the Gates. And there are some who believe that, as Lucian's Elder, John will not attack while your brother is here." Cerberus snuggled beside her and rested his broad head on her stomach.

"John was my Elder, too." Yet John never gave her the patience or attention he lavished on Lucian. The Seraph treated her no better than her father and uncle on Earth. Her brother had been the golden child, prized for his maleness, and she had been nothing more than an inconvenience, useless as the books that kept her brother content.

Catarina took one of the books from her twin's nightstand and opened it. She tore a page out and released the paper to drift to the floor. "He used to read to me."

Cerberus heaved a bored sigh.

By the dying embers of the fire in their nursery, Lucian taught her how to read. Their father spared no expense on the best tutors to groom Lucian as his successor, but her weakling brother desired the priesthood. Blind to Catarina's true worth, their father spent his life trying to teach a bird to swim, because Lucian had no interest in governing their father's province.

In the night, when the adults slept, the twins devised a plan where they both would be happy. Lucian would teach Catarina everything she needed to know to rule their land, and on their father's death, she would rule and Lucian would join the church. They hadn't anticipated their uncle's deceit and the deaths of their parents.

Catarina ripped pages from the book, one by one. "When we were young and I was unhappy, he would do whatever I asked to see me smile again."

"It's been years since our happiness has concerned him."

"He swore to our mother that he would always watch over me." Catarina recalled their mother's haggard face as she shoved their father's bloodied ring on Lucian's finger. She had forced him to kiss the cold metal and swear an oath to watch over his sister and avenge his family.

Then she sent them into the night. They became lost in the forest until the Crimson Veil brought them into Woerld. Lucian, duty-bound creature that he was, kept the one oath he could. He watched over his twin. Catarina intended to hold him to that promise. She tore another page from the book.

Even in Woerld, all had been well between them until Rachael stole her brother's affections. Catarina had warned him to leave Rachael alone, but he'd ignored her. He always ignored her until it was too late. "He'll see the error of his ways," she muttered to the book.

Cerberus said, "He sees only misery now."

"Then he shall have it." Her uncle had taught her the art of brutality. "In abundance."

Cerberus slithered up beside her and nosed at the book until she dropped it to the floor. He whispered in her ear: "Lucian resists our reasonable requests to open the Hell Gates. No sooner than he is out of our sight, he has broken his covenant with the Citadel. The same covenant he repeatedly cited for his refusal to open the Gates for us." The demon's voice dropped to a sibilant hiss. "The jackals took a foundling near Cross Creek. We believe it died. The jackals smelled another, but it eluded them."

To take a foundling before it entered Woerld was a minor victory but a triumph nonetheless. She stroked his brow. "Do you suppose it had a sibling?"

"It's possible. That would be cause for Lucian to justify violating his covenant. If the child passed through to Hell, it's probably dead or mad by now." He relaxed beside her once more. "If the child is alive, it will be in our favor. A foundling will slow Lucian down and give Speight time to reach him." The demon paused, then whispered in her ear, "John has sent Rachael after Lucian."

Catarina smiled. When Lucian saw how Mastema and the Wyrm had maimed Rachael, he'd change his mind about love. "I'm assured she won't survive the Wasteland. The Wyrm is upon her. When the demon takes her, I will call her to me." *Then here we shall be, all of John's foundlings living as a happy family once more.* The Citadel would be without an heir apparent, and should John die, her people were prepared to promote anarchy.

"This evening," she said, "I told the Council that Speight has taken a small party to map a route for our armies. That should adequately cover his absence while he hunts my brother. Lucian knows too much."

"He will warn the Citadel," Cerberus murmured. "If they're prepared for our assault, they could extend the campaign into the next winter."

No, the attack had to be swift and deadly; Catarina couldn't afford an extensive campaign unless she crippled the Citadel quickly. Without the element of surprise on her side, John could be prepared to withstand a siege. If he found a way to extend the campaign into winter, her troops would be cut off from their supply route. The costs of the war would exceed her treasury, and Golan's King Adelard wouldn't support further battles against the other bastions. No, Lucian had to be stopped before he ruined everything. "I won't allow that. If Speight fails to bring Lucian home, I'll go after him myself."

Cerberus nipped her breast playfully. "Have a care you don't place yourself in the Citadel's hands, darkling."

So long as she remained behind the walls of a city of sanctuary, no Katharos could arrest her. If she dared step outside Hadra's gates, she could be returned to their damned Citadel for the trial she had escaped.

"If I could send my spirit far from my body, I would never have to leave Hadra. I could sing him home from the safety of this room."

Cerberus raised his head and nuzzled her ear. "Such power comes at a price."

A price. For everything there was a price, but Catarina knew how to barter with the Fallen. Deprived of God's love, the Fallen's ruined bodies only knew the anguish of their defeat. Mortal emotions were reflections of the divine and gave the Fallen short respites from their pain.

Catarina met the demon's silver eyes. "Mastema gets my soul and my love. Would you cheat your master of my love?"

Cerberus hissed and lowered his head. "Make no such accusations! Never would I cheat my master of his prize, but surely, darkling, surely you can give me sip of one of the lesser passions? In return, I have power that can be yours."

"You've become greedy." She tweaked his ear and he yelped.

"Lucian knows our plans," he said. "Perhaps Speight will find him before Rachael. Perhaps."

Catarina toyed with his ear and gazed at the tapestry. The agony in the stag's eyes reminded her of Lucian, and she felt a pang of guilt. Once they made plans with their secret childhood language, both desiring only the other's happiness. Then he had forsaken her for Rachael.

He was too unstable with his loyalties, and Lucian's love of God combined with his knowledge of her campaign against the Citadel turned him into a dangerous enemy. Only by keeping him at her side could she be assured of his allegiance. Though she hated to hurt him, she refused to tolerate his defiance, and Lucian never learned from his mistakes.

"My compassion," she murmured.

"It's such a small thing to ask."

She despised the remorse that ripped her heart when he forced her to punish him. His latest transgression proved he still placed that whore Rachael over his own flesh and blood. Lucian would always be in need of correction; he had no discipline. Without her compassion, the worthless guilt would be a memory, and Catarina would force him to submit to her will. "Take it," she said before she could change her mind.

Desire softened the demon's gaze as he inched closer to her face and pressed his lips against hers. His tongue slipped into her mouth and down her throat where she felt the pinprick of a needle. Ice ran through her veins as he drew her compassion from her soul. The empathy she once harbored for her twin vanished; all she felt was bleak despair for his betrayal. Her heart grew brittle as coal. The demon finished, and she shuddered.

A sound from the hall distracted her. Cerberus cocked an ear and turned his head as a young servant entered the room with an armload of wood. Obviously not expecting to find his mistress in Lucian's room, he halted mid-step when he saw her on the bed with the demon. He hesitated, looking first to her then to Cerberus. In the semi-dark room, she noticed his eyes were brown, lighter than Lucian's but no less lovely.

She waved him inside as her gaze crawled over his muscular arms and strong shoulders. With the same height and build as her twin, he could almost pass as Lucian's son.

The youth bowed and went to the hearth where he rolled the sleeves of his tunic before he tended the fire. The flames cast red highlights in his dark hair. He worked quietly in a noticeable effort to avoid drawing further attention to himself.

Catarina slid from beneath Cerberus and sat up. One of her diamond clips snagged on the lace of the pillowcase. A section of her long black hair spilled across her pale shoulder to frame her breast.

The sound of the clip striking the floor caused the young man to falter in his work. When she didn't speak, he resumed his labor.

Catarina removed the pins from her hair. She tossed the clips carelessly to Lucian's table where they spilled like glittering tears. "Give me your name," she said to the boy. There was power in a name.

From where he knelt by the fire, the young man froze in the act of picking up another log.

Cerberus jumped from the bed, his tail whipping from side to side as he stalked the youth. "Your mistress gave you a command."

The servant turned and faced her but kept his eyes averted. "Armand, my Lady."

"Armand." She turned the sound into a longing sigh as she untangled the last diamond clip from her locks. "Come here, Armand."

Armand didn't move. Instead, he glanced at the door as if to gauge the distance.

Traitors. All of them. Deceitful traitors. She snapped her fingers and flicked her wrist in the direction of the door. It slammed shut. From the hall, the lock snickered.

With trembling hands, Armand set the firewood down and rose. Wood chips clung to his clothes, and he looked at his dirty hands blankly. He brushed himself off and came to her. Without looking into her eyes, he knelt at her feet and mumbled, "My lady."

She leaned forward and held her hand out to him.

His lips brushed her knuckles and a tingle of desire flew up her arm. His cheek was damp with tears and she stroked his face. He didn't flinch; he wouldn't dare.

Delicately as a cat licking her paws, Catarina rolled her tongue around her finger, tasting his terror. It wasn't his despair she wanted. "Come to me, Armand." She tugged his hand and he rose to sit beside her. "Lie down, darling."

She drew him to the center of the bed and when his dark head was against her brother's pillow, she stretched out beside him, her skirts settling around them. "Tell me who you love, Armand."

Confused by her request, his gaze met hers and she had him. She wrapped her will around his and drew him close. They were simple as sheep, these easily manipulated children, not at all like her twin, who resisted her.

"Your love. Is it a girl? Do you have a girl, Armand?" Her mouth brushed his. "That you love?"

His lips parted, but before he could articulate a sound, a name touched her mind: *Clarissa*.

"You love a girl named Clarissa. Is that right?" She smiled at him as she traced the line of his jaw with a feather touch.

Frozen beneath her spell, he shivered.

Cerberus jumped onto the bed and brought his snout close to Armand's face. The youth tried to squirm away from the demon, but there was nowhere to go. Catarina held him in her enchantment so Cerberus could lick each of the young man's tears as they fell.

"Armand," she whispered. He made a small sound in the back of his throat. She unlaced his tunic, trailing first her fingers then her lips down his chest. "Give me your love."

"Please." He tried to resist her, but he had looked into her eyes. He belonged to her, and in the end he had no choice but to obey.

She kissed his lips and sucked his love from his soul as Cerberus had taken her compassion. Her flesh warmed, yet the relief she derived from this child was a weak mimicry of the respite she took from Lucian.

Her twin's love was pure, and when she kissed him, she drank deep from his soul. Without him, she was ever cold.

We are never the same without you at my side.

Cerberus moved to her side of the bed, his tail snaked up her ankle to her calf as he stepped on the mattress. Fluid as an eel, he slithered up her back, pressing her closer to Armand.

"Lucian," she moaned against the boy's hair. Cerberus' strength flowed through her veins and Armand's passion filled the dark holes of her spirit. Her vision was sharper, her hearing more acute. Motes of power danced through the air like a rainbow of light. No drug made her feel like this. She was invincible.

"Sing him home," Cerberus said, his breath hot against her ear.

She could. The strength was hers. She could find her way to her brother's soul and sing him home. He would have no choice but to obey her, and when he did, she would turn his heart to glass.

The demon nuzzled her hair and said, "Do it. Turn his heart to glass, grind it to powder, and if he speaks…"

"If he dares," she whispered against Armand's throat.

"…crush every soul he has ever loved."

In the darkness, she sang to a man-child and dreamed of her twin. Humming softly…

†

He awoke to a broken lullaby he recalled from his youth. Someone whispered his name. Lucian opened his eyes, wrapped in night so deep that he could not see his breath mist before him in the icy air. His sister's spirit hovered at the edge of their little camp.

Lucian's blood roared through his veins; fear gripped him by the throat at the sight of her. This magic was new, and she'd caught him unawares. Now that he didn't have to guard his every thought against her, life outside of her house had made him careless. Lucian refrained from glancing in Lindsay's direction. For now, the child was safely behind him, out of his sister's sight.

"Lucian, we are never the same without you at my side." Catarina's voice passed through space and time as a nail to his heart, recalling their devotion to one another before her corruption. On a journey with his father, Lucian had written those words to her when they'd lived on Earth. They had been ten, and he knew she pined for him during those trips, so he always tried to write words to soothe her. She was no longer a child and neither was he.

Grinding his teeth against the pain and the cold, he struggled to his feet. "No more, Cate." It was partial demand, partial plea.

"Oh, my darling," she said. "We've had such a misunderstanding."

She shook her head sadly and her dark hair shadowed her face like a veil. He couldn't see her eyes and thought himself safe from her wiles. "I know the thought of my retribution frightened you, but you misinterpreted my actions. My spies have uncovered threats against us. I sent my soldiers because I worried for your safety. The priest told me you were terrified so he helped you leave. What lies you've spread, Lucian. It grieves me that you believe I am such a monster."

He felt her distress, and guilt gnawed his heart. Could his fear have clouded his judgment? He remembered her pleading tone as he'd walked out on her. Rather than demanding that he return, she had implored him.

"Now you are in great danger, wandering the Wasteland alone." She gestured to his leg. "Crippled. What would happen if you fall and cannot rise? How can I live if something happens to you?"

With the special bond they shared, he heard her thoughts as clearly as if she'd spoken. *We are never the same*, her heart whispered to his, *without you*. "Come home, Lucian, where the fires are warm and there is no more pain. I forgive you. We'll forget about this and love one another again."

Each time she said his name her spell wrapped more securely around his heart. He saw his room behind her, enveloped in heat from the roaring fire; the warmth washed over his body and drove his pain away. Wouldn't it be good to rest? To be warm and fed?

Come home, Lucian.

Relief flowed through him. It was all a mistake. He'd simply misinterpreted her intentions. This time would different; they would put aside their grievances. She would listen. Surely she would be reasonable. This time.

"Lucian?" Lindsay whispered as she touched his hand. "What's going on?"

Catarina's hold over him shattered when he looked away from his sister. The remnants of her enchantment spun away, insubstantial as dreams. The chill air of the Wasteland seeped back into his bones and his stomach growled with hunger. Only pain and humiliation awaited him in Hadra. She would never forgive him for running a second time.

He took Lindsay's hand and drew the girl close. How could he have forgotten Lindsay? A week in Hadra would leave the girl insane. All the fires blazing in that haunted house couldn't keep the shadows at bay. There was no reprieve from his sister's malevolence. There never could be.

He wouldn't betray another innocent to Catarina's wrath, not for all the warmth on Woerld. *God help me, please.* Lucian saw his room again; this time, he noticed a young man supine on the bed. The youth had eyes like stones to match his loveless heart, shriveled and black.

Go home where she will grind glass into my heart for eternity. "No more," he said a second time, his voice stronger.

Catarina ignored him and addressed Lindsay. "Tell me your name, my dear."

"Tell her nothing." Lucian tried to shield the girl from his sister, but Lindsay was captivated by Catarina and stepped around him.

"Lindsay Richardson."

"Lindsay Richardson. What a lovely name. And aren't you pretty and pale, like a girl made of glass?" Catarina's apparition flickered then grew clear again.

Lucian took heart; a spell this strong had to be draining her physical body. He only had to wait her out and pray that Lindsay said nothing to give their location away.

"I'm so sorry, Lindsay. My brother is very confused, his mind is not right. Tell me, has he been telling you about demons and Hell? Angels?"

The weight of Lucian's fear almost dragged him down. With his shaggy hair and beard, he probably looked and smelled like a madman wandering the wilderness, raving of angels and demons. The fragile progress he'd made to win the child's trust was broken; he could see it in Lindsay's guarded look. "She lies, Lindsay," he said.

"He thinks I want to hurt him, but I just want him to be safe." Catarina smiled. "He needs someone to look after him."

"Are you?" The girl stepped away from him and he released her hand. "Crazy?"

"No, Lindsay." Lucian shook his head. "No."

"He's just sick and confused," Catarina said.

Lucian stood very still so as not to startle the child. "I swear I haven't lied to you."

"Haven't you, Lucian?" Catarina gestured to the mare. "Have you told her that you murdered the man who rode that horse? Isn't that a lie of omission?"

Lindsay took another step back and tripped. Lucian reached out to grab her arm and break her fall, but she twisted away from him. She sat down hard and looked up at him. "Is she telling the truth? Did you kill somebody?"

"I did."

"Oh, God," Lindsay whispered.

"Tell me where you are, Lindsay." Catarina's spirit drifted forward, and Lindsay pushed herself backward. Catarina halted. "Not everything he told you was a lie. You were drawn to him, and he is your Elder, damaged though he is. I know you're trying to understand your attachment to Lucian. These first days are so hard for foundlings. If you help me bring my poor brother home, you may stay with us. I will dress you like a princess and give you everything you could possibly desire. Have you seen a tree, a house, something you can describe to me so my men can find you?"

Lucian wanted nothing more than to let the child see his heart and know he meant her no harm, but he couldn't manipulate Lindsay's decision. Either she would choose to follow her Elder or she would choose the easier path of the Fallen. Whichever road she desired, the decision had to be hers and hers alone. If he influenced her as he had Catarina, then he would always doubt Lindsay's allegiance to the Citadel.

Lindsay sat on the ground, her gaze flickering from Lucian to Catarina. She was overwhelmed; Lucian saw it in her tears, and his heart was moved with pity. He said, "You owe me no loyalty. If you want to tell her where you are, go ahead. I just ask that you wait until dawn. That will give me time to be away. Will you do that for me, Lindsay?"

"Tell me now, Lindsay." Catarina's image shimmered with her eagerness and she leaned over the child.

Lindsay evaluated first Catarina, then Lucian, measuring each twin with her gaze. Her left eye narrowed at Catarina. Lindsay wiped her eyes and stood to take Lucian's hand. "I'm staying with you. I don't think you're crazy." She whispered, "I didn't think Hell was amusing."

Lucian wanted to weep for joy; his respite was short.

Catarina's shriek filled the night. "You'll tell me where you are, bitch-child!"

Lindsay screamed. "Stop it! Lucian! Make it stop!" She doubled over and pulled at her hair. The band that held her ponytail in place snapped free, and her pale locks tumbled around her face. She yanked handfuls of hair from her scalp. White strands floated to the ground in an ashen heap. Lucian dropped his cane and grabbed her so he could hold her with both hands. Wild with pain, she tried to twist away from him, but he kept his grip.

Lindsay didn't know how to shield herself, and Catarina intended to seize the information from the girl's mind. Lucian had been the victim of his twin's attacks in the past, but Catarina always needed Cerberus to aid her in defeating Lucian's defenses.

As he had in Hell, he concentrated on Lindsay's mind until he felt his soul connect with hers. This time, she was aware of his presence in her mind. He startled her with the intimacy of his thoughts, but she didn't resist him. Under normal circumstances, an Elder and foundling would use an opportunity like this to cement their attachment to one another.

Yet these weren't normal circumstances, and he would not remain her Elder. He had no choice. Catarina would kill the child. Lucian shielded Lindsay from Catarina's assault then turned on his sister.

He had no time to mourn his neglect of prayer. He scoured his memory for a Psalm of protection. Yet the only one he could recall was the Psalm Rachael used whenever she was threatened. "'I cry aloud to—'"

Scalded by his words, Catarina fled from Lindsay's mind. "God damn you—"

"—'that he may hear me.'"

"—Lucian, don't you dare pray against me!"

Free of his twin's control, Lindsay sagged against him. Sobs racked her body.

Catarina's image wavered. "Is this how you treat me after all I've done for you? You pray against your own flesh and blood for the sake of a stranger! Is this how you repay my benevolence? You offend me with your ingratitude."

Oh, dear God, but isn't that grand? He *offended* her. He wasn't prepared for the rage that surged through his chest and flushed his face like a lightning flash.

Suddenly, his head rocked and he staggered beneath the pain shattering his mind. His heart hammered against his ribs as if it could escape its prison of blood and bone. Before he could recover himself, Catarina shot another blow to his mind that was the equivalent to a punch in the face. He barely shielded the child from the brunt of his twin's attacks.

"Lucian!" Lindsay's cry penetrated his agony.

"Lucian!" Catarina's mocking voice echoed. "Silence! Or I'll break you!"

The agony in his head blinded him, and he lost precious moments struggling out of the pain. When the encampment swam back into focus, he raised his head and locked his attention on his twin. "In the day of my trouble I seek the Lord—'"

Catarina flinched and screamed. "You will come home to me now!" Weeping wrath, she pointed one shaking finger at him. "Do not estrange yourself from me, brother. I am all that stands between you and suffering. Do not make that third pronouncement."

"No more!" His voice thundered through the pre-dawn silence, and her features contorted as she shrieked herself back to her warm rooms.

In her absence, nothing stirred. Woerld was silent and the wood not so dark now that death had passed them over. Still, he couldn't slow his pounding heart nor rid himself of the rancid taste of...

†

Fear soured Rachael's mouth, almost bringing her to wakefulness before her dreams drowned her in slumber. On her blanket before the small campfire, she moaned in her sleep as Lucian's terror bumped against her breast. She felt his heart pound; the same heart that had once beat in time with her own. His vulnerability disturbed her, for the Draconian prince she had known never felt so trivial an emotion as fear.

...no more, no more, no more...

We were done long ago, long before this dawn when he denied his sister three times. *We are done, Lucian.*

Through space and time, his answer drifted soft as ashes, *I understand.*

Then the fragile link severed and Lucian was gone from her. She wasn't prepared for the vast emptiness he left in his wake. The darkness his presence held at bay came rushing down on her, engulfing her in a misery deepened by his absence. The Wyrm scratched against the back of her mind, rapping, tapping, seeking a way into her so it could use her for its own, but she cried aloud to God and drove the Wyrm back.

Tossing restlessly, she dreamed Lucian standing before her. She was drenched in blood and thrust her crimson hands forward, her life pooling at her feet. *I can't make it stop*, she said as a fly whined past her face.

In the sky, a great dark cloud boiled on the horizon. Thunder reached the crescendo of a sonic boom. It was coming, hidden in the cloud, something huge, coming straight for Lucian. Her breath came in short bursts. She held up her hand, palm out to the blackness bearing down on them.

no no No No No. "No!" She sat up on the cool ground of their campsite, her arm outstretched like it had been in her dream. She felt Lucian's presence return, nothing more than the faintest sense of his consciousness touching hers, but there with her.

Rachael.

Just her name and nothing more, because he had never called her Rae like the others. He always said her whole name as if he loved the feel of it in his mouth.

Rachael.

Just her name. Then he was gone from her again and so was her fear.

Someone took her wrist and she bit a scream to silence.

"Rae?"

In the small encampment, shapes became clearer in the pre-dawn light that hedged the shadows clinging to her awareness. Focusing on the coals of the fire she and Caleb had allowed themselves, she tried to bring herself back to reality.

"I'm here for you, Rae." Caleb's voice dispersed the last of her dream.

He was beside her, close enough to kiss, and for one wild instant, Rachael expected him to brush his lips against hers. An image abruptly flashed through her brain, and she saw herself with Caleb. They were in her bed naked, straining against one another. He kneaded her breast with one greedy hand and pinched her nipple between his finger and thumb. She clawed his back and bit his shoulder; her hips rising to meet his thrusts as he pushed himself deeper into her. As suddenly as it had begun, the image was gone.

Rachael shuddered. Where had that picture come from? "All right." Her voice was thick with unshed cries and the Wyrm snaked forward. She sent it scurrying. *I cry aloud... oh, God... I cry.* "It's all right," she said.

He nodded but didn't let her go. She extracted herself from his grip; she didn't want him touching her. He frowned like he read her mind and sensed her loathing. She shook off the idea. Caleb's talents were moderate at best. He excelled in sensing the presence of others, but he didn't have the ability to discern their thoughts. Only those with the greater talents could actually hear the thoughts of others.

"Lucian is on the move," she said to break the uneasy silence. "He's coming south with the foundling. Catarina wants him home to her. He's denied her three times."

Caleb blanched at Lucian's name. "How do you know all that?"

"I drift." Lucian's word: drifting. That's what he called the surreal experience of moving between dreams and realities during sleep. "There was a disturbance in the Wasteland last night."

He gazed into the fields again. "The two of you always were too close."

"He was shielding the foundling from Catarina."

Caleb snorted a laugh and rose. He walked to the fire and kicked the dirt more violently than necessary to cover the smoldering coals. "We haven't even reached him and he's already started to deceive you."

"There was no deception. He was protecting the foundling."

"That's what he wants you to think."

Rachael got up and grabbed her saddle. "I'm a judge, Caleb."

"You were a judge when he deceived you the first time."

She choked on her rage and turned on him. His back was to her so he didn't see her scowl. She said, "Which means I'm watching him closely now."

"Are you really?" He threw the saddle blanket onto his mount and the mare danced away from him. He soothed the horse with a touch.

Her tone turned deadly. "I'm watching everyone, Caleb." *And that includes you, my good friend.*

He froze then calmly pulled the saddle's cinch into place. "I'm on your side, Rae. You know that."

Do I?

"After all we've been through, you should know that."

"But I'm deceived so easily."

"That's not what I meant." He turned to face her. "Lucian is complicit with the Fallen, and he has Mastema's gift for lies. That's how he deceived John, Reynard, me, you. All of us, Rae, he deceived all of us. He's dangerous and he'll use your feelings for him against you. That's how the Fallen win. They turn your greatest weakness against you."

She didn't like the fear she saw in his eyes, not at all. Yet it wasn't Lucian that Caleb feared. There was something else, something deeper and the truth eluded her. It had something to do with Tanith. Tanith tried to warn her, but Rachael couldn't recall the older woman's exact words. They had stood close together in the courtyard, whispering so no one would hear, and Tanith said—

"Rae? Are you okay?"

Rachael started and realized Caleb was ready to go; she hadn't begun to saddle Ignatius. "I'm fine." She got to work and finished quickly. What was wrong with her? She couldn't remember a conversation from three days ago, but her past with Lucian remained clear as day.

Caleb didn't pursue their discussion as they took to the road, and she didn't encourage any more talk. She'd had enough barren words to last her a lifetime.

The fields surrounding them were coming to life with farmers and their families working diligently to bring in the harvest. She envied them their normalcy and their easy companionship.

Ignatius trotted effortlessly on the good road, and the Wyrm receded with the strengthening sun. Yet she still couldn't resurrect

Tanith's words. All her mind conjured was the image of Lucian comforting the foundling. He appeared ragged and broken with his tattered dignity drawn around him like a cerecloth.

Catarina was absent from his side and now Rachael understood why: Lucian ran from his sister as fast as his disabled body would allow. This morning's dream had solidified her suspicions that something had broken between the twins.

The recollection of Lucian's haunted eyes moved her heart to a pity she couldn't afford. Yet there was something else, something Rachael could only feel, a desire he guarded jealously, and it had to do with her.

She thought she heard him say he was sorry.

Or maybe that, too, was white noise blowing in the background; words as sterile as the loneliness engulfing her life. The deed was done and though time had not healed her, she had reconciled herself to her emptiness.

His remorse shouldn't matter to her one way or another.

But it did.

CHAPTER SEVEN

melasur

Lindsay buried her face in Lucian's shirt; her ears rang, drowning any sound other than the steady thump of Lucian's heart against her ear. Her head throbbed and she tasted blood on her upper lip. She closed her eyes and tried to pretend that Lucian was Pete. Her dad always pushed her away and told her to stop whining, but Pete rocked her and called her his tough girl and promised to make her pain go away. Pete always made her feel safe.

Lindsay opened her eyes. After a spate of dizziness, she focused on the threads of space mangled by Catarina's departing spirit. Yesterday, everything seemed like an adventure, like stepping through the wardrobe or falling through the looking glass, but Catarina's attack had turned Woerld ugly. The air crackled with static like a disrupted television signal before it eventually solidified into the terrain she remembered seeing last night.

Lucian's large hand rested lightly on her brow and she felt the warmth of his concern. His magic thrummed through her body with a pleasant tingling sensation. Any doubts she had about his intentions disappeared when she saw his commitment to protecting her. She didn't know how to shield her mind against him, but right now she didn't want to push him away.

Immersed in his memories, she saw portions of his life. Though he prevented her from witnessing the worst of the horrors he'd experienced, she saw enough to fear his twin. Catarina didn't love him. She fed on his soul like some psychic vampire and forced him to heal her every ache. When he didn't do what she wanted, she hurt him like she had just now.

Lindsay felt a brief surge of confidence. She'd made the right decision by keeping their location hidden. She just wished she knew how to keep Catarina from hurting her again.

"I will teach you how to keep yourself safe." Lucian's soft baritone thrummed past her headache. "Imagine a wall around you, Lindsay."

She squeezed her eyes shut until stars danced behind her lids. Lindsay imagined a glass dome.

"That's very good. Make it strong and hard. Can you do that?"

Bulletproof, she made it bulletproof so anything that hit her wall bounced off.

"Now make it so no one can see inside you."

Lindsay imagined the wall was opaque like the tinted glass on her dad's SUV; she could see out, but no one could see inside. Not even Lucian. Surprised, she whispered, "It worked."

He didn't answer and she looked up. He remained still with his eyes closed. He tilted his head like he was listening to some sound only he could hear. Lindsay lowered her glass wall and heard him call out Rachael's name, but his lips didn't move.

He had spoken, she was sure of it. Not with his voice, she realized, but with his heart. *He's talking to her with his heart, because he loves her and he's afraid.*

Faintly—and here Lindsay closed her eyes and listened intently—but very faintly, she heard Rachael's reply. Rachael told him they were done, and Lucian fled her jagged grief, unable to bear his shame.

Lucian shielded his mind against Lindsay, and she missed the comfort of his presence. Their encampment swam before her vision; a thick fog obscured the trees. Lindsay blinked; her dizziness was back. "Lucian? I don't feel so good."

"Rest. Another minute. It will pass." He slurred his words as if he was drunk.

But he's not. He didn't smell like her dad did when he was drunk and he wasn't mean. No, he was hurt, worse than her. "What happened?"

"My sister—" He released her and withdrew a handkerchief from his sleeve. "—has become more powerful."

Fear bit into Lindsay's heart. The ringing in her ears was starting to fade, but her head was still pounding. She helped him stand. "Are you sure you're going to be okay?"

"I will be." He leaned on his cane, his head bowed. When he wiped his face, the cloth came away red. A crimson tear slipped from his eye.

"Jeez, Lucian, you're bleeding!" She hated the way her panic drove her voice up two octaves, but she had no idea what to do if he got sick. There were no hospitals here, no ambulances. The realization of their helplessness dropped ten pounds of ice into her stomach. She wished Pete were here. He'd know what to do.

"I'm all right." Daubing another bloody tear, he gave her a wan smile that did nothing to reassure her. "Whenever the Fallen attack a Katharos, it causes us to bleed, often from the eyes. If the attack is severe then from the ears or nose."

She remembered her first aid class at school and how their teacher warned them never to move someone with a head injury. There hadn't been anything about bloody tears, but bleeding from the ears or nose could mean a concussion.

"Like a concussion?" Even as the words left her mouth, she felt stupid. God, why was she always saying stupid things?

"Similar. And you're not stupid. Just inexperienced." He reached down and Lindsay didn't flinch when he touched her upper lip.

When she saw the red on his fingertip, she wiped her nose and stared at the blood. "What does this mean?"

"You are Katharos," he said.

She thought she saw a glimmer of pride in his eyes. Katharos. He made it sound like such an honor, like she'd done something really important. Lucian called her Katharos with the same dignity that her dad gave to Pete's status as a football player. Katharos. Finally somebody was proud of her. Lindsay wiped her blood on her jeans.

Lucian limped to the tack where he picked up the bridle. He motioned for her to join him. In the middle of the halter's brow strap, there was a finely crafted metal emblem.

"Do you see this?"

It was a circle and in the center, two ravens faced one another with their furious wings spread wide. Their beaks were locked in mortal combat. "Yeah."

"This is the symbol that Catarina has devised for Mastema's bastion. Mastema is Beelzebub's general. Do you remember what I told you yesterday about the Fallen?"

It felt like a test, but after seeing his memories, Lindsay understood that everything on Woerld was a test. Only this wasn't a game and one screw-up could mean death. She glanced at Lucian's bad leg. Or worse. "I remember. They want to break out of Hell and take over Woerld first, then Earth, then Heaven."

"Very good. A very long time ago, my sister summoned a demon: Cerberus."

"The three-headed hound of Hell."

He paused and a slow smile crinkled the lines around his eyes. She'd known something he didn't have to tell her and her confidence grew.

"Well," he said, "the Cerberus I know has only one head and that's wicked enough. He persuaded my sister to sell her allegiance to Mastema. This means that she'll serve the Fallen on Woerld while she lives and again in Hell when she dies. In return, Mastema has promised to make my twin a ruler on Woerld."

"What's that got to do with you?"

"When she made her bargain, my sister also promised Mastema my allegiance."

"What did you do?"

"I refused. And you must promise me that you'll never accept anything with this emblem on it. No matter how pretty it may shine, no matter how kindly it's presented to you, never accept anything with these ravens or you will bind yourself in an agreement with my sister and Mastema. Will you promise me?"

Lindsay looked at the emblem and recalled seeing the same design on Catarina's necklace. Catarina's amulet had glowed with a pale green light the whole time she attacked them. What was it Lucian had said about the people who followed the Fallen? They used amulets and incantations. That's what Catarina did. Just like Lucian had said.

Maybe he didn't tell Lindsay about killing that soldier, but when

Catarina brought it up, Lucian didn't try to lie; he told the truth. So far, everything he'd said was true. Pete always told her not to listen to what people say, but watch what they do.

Yesterday, she hadn't known what Lucian meant when he'd called himself her Elder, but now she realized he was like an adoptive parent. If he said to avoid Mastema, then she would. "I promise."

"Good. Very good, Lindsay." He gave her a hint of a smile. "Remember the emblem. It's not well known in the south and some people wear it boldly."

Feeling surer of herself, she asked, "Will you promise me something?"

He slipped the halter over the mare's head. "I'll try." His speech was no longer slurred, and he seemed to be recovering from whatever Catarina had done to him.

She picked up the saddle blanket and brushed the dirt and dead twigs off it before she handed it to him. Unsure how to bring up the soldier's death, she paused, then asked, "Did you have to kill him? You know. That soldier?"

His hands slowed and he turned to face her. His smile was gone, and his eyes looked so sad, she felt a lump rise to her throat. She was suddenly sorry she'd brought the whole thing up, but she had to know the truth. Her fingers found a twig stuck to her coat and she twisted the wood until it snapped.

"I'm afraid I did," he said. "If I hadn't, he would have raised the alarm, and we would be on our way to Hadra right now. Back to my sister."

Lindsay swallowed and nodded. She had no desire to see his sister again. "Let's try not to kill anybody else, though, okay?"

"I can only promise you that I will kill when there is no other way."

Lindsay toed the dirt with her tennis shoe and considered his compromise. "I guess I could go with that. I mean, you're all into this Biblical stuff, you know? Just remember that 'Thou shalt not kill' part, okay?"

A faint smile touched his mouth before he turned serious again. "God will forgive you for defending your life. That's what I did with the soldier. I defended our lives. I was wrong not to tell you about it."

Lindsay winced at the guilt she heard in his words. "Yeah, well, that's okay. Not telling me, I mean."

"I understand." He lifted the saddle and placed it on the horse's back. "Why don't you go down to the creek and wash up?" He unhooked the flask and handed it her before he reached for the cinch. "Fill that up. We need to leave."

"Sure." Relieved that he'd found a way to end the awkward conversation, she grabbed the flask and went to the creek. God, but she could such an ass sometimes. Pete was right; she didn't need to spew every thought that rolled through her brain straight out of her mouth. Lindsay carefully picked her way through the dead leaves to the edge of the water.

The creek was only ten feet away from their camp, but with the foggy morning, she could barely see Lucian working with the horse when she looked back. She squatted on the bank and ducked the flask under the icy water until it was full. She had just started to wash her face when the whisper of voices filtered through the fog.

"...not here..."

"Well, look harder," another man answered. "Speight's going to have our balls if we don't find that son of bitch."

Lindsay froze. She couldn't see anyone, and the fog carried the sounds funny. She couldn't tell which direction the voices were coming from, but she had no doubt who they were. Lucian said Catarina's soldiers were out there, and Lucian hadn't lied. Not once.

"Speight's going to make him walk back to Hadra."

The other man wheezed a short chuckle. "End up dragging 'im back is what. The bastard can't walk for shit."

Lindsay's fear nailed her to the ground. She couldn't move. The soldiers were coming and she couldn't move. She had to warn Lucian.

The soft thud of hoof beats sounded behind her and she squeezed her eyes shut.

"Lindsay," Lucian whispered.

She almost cried out in relief. She turned and saw his eyes narrow to dangerous slits, but he wasn't angry with her. He was looking into the fog where she'd heard the soldiers talking. The air around Lucian darkened visibly. Lindsay blinked, but the dark aura remained with him, threatening as a thundercloud. Unsettled by the raw fury around him, she didn't immediately reach up to take his outstretched hand.

He leaned toward her and afraid he would fall, Lindsay grabbed his hand. He easily lifted her to the saddle in front of him. He hadn't tied his pack to the horse, but wore it on his back. She also noticed he wore his sword on his hip where it would be within easy reach.

He tied something heavy around her waist and she looked down to find his knife hanging from her hip in a leather sheath like a sword. Her spit dried in her mouth. She guessed the blade was six or seven inches long and the whole thing felt heavy and cold.

Lucian's breath moved her hair as he whispered, "You won't be strong enough to push it through their leather."

She gaped at him. He was talking about hurting somebody. "I can't do that." She kept her voice low, but she wanted to scream. She had to make him understand, she couldn't stab somebody. "Lucian, I can't."

He put his arm around her and drew her so close she could almost taste his breath. "Stab any break in their armor. Aim for the neck, the shoulders, the elbows, or behind the knees. Keep it sheathed while we're riding. If we lose the horse or become separated, strike to kill or maim."

Tears stung her eyes. "I can't."

"Your life depends on it."

"Can't we hide until they go away?"

He put his hand over her mouth. "It's you or them. Don't listen to their lies; don't bargain with them. If you have to kill, do it. God will forgive you for defending your life."

She felt sick enough to vomit. Lucian released her and nudged the horse forward. Lindsay gripped the pommel as he guided the mare back to the road. Her pulse started to pound and she felt each throb of blood pass through her veins. Every sound in the woods penetrated the adrenaline washing over her.

The trees loomed like black bones and the dull light rendered the dense fog luminescent. The soft dirt path he called a road muffled the mare's hoof beats. They had barely gone a hundred yards when a horn blew so close Lindsay almost screamed.

Someone shouted and another horn blew three times in answer to the first. The shadows of other riders became visible through the trees.

Lucian dug his heels into the mare's sides and snapped the reins to hit the horse's flank. Their mount shot forward. Two riders came out of the mist on their left, and Lucian yanked the reins hard to the right to plunge them into the forest.

He bent low over the mare's neck, forcing Lindsay forward to shield her body with his own. Grabbing the pommel with both hands, she squeezed her knees around the horse's sides and held tight.

A tree limb snapped at her face and slashed her cheek. Her sob was lost in the thunder of hooves and the shouts of Speight's men. Another horn blew; Lindsay couldn't determine the location. Everything was moving too fast, the trees blurring past.

Their horse reared, balking at a steep slope. The pommel jabbed Lindsay in the stomach and she gasped for breath. She knotted her fingers in the horse's mane. Certain they'd spill to the ground, she waited for the impact. Lucian kept them in the saddle.

When he regained control of the mare, he forced the horse down the hill. She shied and tried to gingerly pick her way down the slope. Lucian didn't give her time. He snapped the long reins again. The mare plunged forward, half-sliding on her haunches. She stumbled at the bottom. Lindsay screwed her eyes shut; the horse regained her balance and took off again.

The sound of horns bellowing around them drowned Lindsay's thoughts as Lucian forced the mare uphill. The soldiers were moving slower through the woods, but they were close, and they were coming at them from all sides.

✝

Had Lucian been alone, he would have fought them until he forced one of them to kill him. The child changed everything, and he had to find a way to lose them. He put his hand on the mare's neck and channeled his panic into her mind. She sideswiped a tree and Lucian took a blow to his thigh. He was grateful it wasn't his knee. Branches flailed at his arms as he pushed the horse to the limits of her endurance.

The forest gave way to a huge field of long grass that tangled around their mare's legs. Though she slowed, she didn't stop. Foundation stones poked through the grass, and Lucian looked to his right to see the crumbling city of Melasur. The remnants of the Zoroastrian bastion and its ruined towers rose out of the gloom, a ghost fortress on the horizon.

He risked a glance over his shoulder to see seven soldiers come out of the woods. Even from this distance, Lucian recognized Speight. The captain led the chase, Catarina's emblem shining on his chest.

A strong wind blew from the south and the sun peeked through the clouds to feather the mists. Within minutes, they had lost the cover of the fog. Their mount struggled up a short hill. Lucian jerked the reins hard to the right a second time to avoid going off into a deep gorge. Over two hundred feet below, whitewater surged through the narrow canyon; he found the view comforting. If worst came to worst, he would send the mare over the edge.

On level ground, the horse picked up a fraction of the speed she had maintained during the ride through the wood. She was growing tired.

Ahead, the Melasur Bridge spanned the gorge. Thick gray columns made of mountain rock rose from the gorge to form graceful arches that supported the deck of the bridge. Before the War of the Great Schism, the Melasur Bridge had transported throngs of people between Ierusal and Melasur.

As they neared, Lucian's hope for an easy crossing faded when he saw the blackened and broken stone. The vestiges of ancient magic hung in the air like a bad smell, though any power from the spells was long gone. All that remained was the result of destruction left in the wake of the War.

Three segments of the original deck had been blasted completely away. The gaps had been repaired with wooden platforms, but when the Wasteland was abandoned, the platforms were left to the elements. The guardrails on both sides were missing or rotted and the platforms were probably in the same sorry state. Huge chunks of stone, some as large as wagons, littered the deck. With Speight on his heels, Lucian had no choice but to chance the bridge.

He steered the mare from the embankment to the deck. Before he could slow her to a walk, she skidded on loose stones. The wind howled around them, and the mare laid her ears flat against her head. Her eyes rolled so that he could see the whites with every toss of her head.

Speight and his six men reached the top of the rise.

The icy wind tore at Lucian and ripped Lindsay's hood from her head. The horse's nostrils flared as she took one skittish, sidling step after another. The mare was spooked, either by the wind or his own terror, and he wouldn't be able to control her much longer.

They were approaching the first wooden platform, and he couldn't take a chance on the horse panicking as they crossed. He dismounted and removed his mantle, keeping a firm grip on the halter. In spite of the horse tossing her head, Lucian managed to secure his cloak over her eyes. With the makeshift blinder in place, the mare calmed somewhat and responded to his soft words. Her mind became easier to control as he soothed her with images of green fields.

Speight shouted and Lucian's heart sank as the soldiers whipped their mounts with brutal abandon.

He maintained a soothing tone and watched Speight's approach. "Lindsay, can you come down by yourself?"

She jumped from the saddle and was beside him, miming his attentive stance.

"What now?" she asked.

The sound of the wind and his heart silenced the victory cries of Speight's party. He glanced at the platform again. It looked solid enough, but appearances were deceiving in the Wasteland. "I want you to go to the next stone section and wait for me there. I don't know how stable the platform is, so watch where you put your feet. Once you're across, I'll come with the horse. Understand?"

"You got it." She turned and sprinted across.

He held his breath until she was safe.

Speight's men were less than fifty yards away.

"Come on, Lucian!" The child was fairly dancing in her anxiety next to a large boulder the size of a barrel. "It's solid."

He prayed she was right; he wasn't sure if the wood would hold the combined weight of him and the horse. There was no time for caution. He led the horse onto the slats. The wood was firm beneath them and he moved as fast as his lame leg would allow.

When he reached Lindsay, he didn't need to turn around to know that Speight had made it to the bridge's entrance thirty feet behind them. The child shuddered not from the cold but from fear. Her pale eyes flickered from the men behind him to the platform Lucian had just crossed.

Speight shouted to be heard over the wind. The captain's words might as well have been knives in Lucian's back. "All right, Lucian, it's over. Come home quietly so I don't have to tell your sister you were a bad boy."

The same flush of fury he felt against Catarina surged through him at Speight's condescension. Lucian reached for his sword and kept his back to the captain. He had no intention of returning to his sister.

"Run," he whispered to the girl.

He prepared to snatch his cloak from the mare's head and send her on a panicked run into the middle of Speight's men. That would buy him enough time to retrieve his cane and draw his sword. He wouldn't be able to stop them, but he could delay them long enough to give Lindsay a good head start. The child was quick, and if she could get across the bridge and into the forest, she could elude them until Rachael found her.

Lindsay ignored him; her eyes were locked on the wooden platform they had just crossed.

"Lindsay." He looked over his shoulder to see the men were close to wooden slats. "Run, child. I'll hold them off."

One of the soldiers cried a warning as several stones began to spill from beneath the platform. Lucian glanced over the edge; more rocks and debris from the original bridge rolled over the side and into the gorge. The wooden slats shuddered.

Speight was forgotten as Lucian turned to find Lindsay's face red with exertion. Her lips were pulled back from her teeth, her fists clenched at her sides. Lucian became aware of the resonance of Lindsay's magic surging beneath the fractured Wasteland spells.

A resounding crash drowned the wind. A rectangular stone the size of a hay bale surged upward through the slats to obliterate the platform. Splinters and shards of wood flew into the air. Lucian ducked and shielded his eyes.

Horses screamed and reared. The soldiers struggled to control their mounts and avoid the debris. Curses seared the air; two of the men retreated to the meadow.

Lucian's mare tossed her head and the mantle slid off her head. The horse danced close to the edge of the bridge as she backed away from him. One hoof stepped into the air and the horse lifted her head. Lucian pulled with all his strength, but his leg betrayed him and buckled. His heart sank; he couldn't hold her. He released the reins in time to break his fall to the stone deck. The horse took her fatal step and went over the side of the bridge.

Lindsay's screams filled his head. The rock she conjured fell back through the chasm. It hit the stone bridge with a crash and a plume of dust shot upward. Lucian glanced into the hole. Ten feet below, the rock landed close to where it had been before Lindsay moved it. Her talents were becoming manifest.

She ran to him and tried to help him stand. "Are you okay? I thought you were going over with the horse!"

"I'm fine." He reached over his back and his fingers found his cane; he pulled it from his pack. He got to his feet and pushed her behind him.

Across the newly formed chasm, the captain and his soldiers were calming their mounts and surveying the damage. Speight and four of his men remained on the bridge.

Lucian drew his blade and glared at Speight, but he spoke to Lindsay. "Go ahead of me like you did before. Quickly."

"Come on," she tugged his sleeve.

He shook her off. "Go!"

She snatched his mantle off the ground and scrambled ahead.

The chasm between the two stone columns was too broad for Speight or any of his men to cross. One of the soldiers raised a bow and notched an arrow. He aimed his shot at Lucian. Speight raised his hand. The man lowered his weapon.

"She wants him alive!" The captain glowered at Lucian. "There's another pass three days down. You and I both know this is going to end badly if you don't do like she says."

Lucian remembered how he had hobbled through Catarina's house while his leg healed. To walk six feet felt like sixty miles, but his twin insisted that he dine with her every evening. If he remained in his room for any reason, she would send Speight and his men to drag him downstairs. The captain had always been happy to oblige his mistress.

"Come on, Lucian!" Lindsay's frightened voice interrupted his reverie. "Hurry up!"

She had stopped on the other side of the next platform, poised to run, but she hesitated. *For me*, he thought, *she waits for me*. For the first time in years, someone depended on him, and he wouldn't fail again. Lucian backed away from Speight and his men.

Lindsay relaxed her stance and waited for him. His mantle was bunched in her arms, and pale hair whipped around her face in the wind. Her features were fierce with her terror, her cheeks flushed. In a flash, Lucian saw the woman she would become and her beauty was terrible, like a diminutive angel full of light and fire ready bring the wrath of God down on her enemies.

Speight's attention shifted to Lindsay, and he grinned through his thick mustache. "Nice looking kid you got there, Lucian. You share?"

Disgust twisted Lucian's stomach. Catarina kept Speight supplied with children Lindsay's age or younger; the man's sexual appetite was insatiable. Lucian would die before he allowed Speight to touch this child. He had failed to save the others; he could save Lindsay.

While Speight talked, several of the soldiers rode toward the next pass at Dervenshire. Lucian stumbled on the loose gravel and glanced over his shoulder to make sure of his path. He sheathed his weapon and started to move faster. Speight loved to hear pleas and retorts; silence drove him wild with fury. Lucian learned long ago how to cheat the captain out of the satisfaction of an argument.

Speight leaned forward, his face as ruddy as his hair. "I'm dragging your crippled ass back to Hadra before the end of this week, Lucian Negru! The harder you make me work, the rougher it's going go! If you've got any fucking brains at all, you'll sit your ass on the other side of this bridge and wait for me!"

Lucian almost stepped on Lindsay, who glared at Speight with tears in her eyes.

"Lindsay?" He ignored the captain's impotent shouts and focused on the child. "Are you hurt?"

"Why are you letting him talk to you like that?"

Speight reined his mount to join his men.

"Because he wants me to shout back at him. It's a game to him, and it makes him angry when I don't return his insults."

She handed him his mantle, and he stroked her hair out of her face. He realized she lost her purple band at the camp. "Let's go," he said gently.

It took them longer than he would have liked to work around the debris, but they made it to the other side with no more adventures. When they reached the meadow, he sat down on a rock and rubbed his aching knee.

Lindsay had stopped crying, but she was pale and drawn. Lucian motioned for her to come to him and she did.

"Are you all right?" He examined her, looking into her eyes for any sign of strain as he checked her pulse. Her hands trembled but otherwise she seemed fine.

"I really sorry, Lucian. I didn't mean to kill the horse."

The horse. Lucian tried to ignore the disappointment raging through his gut. The animal had been a boon to them, but it couldn't be helped. "I know you didn't. We'll do just fine without her."

"Jeez, Lucian, don't you get you get it? That was real animal, and I killed her."

"She panicked, Lindsay. When any creature panics, it loses control of its fate. Do you understand that?"

Lindsay froze. "Like I did at the creek. I panicked. I couldn't move, Lucian."

"I know." He pulled her down beside him and put his arm around her. "I know."

She jammed her elbows on her thighs and leaned forward, her teardrops fell to the grass. "I hate it here. I hate everything about this place."

He could easily heal her grief with a touch, but not without crippling her as he'd damaged Catarina. He wouldn't do it. Lindsay would have to learn to cope with her dark days like Catarina should have done. If he'd been stronger, he would have pushed his twin away rather than give in to her constant demands. Perhaps she would have grown to become self-sufficient, instead of relying on him for her every need.

"Listen carefully." He rubbed her back. "Your talents have started to emerge, and you must learn to control them and your emotions. If you panic, you'll die like that horse."

"How do you do that? How do you keep cool when somebody is bearing down on you like that?"

"Practice." He smiled and tilted her face up so she had to look at him.

"I don't want to practice that anymore, not if it means being scared like that."

He chuckled and wiped her tears away. "Fear is natural. You'll be frightened many times during your life, Lindsay, and you will overcome it every time." He found a strip of leather and tied her hair back. "One thing I learned while I lived with my sister was to celebrate each and every victory, no matter how small it may seem. At the creek, you froze and I helped you. However, you overcame your fear when Speight was bearing down on us. You used your talent to raise that rock. You saved us. That is a victory."

She looked back across the bridge. "For real?"

"For real. Now that we know one of your talents, I'll have to teach you how to use God's power. If you don't learn how to focus your energy, you could end up hurting yourself and anyone around you." He rose and tested his weight on his knee. He was sore, but he could walk. "We've got to move. We have a three-day head start. Let's use it to our advantage."

She glanced uneasily in the direction Speight had taken his men. "Maybe we can get another horse."

He didn't answer but watched his step on the broken paving stones leading away from the bridge. Without the horse, they wouldn't move fast, nor would he have the luxury of taking his time to rest his leg. Speight would ride his men into the ground now that he'd sighted his prey. That meant Lucian would have to push himself on his bad knee, and he knew what kind of agony that would bring.

No help for it, he thought as he paced himself. Speight wasn't the only danger to them; Catarina knew of Lindsay, and that put Lindsay's welfare in jeopardy. Catarina would allow no one to stand in her way of Lucian's affections. She had thought nothing of orchestrating Rachael's ruin; she would easily eliminate a defenseless child.

"Lucian?"

"Yes, child?"

"It's okay to cry when you're scared, right? I mean that doesn't make me whiny, does it?"

He remembered Rachael, who never cried.

Once he had asked her, *Don't ever you weep?*

In the night, she answered, *when I'm alone.*

It wasn't until his sister's betrayal that he understood what Rachael meant. During the eternal dusk that had shadowed his life these last years, he often pondered Rachael's words. He knew what it was like to weep in the night, and he knew what it meant to surrender.

"Lucian?"

"Of course it's all right to cry." He tugged her hood onto her head so she wouldn't take a chill or see his eyes.

He was surprised when he felt Lindsay's tentative touch. When he didn't brush her away, she reached more confidently and placed her hand inside his. He would have to be careful with this child, or she would win his heart in spite of his resolve to keep their relationship distant. Lucian gave her fingers a reassuring squeeze and she rewarded him with a small smile.

For now, that was enough.

CHAPTER EIGHT

the ierusal barren

Translucent clouds veiled the sun as Lucian and Lindsay stopped in front of the dilapidated tavern. A sign creaked in the weak breeze; the proud red bull painted on the board had faded to the color of rust. Beneath the sign, the crooked door leaned into the frame. Brown weeds grew between the slats of the wooden porch. The lone sentry on Ierusal's outskirts, the pub had once been a traveler's last stop before Melasur, but visitors came no more.

"Is that a tavern?" Lindsay whispered and pointed at the inn.

He nodded and found his handkerchief. He wiped the sweat from his face and tucked the cloth back into his sleeve.

Earlier, she had braided her hair and used the leather strip to tie the end. The braid swung over her shoulder as she looked around him. "Think there might be a place for you to sit for a few minutes?"

"No time." He gave her what he hoped was a reassuring smile, but the gesture felt false even to him. His leg throbbed constantly from the forced march he'd subjected them to over the last few days, and he wasn't sure how much longer he could go on.

"You don't have to pretend," Lindsay said. "I can tell it hurts; you're moving slower."

"I'm fine." He gestured to the skyline. "And we're almost there."

Spires rose against the clouds. The jagged edges of wood and stone bore testimony to the acrimony that had wasted Ierusal and the surrounding land. Through the pale, dead trees, he could see the city's stone walls rise behind a hedge of greenery. They were perhaps a quarter of a league from Ierusal.

The faraway sound of a horn silenced any further conversation. They waited for a full minute, but Lucian sensed no one and they heard no further noise.

"Is that Ierusal?" she asked, nodding at the broken spires.

"It is, but we still must be careful." He started walking. "Keep your voice low. If you must talk, let's continue your lessons."

She rolled her eyes. "Can't we take a break, Lucian?"

He said nothing but walked as fast as his lame leg would allow.

She sighed and made no more protests. "Psalms. You were teaching me about the Psalms."

"Ah, now I remember. We use the Psalms to focus our minds on drawing down our power. I think you likened it to drawing down the moon?"

"Yeah, but you called it Avalonian, not Wicca." She ducked a low hanging limb and turned gracefully to walk backwards so she could look at him. "If you're a Christian, how do you know so much about Avalonians?"

"John's wife Tanith is a priestess." He smiled at her disbelief. "She married John, but she didn't convert to Christianity. John would never ask her to give up something so precious as her beliefs. It's how the Seraphs keep peace between the bastions. It is forbidden for Katharoi to proselytize."

"This sure isn't like Earth."

"It's what Earth could be with a little more tolerance." *And a common enemy.* The tip of his cane landed on a loose stone, and Lucian's weight shifted to his bad leg. His knee buckled and he groped for a way to steady himself. Lindsay rushed toward him and grabbed his arm; he clutched her shoulder until he found his footing. She was a good child; it would be easy to love her, but Lucian resisted the temptation. To open his heart to her would only bring them both more pain in the end. He patted her back and resumed his pace with more care. "Go on."

She stayed close to his side and recited what he'd taught her. "When we draw on the Spirit without a clear focus, we can do more damage than good with magic." Lindsay grew quiet, and he waited for her to speak again. "That's what happened at the bridge, didn't it? I panicked and didn't have a clear focus."

"Very good." He liked it when she arrived at her own conclusions.

"So the Psalms will help me focus?"

"Yes. Then you can channel the spell more effectively."

"And not hurt anyone?"

"Precisely." Lucian nodded and they walked in silence until the forest gave way to a small field of yellow grass undulating in the cold wind. Several yards ahead, the grass ended abruptly at the edge of a blackened patch of ground. The scorched area covered several leagues to the left and right.

Though the eastern and western gates were out of sight, Lucian knew the charred area extended to both gates, creating a horseshoe of barren ground around the city's walls. Nothing but burnt earth filled the land from the edge of the field where they stood to the greenery at the base of Ierusal's walls. The skeletal remains of siege weapons rose from the ashes. Strewn across the Barren were lesser tools of destruction mixed with gray and broken bones of soldiers and their mounts. It was a field of death.

The road passed across the Barren to the northern gate. Strangely enough, whatever had burned the earth left the cobblestones unmarked.

Lindsay stared at the carnage. "What did you guys do to this place?"

"This is the result of Mastema's rage. There are five areas like this in the Wasteland; we call them Barrens. This is the Ierusal Barren." John had never allowed them to get close to any of the Barrens; he claimed the grounds were haunted.

Until now, Lucian had avoided the scorched areas, but the road that cut through the Ierusal Barren was the shortest route to the city. Beyond the Barren, at the top of a gently sloping hill, the city of Ierusal lay forlorn and rotten. The only sign of life was a thriving rose bush, the Sacra Rosa, which crawled up the battlements to obscure the gray stone walls surrounding the city. The plant was as green and lush as if it were mid-summer, not autumn.

It was the first living thing they had seen in the Wasteland and Lindsay exhaled with wonder. "It's beautiful."

It was deadly. John had brought his three foundlings here to impress upon them the history of the Wasteland. He had made sure to push back the verdant leaves to show all three the thorns that were long and sharp as daggers. Catarina had merely raised an eyebrow at the legend, but the Sacra Rosa made a deep impression on Lucian and Rachael.

"It's the Sacra Rosa," he said.

"Is it magic too?"

"Yes, it is. You see, this was the last city to fall under Mastema's siege during the War."

"That schism thing, right?"

"It is called the War of the Great Schism, not 'that schism thing.'"

She wrinkled her nose at him.

"There's a legend that says the flowers were born from the bodies of the last four Katharoi to take a stand in defense of the city. When the Fallen's mortal army took Ierusal, the Katharoi commissioned their bodies to the earth, one Katharos by each city gate. The Sacra Rosa grew overnight. The city was open for anyone to enter, but only those with love for the Spirit could pass through the thorns unmolested when they left. Those committed to the Fallen were torn to pieces."

She touched the end of her braid to her lips. "Is it true?"

"What?"

"The legend. Is it true?"

"I don't know."

Lindsay cocked her head and examined the distant city. "So all those evil people are still there?"

There were hundreds of stories to explain the loss of life. They had starved and resorted to cannibalism; they had fallen through a Hell Gate and into Mastema's mouth. While the tales were endless, the result was the same—the city was empty. Lucian chose the least offensive of the lot. "They went mad and fought amongst themselves until there were none left."

She picked up a twisted piece of metal and turned it over in her hands before losing interest and dropping it back to the ground. "Do you people have any happy stories?"

He gave her a weary smile. "Yes, yes, we do. I shall try to remember one for you." He looked to the sky. On the other side of Ierusal, great, dark clouds started to gather. It was early afternoon, and if they crossed the Barren, they might have a roof over their heads before the rain came.

A chill wind ruffled his hair and he pulled his mantle close. "Let's go."

At the edge of the grass, a wagon lay on its side, the iron frame all that was left to give it shape. Lucian hesitated. He didn't like the look of the alien landscape. John had been right in avoiding this place. The eerie silence of the Wasteland coupled with the devastation of the battlefield left Lucian anxious.

Lindsay rubbed her arms. "There's something bad about this place. The magic here buzzes. It almost hurts."

"We'll be all right." When he concentrated, he felt the vibrations as well, but this was simply more of the Wasteland's sour magic. "You're becoming more sensitive to the Wasteland spells as your own talents manifest. Strong magic leaves a resonance. You have to learn to understand the difference between a reverberation and active spells."

"How do you know the difference?"

"Experience. What you're feeling now is an echo. What you felt with Catarina was active magic." He gauged the distance to the city.

John's warning to avoid the Barrens was as fresh in Lucian's mind as the day his Elder had spoken, but the approaching storm was gaining speed. He could smell rain in the cold air, and if they had to take cover outside the city, it would mean returning to the tavern. With the cold and the damp, his leg would become more inflamed, and he might not be able to walk for a day, maybe two.

He looked down at Lindsay. Deep circles shadowed her eyes and she wiped her runny nose on the sleeve of her coat, but she didn't complain. She showed remarkable determination and proved herself resilient in spite of her frail appearance. Though she wouldn't admit it, he knew she was nearing the end of her stamina. He needed to get her inside too, preferably some place where he could dare light a fire.

Waiting was out of the question. "Don't deviate from the road."

Rather than question him, Lindsay simply nodded and stayed close to him. It was obvious she didn't like the area, either. Her pace reflected her anxiety, because twice she pulled ahead of him. He called for her to wait. He wanted her close in case she needed him.

They were halfway to the city walls when the ground began to slope upward. The wind blew a chill breath over Lucian and he paused. Lindsay stopped at his side.

He sensed a subtle shift beneath the resonance of the old magic. He tried to discern the new reverberation from the splintered enchantments left from the war. He couldn't sense Catarina or her twisted spells in the Barren. Whatever caused the change was different from anything he'd ever felt before, something old but still very, very powerful.

He started walking again; the slope seemed to have steepened. He trudged up the hill only to stop every few steps to rest. He leaned on his cane with both hands, his boot tight around his leg. Every step felt like a hot poker was thrust into his thigh and hip. His flesh goose pimpled from the cold; the wind snatched at his hair.

Lucian, the sudden whisper was right at his shoulder.

He raised his head; there was nothing, no one. The words had not been spoken aloud. He wanted to touch the hilt of his sword but feared releasing his cane. The pain in his leg turned to an agony.

Lucian looked up. Lindsay slipped ahead of him again.

He called her name and she turned, the fur of her hood caressed her lips. "Wait for me," he said.

She nodded and waited for him. Gritting his teeth, Lucian took one lurching step after another. Lindsay started to walk back toward him.

What will you do if she needs you? the whisper taunted.

Dark clouds roiled over the horizon.

He stopped and listened. At first he wanted to convince himself it was the wind, but no wind could articulate his fear so clearly. Some *thing* had spoken.

Lindsay reached his side and placed her hand on his wrist. "You okay, Lucian?"

"I'm fine." Cold fingers brushed his cheek. When he turned, nothing was there. Sweat dampened his hair.

"You don't look so good," Lindsay said.

"I'm fine." He scanned the Barren and thought he saw something move on the ground. He stared until his eyes watered.

I'm not there, Lucian.

Lindsay followed his gaze. "Is something out there?"

I'm here.

"Hey, Lucian?"

With you.

"I'm fine." He tore his eyes away from the Barren and focused on the child.

Lindsay nodded. "Okay." She didn't question him although she didn't look convinced. They resumed their journey.

Lucian focused on putting one foot in front of the other. Ierusal looked like it was a thousand leagues away, but he had to get there. A promise. He had promised Rachael something.

You promised you would never leave her, said the voice, *but you abandoned her.*

Lucian was stung by the memory of Rachael's palm sliding across his at the Hell Gate. She had tried to hold on to him, and he had simply opened his hand and let her go.

"Lucian?" Lindsay touched his wrist again.

He jerked away from her and the weight of his pack almost toppled him. He barely kept his feet beneath him. He looked away from her concern, back into the Barren.

Do you know what they did to her in Hell?

The dark ground rose up to meet the black sky. He heard a faint buzzing and saw shadows split and multiply as the hum increased. Flies feasted on the corpses. Their numbers continued to grow until the ground rolled and slithered with their mass. The drone became a roar.

This was an illusion. It had to be an illusion. Lucian stopped.

"Lucian," Lindsay said, more insistent this time, her voice barely rising over the whine of the flies.

What happened to Rachael was done. He could never change that, no matter how his heart begged. Lindsay might be saved if he could step out of his wretched depression and focus on her. He looked down at her. Lindsay's adolescence vanished beneath the creases of worry around her eyes. She frowned up at him, and Lucian realized he'd stolen her youth the same as he'd stolen Rachael's.

The creature following him locked onto his despair. Lucian's anguish became a living thing, rising up and out of his soul only to draw the darkness down around him. A terrible stench radiated from the Barren, the odor of burning flesh mingled with wood and hot metal. The buzzing reached a fever pitch.

Lindsay's expression never changed; she seemed ignorant of the haunting. She was concerned for him, but she didn't appear afraid. Be it demon or devil, the creature hadn't touched the child and she didn't seem to be aware of it.

The wind clawed his face and he jerked his head. His cheek was wet and he winced when he touched his torn flesh.

"Oh shit, Lucian! What just happened?" Lindsay's voice rose in alarm.

Lucian licked his lips. "Do you remember your lessons, Lindsay?"

"You're bleeding!"

"Lindsay. Your lessons."

"Okay. Don't panic," she muttered to herself. "The Psalms? Is that it, Lucian? The Psalms?"

In the Barren, black and purple shadows ebbed and flowed into one another. The reek of burning flesh mingled with howls of agony. The flies tore the flesh of the living and the dead. Lucian looked into the shadows. He glimpsed the outline of a face before the mists swallowed the shapes again.

A shade flickered by on his right, and Lucian turned to find a spirit standing on the side of the road. The creature's feet were mired in the charred ground, buried to the ankles in ash. The ghost's dark hair was wild with tangles and the eyes were as black as the encroaching storm. Four slashes lacerated the creature's cheek as if someone had drawn their fingernails through his flesh. The ghost wore Lucian's face and spoke a dark gospel.

They descended on her, a living Katharos, to vent their rage. They tore her flesh and begged for her bones, but Mastema wouldn't allow it. He only gave them a taste of her, enough to whet their appetites. He saved the best for himself.

Chilled by the spirit's words, Lucian gripped his cane. He never saw Rachael after he abandoned her at the Hell Gate. When they brought her back to the Citadel, they kept her body covered as if she were dead.

And you murdered her.

Lucian swallowed and shut his eyes.

Lindsay said, "I know 'the Lord is My Shepherd.'"

"What?" His voice was so hoarse he couldn't hear himself over the sound of the flies. "What did you say?"

She's here, Lucian. The spirit held out his hand and beckoned. *Rachael is here. You can save her.*

He could save her and undo everything that had been done. Wasn't that why he started this journey? To save Rachael?

Help her and become a Katharos once more.

"The only Psalm I know by heart is 'the Lord is My Shepherd,'" Lindsay said, her fingers entwined with his. "Stay with me, Lucian."

The spirit smiled sweetly and held out his hand.

"Say it for me," Lucian whispered as the need to step off the road and into the Barren became overwhelming. The only thing holding him to the cobblestones was Lindsay. He promised her he would not leave her.

You promised Rachael.

"Out loud?"

"Please." His promise to Rachael he had broken, his promise to Lindsay he would keep.

She didn't hesitate and began to recite the Psalm.

In the flash of a memory, Lucian saw Rachael's eyes pleading with him not to leave her. A fly landed on her outstretched hand and she screamed his name.

Forsake her a second time and she will die forever. Oh, you think you know pain, Lucian, but you know nothing.

Lindsay's voice rose over the sound of the flies.

His suicide wouldn't change the past. Rachael wasn't here. The Barren offered atonement in the form of eternal flagellation, nothing more.

Beneath the strange magic of the Barren, Lucian felt Lindsay's resonance filter into his heart. Her clear, beautiful voice drowned the spirit's entreaties. She prayed, "'Yea, though I walk through the valley of the shadow of death, I will fear no evil.'"

"I will fear no evil," Lucian said and met the ghost's eyes. He backed away from the spirit and turned to face the city once more.

Lindsay continued the Psalm as they walked toward Ierusal again.

He ignored the icy, spectral fingers stroking his throat. The fingers slid away, and the buzzing of the flies faded into the distance. Gradually, the pungent fragrance of the roses overwhelmed the odor of death rising from the Barren's charnel grounds.

Lindsay finished the Psalm and looked up at him. "How'd I do?"

They halted at the top of the hill a few yards from Ierusal's wall. Autumn grass wavered in the wind and brushed his knees. He shuddered when he gazed back over their path through the Barren. "You were magnificent. You didn't panic and you focused on your spell."

She blinked and grinned. "Hey. I didn't panic, did I?" Her smile faded. "Your face is bleeding."

He touched his torn cheek gingerly; the gash wasn't deep, but he needed to clean the wound to prevent an infection. "Maybe we can get inside and find a place to rest."

"What happened back there?" She glanced down the hill, and he gently disentangled his hand from hers.

"It was a haunting. A spirit was drawn to me." *To the darkness within me.* "You kept your head, did as you were told, and drove it off."

She glowed at his praise and he resisted the urge to touch her cheek. Instead, he turned and looked at the Rosa.

The bush grew in a lush mass around the wall. Some of the branches were as thin as twigs, older limbs as thick as Lucian's torso. Each branch sported thorns varying in length from only a centimeter to several feet. The limbs were woven together as tightly as a tapestry, giving only the barest glimpse to the blooms beneath the leaves.

The Rosa grew over the gate in a graceful arch, like a wedding arbor. The portcullis was closed and even a child Lindsay's size couldn't have squeezed between the bars. Next to the main gate was a smaller door that hung from one hinge and was pushed half open so Lucian could see the littered street. He hadn't noticed Lindsay pause to examine the Rosa.

"They look like faces," Lindsay said from behind him. She stood on her toes and examined one of the snowy flowers. She pushed the sleeve of her coat back and reached for the bloom. The branches rustled and the flower withdrew into the shadows.

"Leave it!" Lucian shouted.

She jumped and stumbled away from the Rosa to turn to him. Her eyes were wide with shock, and he realized this was the first time he'd spoken harshly to her. He lowered his voice and tried to calm his pounding heart. "Don't touch it. Never touch it." He remembered those haunting petals that bore striking resemblances to human faces. "Come."

Lindsay approached him cautiously and jammed her hands into the pockets of her coat. "I didn't touch anything."

"It's all right. I'm sorry I yelled. Just—"

"Don't touch it. I got it." She came to his side with several backward glances at the roses. "Did you find a way inside?"

"Yes. Wait here." He unsheathed his sword.

"Okay." She eyed the blade with narrowed eyes. "Just don't be long."

He stepped through the door. The remaining structures were stone, but a few charred, skeletal fingers of wood pointed to the dark sky. Rags flapped in the empty window of a building with only two sides. The other two walls had disintegrated into dust and rubble to block a narrow alley.

The blackened walls gave evidence to the conflagration that had raged through this section of Ierusal. Here the fires had burned naturally; there was no residue of old magic. The houses surviving the fire were jammed close together, causing the street to constrict into tight alleys. Intimate with Hadra's warrens, Lucian recognized Ierusal's slums.

Not even a rat stirred in the silence.

He sheathed the sword. "Come along."

Lindsay came through the door to stand at his side. His knee burned with every step; he needed to rest. Rather than sit, he started to walk with Lindsay next to him. Once they were a few blocks inside the city, he'd sit, but not here.

Lindsay stayed close and asked, "Which church do we need to find?"

"Any one will do. Let's see if we can find one with a roof."

Overhead the clouds grew more ominous as the day faded, and the air grew cold enough for their breath to plume before them. They picked their way through the debris in the street, moving deeper into the city with Lucian stopping more frequently as they left the slums and burned buildings behind.

Shops lined the street, and broken glass littered the rubble scattered across the road. The wind whistled through the empty buildings, moaning a dirge to Ierusal's past. A doll's head stared blindly from the gutter, the porcelain face cracked, the painted smile crooked. Lindsay sidled closer to Lucian to avoid the abandoned toy.

They came to an intersection where the street branched into five directions. Lucian stopped and sat on the stone ledge of a shop window to consider their route. He rubbed his thigh, the muscle tight beneath his palm. He pulled his pants leg up and adjusted the laces on his boot to accommodate the swelling in his leg. The skin around his knee felt hot.

Lindsay winced at sight of his knee. "Does it hurt bad?"

"It's uncomfortable."

She squatted to tie her shoe and looked up at him. "How'd you mess it up?"

He clutched his cane and turned to examine the junction. Despite his effort to remain focused on their journey, a memory flickered like torchlight against stone walls. After years of living in the darkness of his cell, the light had been blinding. They'd strapped him to a wooden table, and he'd felt only dread when he saw his sister. A teardrop of moisture had seeped down the wall.

Catarina's merciless voice commanded her chief torturer. *Cripple him. Don't maim him. I don't want him maimed.*

The torturer secured Lucian's thigh until the leather bit through his dry flesh. Without a word, the man reached down and twisted Lucian's calf to tear the cartilage in his knee. Lucian never forgot that excruciating pain. Catarina kissed his lips, silencing his scream. The walls wept for him, no other, and he knew then that he was alone.

"Lucian?"

A drop of rain touched his cheek and he blinked. "When I was younger, I had an accident." He forced a smile and turned back to her. "That's all."

She stood and a frown drew her pale brows together as she examined his face.

"When I left Hadra," he said and nodded at the intersection,

"Matthew said to always follow the right-hand path. I think we should do that now." He rose and rapped his cane against the road. "I felt rain. Let's see if we can find a church that suits our needs."

Her frown deepened, and she glanced at the sky. "It's not raining."

He didn't respond.

She joined him and asked no more questions as they ventured down the street. They were several blocks away from the intersection when Lucian saw the church nestled between two larger buildings. A narrow dirt alley ran on either side of the chapel. Like the other religious houses in Ierusal, the cross at the top of the steeple had been destroyed, but the rest of the structure appeared intact.

This would have to do. The sky threatened a downpour, and Lucian couldn't go another step. Lindsay followed him up the stairs to the porch. He shoved the door open and prayed his soul-light into being, then sent it into the dim room.

Dirt coated the floor, and shards of wood were scattered throughout the room. The four pews at the rear of the church had been shattered as if someone had taken an ax to them. The remains were strewn from the nave to the altar. The four pews near the altar were intact and dull with filth. Three confessionals lined the wall to the right of the entrance. Although the cross hung upside down, the altar itself remained untouched.

Lindsay closed the door. She summoned her own soul-light and explored the splintered confessionals, sneezing at the dust she stirred. Over the confessionals, a sliver of sky was visible through missing tiles, but the rest of the roof appeared intact.

Lucian used his cane to clear the rubble from his path. He went to the cross and hung it properly. Between the last confessional and the pulpit was another door.

"Lindsay."

She emerged from the confessional closest to him.

He motioned to the door he'd just found. "Let's stay together."

She nodded and he opened the door to find the priest's study. Floor to ceiling bookshelves stuffed with books and scrolls lined the walls behind the heavy oak desk. The books and papers were swollen with moisture and the room smelled of mildew. Lucian picked up an overturned chair. On the desk, he brushed aside the dust to find a half-completed sermon spread on the blotter. The pen had rolled onto the floor and the inkwell was dry. Two more chairs faced the desk. A couch rested beside a door that opened onto a porch in the alley beside the church.

On the opposite wall was the door to an austere bedroom consisting of a wardrobe and a single bed. The mattress was dingy and damp, but serviceable; Lindsay could sleep off the ground and in relative comfort tonight.

From there, they found an entrance to a small kitchen with another exit into a weedy yard at the rear of the church. Outside, the first drops of rain started to fall.

The patter of the cold drizzle hitting the roof was the only sound in the church, not even remnants of the Wasteland's spells disturbed the peace of this building. They had three possible exits, and the locks on the doors appeared sturdy enough. Should worst come to worst and Speight reached them before Rachael, Lucian felt he had a defendable position. Tomorrow he would explore the alley and backyard to see if he could present Speight a few surprises.

"Well?" Lindsay asked.

"This will do."

She smiled when he took off his mantle and dropped his pack in the bedroom. He directed her to help him clean the bedroom and kitchen and taught her to light the fires.

They had managed to scavenge a few pathetic turnips and onions by the roadside, and Lindsay retrieved the vegetables from her gym bag. By the time he had some water boiling on the kitchen stove, the rooms had become warm enough for Lindsay to take off her coat.

"Won't Speight find us with the smoke from the fires?"

"Possibly." He used her knife to chop the turnips. "But Speight is superstitious. I don't think he'll try to cross the Barren or the Rosa." Whether Speight came into Ierusal or not depended on if he was more afraid of the Sacra Rosa or Catarina. "We'll worry about Speight in the morning. In all probability, he's found shelter for his men tonight. They'll move slowly in bad weather."

"How's Rachael going to find us?" She lazily rolled one of the onions with her finger.

"Rachael will have a constable with her, someone who can sense another's presence like I can with the soldiers. It will take them a little longer in a city this large, but if we remain in one place, she'll find us." He wiped his hands on a rag. "While that's cooking, let's get one of the chairs into the bedroom. You shall have the bed tonight, and I will have a comfortable place to sit."

"I could sleep on the couch and you could take the bed." She pushed away from the counter and followed him into the study.

"That's quite tempting, but I'd prefer not to go into a deep sleep tonight. We're not safe yet." While he was sure Speight's superstitious nature would keep him away from the Sacra Rosa, he wasn't so sure about Catarina.

He had stopped trying to second-guess his twin when she stood outside his cell and announced she now knew what to do with him. From that point forward, she became an enigma to him, and his pathetic attempts to decipher her intentions only amused her.

Yet he knew that when Catarina left them several nights ago, she had been infuriated by his defiance. He had learned not to mistake silence for forgiveness, for Catarina did not absolve an injury to her pride. Prolonged quiet from his twin only meant she hadn't devised the perfect retribution. When she was ready, she would come, and she would leave sorrow in her wake.

CHAPTER NINE

simulacrum

Catarina licked her lips. The heat from the fire in Lucian's room intensified the odor of Armand's blood and fear. Propped against the pillows, the youth's body listed to the center of the mattress, his chest barely moved. Black and yellow bruises covered him. From her chair by the hearth, Catarina measured the boy with her dark gaze. She shredded another page from the book in her hand. The paper fluttered to the floor to join thousands of others, a carpet of parchment and vellum.

Cerberus sat beside the nightstand and watched her, his silver eyes inscrutable. The lethargy she endured after her attack on Lucian had departed. While she recuperated, Cerberus watched over her and executed minor administrative decisions in her absence—all the things Lucian should be doing. She pressed her lips together and ripped a handful of pages from the volume. Unlike her twin, Cerberus had no difficulty with loyalty. She narrowed her glare at the battered youth on Lucian's bed.

Cerberus said, "Speight lost Lucian three days ago at Melasur."

She didn't need to ask how he knew; Cerberus never failed her. She dropped the book to the floor and rose. Her silk gown whispered against the paper covering the floor. She retrieved the prism from Lucian's desk.

A bitter smile played across her lips as she retraced the familiar steps to her brother's bed. Armand's right eye darted in her direction, and he clutched the twisted sheets to cover his nakedness. He stopped moving when she shook her head. A lock of hair slipped from her loose coif to caress the ruffles of her bodice. She tucked the errant strand behind her ear.

Armand stiffened when she slid into the bed beside him. Her tongue darted to her lips and she caught her breath. While not as sharp as it had been three days ago, his terror still edged the air. Catarina rubbed the pad of her thumb against the prism. Armand's anxious stare followed her movements.

Lucian's haunted gaze had also followed her when he'd first been bed-ridden. Yet when she had tried to help him, he brushed her aside with shaking hands, refusing her ministrations. So she left him alone and forbade the servants from helping him. She called him an old man as she left the room, not daring to look at the hurt in his eyes.

She examined Armand's pleading gaze. Without her compassion, the guilt that used to accompany her actions was gone. Cerberus had freed her.

The demon said, "Speight lost him at Melasur."

"I heard you the first time."

Armand winced when she lifted the coverlet to wipe his chin. How had she ever seen Lucian in this mewling, fearful child?

Cerberus came to the bed. "Speight believes he is going to Ierusal."

"Lucian thinks the Rosa will protect him."

"As it will."

"The Rosa is as dead as my brother's god." How could he trust in a god he couldn't see and not have faith in the sister before his eyes?

She dug the tip of the prism into Armand's stomach until blood oozed around the point. Armand went gray, but his horror no longer titillated her. He had become as mundane as the furniture, a plaything, like Lucian's little foundling. The girl excited Lucian's need for a purpose. Without the child, he would see no reason to continue his quest; he would come home.

"The foundling is the key," she muttered. Within hours, that filthy child-beggar had claimed Lucian's heart. He would try to protect the girl like he'd tried to save Rachael. Catarina ground the prism into Armand's stomach and the boy cried out. She ·slapped him into silence.

Lucian gave his love freely to strangers while his only family languished from neglect. After all she had done for him. Hadn't she fed and clothed him? Didn't she give him shelter when no other would take him in? And for her multiple sacrifices, he defied and abandoned her so he could undermine her life's work.

"Lucian is just like our uncle Mircea." Catarina removed the prism from Armand's stomach. The boy sobbed, putting his hands over the wound. She pressed her mouth close to his ear and whispered, "Our father harbored a snake at his breast. Mircea lived off our goodwill until he was no longer content to live beside us. Mircea wanted our father's life and he took it."

Like Lucian wanted to steal hers. Jealous, he'd always been jealous of her ability to bring her goals to completion. "He's not as clever as Mircea. He never will be!" She raised the prism and brought it down on Armand's chest.

The boy wailed. The noise was a blade through her head. Armand tried to crawl away from her. She snatched his wrist, digging her nails into his flesh.

The room grew cold in spite of the fire. Catarina felt Mastema's presence. "For you, Mastema, for you. Grant me power so I can bring the traitor home." The ancient language of the angels clawed her throat and surfaced as a guttural moan.

Power surged through her amulet and into her veins as Mastema answered her call. The rush of adrenaline brought her close to orgasm, but Catarina felt she had only scraped the surface of the dark angel's strength. She craved more.

The tapestries rustled and fluttered. The eyes of the stag undulated and seemed to wink at her. Lucian's eyes. Mocking her.

Catarina reached out to the tapestry, and the threads from the stag's eyes flowed from the wall hanging to dance serpentine in the air. The threads slithered onto the mattress, and she guided them to the soles of Armand's feet.

The boy shrieked when the strings wormed into this flesh to become one with sinew and bone. The cords wrapped his toes, his ankles, his calves, inching upward to encase his body.

Cerberus leapt to the bed, delirious with glee. Her power grew with the demon's nearness and she was dizzy with the sudden influx of strength. The colors of the threads twining around Armand grew more vibrant, bursting into a rainbow of color.

The tapestries billowed from the walls as if some huge presence stalked behind them. Catarina shivered in her thin silk gown, but when she pressed her lips close to Armand's, she found no more warmth to be drawn from him. No matter. There were a thousand Armands in Woerld, and though none of them warmed her as Lucian did, they would be suitable surrogates until she brought her brother home.

"Steal her from him," Catarina whispered as the threads encased Armand's body. Without the foundling to distract him, Lucian would come home. Home where he could be watched. "Give her to Speight."

Armand thrashed and tried to push the string away, but it stuck to his fingers, spiraling around his hands.

"We are never the same without you," she murmured, weaving her words into the threads. The cords seared into Armand's flesh, crept through his lips to crawl down his throat and strangle his cries.

"Hush, hush." Catarina soothed as she guided the thread through him and into his brain. "Never without you at my side."

Armand's voice became muffled and his struggles eased as the thread encased his limbs and blinded him. He mewled and scratched the cords concealing his face. Soon he lay still, awaiting her command. The dark thread pulsed with a heartbeat of its own, turning Armand into a life size poppet—a simulacrum ready to do her will.

"Ride the moon and steal her away." She slid from the mattress in a hiss of silk.

"I give you her name: Lindsay Richardson." At the window, she pointed toward the blood-colored moon rising on the horizon. The simulacrum reached out and a thread loosened to travel upward into the night to attach to a moonbeam. Using the thread like a rope, it pulled itself up and over the rooftops to disappear into the darkness.

Catarina sank to the window seat. Already Cerberus' power was receding from her body, leaving her tired. Her veins felt withered, old. She turned the prism over in her hands.

Cerberus hissed as he brushed against her hip. "You promised Mastema Lucian's soul too. My Lord will not wait forever."

"Lucian won't deny me." Dreamily she rotated the prism, trying to capture the light. "He has never been able to look into my eyes and deny me anything. He swore on our dead father's ring that he would always watch over me. So long as he wears that ring, I have his oath. I have to reach him."

"There is a fractured Hell Gate outside of Ierusal." The demon grinned, baring his long teeth.

She shook her head; it would take too long. She needed speed, supernatural speed. "We must go faster. I want to be there in a day, no more than two."

Cerberus' tail slithered up her back then coiled around her arm. "There is a way," he said as he glanced toward a mirror in the corner of the room, "but there is a price."

Catarina looked into his silver gaze. "Mastema has my soul. What more could he want?" She squeezed the hard glass of the prism.

"Your love."

"He has my devotion."

The demon stood on his hind legs and placed his paws on her shoulders. "No, darkling, he wants the love you harbor in your soul."

A sliver of fear pierced her. "My love of Lucian?"

"Your love of anyone. Think on it, darkling. This is not so much a price as it is a gift. Without your compassion, you felt no guilt. Without your love for Lucian, you can bring him to your will." The demon moved closer, his breath frigid against her throat. "What stayed your hand all these years but the weakness of love?"

Catarina hesitated, recalling the moment in the garden with Lucian when their love had surfaced like warmth after the winter. In that moment, she'd remembered their days on Earth when Lucian cherished her. Would giving her love to Mastema rob her of those memories? The prism was heavy in her hand.

Cerberus' tongue caressed her ear. "When Lucian suffered, you suffered with him. Without your love, you may have your way with him. He seeks to destroy you. Like Mircea destroyed your father. You must act first." He nuzzled her earlobe and a chill cascaded down her back. "Think, darkling. What is love without compassion?"

Catarina shivered, cold, always so cold. "Would I still love you?" She caressed his muzzle.

"You don't love me now. You need me." Cerberus dropped to the floor and walked to the mirror. "Tell me, darkling, do you want the power of angels?"

Love. Did she really need such a paltry emotion? What had her love of her twin given her other than grief and suffering? Love had blinded Rachael and damned her to the Wyrm; love had torn Lucian in two. Could there possibly be a more cursed emotion to suffer?

Catarina went to the demon's side. She could give her god no better gift than ease from his pain, and in return, he would give her the power of angels. Devoid of these weak emotions, she would be a goddess. Lucian would worship her.

Cerberus bowed his head and muttered an incantation. The mirror clouded. When the mist parted, her reflection shimmered and disappeared to reveal steps carved into stone. A curl of smoke drifted upward. The stairs led down into the depths of a cavern growling with moans. The odor of sulfur and ash rose into the room.

Love. It was nothing.

✝

Lindsay whimpered in her sleep and Lucian jerked awake. Minutes seeped past as he struggled to familiarize himself with his surroundings. His chair rested against the door to the office so none could enter without waking him; his sword and cane were balanced across his lap. The rain had stopped, and moonlight splashed across the kitchen floor. The vague shapes of their packs formed a lump beside the bed where Lindsay slept.

Though he'd chosen the most uncomfortable chair in the office, the warmth of the rooms combined with a full stomach had lulled him into a deep slumber. He rubbed his eyes and winced when he accidentally touched his torn cheek. The sting of his fingers against the open wound banished the last of his drowsiness. His right shoulder was sore from days of hunching over his cane and throbbed in counterpoint to his knee. He shifted his weight, but could find no relief for his aching limbs.

Lindsay tossed and turned, crying out. He hooked the sword's strap over his shoulder and rose to check on her. When the rooms had warmed, she removed her coat and gloves before going to bed, but the fires in the two stoves had died to embers. Now she shivered beneath the thin blankets, so he covered her with his mantle.

Lucian stroked her hair out of her face, and she tugged his cloak beneath her chin. He had done well to prevent their bond from growing deep, and he felt he could part from her now and feel only a little pain. As badly as he wanted to love Lindsay and make her a part of his soul like any Elder would, he held no delusions.

At the Citadel, they would take Lindsay from him and that amputation had the potential to be devastating for them both. Even with the severity of Lucian's crimes, John had never severed their bond.

You were my son, John whispered to Lucian before they dragged him from the Seraph's presence. Those four words had broken his heart. Though he'd braced himself to be severed from John's soul, the Seraph never completed the act. Lucian had always been grateful to him for that one mercy.

He realized how deeply his actions had wounded John. Rachael wasn't the only person he had harmed, and his deeds had disgraced countless others within the Citadel. No amount of apologies could rectify the devastation he'd left in his wake. Yet he was through hiding, sick with self-loathing, from his errors.

Neither should anyone else suffer because of him. Rachael and John would help Lindsay by blunting the affect on her, and the less attached they were to one another, the easier it would be on him and Lindsay. It was best this way.

Lindsay sighed Peter's name before she quieted.

He and Rachael had spoken four days ago, and if she rode hard from the Citadel, she and her constable should be at Ierusal any day. His earlier anticipation of seeing her vanished into dread. He wouldn't insult her by asking for her forgiveness; there could be no pardon for such a betrayal. The best he could hope for would be her mercy.

Lindsay mumbled in her sleep, and he tucked his mantle around her ankles before turning his attention to the woodstoves. He added wood and stoked the fire to life in the bedroom's small stove. When he finished, he went to the kitchen and knelt to resurrect the blaze in the cooking stove.

Done with the fires, he brushed his hands against his shirt and shut the door. As he stood, a shadow passed one of the windows to momentarily obliterate the light of the full moon. Lucian froze. The lock was in place on the kitchen door. He drew his sword and advanced toward the window. Outside, water dripped slowly from the eaves to the porch where icy moonlight bathed the weed-choked yard. Nothing moved.

The sensation of familiar magic stung his body.

Catarina.

He backed away from the window; a crash from the bedroom caused him to whirl. From where he stood, he saw the door to the study was wide open and his chair was on its side. He couldn't see the bed or Lindsay. Edging close to the counter on his right so he could see into the dark room, he advanced toward the bedroom. His sheath snagged on a drawer and he dropped it to the floor when Lindsay screamed his name.

For one terrifying moment, the child sounded exactly like Rachael when he'd released her at the Gate so long ago. Lindsay's second shriek tore through him as he reached the door.

A man jerked the child up by her arm and she writhed in his grip, trying to tear herself out of his hands. The intensity of Catarina's magic was overwhelming. So was the smell of burning flesh.

Enraged, Lucian shouted and the man turned. The creature had no face. Threads loosened and slashed the air where eyes should have been. A tiny round hole existed in place of the mouth. The creature's breath whistled as it gasped for air. Lucian's horror drained the strength from his limbs.

"Lucian!" Lindsay hacked at the fiend's wrist with her knife. Her blade sliced through the cords, which split and waved through the air like snakes. In the gaps, Lucian saw muscle and tendon, and he realized the monster had once been human. A malicious spell invigorated the threads and caused them to eat into the man's flesh like acid.

The creature whined.

Lindsay screamed. The resonance of her magic mingled with Catarina's, and Lucian's pack flew through the air. He ducked and the bag hit the wall where his head had been. The wardrobe vibrated against the wall. Behind him, the kitchen drawers rattled, struggling to open.

Lucian's blood pounded in his ears so loud it almost drowned the child's cries. He advanced, looking for an opening. "Lindsay! Get down!"

She threw her weight backwards and dropped to the floor like she was sitting. The creature didn't release her. It didn't matter; Lucian had the opening he needed. He slashed at the creature's neck, but his strike went low to slit the fiend's narrow chest.

It howled and struck out. Lucian's shoulder burned when the creature's hand hit him. He staggered backward against the wardrobe and his cane flew from his grasp. He kept his grip on his sword, but his knee betrayed him and he went down.

Lucian searched for his cane and spotted it two feet away. He crawled toward the stick. The fiend kicked out at the cane and missed. Lucian stretched and extended his sword to snag the cane. He rolled it toward him and managed to lumber to his feet. Sweat rolled into his eyes and he staggered from pain and exhaustion.

A deep gash crossed the creature's chest. Threads wiggled and the blood slowed to ooze over them as the wound closed. Lucian realized he could hack at the creature all night, and the fiend would heal itself. Despair rose in his breast; he couldn't win. His sister's magic had grown too strong.

God's power is greater. Matthew's voice broke Lucian's stupor. *God's power comes from love.*

Lucian's hand trembled. Love. He looked at the quivering girl. All the feats he'd accomplished these last days had been achieved through courage born of his love for Lindsay. God had answered his call to open the Hell Gate and his magic was returning to him. Surely if he opened his heart to God and allowed the Spirit to flow through his limbs, God would help him save her again. The words he thought he had forgotten surfaced in his mind and Lucian Negru remembered what it meant to be Katharos.

The monster dragged Lindsay to the bedroom door. Her panicked eyes met Lucian's, and he knew if he didn't act, he was going to lose her forever.

Lucian's voice rolled through the small room, loud as thunder. "Release this child, Lindsay Richardson, I command you through the holy name Iehova!" He felt the power of God surge from within him to pass into his sword arm. The blade of Matthew's sword brightened to burn white-gold in the dark room.

The monster yowled and flung Lindsay away so it could cover its face. Lucian drove the sword deep into the creature's shoulder. Lurching backwards, the fiend peeled itself off the blade and ran. Lucian followed it into the study. The monster bumped its injured shoulder against the doorjamb of the outside door and fell to the stoop. Lucian was upon it before it could recover.

A long thread protruded from the monster's back and disappeared into a moonbeam. Catarina had drawn from the legends of their Walachian youth for her creation. Lucian remembered the tales their grandmother had told them of vampires riding the moon. The old wise woman had told them the secret of killing one too.

The creature howled with fresh agony when Lucian slashed the cord rising to the moonbeam. He thrust the blade deep between the Simulacrum's shoulder blades. The monster pitched forward into the muddy alley, almost jerking the blade from Lucian's hand.

Lucian hooked his arm around one of the posts. Splinters bit into the crook of his arm as he slid from the stoop to the ground. The creature made it to its knees; Lucian brought his blade down on its neck, severing the head. The torso wavered then fell forward.

The frigid night air burned Lucian's throat as he leaned on his cane. The creature at his feet didn't move. The threads fell away from the mangled body to reveal a man's flayed corpse. Lucian crossed himself and muttered a prayer for the man's soul.

The light within Matthew's sword shimmered then faded to leave the blade cold and blue in the moonlight. Catarina's magic died with the monster; she had sent nothing else. Silence filled the night.

He needed to get back to Lindsay, the latest in Catarina's long line of damaged souls. His twin made his life a curse and any who got near him were injured in his wake. It would be safer for all of them if Rachael simply cut his throat when she arrived.

Although he knew it was dead, Lucian backed away from the creature. He almost slid on the thin film of ice covering the wooden steps. He hooked his wrist around the porch's banister and stopped his fall.

Once inside, he slammed the door shut and shoved the desk in front of the door. Lindsay's terrified sobs reached him as he returned to the bedroom. He saw the sheath in the kitchen where he'd dropped it, but he didn't have the energy to retrieve it. He tossed the naked blade on the bed. "Lindsay?"

The contents of his pack were scattered across the floor. The wardrobe and kitchen drawers were still. His blood raged from the fight, and he had to calm himself before approaching the child or he'd do her more harm than good. Her anxiety would make her extremely sensitive to his mood.

If he was angry, she might mistakenly perceive him as the enemy and attack. An injured Katharos could be more dangerous than the Fallen, especially when their powers were developing and their control was minimal.

He summoned his soul-light and the shadows departed. "Lindsay, answer me."

Her ragged sobs were her only response. She huddled in the corner between the wardrobe and the kitchen door, holding her injured arm in front of her like an offering. Her sweater hung in smoking tatters up to her elbow. Fat blisters formed in clusters all along her forearm and wrist where the creature had grasped her.

The image of Rachael's injured arm flashed through his mind. He'd watched from his cell as John lifted the blanket covering Rachael. The Seraph had spoken to her, his words drowned by the inhuman keening rising from beneath the blanket. The sight of Rachael's bloodied hand accompanied by her unearthly moans tormented his memories.

"Lindsay?" He held out his hand. She didn't acknowledge him. "Let me see." He moved into her line of vision and she blinked.

Her breath rose and fell in short, rapid bursts. "Lucian?" She pushed her injured arm up for him to see. "I panicked again. I'm sorry. I don't want to die."

"Hush now." He took her hand and she let him help her rise. "You're not going to die."

A bruise darkened on her forehead; when the creature flung her, she must have hit her head. He probed the wound and though she winced, she didn't pull away from him.

He led her to the bed and sat with his back against the headboard. He drew her onto his lap so he could cradle her in his arms. She didn't deserve this pain.

Lindsay stared up at him, her sobs dying to hiccups. "Hey, Lucian?"

"Yes?"

"Will you call my mom?"

He frowned down at her. She wasn't as lucid as he'd first surmised. Perhaps she'd taken a harder hit to the head than he realized. "Of course." He rocked her and passed his palm over her eyes. "Sleep now." He touched her panicked mind with calm thoughts, easily penetrating her defenses to eliminate her pain and lull her into sleep.

"My phone," she whispered.

"I will call her."

"Pete too."

"Of course." Taking her injured arm in his hand, he closed his eyes and hummed a wordless lullaby he remembered from his youth. She wanted her mother and brother, not her Elder, and that was his fault too. Rather than give the child the comfort she needed, he'd been more concerned for his own welfare, and Lucian saw he was wrong to want to keep her at a distance.

He'd almost lost her tonight; almost lost her without truly knowing her soul the way an Elder should know his foundling. He shouldn't cheat either of them of that special bond, even if it was only meant to be for a short time. Lucian's lullaby shifted to become the soft chant of a healing Psalm.

A shadow moved along one wall, and he faltered, releasing the child to touch the hilt of the sword beside him. The shade lifted his open palms to the ceiling, and Lucian recognized Matthew's spirit. The old priest nodded as Lucian took Lindsay's arm again and resumed his chant.

There was nothing to fear, even in this dark hour, for divine light surrounded them. God had answered his call. Lucian reached beyond himself to the core of his soul where God's love burned within him. He passed this grace to Lindsay's frightened spirit, healing her body, soothing her soul, uniting them as father and child with a tenderness

Lucian had forgotten he possessed. And as he allowed her into his heart, sometime in the night, the precise hour unknown, Lucian's heart of stone transformed to a heart of flesh.

CHAPTER TEN

the citadel

John Shea's footsteps echoed softly on the worn stone steps that led him deeper into the catacombs beneath the Citadel. His soul-light illuminated his path through the dank corridor, driving the black rats from his path. The darkness behind him matched his mood. The message to meet beyond the crypts had come from the Lord High General of the Citadel's armies, Xavier Sarr. These midnight meetings never brought good tidings, and John had enough concerns without Xavier's bad news.

The Rabbinate's Inquisitor Adam Zimmer had left this morning after spending a few days at the Citadel. Zimmer had diplomatically suggested that John might need the Rabbinate's help in bringing Lucian to justice. The Rabbinate didn't want to see the situation get out of control; they felt an earlier intercession by neighboring bastions would have prevented the Zoroastrian schism. John's fingers twitched.

The only thing that prevented him from sending Zimmer on his way prematurely was his respect for the Rabbinate's Seraph. Ephraim Cohen and John had served together in Woerld as Inquisitors then Seraphs for over fifty years. They loved each other like brothers, and John knew that if this situation had involved any of his Katharoi other than Lucian, Ephraim never would have sent Zimmer. Yet it was Lucian, and had their positions been reversed, John would have seen fit to send his Inquisitor to make sure the situation was firmly in hand. Although he understood Ephraim's reasoning, he didn't like the insinuation that he couldn't control his Katharoi.

At the bottom of the stairs, John veered left down a long tunnel until he reached a wooden door held together with rusting iron bands. This set of corridors branched away from the Semah River, and though the air was drier, dampness still seeped down the walls. John found his key, and the oiled hinges allowed the door to open without a sound. Xavier's spies kept these routes immaculate.

It had taken John years to fully develop his network of agents, and longer years before he was satisfied with who could be trusted. After Lucian's betrayal, John swore he'd not be caught off guard again. He would not tolerate another Lucian. Ephraim had nothing to worry about.

He rounded a bend in the tunnel and saw Xavier's dark form illuminated by his own soul-light. The General dwarfed the two guards that flanked him; he looked like a great black lion with his dreadlocks framing his face. Like John, he'd forsaken his formal robes of office for a shirt and heavy pants to ward off the tunnel's chill.

The guards snapped to attention and Xavier bowed.

John waved their deference aside. Xavier gestured to the guards and they split up. The woman went to the right, the man to the left. They moved several yards away to watch the branches in the corridors to make certain no one stumbled on the meeting.

Xavier stepped aside so John could approach the cell. He opened the metal door that covered a small barred window. Through the opening, John saw a rough wooden table with a bench on either side. Torches blackened the walls of the windowless room with acrid smoke.

On one bench, a young man sat with his wrists chained to the table. The youth stared at the opposite wall with red-rimmed eyes. His olive skin gleamed with perspiration. He sat perfectly still, his breathing shallow.

Victor Ramos. The youth was around fourteen years old, just the age to get into trouble without firm supervision. What had the boy gotten himself into while Aldridge was gone? John clasped his hands behind his back.

A shadow moved in the far corner of the cell. John caught the faintest sheen of coal black hair and recognized Gayane Balian, the Citadel's Chief Intelligence Officer. If she was here, the news was dire.

John stifled his anxiety. Xavier and Gayane were veteran warriors, and they would sense his disquiet. John's Elder, Miriam, had instilled in him the same code that she lived by as Seraph. The first rule was never let the members see their Seraph doubt himself. Regardless of his inner turmoil, he must always show a calm facade. John stilled his soul and closed the metal door that covered the window. He turned to Xavier. "What's going on?"

"That is Victor Ramos," Xavier said. "Caleb Aldridge is his Elder."

"I know who he is."

"He's one of Gayane's cryptologists. He came to her this morning with this." He produced a piece of yellowed silk from his pocket.

John took the swath and unfolded it. He gazed at the incomprehensible sigils splayed across the page long enough to recognize an encrypted message. "What does it say?"

"It's a report from one of our spies in Hadra."

That was a rare spot of good news. "So, our people in the northern provinces aren't dead?" He handed the cloth back to Xavier.

"No. This one is only a few weeks old." Xavier leaned close and lowered his voice. "I've suspected for some time that our messages were being intercepted. I thought the messengers weren't making it out of Hadra, but it seems I was wrong."

"How so?"

"This one was found in Constable Aldridge's satchel. Victor brought it to Gayane this morning. I'll let her tell you what happened." Xavier opened the door and stepped aside so John could go in first.

What was Caleb Aldridge doing with an encrypted message? John couldn't staunch the dread rising in his chest. Rachael had all she could handle with the Wyrm. What if he'd misjudged Caleb?

Victor turned his panicked gaze on John and went so white that John feared the boy's heart had burst. A tear leaked from one eye and Victor reached up, but the chains stopped his hand just short of his face. He had the wild look of a trapped animal.

Unbidden, John recalled seeing the same terrified look on Lucian's face when he'd been arrested. John's pity rose for the boy, but he'd show

Victor Ramos no more mercy than he'd shown his own foundling.

Gayane stepped forward and bowed. In spite of the ragged scar that crossed her proud nose to fall across her cheek, she was a beautiful woman. She was also a killing machine with a cunning mind. John trusted her and Xavier with his life.

"Your Eminence," she said.

Xavier closed the door and took his place at the head of the table, his stance relaxed.

John acknowledged Gayane then sat on the bench. He looked into Victor's eyes but spoke to Gayane. "Tell me what you've found, Commander."

Her soft voice was barely audible beneath the sound of the torch flames. "Victor came to me this morning with a message from one of our spies in Hadra. He said he found it in his Elder's satchel. Victor, tell the Seraph what you told me."

Victor blanched like he'd been struck.

John knew from experience it was better to come off tough at the beginning. "Well?"

"I stole the missive," Victor whispered. "I took it from Master Caleb's satchel."

"When?"

"The morning the Hell Gate opened. When Master Caleb got your summons for the directive, he left his satchel in his office. He usually locks the bag in his desk, but I think he forgot about it in the excitement. I know I shouldn't have, but I was curious. I looked inside." He absently pushed at the chains' cuffs as if he could slide them off. "There were several missives there. I took the one on top."

John glanced at Gayane.

She said, "Victor is learning the more complex codes. He told me he wanted to practice deciphering the message. He initially thought he had a ciphered message from one constable to another. He put it in a drawer in his room and forgot about it until a few days later. He started working on it. He correctly deduced the message was from one of our spies."

Xavier spoke up. "Not the kind of information Caleb Aldridge would be privy to."

Gayane nodded. "When Victor realized what it was he came to me."

John's trepidation grew. "And you think the other missives in the satchel were also from our spies?"

"That's my theory," Gayane said.

"Where is the satchel now?" John asked. *And those missing reports.*

"It seems to have disappeared, your Eminence." Xavier glared at Victor, who refused to meet the General's eyes.

Gayane took over the narrative again. "Victor attended Peter Richardson's funeral with everyone else. I'll vouch for his presence there; he stood next to me. He didn't go back to the apartments he shares with his Elder until the evening of the funeral. That's when he noticed the satchel was gone."

John looked at Victor. "Why didn't you tell someone, son?"

Gayane put her hand on the youth's shoulder. "Tell him, Victor."

John saw Gayane's fondness for the youth in that one gesture.

Victor took three deep breaths before he could continue. "That night, before I went upstairs, I saw Commissioner Dubois in the atrium with a similar satchel. I didn't think anything of it until I saw Master Caleb's was missing."

The boy was lying. John saw it in his eyes, read it in his words. He had been a judge, and he knew the signs of deceit. "Why did you wait so long, Victor?"

"I just deciphered the message today." He glanced up to Gayane, but she remained silent.

John didn't believe him. "You noticed the satchel was in Dubois' hands, which meant that someone other than staff was in your rooms. Didn't that disturb you?" Out of the corner of his eye, John caught Xavier's smile of vindication. John placed his elbows on the table and steepled his fingers beneath his chin. "I think you deciphered that message the same night you saw Dubois with the satchel. Now you tell me why you waited so long to notify Commander Balian about the message."

Victor stared at his hands miserably. "*Miserere mei, Deus,*" he whispered and choked on a sob before he could finish the prayer.

Miserere. Have mercy. John kept Rachael's ruined face before his eyes. God Almighty, what if he'd misjudged Caleb, and Rachael, half devoured by the Wyrm, was riding with a traitor at her side? A traitor he had appointed. He had no mercy left in him for the likes of Victor

Ramos. John slammed his palms on the table. "Tell me the truth, boy! Or your suffering has just begun."

"I was afraid!" The youth's words were barely intelligible. "I didn't want Master Caleb in trouble, because I knew—"

"You knew he'd drag you down with him?"

"He's my Elder, your Eminence."

Now John saw it. If Caleb was suspected of any wrong-doing, his foundlings would also be alleged to be corrupt.

Victor met John's gaze. "I swear before Christ, your Eminence, I did not know."

John raised his hand, and Victor stopped talking. If what Xavier and Gayane implied was true, then Dubois and Caleb were obstructing information to the Seraph. John turned to Xavier. "Speak plainly to me. Do you believe that Dubois and Aldridge are intercepting our messages?"

"We don't know anything for certain, your Eminence. All we have are suspicions," Xavier said. "I had a brief message via carrier pigeon that Judge Boucher and Constable Aldridge stopped at the Eilat outpost for provisions. That would have been two days ago. The message indicated that all was well." Xavier paused, and John wondered if the General wasn't trying to reassure himself too. None of them wanted to believe Rachael was riding with a complicit member. Xavier continued. "It's possible that Aldridge didn't know what the missives were, your Eminence. Dubois could have been using him as a courier with Aldridge thinking the notes were being sent to you."

John desperately wanted to believe him. He struggled to reel his emotions under control, but he couldn't shake the horrible feeling that he'd sent Rachael to her death. *I've killed her. Lord God, I've killed the one I loved the best.*

John's fingers absently found the cloth and he returned his attention to Victor. The boy was in a no-win situation. If he accused Dubois, it would be the word of a protégé against the word of the Commissioner, and Dubois was known for his retribution against perceived enemies. Regardless of whether they were loyal to the Seraph or the Commissioner, the constables would see it as their duty to make Victor's life a misery, just as they had with Lucian.

John pressed his thumbs against the corners of the silk. "Who else have you spoken to about this, Victor?"

"No one, your Eminence. I swear before God, no one!"

Gayane's fingers tightened on the boy's shoulder, but he didn't calm. It was obvious Gayane thought Victor was innocent, but John wondered if her fondness for the boy was clouding her judgment. If he had not allowed love to blind him, he would have seen Catarina and Lucian's downfall coming. Gayane needed to stand back from this boy's fate.

Xavier glanced at the door. "The only ones who know about this are the four of us and my two guards out there."

John looked at Victor, but all he could see was Lucian's misery staring back at him. He didn't temper his words. "You're under arrest, Victor Ramos. I won't forget you went to Gayane with the report, but you've lied to me. I can't trust you. Whether you're guilty or not, if Dubois or any of the constables, including Master Caleb, find out what you've told me, your life will be forfeit. Do you understand?"

Victor bit his lower lip. A trickle of blood reddened his teeth.

"Do you have a place to keep him, Gayane?" he asked. "Some place where he won't be found unless I need him?"

Gayane's face betrayed no emotion, but John sensed she wasn't pleased. "We have some cells down here. It won't be comfortable, but he'll be out of sight. I can arrange a reason for his disappearance so no one suspects he's been arrested."

"Excellent, have it on my desk in the morning and I'll sign off on it. Get him out of here."

Gayane took Victor to the door and waited until one of the guards came to her. She spoke briefly to him, then he disappeared with Victor in tow. When Gayane returned to Xavier's side, the General lowered his voice. "Should I order Dubois' arrest, your Eminence?"

"On what charges?" When Xavier didn't answer, John shook his head. "You can rest assured that Aldridge's satchel and those missives have disappeared by now. We've nothing to charge Dubois with. We need proof. So, we watch them and we act as if we know nothing. Give them enough rope; they'll hang themselves without the least effort from us."

"I've already arranged for my people to watch Dubois," Gayane said. "And Bartell."

John raised his eyebrows at her. "What does the Lord Inquisitor have to do with this?"

"Nothing," Xavier said. "Yet."

John examined the General's stony features. Xavier, like Rachael, hated Reynard Bartell ever since he used Lucian's conviction to advance to Inquisitor. Prior to Lucian's betrayal, Xavier and Lucian had been the best of friends. Both were excellent strategists and thoroughly enjoyed their friendly rivalry during war games. John had no doubt that to this day Xavier felt Lucian was wrongly convicted.

Reynard certainly hadn't been John's pick as Inquisitor, but the Council had been unanimous, and at that time, John was in a poor position to argue. However, he refused to allow his personal feelings for the man color his judgment. "Is this your vendetta against Reynard, Xavier?"

Xavier's features remained impassive. "Reynard and Dubois are close. If Dubois is under suspicion, then we must do everything we can to assure ourselves of our Lord Inquisitor's absolute innocence."

John's smile felt tight. "Nice hedge, General."

Xavier didn't blink. "Thank you, your Eminence."

"They won't make a move without us knowing it," Gayane promised.

"And you—" John pointed at her. "—watch that boy. Might I recommend that you don't get too attached to him? Just in case."

She arched a shapely eyebrow at him. "In case he's using me?"

In case he's another Lucian, John thought. "Guard your heart, Gayane. I speak to you from experience."

Her expression didn't change, but he saw concern flicker in her eyes.

John caressed the silk and pushed it toward her. "What does it say?"

Gayane didn't bother to look at the cloth. Her confidence returned; she was back in her element. "It's from Matthew Kellogg, written three weeks ago. He states that Catarina has solidified her position in Hadra. She has not moved on the churches and temples, but it's merely a matter of time before she does." Gayane hesitated and glanced at Xavier. "The last portion is a personal message for you, your Eminence."

John closed his eyes. "Go on," he whispered.

Gayane cleared her throat. "He says: 'I have dreamed and the Lord has spoken to me. A lost sheep will seek his way back into the fold. Miserere.'"

PART II

...do not weep,
not yet, that is, for you shall have to weep
from yet another wound. Do not weep yet.

—Dante
Purgatorio

CHAPTER ELEVEN

ierusal

Droplets of water clung to the trees in spite of the frigid breeze, and Rachael monitored the sparkling limbs with a worried gaze. More clouds were rolling through the sky this morning, and the smell of rain was in the air. The horses weren't shod for ice, so if the temperature continued to drop, they could be in for a rough return trip. The muddy ground was still too warm to freeze, but the Wasteland's weather patterns had never been predictable.

Like everything else here, she thought as she drew her coat up against the chill. She glanced back to check the spare mount; the chestnut gelding walked docilely behind Ignatius. The road sucked at the horses' hooves as if to draw them down into Woerld's musky womb.

The absence of wildlife added to the Wasteland's desolation. No quail burst from the fields, no birdsong haunted the air; it was like moving through a tomb. Scattered farmhouses began to take the place of trees as she reached Ierusal's outskirts.

The empty cottages were mute markers of the people who had occupied the thriving country of Norbeh before the war. Fields overgrown with weeds and shrubs littered what had once been farmland. The houses were set well away from the road, yet even from a distance, it was obvious the buildings were empty.

A door banged, and Rachael pulled Ignatius to a halt. The noise was too rhythmic to be anything other than the creak and thump created by a broken latch and the wind. She located the sound's origin at a dilapidated cottage with ivy snaking through the blind windows. The front door swung in the wind and slammed against the frame. Near the house, a plow leaned against a barn wall, but the rest of the building was gone, perhaps blown away by some other savage Wasteland storm.

Ahead, the walls of Ierusal loomed behind the Rosa, which had grown substantially since she had last been here. She recalled her dream: Lucian standing before her in a city of death while her blood pooled at her feet.

I can't make it stop.

Mouth dry, she took a sip from her flask, then nudged Ignatius back to his slow walk. The Wyrm had been silent for the last three days, not offering the slightest push against her consciousness. The demon's lack of activity was unnerving. Twice in the last sixteen years the Wyrm had withdrawn, only to resurge with a fierce assault. Both of those times, she had resided at the Citadel and John had helped her put the demon down.

She would have no help in the Wasteland. Caleb simply wasn't strong enough to be any assistance against the Wyrm. His lack of skill would do more to imperil her than save her. She was better off fighting alone.

The thump of hoofbeats caused her to turn, and she hated the way her neck ached in the cold. Caleb emerged from the forest and caught up to her, his mare tossing her head as she slowed.

"Everything all right?" Rachael inquired.

"Oh, yeah, I just like to look behind once in a while." He took his gloves off and blew on his fingers. "You know, I've been thinking, Rae."

She made a noncommittal sound in the back of her throat and nudged Ignatius to a fast walk with Ierusal's gates in sight.

"Don't you think it would be better if I went in and brought Lucian out to you?"

The wind gusted and lifted her hair out of her face as she reined Ignatius to a stop again. Between the cold and damp, her joints ached with fierce pain. "Say again?"

"Well, I've been thinking."

"Hmm?"

"About the Rosa and the Wyrm."

She said nothing. John had taught her to wield silence with deadly skill.

"If the Wyrm is strong in you when you leave Ierusal, it's possible the Rosa will strike against you. It'd be safer for you if I went in and got Lucian. I could bring him and the foundling out. Nobody would ever know you weren't there for the initial arrest."

"I would know." She'd made her peace with death soon after she discovered the pain of living. If the Wyrm was so strong as to attract the Rosa's wrath, then let the Rosa have her. Rachael had no intention of prolonging her demise.

"I'm worried about you."

"Duly noted." She kicked Ignatius to a trot, hoping to dissuade Caleb from sharing any more of his concerns. "Now do your job so I can do mine."

His mare kept pace, and he was quiet, his expression grim. The odor of wood-smoke hung just under the scent of the Rosa; Lucian and the foundling were close.

The city's southern gate was open. Rachael slowed again, distracted by the evanescence of a fractured Hell Gate somewhere nearby. The Gate strained to swing through the threads of time and space, seeking a way to open. Rachael slowed Ignatius until she was sure the ancient spells locking the ruptured Gate were secure.

"You feel it too?" Caleb asked as he reined his mare to match Ignatius' pace.

"We'll be fine." She returned her attention to Ierusal and the Rosa. The leaves rustled like a murmur in the light breeze, obscuring the flowers hidden amongst the thorns. As they passed beneath the bower outlining the gate, Rachael felt the tingle of the Rosa's magic caress her flesh.

The feeling faded as they passed beneath the portcullis. Although dim, the entrance tunnel was clear of debris, and they soon re-emerged in the pale morning light. The horses' hooves echoed against the cobblestone road. Wind whistled through the buildings and alleys.

In the back of her mind, the Wyrm slithered before it quieted again. Rachael shuddered. Wagon frames jutted from the rubble of a collapsed building. Jagged piles of bones littered the street where people had died on top of one another in the assault. A horse's skull lay several feet from the disaster, the empty sockets fixed on Rachael.

Across the street, a missing wall from another building revealed a table and broken chairs. A bundle of rags fluttered in one corner of the room. The only sound was the moaning wind.

She allowed Caleb to pass her and followed him onto a back street to avoid the carnage. They wound their way through Ierusal's alleys, stopping every so often so he could listen. Rachael tensed each time he stopped. She wanted to be done with this whole mess.

The morning slipped away from them and the clouds grew heavy with rain. It was early afternoon before Caleb held up his hand. They dismounted and tied the horses to the post of a house. The signature of Lucian's magic flowed over her, as familiar as his touch. She knew without a doubt Caleb had led her true. Lucian was close.

Caleb pointed to what she thought was a small house a block away. She examined the roofline and saw the steeple had been damaged. It was a church.

Where you always knew to find me when I was troubled.

A thin stream of smoke filtered through the chimney; the fire was all but out. As they neared, she noticed two back entrances, one through a partially demolished picket fence and the other via a porch from the alley. Rachael glanced at the windows. No one moved inside.

They drew their swords. She motioned for Caleb to take the alley entrance as she stepped through a gap in the fence. She lost sight of him when she stepped onto the porch. Through a dirty window, she saw the kitchen. An empty scabbard was abandoned on the floor. A pot lay on its side in a puddle of liquid. The presence of Lucian's magic was overwhelming, and she remembered his voice rumbling through her bones when he had opened the Gate.

Biting the inside of her cheek until she tasted blood, she waited until she had her heart under control. She twisted the knob; the door was locked. She knelt before the keyhole and reached into her pocket to retrieve a thin piece of metal, which she used to pick the flimsy lock. The kitchen door opened. Rachael paused, listening.

She made a full count to ten before she eased into the room and with five steps she was at the sheath. The scabbard was old, but when she looked closely, she saw it bore the unmistakable Citadel emblem. *Where had Lucian gotten a Citadel sword?*

Lucian's weapon was broken when he was exiled. John had presented the destroyed blade to her in a formal ceremony as a symbol of the Citadel's retribution. She wrapped the pieces in a blanket and curled up in bed with the remnants of the shattered steel. For three days she had not moved until John lost his patience and forced her to accept the truth of Lucian's betrayal.

Rachael blinked against something in her eye. If Lucian used the blade, then it was a gift, because a stolen Katharos's sword would bring agony to a thief. But what Katharos would give a renegade something so precious?

She cocked her head and listened. Someone moved in the next room. How and why he'd come by the weapon were irrelevant. He was armed.

A shadow moved and when she looked up, he was there with his sword only a few feet from her chest. She reflexively brought her blade up as she stepped into a fighting stance. The kitchen was too narrow for either of them to swing their blades so it would be a fight of thrusts. He held the advantage with his longer reach. She needed to draw him into the open.

Lucian kept his right leg away from her and leaned heavily on his cane. Blood seeped into his beard from a wound on his cheek. Beneath his tan, his skin was sallow, the circles beneath his eyes black.

In his gaze, Rachael immediately recognized the agony no drug could heal. She knew that look well. She had broken all her mirrors so she wouldn't have to see her own distraught stare day after day.

Now her pain looked back at her through obsidian eyes and for one blind moment, she wanted to run him through with her sword. Just to make their anguish stop. For once she wanted to let the rage she harbored in her heart give her license to kill.

But she didn't. She wouldn't allow herself the luxury of becoming like the Fallen, like Catarina. Though it meant staring back at her grief, she forced herself to look at Lucian. Maybe this terrible misery wasn't meant to end; maybe they were meant to bleed on one another forever.

The tip of his blade wavered. "Rachael?" His voice cracked halfway through her name. He knelt before her, crumbling slowly to the dirty floor. He reversed the sword to present it to her hilt first.

Her heart twisted, but she brought a hob-nailed boot down on her pity. "I have a directive from the Seraph that you are to surrender yourself to my authority." Her voice didn't belie the doubt gnawing her resolve. John would have been proud of her.

"I will."

She accepted his sword and power surged from the weapon into her palm. He had recently summoned God's authority through the blade. Rachael frowned and sheathed her weapon before she retrieved Lucian's scabbard from the floor. As she rose, she noted the disarray in the room beyond the kitchen. *Where was the foundling?*

Caleb entered the other room and barely glanced at the scattered possessions. He carried his sword in one hand and manacles in his other. "The other door was blocked. I had to come through the chapel." He stepped into the kitchen as she draped the strap of Lucian's weapon over her shoulder. Caleb threw the manacles at Lucian, who caught the cuffs before they fell to his lap.

"Put them on. Then hand over the cane." Caleb pushed the point of his blade against Lucian's throat.

"Wait," she said to Lucian and he froze. Even as an exile, Lucian's status from his days as a Council Elder demanded a modicum of respect. "I have his sword. He's surrendered to my authority. Why don't you take care of the horses?"

Caleb's blade pressed into Lucian's flesh and a drop of blood wept across the steel. "As soon as he's subdued."

Lucian stared at the scarred cabinets, his head against the wall. It was evident to her that his subjugation had come long before this day. She bit down on her anger at Caleb and said, "Go get the horses."

Caleb shook his head. "I'll stay with him. Just so there's no appearance of impropriety."

Was he deliberately trying to undermine her authority with Lucian? Rachael's eye narrowed at the constable. Caleb usually threw his weight around with prisoners, but he was never unnecessarily violent. Yet if Lucian made one wrong move, Caleb's blade would open his jugular.

Rachael felt Lucian's fear as clearly as if it were her own. Stunned by his willingness to open his thoughts to her, she looked down to find his eyes on her. Pleading. Something was very wrong.

Both men awaited her decision. To allow Caleb to stay while she retrieved the horses would make her weak in Lucian's eyes. "Get the horses, Caleb."

The constable wavered for another second then jammed his sword into its sheath. Lucian closed his eyes and sagged against the wall.

As Caleb brushed past her, he leaned close. "I need to talk to you." He went to the porch.

Rachael reached down and grabbed the manacles out of Lucian's hands. "Don't move until I get back."

He nodded and she met Caleb outside, leaving the door open so she could see Lucian. "Talk."

Caleb whispered, "There's a body in the alley. It's been burned beyond recognition. The remains stink of Mastema's spells."

"What is it?"

"I've never seen the like. It reminds me of a golem. That one," he whispered as he nodded toward Lucian, "probably created it for protection and it turned on him."

"So he destroyed it?"

"Obviously."

"With Mastema's magic?"

"What else?"

A Citadel sword, perhaps? she thought as she fingered the strap on her shoulder. Caleb apparently hadn't paid attention to Lucian's blade. She made sure to keep the scabbard aligned with her body and out of his sight as she untangled the layers of magic surrounding the church.

She sensed an echo of Lucian's magic and another reverberation from someone she didn't know, possibly the foundling. The child's spells were fragmented, prayers started and ceased without focus until her charms became wild with her panic. Yet there was nothing dark about these enchantments.

Something else had walked the streets, and Rachael sensed Mastema's tainted resonance. Lucian and Mastema were in her blood and bones; Rachael would know either of them by the vibrations they left in the air. Beneath Mastema's taint was a fourth layer of magic that carried a weak malevolence, barely remembered like a tickle at the back of her throat.

Caleb leaned forward, but before he could speak, she reached out and put her hand on his shoulder. "Good job." When he started to move away, she seized his arm. "And Caleb," she whispered so Lucian wouldn't hear, "regardless of his crimes, past or present, he was once a Council member. I will not have him manhandled like a common thief. Am I clear?"

"You are."

She released him. "Take care of the mounts. I'll be fine until you get back."

He nodded and stepped off the porch. "Mind your blind side."

It wasn't bad advice. She turned so he couldn't see the sword and waited until he rounded the corner before she returned to Lucian. She wanted to say something to tear his heart from his chest, but every clever riposte fled her mind. All her words had been spent through the years, and though she had once yearned to see him debased before her, she found no joy in his degradation. Revenge was highly overrated. She placed the manacles on the counter and held out her hand.

"Rachael." He took her hand but didn't rise. "I'm so sorry."

"Don't even start." She cut him off. His fingers stiffened around hers. "I'm not interested."

Instead of a rebuttal, he knelt before her and offered no resistance. The relief and hope she had seen on his face when she'd first entered the kitchen was gone. His palm slid across hers to leave her hand empty. He had let her go again, this time at her request. The edge thinned around her anger. She offered once more to help him stand, but he rose unaided.

"Where's the foundling?" she asked. The question rang hollow, a white noise to fill the empty space of his silence.

He gestured at the adjoining room with a casual wave along with a tilt of his head. It was a movement so uniquely his, Rachael felt a surge of nostalgia. "Lindsay was hurt last night when we were attacked," he said as he limped into the room.

"Who attacked you?" She followed him, wincing at his pained steps. Caleb's golem?

"One of my sister's creations. It's dead." His contemptuous tone wasn't lost on her as they reached the bed where a chair sat by the headboard.

Of course, that was the resonance she couldn't place. Catarina. Now that he named it, Rachael didn't see how she could have missed his twin's spell. Yet she'd always been blind to Catarina's magic. Lucian was a part of her, but his sister kept herself inviolate, cold as a winter queen, sharing herself with no one but Lucian.

Rachael redirected her attention to the foundling. Lucian had obviously been in the midst of bandaging the girl's arm when Rachael entered the kitchen. Her wrist and forearm were still swollen and red, and a few deeper blisters festered in her flesh, but Rachael saw where Lucian had healed the worst of her injuries. The girl's arm still glowed in the room's half-light. To have healed her meant he called on the name of God, because the Fallen couldn't heal. Never had Woerld known a Katharos who could walk between God and Hell's Fallen with impunity. Rachael was pragmatic enough to know she wasn't witnessing a new phenomenon. Lucian was not complicit; he couldn't be and do what he'd done.

Lucian lifted the girl's wrist and finished bandaging her arm. "Her name is Lindsay Richardson."

She started. "What?"

"Lindsay. Her name is Lindsay Richardson."

"Her brother's name was Peter." She resisted the urge to touch Peter's wallet.

"Was?" Lucian tied off the bandage and turned to Rachael.

"I told you. Jackals took him while he was in the Veil."

The girl murmured Lucian's name, and he brushed his fingertips across her forehead. She quieted and fell back into peaceful sleep. "The Veil closed and broke the connection before I heard your answer. I didn't know."

Lindsay's pale lashes were still against her dirty cheeks. Only people who had never known privation slept with such abandon. Like Lucian, she was obviously a child who had always been loved.

He limped to the chair and eased himself down, holding to the bedpost as he sat. "I'll tell her when she wakes."

"The sooner you start withdrawing your influence, the easier it'll be on her. I'll break the news to her."

"That is up to you. As Judge." The only sign of his agitation was his white-knuckled grip on his cane. He tilted his head against the wall and closed his eyes, his movements heavy with grief. "Just don't let them say I corrupted her. I have not."

"That's out of my hands and you know it." This was his foundling, his burden; he should have maintained an emotional distance from her. *Don't make this my responsibility. I can barely take care of myself,* but she halted the words before they spewed from her lips and said, "John will judge her impartially as he's judged every child before her. If he says she's pure, they'll accept her."

"They will talk about her no matter what John does. You can teach her how to survive, Rachael."

"All I know is how turn a heart to stone. Would you have me teach her that trick?" She realized from the look on his face it would have been kinder if she'd struck him. She rubbed the patch covering her eye as a headache whined through her brain.

He pressed his lips together and said nothing else. She wasn't quite sure what to do with the tense silence so she let it stand between them. She feared when the wall came down her defenses would be laid bare.

Lindsay's eyelids fluttered; she would awaken soon. Lucian's magic was losing its hold as her body finished healing. Rachael couldn't take her rage out against this child. Peter had wanted his sister saved, and though he'd asked Rachael, it had been Lucian who had rescued her. In spite of all his failings, he had Lindsay's best interests at heart. A person didn't have to be a judge to see it.

Outside, she heard the jingle of tack as Caleb led the horses into the backyard and within minutes he appeared in the bedroom. "It's starting to rain again."

Rachael didn't acknowledge him; she didn't trust her voice.

"Gonna rain," he said.

Gonna come a drowning rain, she thought as she swallowed past the knot in her throat. "Is there a place to stable the horses?"

"There's a carriage shed out back that'll give them some shelter."

"Take care of it."

He left them after a lingering look, which she didn't acknowledge. When she was sure Caleb was gone, she went to squat beside Lucian. She lowered her voice and spoke as gently as she knew how. "I believe her Elder should tell her about her brother." She reached in her pocket and, though it broke what was left of her splintered heart, she pressed Peter's wallet into his palm. "Give it to her. It's all I was able to save of him."

He looked at her as if calculating her intent before he accepted the wallet. "Thank you."

"We'll wait out the storm and leave in the morning if we can." She reached up and touched the gash on his cheek. "You can rest this afternoon. Then we'll talk."

He looked away from her and she followed his stare to the shadows hovering in the corners. She hid behind his stone silence and waited. Minutes passed before he spoke again. "I will tell you things," he said.

Just that.

Nothing more.

CHAPTER TWELVE

lamentations

Lucian stared into the shadows to avoid Rachael's gaze. She gave his arm a gentle squeeze, but he didn't respond. If he touched her, he was afraid he wouldn't stop. Beneath her scars, he saw the woman he loved.

The Wyrm was close to taking her. Only an exorcist could see the blue-black shadow in her eye that indicated her possession. Lucian calculated the depth and color of the Wyrm's reflection; Rachael didn't have long. Worn down by her constant battle against the demon, she was too weakened to survive a sustained attack. Yet he could only exorcise the demon with her permission. There would be no opportunity to save her if he couldn't win her trust.

The kitchen door slammed, causing both of them to jump. Rachael rose as Caleb stalked into the room and tossed their packs into a corner. He shook the rain from his coat and hung it from a peg by the stove. "Nasty out there." He dropped the manacles on top of the packs.

Lucian touched the cut on his throat where Caleb's blade had nicked him. He remembered Caleb from the group that had brought Rachael back to the Citadel. Even as John stepped onto the wagon beside her, he'd singled the constable out with praise for rescuing

Rachael. The other Katharoi took note, and Caleb preened in his sudden celebrity.

Now the constable went to Rachael and put his hands on her shoulders. She tilted her head as he whispered in her ear. He slid her coat off, and Lucian noted Caleb made sure his knuckles trailed down her arms. She nodded and murmured a reply. She didn't chastise him for his intimacy; she seemed to take it in stride. Caleb smiled at Lucian over her shoulder.

His touch bespoke familiarity with Rachael's body. Lucian's fingers massaged the head of his cane. Apparently she had wasted no time mourning his exile before she decided on his replacement. He observed them through his lashes as he tried to dampen his jealousy. Had he seriously expected her to spend the last sixteen years pining for him after he'd sent her Hell?

Caleb had rescued her, so she should be grateful to the constable, but even gratitude had its limits. The man was so utterly beneath her in both intelligence and station. She should have thanked him and moved on to a more suitable arrangement with a man of her rank.

Rachael touched Caleb's wrist lightly as she spoke to him again. The constable was so distracted he didn't notice her check the Citadel insignia on Matthew's sword before she put the strap over her head. She made sure the side of the sheath bearing the Citadel's motif was to her back and out of Caleb's sight.

Lucian frowned. She must want him dead very badly to hide his use of the Citadel blade. His ability to call on the power of God through the sword might be the only evidence standing between him and a noose. A new ache filled his chest. While he hadn't expected her love, he had not anticipated her to use subterfuge. He had hoped she would at least find it in her heart to forgive him. Instead, she planned to subvert his chance for a fair trial.

Caleb went into the office. Rachael lingered on the threshold and spoke to Lucian. "I'm leaving the door open."

There was nothing veiled in her warning; she would be listening for his movements. Lucian didn't bother to answer. She frowned, but she must have thought he dozed, because she didn't push the point. She left him alone, and he was grateful.

Fingers brushed the back of his hand and he sat up with a start.

Surprised to find his cheeks wet, he rubbed his face dry and found Lindsay's pale gaze fixed on him. She must have sensed his discomfort, because she looked away while he composed himself. Her hand never left his.

"How do you feel?" he asked.

She looked down at her left arm and wiggled her fingers. "It still burns, but I can handle it. Did you fix it?"

He nodded.

"Thanks." She nodded toward the office. "Is that Rachael?"

"Yes." He wondered how long the girl had been feigning sleep.

Lindsay craned her neck to look into the other room. "There's something wrong with her. She's got some kind of shadow in her eye."

"What?"

"In her eye, there's a shadow. It makes her pupil shiny and blue, but it moves like a cloud. It's never in one place for long. What causes that?"

"You saw it?"

"Can't you?"

Now he knew why the child had been drawn to him; she was an exorcist. The telekinesis alone was a worthy talent but her ability to detect a possession made her a rarity. When John saw her talents, he would know her potential and her future at the Citadel would be assured. Lindsay would be safe.

He realized he would never see her take her vows against the Fallen. She would grow up and he would be nothing but a memory of her first days in Woerld. "The Wyrm," he said and swallowed past the hollowness in his throat. "You are seeing the evidence of Rachael's possession. Whenever a demon possesses a mortal, the demon casts a shadow in the person's eye."

"Can anybody see it or is this another talent?"

"Only an exorcist can see it. It's your talent. Like it's mine."

Out of the corner of his eye, he noted Rachael had slipped back into the room to watch them. He knew she expected him to use the ritual words to renounce his rights as Lindsay's Elder, but he couldn't summon the phrases to his mouth. Not yet. He didn't speak until he was sure he controlled his voice. "Lindsay, this is Rachael Boucher, the Judge I've been telling you about. Present yourself to her and do as she says."

Lindsay hesitated. "You okay?" she whispered.

He nodded. "Go."

Lindsay didn't ask any more questions. She glanced back at him as she crossed the short distance to Rachael. She walked up to Rachael and thrust her chin out and cocked her hip; her arms crossed her thin chest. Lucian held his breath, although her stance indicated defiance, Lindsay didn't openly challenge Rachael. Yet.

"Let's go in here," Rachael said. "We can talk in private." She gestured for Lindsay to go into the office and, after another quick nod from Lucian, Lindsay obeyed her.

In her own way, Lindsay let Rachael know where her allegiance rested, and it was with Lucian. He was simultaneously proud and frightened for her.

Caleb emerged from the room and almost ran into Lindsay. "Hey." He smiled. "You might want your coat." He stepped around her and plucked her jacket from the peg. "It's still a little cold in there."

She took her coat and put it on before she disappeared into the other room. Rachael followed the girl and shut the door.

Caleb lounged by the stove. He waited a few minutes before he said, "It wasn't enough to ruin her life once, was it?"

Lucian dropped his gaze to the floor.

The constable warmed to his topic. "Now the whole ordeal is going to be dredged up again. Did you stop and think what that's going to do to her?" He paused as if he was expecting an answer. "You're like a cancer, Lucian. You just spread grief wherever you go."

Lucian tried to merge Caleb's voice with the sound of the rain. When his twin and her cohorts had taken their amusement in his disgrace, he'd never had any difficulty shutting them out. He'd learned to calm his mind and not hear them, but he found himself unable to draw Caleb's words behind a convenient fantasy. The constable was too close to the truth.

Caleb crossed the room and bent down so Lucian had no choice but to look at him. "I love her, Lucian. I love her like you never could." The constable lowered his voice until he could barely be heard over the rain pounding on the roof. "I'm going outside to walk the perimeter. Make a run for it. Take one of the horses and go back to your sister, go to some other city of sanctuary. Open a Gate and go to Hell, I don't care, but just get out of everybody's lives forever. I'll take care of Rachael and the girl."

It was the easy way out. Lucian knew once he cleared the back door, the constable would kill him, and Rachael would be none the wiser. He might have considered the offer a week ago. Not now, not after last night. The Spirit had touched him and he had found his courage. He understood how Matthew had been able to calmly give himself to save Lucian. Now Lucian would give himself to save Lindsay. There was no going back.

"I swear you'll live." Caleb drew his blade and kissed the hilt. "I swear before God Almighty and the Citadel I serve." He sheathed the blade and rose, backing toward the door. "You be gone when I get back."

The constable slipped away, but Lucian looked to the door shielding Rachael and Lindsay. He wouldn't abandon them. Even if they took Lindsay from him and Rachael hated him enough to lie about him, he wouldn't abandon them.

Not this time.

†

The fire Caleb built warmed the room, and Rachael lit two candles to drive away the late afternoon gloom. She caught Lindsay staring at her scarred face in fascination. Lindsay looked away guiltily, but Rachael didn't chastise her. Instead, she observed the thin girl with white-gold hair and pale blue eyes. She seemed to be made of glass; such a fragile child, and the delicate ones never lasted long.

"Are you in pain?" Rachael gestured to Lindsay's hand.

"I'm fine." She touched the bandage absently. "Lucian fixed it."

"Has Lucian told you about me at all?" Rachael sat on the couch beside the trembling girl, hoping to reassure her.

Lindsay got up and moved to sit in the chair facing Rachael. "Yes, ma'am."

The Wyrm. Even this new to Woerld, she was sensitive to the evil Rachael carried. She didn't try to encourage Lindsay to return to the couch. "What did he tell you?"

"That you're a judge. And that Pete is with you."

"That's all?"

Lindsay shrugged and kicked one foot back and forth in her nervousness. "Is Pete okay?"

Rachael thought about saying yes, because he was okay, much more so than if he'd lived, but she couldn't bring herself to lie so glibly. "Have you ever promised someone something?"

Lindsay nodded and twisted a strand of her hair through her nervous fingers.

"Well, I made a promise to Lucian, and it's very important that I keep it." *Because trust is hard earned and easily betrayed.* "Be patient a little longer and when we're done, Lucian will talk to you." Rachael watched her chew her lower lip. She wished she could send Lindsay straight to Lucian, but the news of Peter's death wouldn't be easy on her. Impaired by her grief, Lindsay's testimony would be muddled at best, non-existent at the worst. No, it was better to question her first. Once Rachael acquired the information she needed, Lindsay could grieve in peace.

"This won't take long, will it?" The hope in her voice was heartbreaking.

"No. It shouldn't take long at all." Rachael noticed Lindsay's eyes were the same color and almond shape as Peter's, but Peter's hair had been darker, almost brown. An image flashed in her mind of Lucian and Catarina laughing together over one of Catarina's asides; their eyes were identical too. She recalled standing across the room, watching them enviously.

"Well." Rachael pulled herself out of her memories and back to the present. "I'm a Citadel Judge. That means anything that you tell me I will have to report back to the Seraph and the Council. Do you understand?"

Lindsay nodded.

"Why don't you tell me about meeting Lucian?"

Lindsay's foot swung faster, and she narrowed her eyes at Rachael. "I know how this works. I'm not getting Lucian in trouble."

Rachael wondered what lies Lucian had used to twist the girl's allegiance to him. "Who says he's going to be in trouble?"

"He told me he shouldn't have opened the Gate."

No, he shouldn't have opened the Gate. Rachael slipped into a dream. She remembered her excitement when Lucian had promised to teach her the Psalms to open the Gates. In the potter's field, they had stood so close she felt Lucian's heart beat against her back. *John says I'm not ready for the Gates.*

John's a fool.

Rachael started when Lindsay's voice disrupted the memory. "He said when you got here, he was going to be under arrest. And I wasn't supposed to be upset about it because he broke a promise." Her glare deepened and a tear slipped from the corner of Lindsay's eye. She wiped her face.

Perhaps Lucian wasn't twisting the circumstances to win Lindsay's sympathy. Rachael remembered Caleb's eagerness to see Lucian in chains. It was possible he'd been trying to prepare Lindsay for just that scenario. "What else did Lucian say?"

"He said that I had to do what you said, nobody else. Then when we get to the Citadel, I could trust you and John and John's wife Tanith. He said to trust nobody else."

"John, Tanith, and me. No other names?" Surely he would have given the child the name of a compatriot, someone within his and Catarina's intimate circle, not the Seraph's family.

"Nobody else. Why's he in so much trouble?"

"Lucian made a very solemn promise never to open a Hell Gate again. We call that promise a covenant. In return for promising not to open the Hell Gates, the Council banished Lucian." Because John couldn't order Lucian's death, not with her life hanging so precariously in the balance. To lose Catarina to the Fallen had been demoralizing, but the loss of all three of the Seraph's foundlings would have been devastating to the Citadel's future.

"He didn't leave Hadra to open a Gate. He left because of you," she said.

Rachael licked her lips. "What?"

"He just happened to be there when Peter and I came through the Veil. You're the whole reason he left Hadra. He still loves you and wants to make you better." Lindsay held up her hand. "Like he fixed me."

Rachael's pulse jumped. This didn't make sense. No matter how desperate his situation, Lucian was far too reticent to tell a child something so intimate. "Lindsay, I know Lucian would never tell you that."

"He didn't." She met Rachael's eye, defiance radiated off her small body. "I saw it in his heart when Catarina attacked us and he protected me. You remember. You were there too. You told him to go away and he did, not because he wanted to, but because staying would hurt you more." She sat up in the chair and leaned forward. "And you know it," she whispered.

Rachael rubbed the patch over her eye. She wanted nothing more than to look into Lindsay's heart and see if the girl spoke the truth or only her version of it. Yet she restrained herself. Without the Wyrm, searching a foundling with the intimacy of a soul-touch took finesse; foundlings couldn't shield themselves from the stronger Katharoi. With the danger of the Wyrm, Rachael didn't dare broach Lindsay's frail defenses. The only way she would know the truth is if the child slipped in her story. "Tell me everything, Lindsay." She reached out to touch Lindsay but stopped shy of making contact. "Help me understand."

✝

Caleb still hadn't returned when the door to the office opened. Lucian gripped Peter's wallet. It weighed like a rock in his hand.

Lindsay emerged first, and she came straight to him. "She wouldn't tell me about Peter. She said you had to. It's bad, isn't it?"

He stood and she reached out to him; he put his arm around her as Rachael entered.

"Where's Caleb?"

"He went out. Rachael." The kitchen door closed, and Lucian stopped talking. Too late. He couldn't risk discussing his concerns with Caleb in the room. It was possible that when Rachael questioned him privately, she would have Caleb stay with Lindsay. He doubted the constable would take his aggressions out on the child, but Lucian was taking no chances.

"Yes?" Rachael prompted.

"I'd like to talk with Lindsay alone. If that's all right."

Caleb gave no sign anything was amiss.

"Certainly," she said. "Let's go look at your golem, Caleb." She grabbed her coat and gestured for the constable to lead the way.

When they were gone, Lindsay pulled away from him. "Lucian? Is it bad?"

"I'm afraid so." He motioned for her to sit on the bed and she obeyed him.

"It's okay if he's hurt, even if he's like Rachael." She whispered, "I'll love him anyway."

There was no easy way to tell her. "Lindsay, Peter didn't make it through the Veil."

Tears were already brimming over her lashes and she rocked herself. "He did too. He's just lost." She turned to him.

He wanted to lie and tell her she was right. He wanted to tell her anything to make the grief leave her gaze. Instead, he pressed the wallet into her hand. "Rachael said he died bravely. They've buried him at Citadel. I'm so sorry."

"She's wrong." Lindsay took her brother's bloodstained wallet and turned it over in her hands. "This isn't his."

Lucian refused to take the billfold when she tried to hand it back.

"It's not his." She insisted and opened the wallet.

A piece of paper floated to the floor, and Lucian bent down to retrieve the photograph. Two children on a beach, one was definitely Lindsay, the boy was surely Peter. He held the picture up to her.

Her body hitched with sobs. "Are you sure he didn't go back to Earth? I mean, that would be okay, even if he went back without me."

Lucian shook his head as he reached out and drew her to him. He took her shuddering body in his arms and held her. "Let yourself grieve for him so you can let him go."

"It's not fair."

"No," he admitted, "it is not." Her sorrow went through his heart and for a moment, he was tempted to heal her grief as he had healed Catarina whenever she felt bad. The temptation lasted but a second. He reaffirmed his vow not weaken this child as he had his twin.

He looked up to see Rachael in the doorway again, their bleak guardian angel. He felt her magic steal into his heart for a glimpse of his soul before she withdrew. His pulse quickened.

When they were young, she would test his love by watching him with her soul's eye when she thought he was too preoccupied to notice. One day he'd asked her to stop, because he wanted her to trust him without resorting to prayers and spells. To keep his love, she had acquiesced, and he had turned her heart to glass. So now he opened himself to her and let her see he had nothing to hide.

Lindsay trembled in his arms. He rocked the child, rubbing her back as he had when he first found her in Hell.

Rachael hung her dripping coat on a peg and came to the bed. She sat beside him, but she spoke to Lindsay. "Peter was very brave. He saved your life and even returned after his death to tell me you were in danger. That was his last request, that someone save you." She stared at her hands and made no effort to touch the child. She started to say something else, then thought better of it and remained silent.

"He was your foundling, wasn't he?" It was a rude question, and Lucian wanted to bite his runaway tongue, but he'd held his silence for too many years. His time was short; he would waste no opportunity to touch her.

Rachael rose and occupied herself with tidying the room. She moved so quietly, Lucian almost forgot she was there. He lost track of time while the rain pattered against the roof. Lindsay's sobs trailed off into distressed hiccups. With his back against the headboard, he held the child through her grief and watched Rachael with half-closed eyes.

As he hovered on the threshold of sleep, he felt Rachael's breath tickle his ear. "He was mine."

He started, but even as he opened his mouth to tell her he was sorry, she put her finger against his lips.

"I know," she said.

CHAPTER THIRTEEN

revelations

Rachael lit the last wick and examined the altar with a critical eye. Caleb had found several candles to give the chapel enough illumination for Lucian's inquisition, and she had cleaned the altar of its surface dust. The old church was a miserable substitution for the Citadel's cathedral, but she would make do with what she had. She always did.

"I don't see why this is necessary," Caleb said as he nourished a fledging fire in the woodstove.

"Field interrogations are at the discretion of the arresting judge." She cited the law to silence his objections. "I want the facts in hand when I make my report to John." Rachael had grappled with her memories until Tanith's words resounded in her mind again. She held on to the warning, repeated it to herself and drove it into the depths of her memory.

Trust no one. No problem. She didn't trust Lucian or Caleb. One of them was lying to her and she had to isolate which one. An interrogation would allow her to evaluate both men and the honesty of their statements. Their interaction with one another would tell her more than all the words in Woerld.

Rachael placed Lucian's blade on the altar, making sure the Citadel insignia was facedown, although she wasn't sure whom she thought she was fooling. She and Caleb examined the golem together. Even in the miserable rain, the fading glow around each of the golem's wounds indicated strikes by a Citadel blade.

Yet he tried to convince her that Lucian used Mastema's power to create then destroy the golem. Rachael didn't dispute his claim, although a protégé could have deduced the golem spell belonged to the Fallen, not a Katharos. Did Caleb believe she was so taken by the Wyrm she couldn't analyze the evidence before her?

The stove's metal door screeched like a demon when Caleb closed it. Rachael shivered. For one wild moment, her vision blurred as if a reptilian wing brushed her eye.

The altar disappeared behind a memory of ruined lips pressed close to hers. Open sores had wept across Mastema's once beautiful face and he clutched her close with his twisted arms. He promised to return her to Woerld. All she had to do was give him her love.

She almost acquiesced, then she looked into the angel's eyes. Twin orbs bereft of joy stared back at her and she felt the emptiness of his spirit. Had she never tasted Lucian's love, she might have complied with the angel's demand. But she had, and with the memory of that warmth encompassing her heart, she refused Mastema. The dark angel had expelled his rage on her body.

Rachael dug her nails into her palm until the pain drove the recollection deep. The blurriness dissipated from the edge of her vision, and she took a ragged, shallow breath. She focused on Caleb. Over his head, a thin stream of smoke oozed through a crack in the stovepipe.

He brushed his hands against his pants. "I'll go get him."

She unbuckled her sword and laid it beside Lucian's on the altar. "Give me your sword."

"What?"

Rachael kept her attention on the altar. "John doesn't want the prisoners intimidated by armed judges."

"Judges," Caleb said as he pointed at her. "Constables keep theirs."

"If you remain in this room during my interrogation, you're fulfilling the role of a surrogate judge." It was a lie but one that she could live with. "You'll do it unarmed." She held her hand out for his weapon and hoped he didn't question her. She preferred not to elaborate on the deceit, but if he pushed her for an explanation, she could devise details. She didn't want Caleb armed while her sword was out of reach. Not until she knew whether she could trust him.

His fingers toyed with the hilt of his blade, and out of patience with him, Rachael played her trump card. "If you're afraid of a crippled man, then you can wait with the child."

Caleb flinched at the suggestion and unbuckled his sword. "This is a bad idea."

Perhaps, but it was all she had. She put his weapon on the altar and said, "Wait here. I'll get Lucian."

Silent as a hunter, she walked through the office and stopped at the bedroom door. Lucian still held Lindsay, who rested in his arms, half-asleep. He stroked her hair and murmured to her, his voice a soothing rumble beneath the rain.

Feeling like an intruder, Rachael cleared her throat and Lucian turned his head. "It's time," she said.

"Of course," he whispered and slid off the bed, easing Lindsay down to the blankets. She murmured her brother's name, and Lucian quieted her with a touch. He took something from his pocket and pressed it into the child's hands.

Rachael moved into the room, and a flash of color triggered a sense of déjà vu. She frowned as she neared the bed and recognized the pattern from one of her favorite scarves. She gave the scarf to Lucian years ago. Shocked he'd kept it all this time, she stopped walking.

"You said it wasn't magic," Lindsay said.

"Shh." He passed his palm over her eyes and she slept, the edges of the scarf barely visible in her arms.

"What isn't magic?" Rachael asked.

"It's only my Psalter." He rose and met her gaze. "She was frightened once, and I gave it to her to hold. It seemed to give her comfort. Do you need to see it?" There was no challenge in his tone, and she had no doubt he'd produce the Psalter at her command.

"No, I don't. Let's go." She gestured for him to lead, but she lingered to look down at the scarf. The flowers had faded, and the seams were frayed. *He kept it all these years.* He had to know she would recognize it. Was he trying to determine if she still had feelings for him? She kept her face impassive as she turned.

He was at the door, waiting for her. He clearly misinterpreted why she remained by the girl and said, "She will sleep, hopefully until we're done."

"Good." She followed him into the church where Caleb waited.

Lucian limped into the room and stopped long enough to genuflect at the cross. She gestured for him to sit on the first pew and he obeyed her as she took her place by the altar.

"Give me the cane." Caleb barked the command and held his hand out.

In the candlelight, Lucian's eyes sparkled with anger. His actions since his arrest were above reproach; he didn't deserve Caleb's disrespect.

Rachael clenched her fist and glared at the constable. This was nothing more than another power play on Caleb's part, and he placed her in a difficult position. To leave the cane with Lucian would make her appear lenient, and Caleb would lose face in front of the prisoner.

She snapped at Lucian. "Give it to him."

The gesture was a symbolic victory for Caleb and both men knew it. Caleb took the cane to the office door and leaned the stick against the doorjamb. He was pleased with himself but wisely kept his mouth shut.

Lucian pressed his right hand against his thigh, seemingly lost without the cane. Until now she hadn't realized how much the walking stick was a part of him. It was like he had lost a limb.

Rachael shifted her stance so that she could keep the constable in her peripheral vision. Satisfied with her position, she turned her eye on Lucian and spoke the ritual words. "I am before you, Lucian Negru, not as your confessor, but as your judge. Any words that pass from your lips to my ears will be taken before the Seraph and the Council to condemn or exonerate you. Do you understand?"

"I do."

"Do you accept the authority of the Citadel that I bear in the name of God the Father Almighty, maker of heaven and earth and of all things seen and unseen?"

"I do."

"In the love and light of God's law, do you solemnly swear to speak the truth?"

"I do."

All three Katharoi crossed themselves.

Rachael said, "In the fall of 5858 you were exiled from the Citadel."

Lucian interrupted her. "5857."

She blinked and for a split second, she groped to remember what she'd said. Surely she hadn't forgotten the year this living hell began, but for the life of her, she couldn't recall the words she'd just spoken.

Caleb bristled at the interruption. "Don't correct the Judge."

She held her hand up to silence him. "He's right." She didn't like the genuine worry she saw on Lucian's face. Lowering her hand, she nodded and spoke to Lucian. "You're right. It was '57. In the fall of 5857 you were exiled from the Citadel." She sought to regain her former rhythm. "You were exiled for serving as an accomplice to Catarina Negru's treasonous pact with the Fallen and for aiding her to escape from the Citadel's justice. Is this the truth?"

"It is."

"And where did you go upon your exile?"

"I went to Hadra where I'd sent Cate. When I arrived she told me she had secured a patron, Bernard De Jonge."

"The governor of Golan's Negev province?"

"Yes."

A chill descended over Rachael. "He's complicit with the Fallen?"

"Yes."

"And the Citadel's allies in Negev?"

"Eradicated."

The rain pelted the roof.

Lucian continued. "De Jonge was waiting for Cate when she arrived in Hadra. He helped her set up her household and introduced her to Hadra's mayor."

Rachael struggled to remember the mayor's name. As the Seraph's heir, she knew the names and titles of all the major houses so she could summon them at will. What had been the man's name? Witherspoon? Waithright?

Lucian seemed to sense her discomfort and offered her a lifeline. "His name was Wright. James Wright. He was also complicit."

"Was?"

"He went mad last year. When they couldn't control him anymore, they murdered him."

A hint of movement distracted her as Caleb shifted his weight uncomfortably. Rachael returned her attention to Lucian. "Who murdered Wright?"

"Cate, Malachi Grusow, De Jonge, and seven others." He rattled off their names in succession.

She tried to memorize each one, but the surnames kept tripping around the given names until they were nothing more than a jumble of foreign sounds. Rachael gave up; Lucian was speaking again.

"They made Cate Seraph on the morning I escaped."

"Don't you mean when you left?" Caleb interjected.

Lucian didn't acknowledge the constable.

Rachael held Lucian's gaze. "Who was holding you prisoner?"

"Cate."

Caleb asked, "What changed? You just said you went running to her."

Lucian didn't respond.

"Answer him," Rachael snapped.

"For a few years after I arrived, Cate feigned repentance while it suited her." Lucian looked at her.

She had forgotten how dark his eyes, and the pain she saw reflected in those bottomless shades of black terrified her. The silence stretched between them like the years. She thought he wouldn't continue.

Finally, Lucian said, "One evening she returned home with the demon Cerberus on her heels. She tried to convince me the creature was a hound, a gift from a patron, but there was nothing mortal about the beast. When I challenged her, she dropped all pretensions and announced there had been no revocation of her pact with Mastema." He stopped talking, his eyes full of mist and memories.

Caleb sidled closer to her. "Watch him. He's playing for your sympathy."

Rachael waved him aside. Lucian wasn't faking. She had witnessed his shame over Catarina's actions in the past. Yet when the Seraph chastised Catarina over her misdeeds, Lucian always stepped forward to take the blame for his twin. Rachael wondered if he would accept the blame for the mess in Hadra too.

Lucian whispered, "Cate lied to me to implicate me in her plot. Mastema weakened you with the Wyrm so the Katharoi wouldn't accept you as John's heir."

A thin headache started behind Rachael's right eye. "What are you talking about?"

"Cate summoned the demon Cerberus at the Citadel. In exchange for her everlasting fealty to Mastema, Cate would have power over Woerld. She told me Mastema would revoke his claim on her soul if I led you to the Hell Gates."

The pieces slid together in her mind. Cate involved Lucian to incriminate him, and Mastema intended to debilitate Rachael. Whether by taking her love or destroying her through possession, it was all the same to the angel. In the event of John's death, none of the heirs would be able to fulfill their responsibilities, and Mastema would install a corrupt Seraph loyal to the Fallen.

A simple plan to discredit the Seraph's heirs, and the three of them had walked right into it. She said, "The Seraph suspected that was the Fallen's intent, so he made Reynard Bartell the Citadel's Inquisitor. If I become incapacitated, Reynard will serve as regent. The Fallen's plan has failed."

Lucian shook his head. "Reynard Bartell is complicit with the Fallen."

Caleb bristled as if he'd been accused. "That is a lie! Don't you see what he's doing, Rae? He's trying to break us from within, just like the Fallen did during the Great Schism."

Lucian overrode the constable's objections without raising his voice. "Before she left the Citadel, Cate gave Bartell her Psalter. They inscribed their pledges to one another in the pages, along with the names of their co-conspirators. I have it from Cate's lips."

"Good God," Rachael whispered.

"I don't believe this." Caleb advanced on Lucian. "There's not a more devout member in our service than Reynard Bartell."

"Shut up." Her voice echoed in the church. A thump of fear pounded her heart. Lucian knew the penalty for falsely accusing another member. Rachael had been no more than fourteen when John ordered Adelain Wilson's tongue cut out for falsely accusing another member of being complicit. No one dared charge another member without immutable proof after Wilson's trial.

Certainly Lucian, two years older than her, remembered the incident, but the law dictated she must assume nothing. "You know the penalty for falsely accusing another member, Lucian."

"I do."

"Do you recant?"

"I do not."

Caleb came to her side, his back to Lucian. "Don't listen to these lies, Rae. Reynard has your best interests at heart. He always has."

Has he? The words remained stuck in her mouth. Reynard claimed to seek the Wyrm's true name, but after each exorcism attempt, the demon drew closer to taking her body. Reynard smiled to her face, but what wickedness did he promote behind her back? She visualized the three Katharoi making the sign of the cross as she rode through the Citadel's gates. Tanith's words hissed through her mind: *We are infiltrated.*

Rachael's malignant headache spread across her forehead; she resisted the urge to massage her temple. She couldn't afford any sign of weakness in front of either man. "So," she said to Lucian, "you were imprisoned because you knew all this?"

"No." Lucian made no attempt to elaborate.

"Why then?" Rachael's patience dissipated like the smoke winding up into the rafters.

"Because I refused to renounce my vows to the Citadel and open the Hell Gates on Cate's command."

"Catarina imprisoned you for that?" she asked.

Lucian looked away and didn't answer.

"We've got the important information, Rae," Caleb said.

She held her hand up and he stopped talking.

"The constable is right," Lucian said. "You have what's important."

"You said you would tell me." She clasped her hands until her fingers ached. "What happened?"

He sought his cane and finding it gone, rubbed his knee absently. "When Cate told me there had been no revocation of her pact with Mastema, I left Hadra. She sent her soldiers after me, and they dragged me back to her chained like a criminal." He clenched his jaw, a muscle beneath his cheek throbbed with his pulse. He took a deep breath and said, "They locked me in Hadra's prison."

The light made her uncertain, but Rachael thought a tear slipped over his lash.

"It was weeks before Cate came. She said I was to be tried for sedition. She said she would try to mitigate the charges if I would agree to come home and submit myself to her authority." He tried to skim over the experience as if it meant nothing, but the misery enveloping his countenance told her another story.

"And did you agree to her terms?" Rachael asked.

"No. I did not."

Her headache slivered through her brain and Rachael pressed her fingertips to her temples, closing her eye. Bright stars danced against her eyelid as she took a slow, deep breath to push her nausea down.

"Rae?" Caleb's voice penetrated her agony. When she opened her eye, it was Lucian she saw.

He leaned forward. "It's the Wyrm, Rachael. I can see it."

She lowered her hands and the pain receded marginally. "I know what the Wyrm feels like. This is not it." Since her return from Hell, headaches were an affliction she'd learned to live with. "Did Catarina give you a trial?"

Several minutes passed as he examined her. She was ready to repeat the question when he said, "A year later, she had me brought before her mock court. They sentenced me to five years and sent me back to prison."

Caleb stepped forward and said with finality, "And when the sentence was done, you went back to your sister."

Rachael glared at the constable and rephrased the question. "Is that what happened, Lucian? Did you go back to her of your own free will?"

"No. Cate wanted me to swear fealty to her. When I refused, she had her torturer cripple me." Lucian bowed his head and closed his eyes. Outside the rain beat a merciless rhythm against the roof. "They took me to her house."

"See how he twists the facts, Rae?" Caleb gestured at Lucian. "He says he was a prisoner, but he was merely her hostage."

"Call it what you will." Lucian addressed Caleb for the first time. "But whenever I left her house, I was under guard. She forced me to be at her side for every public appearance so her soldiers knew my face as well as they knew hers. Had I not found Father Matthew, I would still be there. He showed me the catacombs beneath Hadra so I could escape into the Wasteland."

Lucian paused, then said to Rachael, "And that is where I found Lindsay. When she entered Woerld, she accidentally passed through a fractured Hell Gate and into Hell. Her bag dropped beside me, and I used her cell phone to determine her whereabouts. I had a choice to open the Hell Gate or let the child die. You know the rest."

When he didn't speak again for several minutes, she swallowed past the burning in her throat. "Do you have any more questions, Constable?"

"No," Caleb murmured.

"Is that all you have to say in your defense, Lucian?"

"Yes." Lucian nodded.

Rachael swiped her cheek, surprised when her glove came away damp. "Give him his cane, Caleb."

"I don't think so, Rae."

She turned to the constable, but his image wavered before her. The headache slammed against her consciousness, causing her to cry out. Through her pain, she heard the sound of wood scraping against wood, followed by a long, slow creak.

Rachael turned to find the cross swaying gently against the wall. Upside down. The temperature in the room plunged until she could see her breath cloud the air. Wetness trickled across Rachael's upper lip and she tasted blood.

The Wyrm uncoiled in her brain.

CHAPTER FOURTEEN

the wyrm

"Rachael!" Lucian stood; his bad leg buckled beneath him. He twisted as he fell and caught the brunt of his weight with his arms. Before he could rise, Caleb's boot slammed into his chest. The room dimmed and he fought for consciousness. Precious seconds flew past as he gasped for air.

Caleb kicked him again. This time, Lucian caught the constable's foot and twisted. He lost his grip on Caleb's boot, but his blow disrupted the man's balance. Caleb fell sideways onto the pew.

Lucian's vision cleared as Rachael reached out to the altar. Her palm brushed against one of the blades and smoke rose in the cold air. She ripped the glove away from her burning flesh. "It's all right." Her hoarse whisper was barely audible beneath the sound of thunder.

Caleb went to the altar and grabbed his sword. He pushed the other two weapons into the floor, well away from Rachael and Lucian.

Rachael coughed; her blood misted across the altar. She wiped her mouth and fell to her knees. Lucian had no idea how long she could hold out against the demon. He forced his numb lips to move. "She has very little time, Caleb! I can help her!"

"You can't fix this, Lucian." The constable stroked Rachael's hair then stepped away from her trembling form. "I have strict orders. You're going back to Hadra."

The icy air had nothing to do with Lucian's shudder. He'd thought they would be safe once he gave himself over to Rachael's custody. Instead, he'd thrown them into Abaddon's pit.

Lucian struggled to his knees. He glanced at the office doorway where his cane rested against the frame. It was only eight feet away. It might as well have been eight leagues.

Caleb unsheathed his blade and left Rachael's side.

Lucian scanned the filthy floor for something to use as a weapon. A piece of wood about three feet long lay on the floor between him and the office door. Lucian pushed himself backward as if in fear of the constable. *Keep him talking.* "You're making a mistake, Caleb. Cate's promises are worthless."

Rachael moaned the first words of her prayer. Her soul-light encompassed her body only to ebb, eaten by the Wyrm's darkness. The demon grew stronger and she gagged.

She looked at Lucian, tears of blood streamed down her face. The rain drowned all noise inside the church. Rachael extended her hand to Lucian and mouthed, *Help me.* Her body convulsed, then she found the rhythm of her spell again.

Caleb circled to cut off Lucian's slow crawl toward the office door. "Even a Seraph as strong as Catarina can't intervene in Mastema's will. Rachael is mine."

Lucian glimpsed Lindsay's dark green coat as the girl darted behind the office door. He averted his gaze. He didn't want Caleb to realize she was up. "Who promised you such a thing?"

"Mastema. Once the Wyrm comes, I'll be Rae's groom." Caleb kicked the stick of wood into the confessionals. The constable smiled, enjoying his game.

Lucian changed direction and worked his way toward the pews. "You're a fool, Caleb Aldridge."

"There was a ceremony. We took vows."

"With Rachael?" She wasn't complicit or she would have succumbed to the Wyrm years ago.

"Another woman took Rae's vows, but a marriage by proxy is valid. I consummated the marriage with Rae."

Lucian recalled the familiarity with which Rachael and Caleb had touched. He took a shuddering breath. Long years in his sister's house had taught him to strangle his emotions. *Lies; half-truths and lies are what they tell.* He had to be careful he didn't allow the constable to manipulate him into a rage. The Wyrm fed on hate.

Caleb closed the distance between them and leaned down to grab the front of Lucian's shirt, jerking him forward. "The Wyrm will know me for her groom."

Lucian crossed himself. "Lord Jesus, I hope so."

A hint of doubt shaded the constable's eyes and he relaxed his grip. "What do you mean?"

"When it's born, the Wyrm will have to feed. And if you've vowed to become the groom, you are its first meal." It was a lie, but it was the only lie he had. Lucian prayed it would work.

Rachael inhaled sharply and arched her back, her body rose several inches off the floor.

Caleb glanced at her uneasily.

Lucian said, "The Wyrm devours the host's mind to take the body, but it requires sustenance upon its birth. The demon consummates the marriage by eating you alive, prolonging your terror. Your consciousness does not die. You become part of the demon, residing within her. Forever."

Sweat beaded across the constable's forehead; his sword hand trembled, but he kept the weapon out of Lucian's reach. "You're a liar."

Lucian whispered, "I'm an exorcist."

Thunder roared through the night and when the blast faded, Lucian saw Caleb's eyes widen. The constable's head rocked forward, then back. He released Lucian and whirled, but Lindsay was already cocking Lucian's cane back for another strike. As Caleb straightened, she brought the stick forward to hit him in the face.

"Leave him alone!" she screamed.

Caleb's nose broke, and he grunted in shock and pain.

"You're one of them!" Tears poured down the girl's face as she pulled back for another blow.

Lucian snatched the cane from her grasp and jabbed the tip into Caleb's temple. The constable's eyes rolled back in his head and as he fell sideways. Lindsay moved nimbly out of his path. Lucian struggled to his feet. He picked up Caleb's sword.

Lindsay kicked Caleb's leg. "They killed my brother." A sob hitched her shoulders. "I'm not going to let them get you too."

Lucian pulled her into his arms and hugged her. "It's all right. I understand." He kissed her cheek. "You did wonderful." Lucian hefted the constable's blade and turned to Caleb's prone form. He couldn't leave the man there. If Caleb returned to consciousness during the exorcism, Lindsay would be helpless against him. One strike would suffice. The death would be quick, almost painless.

Lindsay grabbed his arm. "We said no more killing. We said that. You promised, Lucian."

He looked from the girl's horrified eyes back to Caleb, and he knew he couldn't murder the man in front of her.

"They're the killers, not us," Lindsay said, her fingers digging into his forearm.

With a sigh, Lucian flung Caleb's sword into a far corner of the church. "All right." He would have to trust God to watch over them.

Rachael's breath rattled horribly as she struggled against the demon. Lucian guided Lindsay away from the prone man to the inverted cross. Lindsay held his cane while he forced the cross back into place then retrieved Matthew's sword.

He unsheathed the weapon and Lindsay cringed at a burst of thunder from the storm. "Hush now." He soothed her.

Rachael's prayers had stopped, and Lucian knew from experience the cessation of prayers indicated the demon was close to victory. He had no time to waste.

Lucian positioned the blade in front of Lindsay with the point down. The cross of the hand-guard was before her eyes and though she was frightened, she had not panicked. He placed her trembling fingers on the hilt, wrapping his large hands around hers. The inscription flickered to life, and her eyes went wide with wonder.

Lucian couldn't recall his last confession, and he had no idea if Lindsay had been confirmed in any religion, but there was no time to debate spiritual purity. For an exorcism of this magnitude, there should have been at least three other experienced Katharoi present. Instead, he had a frightened child.

"I can't do this alone, Lindsay. I need your help."

She bit her lower lip and nodded. "I can do this."

He took heart from her courage and continued. "I need you to help me fight the demon with prayer like you fought the haunting in the Barren."

"You want me to say my Psalm out loud." Her voice was stronger.

"Exactly, and you can't stop until I tell you. Can you do that?"

"I remember. Say the Psalm and use the magic inside me," she said, locking gazes with him.

"First we're going to pray. Bow your head." When she complied, he tried to shut out Rachael's groans. "Bless this child, Lindsay Richardson, and to send thy grace upon her, that she may execute her service to you as a true and faithful Katharos." He paused and was surprised when Lindsay gave a response.

"Lord, hear our prayer," she whispered.

It wasn't the proper response, but he didn't correct her.

"I hear thunder." Rachael's whisper broke his concentration only for a moment.

"Hearken unto our voice, O Lord, when we cry unto thee."

"Lord, hear our prayer." Natural as breathing, the girl slipped into her trance. The blade of the sword shimmered with white light that spread upward into Lindsay's arms.

"And let our cry come unto thee!" He released the sword and traced the sign of the cross between Lindsay's pale eyebrows. The child's soul-light surrounded her small body.

"In the name of the Father, the Son, and the Holy Spirit," Lucian whispered.

Without being told, she began to pray.

When he turned, he found Rachael on her knees beside the altar. She extended her burned hand to him. He snatched her wrist. Another seizure rattled her body and she dragged him to the floor beside her. Lucian released his cane and forced her to face the cross and Lindsay, then he pinned Rachael's arms with his right arm. She didn't resist when he placed his left palm over her forehead.

A foul wind blew through the chapel, dousing the candles, but the light emanating from Lindsay and the sword illuminated the entire area around the altar. Rachael stiffened against him. A screech vibrated through the church. The doors slammed open and closed.

Lucian ignored the distractions and focused his gaze on the sword Lindsay held. "'God hear my prayer; hearken to the words of my mouth.'" The words of the Psalm came back to him as if he had never left the Citadel.

The musty church faded as he sought to join his consciousness with Rachael's. With the strength of his voice and the power of God's name, he bound his soul to hers until he saw her thoughts as clearly as his own.

✝

Lost within a memory, Rachael crawled through a cave. The walls around her throbbed with scarlet veins. A hot wind swirled ash from Hell's landscape into the cavern's depths. She choked on her prayer as she had when Mastema had first left her here. The tunnel narrowed and she scraped her raw back against the low ceiling. Her scream strangled the last of her prayer.

Doubt threaded through her mind. God had abandoned her and left her to the Fallen. A dry sob rattled through her heat-seared lungs. Someone called her name. She froze, holding her breath. Her blood trickled to the cavern floor. How could she lose so much and still live?

Again she heard her name carried on the wind. The walls constricted around her. A low whine burned the back of her throat.

The Wyrm clawed through her brain, pushing her deeper into her memories. Helpless before the demon's onslaught, fear seized her heart. She closed her eye and concentrated on being still. Perfectly still.

"Rachael." A voice like thunder rolled through her thoughts. She flinched from the sound and drew the walls more firmly around her.

It was Lucian. He sought her soul so he could heal her, but she couldn't let him find her. Soul to soul could not lie, and if he saw her, he'd know her secrets as she'd know his. Better she bleed alone than let him see her black heart. She pulled herself into the crevice and tried to stop the panic racing through her veins.

"Rachael." His voice was close. "You're not evil."

She wanted to risk a peek at the cavern entrance where light flickered at the rim. She kept her eye shut. A long time ago, the Wyrm had made her look. The demon had burrowed through her eyeball and into her brain. She'd not fall into that trap again. *I can't see you; you can't see me.* Blood poured through her lips when she failed to restrain her giggle.

Her chuckle turned into a wheeze. *I'm dying.* The thought was weak, an echo in the night. *Oh, God, I'm dying and I don't care.* The Wyrm trembled through her body; Rachael couldn't summon the will to fight. Not anymore.

Breath tickled her ear, and Lucian whispered her name. She opened her eye and saw his arms around her. Somehow he had penetrated her mind and found her soul's hiding place. He took her hand and lifted her bloodied fingers to his lips. Her pain fell away at his cool touch.

"I'm here." His love enveloped her and he drew her into the light of his soul.

She tried to pull away from him but couldn't. There was nowhere left to go.

"Be still," he said. "You called my name. Let me help."

She despised needing him. "I hate you."

"Hate me then," he said. He didn't turn away from her pain. Instead, he surrounded her with love. The scars on her arms began to heal beneath his fingers. He drove her darkness down, back to the Wyrm.

The demon shrieked with rage. Rachael cringed. She couldn't hide from the truth in her heart. No matter what she told herself over the years, her love for Lucian had never died. The hurt from his betrayal followed her days and nights, an open wound that bled forever and ever, Woerld without end. All because her love for him never died.

"Rachael." He gently turned her head until she had no choice but to look at him. Of all his features, it was the compassion in his eyes she adored the most.

"I refused Mastema," she whispered. "Because of you. I refused him because I didn't want to lose our love. And you left me anyway."

He didn't flinch from her accusation. "I didn't want to go."

"You left me alone."

"You were never alone, Rachael Boucher." He smiled. "God was always with you."

"I wanted you."

His great booming laugh encircled her soul. "And I wanted you," he said, and she knew it was true. "Our love is but a pale reflection of the divine." He pressed his lips against her ear and whispered, "I am here with you. God is with us. And I will not leave you. So help me God."

The Wyrm felt Lucian's presence and surged forward. Rachael's body jerked in Lucian's arms. The demon slithered through her veins, into her memories to fire a montage of images into her brain. She was helpless against the onslaught.

...remember...

Her father stood in her bedroom door, a swath of moonlight illuminated his naked body; she burrowed beneath her covers and feigned sleep, but his hand found her breast and; Tanith came close, her breath whispered of traitors and monsters in the night; do not fear them, they are not here, are not here but; Mastema's eyes are full of poison, don't look in his eyes, never look in his eyes; where cracked mirrors fell from the walls, shattered and broken like her faith; and John stood over the Eucharist, stained-glass light bathed his robes in shades of azure-gold-crimson; he spoke of God, of God, God, God, God...

Lucian said, "I command you, unclean spirit, by all the mysteries of the incarnation, passion, resurrection, and ascension of our Lord Jesus Christ, that you give me your name."

Agony soared through Rachael's body until she thought her head would explode. She couldn't escape the visions assaulting her mind...

Her mother opened her arms and smiled; blood poured through her lips and; her father's ax rose and fell when; the Crimson Veil opened, but her father's voice followed her through and she wasn't safe, never safe, even here where; shadows and deceit broke the night with eyes as dark as a storm, and; eyes, she should never look in his eyes...

The Wyrm snarled and tried to withdraw, but Lucian seized the demon's spirit with his words.

"I command you, moreover, to obey me, I who am a minister of God despite my unworthiness; give me your name."

Her heart seized and for a moment she was afraid it stopped beating, then she was afraid she would never die, and her memories would surge forever...

Lucian's arms around her; the moon blessed their passion and she raised her head; but Catarina promised misery upon misery; what was hers was hers alone and whosoever did not love her, she drank their blood while; John held her; Tanith's cool hands soothed her and; Tanith whispered of; poison and traitors; their eyes...

The Wyrm struggled. Lucian refused to release the demon's spirit.

"Give me your name!"

Anguish shot across her face. Rachael's scream blistered her throat and blood poured into her mouth. She gagged and vomited, but she wasn't alone. The power of God thundered through Lucian and into Rachael's body. She thought her bones would dissolve in the wake of his strength.

The Wyrm thrashed and wailed its name. *Vúmis.* It was called Vúmis, and with the Wyrm's name, Lucian's power over the demon became complete.

Rachael gasped for air and felt a thread of hope wind through her soul. Maybe the fight wasn't over yet.

Lucian began the Litany of the Saints. The visions receded, back to the depths where her ghosts would sleep uneasy until resurrected in dreams. All that remained was the sound of Lucian's voice, a memory of his hands in her hair as he lulled her to sleep and deprived the specters of their power.

"Lord have mercy," Lucian prayed.

He would tell her to believe in God's pure love.

"Christ have mercy."

And if she couldn't believe, then she need only believe that he believed.

"Lord have mercy."

Midway through the Litany of Saints, she found her voice.

Lucian said, "Saint Mary Magdalene."

"Pray for us," Rachael whispered.

†

The air pressure shifted, and Lindsay's ears popped. From far away, she heard Lucian and Rachael's voices rise in prayer. She had no idea how long she'd been standing still, holding the sword; it felt like hours.

Without ceasing her prayer, she opened her eyes to slits. Lucian knelt with his head bent close to Rachael's, and each time her body twisted, he moved with her. Rachael's face was almost invisible in the twilight, covered in blood. Every so often, Lucian would make the sign of the cross on Rachael's brow or over her heart as he chanted. They blazed with pure, white light.

The same light poured over Lindsay's arms and infused her body. She wasn't tired and knew she could hold on to the sword for as long as Lucian needed. God's love surged through her small frame to hold the darkness at bay. Her grief for Peter was washed away by the knowledge that he was with the god who made this light.

Lucian's invocation rose over the sound of the wind outside. "I call on the pure name Schemhamphoras, a reflection of the perfect essence of God Almighty to aide me in summoning and adjuring the demon Vúmis that afflicts this woman, Rachael Boucher." Rachael stiffened in his arms, but he held her tight. "In the name of Iehova, also called Tetagrammaton—Iod, Hè, Vau, Hè—the manifestation of the trinity and unity of the divine essence, I summon you."

As Lucian spoke the strange sounds, Lindsay heard a groan. She glanced over to see Caleb reach up to touch his face, which was a mess. Lindsay didn't care; he deserved it. Her rage and grief returned, causing her to lose her rhythm. He made Pete's death possible by working with the angels who murdered her brother.

Lucian's hand moved, and she looked at Lucian and Rachael again. Lucian needed her help, and if that would take out Caleb, then she wouldn't screw up. Lindsay regained the cadence of her prayer. She prayed faster, though, hoping Lucian would take her cue that something was wrong, but he seemed unaware of the threat.

Lucian said, "I adjure you, Vúmis, by the judge of the living and the dead, by the Creator of the whole universe, Him who has the power to consign you to Hell." He made the sign of the cross on Rachael's brow.

Outside, the rain hammered the roof. A howl of rage from the Wyrm vibrated through the air. The bitter taste of fear flooded Lindsay's mouth and she hated the feeling. She wanted to be like Lucian; he wasn't afraid of anything.

Rachael pitched forward; instead of letting her go, Lucian moved with her. He pushed the patch covering her blind eye out of the way. Rachael heaved and a thick reddish substance poured through her mouth.

Oh, God, please don't let that be blood. Lindsay shoved her own sick down.

The storm raged overhead. The wind widened a hole in the roof over the confessionals.

"God the Father commands you; God the Son commands you; God the Holy Spirit commands you. The mystery of the cross commands you."

Rachael struggled against Lucian and lifted her head. Where Rachael's right eye should have been was a black hole without even an eyelid to cover the cavity. Lindsay's stomach lurched; she pushed her bile down.

The tip of a horn emerged from Rachael's empty socket. The Wyrm was coming out and Lucian hadn't told her what to do. Lindsay faltered in her prayer, her fear rising up to darken her light.

"Stand firm, Lindsay Richardson!" Lucian's shout snapped her attention back to her task. His face was shiny with sweat, and tendrils of black hair clung to his forehead. His dark eyes burned with fever, and over his head, a light like a flame seared the cold air.

Lindsay gripped the sword tighter, leveled her gaze at the monster, and resumed her prayer, relieved that Lucian knew what was going on. He'd tell her what to do when the time was right. He hadn't let her down yet.

Lucian continued his invocation as if there had been no interruption. "I adjure you in His name, begone from this woman, Rachael Boucher, who is his creature."

Hissing and spitting in defiance, the Wyrm filled Rachael's empty socket as it slithered out. Lindsay swallowed hard. The demon hit the floor with a wet slap.

True to its name, the white body was shaped like a maggot, but there the resemblance to a worm ended. The demon had a single horn in the middle of its forehead. Its maw gaped to show row upon row of sharp teeth. Four lines of burned, stunted wings rippled along the Wyrm's back.

The acrid air of Hell stung her nostrils as if she was standing in the ash again. She remembered the man with the worms in his throat and the other people moaning together. The ghostly tentacle that shot upward from the hole she and Lucian had almost fallen into rose before her frightened eyes.

The demon hissed and squirmed toward her. Six sets of eyes, black pinpoints of hate, covered its face and locked on Lindsay. She saw its lust. It wanted to possess her body like it had Rachael's. Lindsay's knees went weak.

"Stand firm, Lindsay!" Lucian's voice rolled beneath the thunder.

Lindsay saw jackals with long yellow teeth following her brother into the mist. They got Pete. She snapped herself out of the trance and redoubled her effort at prayer. The Wyrm whined and shrank back.

Lucian's shout startled her. "Kill it, Lindsay! Use the sword!"

She tried to lift the sword and couldn't do more than scrape the point across the floor. Lucian said to focus; she had to focus. Cursing her size, she concentrated on her prayer and tried to use the light to help her lift the blade. The second time, she managed to bring the tip several inches off the floor. She brought it down, but the Wyrm shied away from the light.

"You bastard!" Caleb's cry sent the hair on Lindsay's arms up, and she almost released the hilt. The constable staggered to his feet, his damaged face purple with rage. "What have you done?"

The Wyrm crawled back toward Lucian and Rachael.

"No!" Lindsay yelled.

Lucian cradled Rachael's limp form and raised his hand. The demon snarled at him.

Sweat soaked Lindsay's hair as she concentrated all the power from the light into her arms. *Come on, God.* She raised the heavy sword but the Wyrm evaded the blade again. Her light dimmed with her frustration.

Caleb spoke to the demon. The Wyrm lifted its head as if listening. The constable continued to mutter, beckoning the Wyrm. The demon slithered toward Caleb.

Lindsay followed it, but her arms shook and an overwhelming exhaustion fell over her. Her light withdrew back into her body and no matter how hard she tried, she couldn't summon it again. She realized this is what Lucian meant when he said the Katharoi get tired, and without her light, she was powerless against the demon.

"Lindsay! To me!" Lucian attempted to stand, and though his light still encompassed his body, it wasn't as bright.

Backing away from the Wyrm, Lindsay dragged the heavy sword toward Lucian. He was stronger; he could keep her safe from that thing. Her heel slipped on his cane and she fell backwards, landing hard. Her teeth clicked together and she tasted blood. She squealed when Lucian grasped her shoulder.

He held his cane in his right hand. He took the sword from her, but he seemed disoriented with the same drunken motions he'd exhibited after Catarina's attack. He gestured for Lindsay to get out of the way.

All she could see was the Wyrm, slithering toward Caleb. If the demon saw her on the floor, it might come back. Terror infused her limbs at the thought of that thing in her head, eating her brain. Lindsay used her palms and heels to scoot her body backward to the altar. She recalled the desire in the creature's eyes. It wanted her body. What if it turned on her? Would it try to go through her eye? "Kill it, Lucian! Kill it! Kill it! Kill it!"

The storm lifted off another section of roof near the confessionals and the wind yowled through the church. Darkness coalesced around Caleb; the Wyrm reached the constable. Lucian stood. Even as Caleb picked the demon up and brought it toward his face, Lindsay knew Lucian was going to be too late.

†

Rachael felt Lucian slip away from her, heard him shout at the child, his words filtered into her brain with a clarity she had forgotten she possessed. She pulled her patch back over her empty socket and got to her knees. She groped through the shadows for her sword. Unable to get her sluggish limbs to obey her, Rachael cursed her clumsiness and prayed her soul-light into existence.

She froze in surprise. Her soul-light shined pure and clear for the first time in years. Her right hand felt odd and she pulled her glove off to find the deep scars erased from her flesh. Gingerly, she touched her face and found it likewise healed. Something bumped against Rachael's foot and Lindsay screamed.

Rachael whirled and grabbed Lindsay before she could dart away like a frightened rabbit. Her hand closed on the child's wrist and Lindsay cried out. Rachael wrapped her arms around the girl and drew her against the safety of the altar.

"Easy, easy, easy," Rachael murmured.

"It looked at me," Lindsay said. "It wants to get inside me." The girl was pallid with fear.

Rachael squeezed Lindsay's hand. "We're not going to let it hurt you." She spied her weapon next to the girl's leg. "I promise. I've got to help Lucian."

Lindsay nodded, and Rachael reached around her to snatch her sword. Holding to the edge of the altar, she pulled herself up and turned to find Lucian moving toward Caleb.

His sword blazed with light, but he was too late. Rachael saw the Wyrm's tail flicker once before it disappeared into the gaping hole where Caleb's nose had been. Caleb moaned and stumbled backward, throwing his shoulders left, then right. The constable's yells went higher in pitch as the Wyrm burrowed into his brain. He fell backward onto a pew before he slid to the floor where he thrashed helplessly.

Lucian took another staggering step forward; Rachael got in front of him and put her hand against his chest. His heart pounded against her palm, and she felt his love wash over her again.

"We've got to get out of here," he said and sheathed his weapon.

"I'll take care of him while the Wyrm has him."

"No!" Lucian grabbed her wrist. "You can't kill him."

"I'll make it quick."

"And where will the Wyrm go next once its new host is dead?"

Rachael glimpsed Lindsay's face by the altar, the girl's words still ringing in her head. Of course, the Wyrm would want a child; it would take the path of least resistance. If the demon left Caleb and reached Lindsay, she would succumb to the Wyrm within minutes.

Lucian released her arm, and Rachael immediately missed his warmth. "Lindsay," she said, "come quick."

The child scrambled to join them; she grabbed Lucian's hand and he pulled her close. Lindsay was holding herself together, but just barely. Between Caleb's cries and the Wyrm's dark desire to own her body, she was terrified.

Rachael said, "Go with Lucian."

Lindsay nodded, relief washing over her features.

Lucian paused. "I'm not leaving you."

"Yes, you are." She touched his cheek. His skin was cooling, but she still felt the fever of God's Spirit clinging to him. The exorcism had taken more from him than he wanted to admit. "You'll never make it on foot. Go saddle the horses. I'll be right behind you."

"You promise."

"I promise."

He patted Lindsay's shoulder. "Go."

Lindsay ran through the office door without looking back, and Lucian followed, glancing in Rachael's direction only once before he left her. Relieved, she returned her attention to the constable.

"I'm sorry." Caleb's gasp was barely audible beneath the thunder. His body wrenched upward then slammed to the floor.

"For what, Caleb? What are you sorry for?" She advanced a step, but she knew. She remembered now. Caleb seducing her, taking advantage of her loneliness, stroking flesh no man would touch. He'd used her body while her mind drifted into dreams, raping her more times than she could count. She felt dirty, violated. She wanted to drive her sword through his face, but she held her anger in check. "Tell me, Caleb."

"I love you." His voice broke and he gasped. "I never—" His nails scraped the wooden floor. "I never wanted to hurt you. Never. They said if I helped get rid of Lucian, you'd love me. Don't you love me, Rae?"

Rachael wanted to smash her fist into the man's hopeful expression. "No," she said. "I do not."

"You do! You love me! I'm strong enough for you." The constable's magic filtered beneath the Wyrm's influence. She frowned. Caleb called on God, the very God he'd renounced. He muttered from where he lay on his back.

Rachael stepped backward and the floor creaked.

Caleb's head turned and his eyes shot open. "Lu-Lucian? Lucian? Are you there? Help me, God, please."

A chill ran through Rachael's body as she realized the constable was repenting. *Or it's a trick.* If Caleb asked, Rachael had no doubt Lucian would try to adjure the demon again. Lucian's haggard face rose before her eye. Another exorcism tonight might very well kill him.

"I can't control it." Caleb's whine grated on her nerves. "I thought it was easy. Rae? Is that you?" He gasped and dropped his arms to his chest. "Rae? Get Lucian. I'm begging you."

Rachael kept her sword level and backed toward the office. "I'm sorry, Caleb."

"No! Damn it. You get him. Right now!" Caleb wheezed and clawed his bloody face. "Now! It's eating me! God, Rae! It's eating me alive!"

Rachael stepped across the threshold.

Caleb sobbed. "I can't make it stop."

Rachael closed the door.

CHAPTER FIFTEEN

the sacra rosa

The candles in the office guttered as Rachael ran into the bedroom. The packs were gone. She snatched her coat as she passed the stove. Caleb's cries followed her through the kitchen and out the back door where she almost collided with Lucian and Lindsay.

Why weren't they at the shed? The packs were in a heap by the door. When she moved to go around him, he blocked her path with his cane. He held Lindsay close and whispered, "Look."

Somewhere in the darkness, the horses neighed and shuffled, but Rachael couldn't see them through the storm hammering Ierusal. Wind gusts blew sheets of rain across the yard. The metallic smell of ozone singed the air.

Leaves rustled in an ominous undercurrent to the storm. A triple flash of lightning illuminated the yard. When the darkness descended again, the image of a lush tangle of branches and thorns was seared into her brain. White flowers with human features clearly discernable in the petals emerged from the leaves. The Sacra Rosa flowed into the yard like a wave and moved straight for the church.

The limbs of the plant ranged from thin tendrils no larger than a garden snake to boughs as thick as Lucian's thigh. On the bigger branches, the thorns were as long as Rachael's sword. The acid weight of fear hit her stomach.

The resonance of magic filtered beneath the storm. Her hands and arms tingled with the reverberations, but this spell wasn't coming from the Wyrm. With another flash of lightning, Rachael saw the roses' mouths move, and what she had taken for the hum of the wind turned into a chant. The timbre of the incantation felt both alien and familiar.

She scoured her brain to remember all she'd heard of the Rosa, but no one, not even John, had ever seen it move. She didn't know if the bush was sentient or acting from instinct. The spikes protruding from the branches left her no doubt of their fate if they remained in the Rosa's path. The Rosa's thorns would rip them to shreds.

"We have to go back inside," Lucian said as he lowered his cane.

Lindsay broke away from him. "No! We can't go back in there!"

"Lindsay, stop!" He took a step, but she stumbled out of his reach, toward the edge of the porch.

Rachael eased around Lucian. She would only get one chance. She lunged forward; her fingertips slid across the wet fabric of the girl's coat. She clenched her hand and snagged the strap of Lindsay's gym bag. Closing her fingers around the thin band, she yanked and succeeded in pulling the girl into her arms. Lindsay wailed, and Lucian held his hand out for the child.

"Inside! Now!" Rachael gestured with her head, and Lucian obeyed her without question. Lindsay kicked backward and caught Rachael's shin with her heel; sharp pain twisted up Rachael's leg. She grasped Lindsay to half-carry, half-drag her back into the kitchen. The rancid odor of sour magic filled the air. Caleb's screams had stopped.

Rachael kicked the door shut and wrapped the terrified girl in her arms to keep her from plunging back outside and into the Rosa. "Hush. Stop it. You've faced worse than this, Lindsay. Now stop."

Lindsay made an animal noise in the back of her throat and her elbow shot backward toward Rachael's head. Rachael ducked and held her tighter. She pressed her lips against Lindsay's ear. "Calm down! You have to calm yourself, Lindsay. That's what Peter would do."

Lindsay froze at the mention of her brother's name. She shivered in Rachael's arms, but she appeared to be listening.

Rachael summoned her soul-light. "He kept his head and gave his life to save you. Think about Peter. What would Peter do?"

"Rachael," Lucian said.

Rachael ignored him.

"It wants me," Lindsay whispered. "And I can't make my light come."

"I know. I know." She stroked the girl's hair. "But you're not alone like I was." She passed her soul-light into Lindsay's palm. "We won't let it hurt you, Lindsay. You have to trust us. Trust Lucian. Can you be brave?" She didn't relax her hold until Lindsay nodded. The girl was still frightened, but her terror no longer overwhelmed her.

The Rosa scratched against the side of the church. A branch screeched against a pane of glass, setting Rachael's nerves on fire. The window splintered and cracked. An ominous creak drew their attention to the door bulging in its frame. Leaves, thorns, and flowers pressed against the windows. The blooms' lips moved in the mournful chant that grew more intense with every passing second.

Rachael shoved Lindsay toward Lucian. "Go!"

Lucian grabbed the girl's hand and went into the bedroom. The kitchen door burst from its hinges. In the bedroom, Rachael edged around him to lead the way. Lucian was in no condition for a fight. She wanted to be first inside the church.

The Rosa leaked around the office door, leaves pushing into the cracks, slithering past the hinges. A huge thorn burst through the center of the outside wall, splintering the wood. Rachael jerked the church door open and veered into the sanctuary with Lucian and Lindsay close behind.

The air crackled with static. Rachael heard Caleb's voice, but his words were unintelligible. The wind howled and lifted more of the roof away. The Rosa oozed through the opening.

Lucian snatched Rachael's arm and pulled her directly beneath the cross. With his back against the wall, he put his right arm around her, his cane gripped in his fist. His left arm encircled Lindsay, who shuddered and buried her face in his side. Rachael felt his heart pound against her back.

A shadow moved in front of the pews. It was Caleb, or what was left of him. Rachael put her hand on her sword, but Lucian lowered his cane to rest on top of her knuckles.

Lucian said, "Make no sign of aggression."

A moan rippled through Caleb's throat as thin rope-like striations swelled across his face and neck. Caleb's eyes were bottomless black orbs with neither pupil nor iris, not even the whites could be seen. Blood gushed into his face when his scalp split open to reveal a curved horn growing from the top of his head. His body jerked; the Wyrm commanded his limbs. The demon clenched Caleb's sword. The blade had turned black. The possession was complete; this was the Wyrm manifest.

Rachael tried to swallow her horror. This is what she would have become if Lucian had abandoned her. Yet he didn't leave her; he stayed and risked his and Lindsay's lives to save her.

Lucian's arm tightened around her waist. His pulse throbbed in time with hers just as it had when they had gone through the Hell Gate a lifetime ago. He had been afraid then as he was now, but in her lust for power, she had mistaken his fear for excitement. She placed her sweat-slick palm on his arm.

The voice that emerged from Caleb's mouth was not human. The words were garbled, meaningless, until Rachael understood the demon wasn't trying to speak in any of Woerld's languages. The Wyrm sought the angelic language it remembered from its days in Heaven, the language it had lost when it was cast out.

The Rosa slowed its approach, creeping more cautiously as it surrounded the Wyrm. The leaves no longer roared but hissed beneath the mournful chant of the flowers. Stems from the Rosa flowed around their ankles. A tendril slithered over the toe of Rachael's boot and she jerked her foot to the side. A thorn pricked her calf before the branch withdrew and sought a way around her.

The room brightened as four flowers, twice the size of the other roses, swayed upward on huge branches. These four were older than the rest, their petals tinged with yellow. As the elder roses came forward, the chant intensified. The tingling sensation of the Rosa's magic filled Rachael's chest and she felt cleansed by its song.

The storm resounded around them, the walls vibrating with each clap of thunder. The Wyrm backed away from the plant. Rachael flinched when a branch of the Rosa shot forward. The stem wrapped itself around the Wyrm's distended neck, barbs puncturing Caleb's flesh. The demon slashed wildly with its sword and sliced through the stem. Blood flowed from the severed branch. White petals fell from the three faces that had been attached to the stem.

The Wyrm spun around, his black gaze on Lindsay. Rachael saw the demon's lust. A child of Lindsay's capabilities would prove fertile ground for its malice. Behind her, Lucian stiffened as he realized the demon's intent. He held Lindsay tight against him so she wouldn't see.

The Wyrm snarled and charged them. The Rosa flowed around him, but Caleb ducked and avoided the larger branches.

Rachael pushed away from Lucian and drew her blade. He drew his own sword, but he was too tired to do more than hold a defensive position with Lindsay at his side. "Rachael, no!"

She didn't answer him but met the Wyrm's assault head on with a battle cry of her own. The Rosa parted for her, slithering away from her feet only to slide back over her path. She saw Caleb's sly smile reflected in the broken mirrors of her house, his hands on her body, the Wyrm dulling her mind. *We are infiltrated.*

A branch of the Rosa shot forward, and the Wyrm sliced it from the mother plant before it could touch him. The floor grew slick with the Rosa's blood. Rachael raised her blade, and the demon rounded on her. Caleb's black sword swung toward her head, but Rachael ducked and brought her own sword in a sweeping arc to push the Wyrm's assault aside. Her counter-slash opened a wound on Caleb's chest. They circled one another.

The Wyrm lunged, and Rachael was too slow to parry the blow. Her left side exploded in white pain. She staggered backward and her hip caught the edge of a pew; she spun in time to avoid another blow. Barely. The whistle of Caleb's blade sliced the air by her ear. Strands of her hair fell to the boards.

Several more branches of the Rosa plunged toward the Wyrm. A thorn snagged Rachael's cheek, a branch wound into her hair. The Rosa's song hummed through her body like an electric current.

Overhead the four massive blooms hovered near the ceiling like generals, monitoring the war below. She intuitively knew those great blooms were the original Katharoi who sacrificed themselves to become the Rosa. The Rosa's melodious chant suffused the air with a web of magic that bound the Rosa to its duty. Great tears rolled from the ancient roses' eyes whenever a branch died.

Rachael glimpsed Lucian and Lindsay, but the Rosa flowed around them, sealing them behind protective thorns. Lucian tried to push through the stems, but the Rosa barred his path, and Rachael was glad. He and Lindsay were safe. This was her fight.

The Wyrm pressed its attack. Rachael blocked another blow, her own sword accidentally severing a branch of the Rosa. Rather than turn on her, the plant flowed around her. Three limbs wove together to create a shield for her and deflected the Wyrm's blade.

Rachael saw her opening, and lunged, driving her blade into Caleb's chest. The Wyrm shrieked and bucked Caleb's body. The demon used its horn to slice into the leaves. More petals fell, covering the floor with a carpet of ivory.

One of the ancient roses drifted down from the ceiling toward the demon. The great flower turned, and Rachael saw the bloom's sad resignation. Two huge tendrils held long vicious thorns extended on either side of the main stem.

The demon howled and thrashed, but the light diminished from Caleb's eyes. He went to his knees and Rachael stepped backward. Recognition flashed in his gaze, and just before he died, Rachael saw the man she remembered. She couldn't summon grief for his passing.

The Rosa's chant shifted in pitch. The Wyrm burst through Caleb's bloodied nose.

Rachael followed the demon until the Rosa blocked her pursuit. She tried to circumvent the barricade, but more limbs intertwined to create a living fence. She barely made out Lucian's shadow behind the green barricade the Rosa had formed around him and Lindsay. She called out a warning to him. He didn't answer, but his blade caught the light from a flash of lightning. He watched. Lindsay was out of sight, probably behind him.

The old rose swooped over the demon. The Wyrm crawled toward Lindsay, and the ancient rose brought a huge thorn down onto the creature's body. Howling drowned the wind as the Wyrm thrashed on the spike. The rose lifted the struggling demon to its lips and devoured the Wyrm. The petal's yellow stains deepened.

From a branch below the old rose, a younger flower swayed

forward to hover over Caleb. The face within the petals opened its mouth and struck to bite the top of Caleb's head. The jaws expanded to engulf his face before it encompassed Caleb's body, wrapping him in a pale shroud.

As it ate, the flower turned red with Caleb's blood and the leaves grew darker, more vibrant. Soon nothing was left of Caleb but the sword and his ragged clothing. The red rose withdrew back into the leaves. A rosebud appeared on one of the branches. The flower matured and opened to reveal Caleb's startled features embedded in the bloom. Rachael saw his horrified expression, his eyes darting left and right.

The spit dried in her mouth when another of the ancient blooms drifted down toward her. The petals framed a face that had once been beautiful with almond eyes and full lips but now was so androgynous that Rachael couldn't determine a sex. The lips parted and Rachael thought it would speak. A branch slithered forward to prick the side of her neck. It happened so quickly; the limb retreated before a small cry escaped her throat, and she felt a trickle of blood on her skin.

The flower smiled and came close. Rachael closed her eye and forced herself to remain still. The smell of the rose was overpowering, filling her senses, bringing tears to her eye. Something dry and cool licked the blood on her neck. The air wafted in front of her and she dared to look. The rose was moving away, and branches that had twined in her hair released her.

The Rosa retreated to flow from the room and recede into the night.

Minutes ticked past before Rachael felt she could move. The sting of minor scratches covered her hands and face, and her left hip was wet. She lifted her torn shirt and tried to examine the wound. She sensed Lucian's presence and looked up. He sat down on an undamaged pew and pulled her to him. His soul-light hovered over the injury and he pushed her probing fingers out of the way.

Lindsay watched her with red eyes. "Is it gone for good?"

Rachael nodded. "The Wyrm is gone. For good."

"Are you okay?"

"I am. Are you?"

She craned her neck to see Rachael's side. "I guess."

Her haunted eyes said otherwise, but Rachael didn't push the point. Lucian's hands came too close to the cut and Rachael almost dropped her sword. "Careful! That hurt."

"It's not deep, but it should be bound."

She gently disentangled herself from him and pulled her shirt down. "Just leave it alone." She sheathed her sword, using the motion as an excuse to look away from his concern. "It will be fine."

Rachael summoned her soul-light. Petals and leaves were scattered through the chapel, but the sound of the chant was gone, the spell faded into the night. The floor was slick with blood, and outside, the rain pounded against the roof. She cleared her throat. "Maybe we should sleep in the shed tonight."

Lindsay went to Lucian and put her head on his shoulder. "I don't want to sleep in here either."

Lucian put his arm around the girl. "All right. Outside, it is."

He sighed, and Rachael looked down at his leg. Without a word, she offered her hand, and he allowed her to help him rise. She slid his arm around her shoulders. "Lean on me."

"I'm all right," he said, but he leaned heavily on her.

Lindsay went ahead of them and moved pieces of wood out of the way that might trip him. They kept a slow pace and reached the porch where the storm still drowned Ierusal. Without the combined powers of the Rosa and the Wyrm, the wind had died. Rachael navigated Lucian around the worst of the puddles. Lindsay stayed at his side and tromped through the water as if she could wash herself clean of the Wyrm's foulness.

In the shed, the horses stamped and shook their manes, agitated but unharmed. Rachael guided Lucian and Lindsay to a dry area at the back of the building. Lucian put his cloak on the ground, and gestured for Lindsay to lie down.

"I'm not sleepy." In spite of her protest, she sat down on the cloak.

"You will be," he promised.

"I'll be right back," Rachael said; she didn't wait for their answer.

She went inside the church and retrieved first Caleb's coat, then his sword. The blade was no longer black, and she wrapped the weapon in Caleb's long coat for now. Each sword held something of the owner's spirit, and though Caleb had been complicit with the Fallen, Rachael had no intention of leaving his sword behind. Let the Citadel bury his sword. The Rosa had his soul; that was enough.

As she left the church, she paused by the back door. Her saddlebags were intact, but Caleb's pack was shredded as if the Rosa tore through the leather to find the owner. The soft glow of her soul-light hovered over the manacles lying beside her bag, an ugly reminder of her duty.

A niggling doubt creased the back of her mind. Could she depend on Lucian? Rachael bit her lip. She'd seen into his soul, yet a glimpse into someone's soul only showed the feelings of the present, not the future. Lucian loved her tonight. Tomorrow might be different, especially if she became a threat to him or Lindsay.

Rachael picked up her pack and left the manacles on the porch. Lucian posed no menace to her now, and they still had Speight and his men out there somewhere. She wouldn't deal with it tonight, not with the cobwebs of fatigue masking her thoughts. The manacles and Lucian's arrest could wait until morning. Besides, there was no sense in upsetting Lindsay anymore. The child had been through enough.

As she walked back to the shed, the rain washed her blood from her hair. She used the sleeve of her coat to wipe her face but only succeeded in smearing the gore. By the time she returned, Lindsay was asleep beneath Lucian's mantle. He stood beside the girl, his back to the wall, and Rachael knew from his expression he'd seen her linger beside the manacles.

Guilt wormed into her chest before she could slam the emotion down; she'd done nothing wrong. She wanted to extinguish her light so he couldn't see her face. Instead, she set Caleb's sword down beside his saddle. "How did you get her to sleep so fast?"

"I helped her."

"Like you used to help Catarina?" No sooner had the words left her mouth than she wanted to take them back.

"No." His voice didn't belie the hurt in his eyes. "I didn't take her grief or her fear from her. I eased her into sleep. That's all."

She nodded and looked away.

Lucian asked, "What now?"

"I don't know." Her body still hummed with adrenaline, and in spite of her pain and exhaustion, she knew sleep was far away for both of them. "Lindsay told me about Speight. He could be waiting anywhere. We're badly outnumbered." She paused then said, "Where do your loyalties lie?"

He stiffened, and she noted how his fingers massaged the head of the cane. His voice contained a false calm she'd never heard before. "I told you everything, Rachael. I take responsibility for my part, but I've changed."

"So you say." She met his gaze. "How do I know you won't find me expendable again?"

"How can you say that?" He took a step forward before he caught himself, his fury black as the night around them.

It was good to know he could still get angry, and she savored a bitter satisfaction in provoking him.

"Rachael." He turned his head and released his anger into the storm with a sigh. "I never thought you were expendable." He limped forward until they were inches apart. Rachael slid her hand into her coat to stroke the hilt of her knife.

Lucian said, "You were never meant to be hurt. Cate told me we could cheat Mastema, that she'd made arrangements for your rescue."

Rachael shook her head; he still didn't understand. "Why didn't you come to me?"

He gaped at her. "What?"

"Why didn't you tell me about her pact? Why didn't you let me help?"

"You and Cate hated each other. Why would you have helped her?" He dropped his defenses. His confusion was real.

"I wouldn't have helped her." Rachael wanted to slap him. Why couldn't he see? "I would have helped you. Even if it meant Catarina benefited. All you ever had to do was ask. You never gave me a chance."

"A chance for what? Your own trial and exile? Is that what you wanted?" Lindsay murmured in her sleep as if she felt his anger thrum through her dreams. Lucian lowered his voice and leaned close. "I was protecting you. The less you knew, the less likely you'd be implicated if something went wrong."

"So you didn't trust Catarina either. But you made a decision for me when it was my risk to take, not yours. You," she said, hating the way her voice broke, "you should have trusted me with my fate."

Slow comprehension dawned across his features. She watched him wrestle with her words, seeking a way to mitigate his error, and she saw him fail. He paled, but to his credit, he didn't deny his mistake. "I was such a fool," he whispered. He sounded so lost. "Rachael."

No elation suffused her; his admission was an empty victory that did nothing to erase their suffering.

"Can you—" He reached out to her; she tilted her head away from him. He withdrew his hand as if burned. "Of course." He started to say something else, then slowly retreated to Lindsay's side.

The weight of the years pressed down on him, and for one ragged moment, Rachael wanted to call him back to her. She had rehearsed this scene, and now that it had passed, she felt no vindication for hurting him. She held her breath as he eased himself down beside the sleeping girl.

An opportunity had passed, a ghost between them, and she didn't know how to resurrect it, or even if she should. She stroked the leather of her pack and listened to the silence dragging against the night. The mare shuffled, nudging Rachael from her stupor.

She folded the pack into a makeshift pillow as she went to Lucian. The shadows deepened the creases around his eyes; Catarina had shorn years off his life. Rachael knelt beside him and lifted his head to slide the pack beneath him. He opened his eyes, but his dark gaze was far away.

When he reached up this time, she didn't withdraw. His fingers stroked her cheek lightly as if anything harsher would cause her to fly away. Once, she would have pressed her lips to his palm, once, long ago, when they were young. Now she took his wrist and eased his hand to his chest, then covered him with her coat.

Lindsay muttered in her sleep and rolled closer to Lucian when Rachael slid under the mantle beside her. With a word, Rachael extinguished her soul-light, and in blackness deep as silk, she lay awake, thinking of ghosts and lost opportunities.

CHAPTER SIXTEEN

sigils

Rachael struggled out of a sleep devoid of dreams. The smell of horse piss stung her sinuses. God, had she been sleeping in the stable again? She wondered how much time she'd lost to the Wyrm.

Something moved beside her; she jerked upright to see Lindsay roll over, taking Rachael's small share of Lucian's mantle with her. Sharp pain in her side knocked the last of her drowsiness away. Rachael put her face in her hands. Her head felt swollen, but even as she automatically sought the Wyrm's presence, the memory of last night's events drove the remnants of sleep from her brain. The Wyrm was gone.

Lucian. Rachael dropped her hands, her heart stammering for fear he'd taken one of the horses and fled in the night. She opened her eyes to find him where she'd left him, on the other side of Lindsay. He was obviously spent.

She could use a few more hours herself, but when she staggered to her feet and looked outside, she realized they'd already slept through half the morning. She forced herself to move. Another night behind Ierusal's walls held no appeal for her.

The rain had given way to a clinging mist that left the church a vague outline in the gloom. Ignatius nickered at her when she loosened his reins from the post. She led the three horses into the yard one at a time and hobbled them where they could graze on the sickly yellow grass.

The more she walked, the less pain she had in her hip; she peeled her waistband back to find a righteous bruise from her hip to her thigh. Blood glued her shirt to the cut on her side, and Rachael winced when she tried to loosen the cloth from the wound.

Beside the shed, she found a trough full of water from last night's rain. She wet her shirt until she could examine the cut herself. Lucian was right; it wasn't deep, but it was sore. Rachael cupped her hands and plunged them into the icy water to splash the last of the dried blood from her hands and face. Cuts from the Rosa's thorns crisscrossed her skin. Her reflection wavered on the surface of the water, and her hair framed a face she'd forgotten she owned.

Neither Lucian nor Lindsay was in sight. She returned her attention to the water and lifted the patch but wasn't surprised to find the socket still empty. She should have known he couldn't heal what wasn't there.

Yet he had healed her, and she tried to reconcile this new image of herself with the mutilated face she recalled. Instead of the ropy scars left by the Wyrm, her skin was smooth, and she touched her cheek in wonder. She would never be accused of being pretty—her aquiline nose rendered her features too strong—but with the scars she'd been gruesome.

The water muddied her hazel eye so she couldn't see if it was green or brown today. Lucian had once claimed to know her moods by the color of her eyes.

Focusing on the left side of her face, she could almost imagine she was whole again. She saw the woman Lucian had loved, and Rachael smiled at the memory until a slight tilt of her head revealed the patch covering her right eye. The blank eye of a cadaver stared sightlessly back at her, and her recollection turned bittersweet. She touched the water to shatter her reflection.

Rachael straightened to find Lindsay standing at the corner of the shed. The sight of the girl startled her, and her pulse rattled in her ears. She had to get a grip on herself. If that had been Catarina's soldiers, she would have been dead. When her heartbeat slowed, she asked, "How are you this morning?"

The girl stared at her with haunted eyes and shrugged.

"Do you want to talk about what happened last night?"

"No," she said quickly and jammed her hands into the pockets of her coat. "I'll talk to Lucian when he wakes up. He's my Elder."

The child's words dared Rachael to contradict her, and she decided to back off; let Lucian handle her for now. He deserved credit for guiding her so well through the traumas she'd already suffered. Perhaps he'd know how to ease her through her grief for her brother.

Lindsay turned the subject away from herself. "Your eye isn't all cloudy anymore."

Rachael raised her hand halfway to her face before she stopped herself. "What do you mean?"

"Lucian said when somebody is possessed, you can see the shadow of the demon in their eyes. Last night, your eye had a shadow over it and it's gone now." She lifted her chin in a mannerism so reminiscent of Lucian that Rachael took a mild chill.

Lindsay and Lucian had become too close. Elders and their foundlings risked becoming so immersed in one another's existence the death of one could kill the other. If it hadn't been for the Wyrm, she would have seen the danger last night when she'd talked to the girl. Lucian and Lindsay needed a period of physical separation soon or their bonding would be irreversible.

Lindsay asked, "Can you see better?"

"Yes. I do."

Lindsay nodded as if the admission acknowledged her suspicions. "You were with Peter when he died. Did Pete say anything?" She hugged herself and looked down, then back up to Rachael hopefully. "About me, maybe?"

Relieved by the girl's question, Rachael relaxed; Lindsay seemed herself again, not a shadow of Lucian. "I'm afraid I don't have much to add to what I told you last night. He only regained consciousness long enough to tell me about you. That was his last request. That someone save you."

"Lucian saved me," she said as she glanced at the shed where he slept. "He's been taking care of me just fine."

"Yes, he has." She took a step forward, and Lindsay backed up a step. Rachael halted and reminded herself to be patient. The girl had suffered one shock after another; she wasn't made of glass as Rachael had first supposed, but she could still break. "Lindsay, I'm not here to hurt you or Lucian."

"Then don't take him back to the Citadel," Lindsay whispered.

"What?"

"I said—"

"I heard you," Rachael snapped. She closed her eye and rubbed her forehead before she focused on the girl again. No, Lindsay Richardson's fragility was a façade; her small body housed a determined soul. "Lindsay, I can't turn my back on my responsibility."

"He gave you a second chance. Why can't you give him one?"

Rachael bit back her retort. She wanted to tell the child she never would have needed a second chance if Lucian hadn't betrayed her in the first place. Yet an insidious part of her questioned her own reasoning. Hadn't she willingly followed him to the Gate, knowing he lied?

He'd dangled the one treasure Rachael could never turn her back on—power over the Hell Gates—and she'd followed him like a lamb. What had Caleb said? *The Fallen win by turning your greatest weakness against you.*

"You can go away and pretend you didn't see us," Lindsay offered as she took a tentative step forward.

Rachael evaluated her. *This one will bear watching. She is as sly as a judge.* "Do you really think Lucian wants to live the rest of his life as a renegade?" The girl looked down at her feet. She didn't move away when Rachael approached her. "Lindsay, no one has denied him a second chance. He will get a fair trial, and he will have an opportunity to defend himself."

"He's not one of them."

She felt the girl's intense gaze like an accusation. "I know that."

"He hasn't done anything wrong."

"I know he's not complicit with the Fallen. I know why he opened the Hell Gate, and the Seraph will take Lucian's circumstances into consideration. We're not unreasonable, Lindsay, but we have to be careful. We have to hold our members to their promises."

"You could speak for him. That would help him, wouldn't it?"

Rachael's stomach churned. "You don't know what that means."

Lindsay went on as if she hadn't heard. "If you speak for him and tell them he's okay, they'll listen to you."

Had Lucian put the child up to this? "Do you understand what it means to speak for someone?"

Lindsay met Rachael's gaze. "It means you believe in someone's innocence enough to stand up for them."

"It also means that you share their fate if they're found guilty." When Lindsay didn't drop her defiant glare, Rachael asked, "Who told you about speaking for someone?"

Now the girl blushed and diverted her attention to her shoes, kicking a twig beside her foot. "I saw his memories. He was sad because nobody spoke for him at his trial. He understood why, but it still upset him. He didn't have any friends anymore."

No, he didn't have any friends. He had Catarina and look at what she did to him. Rachael ran her shaking hands through her hair.

Lindsay scuffed the dirt with the toe of her shoe then looked up. "Forget I said that, okay? He'd be mad if he knew I asked you to speak for him."

The girl's concern was too powerful to be feigned; Lucian hadn't put her up to any of this. She thought she was helping him. Rachael nodded. "Okay, between us."

An uneasy silence grew as they regarded one another beneath the weeping sky. Rachael hoped that with a secret between them, the girl would come to trust her. Lindsay's stomach growled and Rachael asked, "Are you hungry?"

Lindsay hesitated then said, "Yeah, I guess so."

Rachael relaxed and recalled giving her saddlebag to Lucian for a pillow. "Let's see if the Rosa left us anything in Caleb's pack. Lucian is using mine."

Lindsay trailed behind her as she went to the porch where deep gouges from the Rosa's thorns splintered the wood. The door sagged in its frame, forlorn and broken as the shattered windows. Holes gaped along the back wall, and Rachael could see inside the kitchen and bedroom.

Caleb's pack lay where she'd left it, next to the manacles. Without stepping onto the fractured boards, Rachael reached over and dragged the torn saddlebag to her.

Lindsay leaned close and pointed to the brand on Caleb's pack. "That's Catarina's emblem."

Frowning, Rachael lifted the flap so she could better see the brand. A garland of leaves formed a circle, and inside the circle were two ravens facing one another. Between the birds was the Citadel's alpha/omega sigil.

"Two ravens fighting in a circle. Lucian said that's Catarina's emblem for Mastema. He said all of Catarina's followers wear it. That's how they know each other."

Three houses of Elders in the Citadel incorporated a variation of this emblem into their standards. Rachael traced the crest with her finger and wondered how many Elders were involved in the original plot. They'd made a fool of her once; she'd not give them a second chance. "What else did Lucian say?"

"That I was never to accept anything with that emblem on it, no matter how pretty it was, because then I'd be showing allegiance to the Fallen. He made a big deal out of it and made me swear." Lindsay peered around Rachael. "We can't take it or we're joining them."

"I believe there's a little more to it than that." Whatever else he'd done, Lucian had impressed upon her the need to avoid Catarina's seal and any who wore it. "We can take it without being complicit."

"How do you become complicit then?"

"You have to renounce your vows to the Citadel, then there's a ceremony for those who choose to follow the Fallen." Rachael folded the flaps of leather to cover the pack's contents and gathered it in her arms. She wanted to see what other surprises Caleb had for her, then she remembered the manacles.

"Why don't you—" Rachael stopped. What was she thinking? She'd started to ask Lindsay to grab them for her, but that would be cruel, especially after gaining a small measure of her trust.

Lindsay cleared her throat.

Rachael said, "Why don't you go ahead and cover Lucian with his cloak? It's going to be colder in the shed with the horses gone."

Lindsay glanced at the manacles but made no remark before she walked to the shed. Rachael cradled the pack in her arms; she would come back for the chains later. She turned her back on the church and joined Lindsay.

Rachael found a spot a few feet from Lucian where she could see through the shed's slats on both sides. She didn't expect anyone would be brave enough to enter Ierusal after last night, but she wouldn't get caught dreaming again. "Here," she whispered to keep from waking Lucian, and Lindsay joined her in the corner.

Rachael unfolded the ruined pack and soon discovered a few pieces of jerky. She handed Lindsay a strip of meat.

"Shouldn't we save some for later?" Lindsay watched Rachael remove items from the pack.

"We're only a day or so from the Eilat outpost. They'll have provisions there." Rachael chewed a piece of meat. She removed the items from Caleb's pack and set them on the ground beside her. He hadn't carried much: a change of shirts, woolen socks, a small kit with first-aid ointments for abrasions and infections, some willow bark, a pot for boiling water, a brush and comb, and a shaving kit.

Rachael sighed. She checked all the pockets a second and third time but found nothing.

"What are you looking for?" Lindsay inspected the items.

"I don't know." A signed confession, a note implicating Reynard, some piece of hard proof she could take back to John. She tossed the empty pack aside in disgust. A miracle. "Nothing, I guess."

The emblem was meaningless unless she could tie Caleb and Reynard directly to Catarina and the Fallen. The Rosa had torn Caleb's clothes to rags. If he'd carried any sign of his complicity with the Fallen or Reynard on him, it was confetti now.

All she had was Lucian's word against Reynard, a begrudged allegation if ever there was one, and a phantom prayer book supposedly in Reynard's possession. Reynard would see her ride into the Citadel with Lucian and that piece of evidence would be destroyed or hidden forever. Then what? The word of one liar against another.

Lindsay finished her breakfast and wiped her hands on her jeans. "Where's his coat?"

"What?"

"Caleb's coat. Maybe he had something in his pocket."

Rachael turned to the corner where she'd left Caleb's sword wrapped in his coat. Maybe she wasn't done after all. "Excellent idea," she said, and Lindsay rewarded her with a smile. Rachael went to the garment and disentangled it from the sword.

At the edge of the shed, she went through the pockets but found little more than lint. The tightly woven wool made the coat rainproof, and the inner lining was quilted to be warm.

Lindsay wandered over as Rachael knelt and spread the coat on the dry ground inside the shed. With her knife, she sliced through the threads holding the lining to the wool.

Lindsay squatted beside her. "Be careful."

"Why?" Rachael frowned at the coat.

"Can't you feel it?"

Rachael looked up. "Feel what?"

"You know, when the magic is sour."

Rachael felt nothing. She passed her hands over the coat, but she didn't feel the first resonance of any kind. "Where is it the strongest?"

"Here." Lindsay indicated an area between the lapel and the collar.

Rachael ran her finger along the seam and sensed the first indication of a spell. It was wound tight and buried deep within the fabric; only someone who knew where to look would find it easily. "You're very sensitive."

"Is that good?"

"It is today." Rachael tried to see if a ward protected the spell. Sure enough, so faint she might have mistaken it for an aberration of the Wasteland's fractured magic, she found a charm embedded over the seam. The longer she focused on it, the more violence emanated from the enchantment.

How had she traveled with Caleb for all this time and missed it? Even as the question crossed her mind, she knew the answer: the Wyrm. The demon had deadened her senses to God's Spirit.

She had been able to dream and feel the reverberation of other people's magic, but those forms were reflexive unlike the intentional use of her other talents. When she thought back on the last eight— no, ten—years, she couldn't recall a single time when she had allowed the Spirit to flow through her.

"Maybe we should say a prayer," Lindsay suggested.

Probably not a bad idea at all; it would be a good way to test herself. "Stand back. Just in case something goes wrong."

"I'll get Lucian." Lindsay stood and backed up a few paces.

"No, let him sleep." She didn't want him to see in case she failed. "You can pray with me. If you like."

"From over here?"

"If you like." Rachael held the offer open like a truce and waited while Lindsay thought about it.

She nodded. "Okay." She knelt in the dirt and bowed her head.

Rachael took a deep breath and placed her fingertips over the ward. A mild burning tingled into her flesh as she began. "Pray with me then, Lindsay Richardson, that we are strong in the Lord and in his mighty power." Rachael felt the Spirit flow through her veins like a current. She'd forgotten the beauty of channeling the Spirit. "We have nothing to fear." Unbidden, Lucian's words tumbled into her mind: *Do not be afraid.* Beneath her fingertips, the threads writhed, and she winced but didn't move her hands. "For our struggle is not against flesh and blood, but against the powers of darkness, against the spiritual forces of evil in the heavenly realms."

Her hands were bathed in light, a light she'd forgotten she possessed. Beneath her fingers, darkness seeped from between the fibers like blood oozing from a wound to flow harmlessly into the ground. "We take up the shield of faith, with which we can extinguish all the flaming arrows of the evil ones." Rachael poured her light into the cloth, and she felt Lindsay's magic drift over her. "Protect us with Your might and Your love. Amen."

The darkness dissipated into the ground, and Lindsay opened her eyes. "Did we do it?"

"I think so." Rachael felt around the collar. "You did very well. I can see Lucian has been working with you."

Lindsay blushed and looked into the yard.

Rachael returned her attention to the coat. The only magic she sensed came from something beneath the fabric. It was unpleasant but no longer violent. She picked up her knife and worked the threads loose around the collar, inching along the border until she was able to peel the lining away from the wool.

"Look." Lindsay pointed to the left side of the collar where a strip of white flashed against the dark wool.

A piece of silk was folded three times. Silk. Of course. They often used silk rather than parchment to send messages. Holding her breath, Rachael unfolded the handkerchief.

"What's it say?" Lindsay scooted around and peeked over Rachael's arm.

"It's just Catarina's seal," Rachael murmured as she stood. Dead center was Catarina's sigil for Mastema. The ink was the brownish-red of dried blood. Rachael ran her finger over the lines and sensed the signature of Reynard's magic, faint like a whiff of cologne beneath wood smoke but there nonetheless. She examined the markings, remembering how John had taught her how to know each Katharos by their blood.

She opened her heart to the Spirit and prayed to be shown the truth. After a moment of squinting at a small section of brown slashes, she saw the first spiral chain embedded in the bloodstain.

"What are you looking for?" Lindsay stood on her tiptoes.

Rachael lowered the silk so the girl could see. "Every Katharos has a distinctive signature to their blood. It looks like colorful chains."

"Like DNA?"

"Yes, exactly."

Lindsay squinted at the handkerchief. "And you can see it without a microscope?"

"Some of us can." Rachael smiled at the girl's incredulous expression. "God has given us talents to compensate for the lack of technology."

"Is that why my cell phone won't work here?"

"Yes. Electronics affect our brainwaves and impede our ability to make conscious contact with the Spirit. For some reason, electronics like your cell phone will only work when the Veil between Woerld and Earth is open."

"And when the Veil closes they turn into something else?" Lindsay asked. "Lucian called them portals for the damned."

"That's a fitting description. You have to understand, angels are made of light, electricity, and their presence disrupts the signals within Earth's devices."

"What about demons?"

"Demons are angels who have fallen from grace. Demons and angels can take many forms, but the essence of their nature does not change." Rachael returned her attention to the emblem. Caleb's signature was instantly familiar; it took her another minute to identify the chains belonging to Reynard. A third person had been involved, but she couldn't discern who.

The spell was bound tight, and the presence of all three individuals had been necessary to leave such a distinctive feel to the sigil.

"Do you know what it means?" Lindsay asked.

"No, I don't." The cloth wiggled beneath her fingers. The silk felt oily, and she resisted the urge to toss it aside.

"What have you found?" Lucian's voice almost caused her to drop the handkerchief.

She turned to find him standing at her left, and she stepped closer to him, holding the cloth up for him to see. Their shoulders touched as he drew his finger along the outline of the emblem. The scent of roses was embedded in his clothes and hair, but underneath the powerful odor of the Rosa, she detected the musky aroma that was uniquely his. With her eye, she traced the curve of his jaw to his full lips.

Lucian frowned at the symbol. "They only carry a missive like this when they enter a broken Hell Gate and walk across Hell. It gets them past the lower demons. You see the brush marks." He took one corner of the silk, and his hand touched hers before he adjusted his grip. His finger hovered over a stray mark. "They mix the blood of the members for the ink. The brush is made from the hair of the person who will use the missive. In this case, Caleb."

"They can do this at any Hell Gate?"

"No, there are only three Gates that are so badly damaged they can be used in this manner: the Gates at Ierusal, Batheba, and Carlenta."

She made an effort to ignore the effect his nearness had on her and concentrated on the silk. The bold strokes on the cloth were vaguely familiar, but she couldn't recall where she'd seen a drawing like this. "Why walk through Hell?" She thought of the weakened Hell Gate she'd sensed when she and Caleb had entered Ierusal.

"Less likelihood of capture."

"Now it makes sense."

"How so?"

"Right before we reached Ierusal, Caleb wanted to ride back and look behind us. Knowing what I know now, I suspect he met with Speight's men. When Caleb rejoined me, he tried to talk me into waiting outside Ierusal while he came in to get you. I thought he wanted to kill you."

Lucian looked down at her. "Last night, when you were speaking to Lindsay, he tried to get me to leave. I thought he wanted me dead. He wanted me out of the way so I wouldn't exorcise the Wyrm."

She looked into his dark eyes so full of pain. Rachael whispered, "Would you have turned yourself over to him if I hadn't been there?"

His frown deepened as the implication of her words hit him. "Probably."

Not probably. "Yes. Yes, you would have." Lucian would have walked right into Caleb's plan. Then once the Wyrm had taken her, Caleb would have dragged Lucian and Lindsay to the fractured Hell Gate and proceeded to Hadra with Speight and his men. "This is strong magic they're working, and no one at the Citadel suspects a thing. How are they doing this right under our noses?"

Lucian shook his head. "They are neither careless nor stupid. They aren't working these spells in the Citadel. They're probably using a holding, someplace far enough away that other members won't stumble on them. Or they're using some area already known for its malevolence, some place that would mask the stench of their spells from other Katharoi."

Rachael went cold. She knew just the place. "Cross Creek," she whispered. Of course. Merciful God, they'd been working their magic in her house.

"Rachael?" Lucian's arm slipped around her waist.

"I moved out of the Citadel several years ago to my holding at Cross Creek."

The blood. She gripped the silk with numb fingers, staring at the marks. What if the third person's blood was hers? Her breakfast rolled uneasily in her stomach. "What if I'm complicit?"

"No." Lucian's hold on her waist tightened.

Lindsay moved into Rachael's line of vision. "Is that how you know about renouncing your vows, Rachael?"

"Lindsay!" Lucian glared at the girl.

"Why are you so scared, Rachael?" Lindsay demanded.

Rachael straightened. She had to get a grip on herself. "I'm not frightened."

"You looked like a ghost! You said everything would be okay for Lucian's trial, but now that you're looking at one, you're scared to death. Won't they give you a fair trial too?"

"That's enough!" Lucian turned on Lindsay and she flinched at his anger.

Rachael blanched, realizing now how feeble her earlier assurances must have sounded. John condoned savage measures to root out the complicit, and she could expect no mercy with Reynard as Inquisitor. A breeze snatched at the silk, and Rachael balled her fingers into a fist to keep the note from fluttering out of her hand.

"They were working their magic in my house. While I was there." What if she'd renounced her vows to the Citadel while under the thrall of the Wyrm? Days of emptiness at Cross Creek stretched before her. Sick with terror, she turned away from Lucian.

"Listen to me," he said. "Not five minutes ago, you let the Spirit move through you. Your prayer awakened me."

Rachael shook her head; that had been a small charm. It was nothing compared to calling upon her greater talents.

"Rachael, you can only give yourself to the complicit through your free will. You know that." He gently extracted the cloth from her hand. "Do something."

"What?"

"Anything. You have other talents. If you're complicit, you won't be able to draw on the power of the Spirit." He gestured to her as if she was a foundling again. "Command the earth."

Rachael directed her gaze to the sodden ground. She tried to still her heart but doubt redoubled her anxiety. She closed her eye and took a deep breath, seeking the calm she needed.

Minutes passed before she felt confident enough to whisper a prayer. As the first word left her mouth, she focused on the thick clay earth at their feet. Peace descended over her and she willed the ground to part. The Spirit moved through her body, and as she opened her hands, a crack appeared in the ground.

The full force of the Spirit coursed through her body and the fissure widened, clumps of soft ground fell into the hole. When the crevice was a foot wide, she ceased her prayer and allowed the gap to close. Sweat beaded on her forehead as she stared at the ground.

Lindsay looked at her with new respect.

Lucian reached out and took Rachael's wrist, guiding her back to him. "Look at it again, Rachael." He spread the handkerchief open. "Is that your blood?"

Rachael licked her lips and forced her gaze to the brown stains. Scrutinizing the blood again, she stared until her head ached. She disregarded Caleb's and Reynard's patterns, unraveling them from the third set of chains winding deep into the silk.

She remembered the account ledger Caleb had left open on her kitchen table. Caleb had convinced her that the sketches were hers, but she couldn't draw, not like that. The same sure hand that had sketched those images of agony in her ledger drew the sigil on the handkerchief.

Studying the blood, Rachael saw the first clue in the chain. Clearing her mind, she followed one link to another until she recognized the pattern. Dubois. Charles Dubois, the Citadel's Commissioner.

"Dubois." She felt Lucian's hand leave hers as she relaxed. "It's Charles Dubois' blood." Rachael raised her head. He looked down at her with a concerned gaze, and she became aware of his hand at the small of her back.

"Not yours."

She shook her head and stepped back. "No." His fingers lingered a second too long on the curve of her spine.

He seemed to sense her discomfort and stepped away from her. "Good."

"I need something to carry the silk in so it doesn't get damaged."

"I got something," Lindsay said. She rooted in her gym bag and retrieved a small tin that had once carried some kind of peppermint. "You can have it." She offered the box and glanced down. "And I'm sorry. I shouldn't have said that. About the trial. And stuff."

"It's all right." Rachael slipped the note into the box and snapped the lid shut. "Really," she said as she held her hand out to the girl, "it's all right."

Lindsay made a fist and held it up. "Good."

Uncertain of the child's meaning, Rachael turned to Lucian, but he'd left her side as silently as he'd appeared. She saw him at the back of the shed where he stood near the packs. Rachael thought he smiled as he made fists and bumped his knuckles together gently.

Rachael returned her attention to Lindsay and tapped the girl's knuckles with her own. Lindsay nodded as if that settled everything and went to help Lucian gather their hastily thrown gear into some semblance of order. He hooked his cane into the strap of his own pack and lifted it. Lucian spoke to the girl and Lindsay answered him in a whisper.

Rather than eavesdrop, Rachael grabbed her pack and went back to the porch. The manacles were curved like a question mark on the wood, and she dropped her bag to open the laces.

The fear of her own corruption still pounded in her heart, and she touched the cold metal, wondering if she would have had Lucian's courage. He had known the minute he left Hadra what returning to the Citadel would mean for him, yet he had come regardless. Rachael gathered the chains into her hands so they wouldn't make a sound before she crammed them deep into her pack.

He had not returned to give her a second chance like Lindsay thought but to make amends. Just a few minutes ago, he could have lied and made her believe she was corrupt. She had witnessed a few Inquisitions, so he might have had little trouble convincing her to turn renegade with him.

Instead, he'd calmed her and made her see the truth, and in return for his sacrifice, she intended to drag him back to the Citadel where a jury of liars and frauds awaited his arrival. Rachael jerked the laces tight with more force than necessary, ignoring the burning in her throat. Lucian had his faults, but cruelty wasn't one of them, unlike those who wore the cloak of sanctity to shield their corruption.

She glanced over her shoulder, and in the depths of the shed, she saw him watching her. Maybe she had to take him back to the Citadel, but she didn't have to abandon him once he was there. She owed him that much at least.

CHAPTER SEVENTEEN

a wish

The pungent scent of roses filled Lucian's senses. In the alley he and Lindsay occupied, a twisted wagon frame rested against one wall. Otherwise, the lane was clear of debris and well sheltered by a row of buildings on either side. The clouds had dissipated; late afternoon shadows lingered over the cobblestones.

Lucian leaned against the corner of a building and looked down the empty street where Rachael had disappeared. She'd departed over an hour ago to mark Speight's position. Behind him, Lindsay held the reins for the three horses.

The wind whistled through the empty buildings, a low, lonely sound. The noise did nothing to soothe Lucian's raw nerves. Rachael's concern was Speight, but his thoughts turned to his twin. Surely she'd felt the disturbance of the Wyrm's passing and knew he was involved. She would interpret his interference with Rachael's possession as an act of war.

Yet what could she do? Catarina wouldn't jeopardize herself by leaving Hadra, and even if she did, how would she reach Ierusal? Lucian kneaded the head of his cane and sighed. He was doing himself no good worrying over a future he couldn't control. He left his post and returned to Lindsay. "Would you like for me to hold them?" He indicated the horses.

She shook her head and continued to stroke Ignatius' nose. "I'm okay." Her expression said otherwise, and a tear slipped from her eye. She swiped it away. "I miss Pete."

"Of course you do."

"Do you ever cry for Catarina?" She sniffled and glanced at him.

"I used to." He stroked the gelding's mane and remembered a time when he didn't fear his sister. "I used to think that if I loved her enough, she would turn away from the Fallen and return with me to the Citadel." He had used that vain dream to sustain himself during those first years of his exile. Somehow, he thought they could return in triumph if Catarina went back to the Citadel repentant.

Lindsay unzipped her gym bag and handed him his Psalter. "Here. I don't need it anymore."

She had rewrapped the book in the scarf, and he felt the resonance of her spells tingle through the cloth. Lindsay was everything he wanted his sister to be. He handed the Psalter back to her. "You keep it."

She slipped the book into her bag and looked up at him. "You think I might need it again?"

She was such a solemn child. "Perhaps," he said.

A rock clattered in the street and Lucian turned to find Rachael standing at the mouth of the alley. He patted Lindsay's shoulder. "Will you be all right?"

"Sure." She knotted the reins in her hands and acknowledged Rachael with a nod.

Rachael rewarded the child with the ghost of a smile and gestured for Lucian to join her.

He couldn't keep the sound of relief from his voice as he reached her side. "I was getting worried."

Her palms were scraped and bloodied, and she wiped them on her pants.

"You're hurt," he said.

"It's nothing." She glanced at Lindsay, then moved around the corner. When they were in the street and out of Lindsay's earshot, Rachael stopped. "Is she all right?"

"She will be." Time would heal her better than any spell he could conjure for her benefit. "About this morning, when she accused you."

"It's forgotten, Lucian."

He saw the truth in her eye; she wouldn't mention Lindsay's accusation to John, he was sure of it. Relieved by her assurance, he looked over Rachael's shoulder. The portcullis of Ierusal's southern gate lay about fifty yards away. A patch of long grass bent from last night's rains darkened in the wake of the setting sun. The leaves from the Rosa obscured all but a small sliver of the field. Twilight shadows slid over the streets; full dark was still an hour away.

"They're out there," Rachael said as she followed his gaze, "about a hundred yards southwest of the portcullis. They've pulled back into the field between Ierusal and the woods. They're rotating watches, so we'll not slip out unseen. I can't fight seven men by myself." She reached behind her and handed him a knife with a wide blade. "It was Caleb's. Hold on to it. Keep your sword. Lindsay has your knife, and I suppose that's as armed as we get. How good are Speight's men?"

At least she didn't intend to deliver him trussed and ready for the trip to Hadra. Lucian slipped the knife into his belt. "Well trained and vicious. Participate in no parley; it will be lies. Give no quarter and expect none. Once we engage, it will have to be to the death."

Rachael frowned at her boots as she absorbed his words. "Lindsay is going to be a liability."

"You can't let them take her."

"I know," she whispered.

Neither of them spoke, and Lucian fingered the hilt of Caleb's knife. At the Melasur Bridge, he had thought he could kill Lindsay rather than see her captured. Now he knew he couldn't perform such an act. One look into Rachael's cold features told him she'd have no trouble saving the child from a fate she'd endured, even if it meant Lindsay's death by her hand. He found no comfort in the thought and was glad when she spoke again.

"We could try slipping out of one of Ierusal's postern gates."

"Into the Barren?" He pulled his mantle tight around himself.

"We could skirt the Barren by staying close to the Rosa."

"Rachael, I came through the Barren. If it hadn't been for Lindsay, I would still be there. She made it through the first time because no darkness shadowed her." He lowered his voice. "Now, after all she's been through." He shook his head. "John was right to tell us to avoid it. The Barren isn't an option. Besides, we'd still have to pass them at the edge of the wall. We'll delay the inevitable and do nothing more than tire the horses."

She crossed her arms and stared at the ground in a hauntingly familiar pose. Lucian found the well-known signs of her frustration comforting; it was nice to find not everything had changed while he was gone. He offered an alternative to the Barren. "We'll wait until midnight and try to slip past them."

"With three horses in an open field?"

"Not with silence, with speed. We can outride them. I did it once with Lindsay."

"In the daylight, Lucian. Not at night. This is hopeless."

"Getting out of Hadra and defeating the Wyrm was hopeless, but God led me through. You said yourself we narrowly escaped Caleb's plan to divide us. God kept us safe. God will lead us through this too."

Rachael raised her eyebrows. "Has it occurred to you that God just might be saving us for something really spectacular?"

"Don't blaspheme, Rachael."

A wicked gleam ticked in her eye, then she turned serious again. "I have an idea." She drew close to him, and with the nearness of her, he forgot his distress. "It's risky, but I believe it's our best chance."

He was on his guard again. "How risky?"

"They won't expect us to ride straight toward them."

"And why should we?"

"Because I'm not fully recovered and neither are you. We'll have to work together. I can bring a chant to open the ground, but Speight and his men will have to be close and riding fast to fall into the crevice."

Lucian kneaded the head of his cane. It could work.

"Do you remember how to engage St. Peter's Cross?"

He recalled the maneuver; two Katharoi could draw their powers together by crossing their blades close to the hilts. The dominant Katharos channeled the chant while the secondary Katharos fed the first his strength. Done properly, they could move mountains, but the effect on their strength could be crippling.

"How close will Speight's men have to be?" he asked.

"Twenty yards. Maximum. Ten would be ideal."

Lucian's chest constricted as he imagined watching Speight and his men ride down on them. "We can't do this from horseback."

"That's the risky part. There's a hillock, midway between the Ierusal gate and where Speight's men are camped. It slopes down then rises again to leave a small gully. They'll have to ride right through it. We can open a chasm in the gully. They will crest the hillock and plunge in. The rear riders will be expecting the forward riders to momentarily disappear in the ditch, so they'll suspect nothing. By the time they realize they've lost part of their force, they won't be able to rein their own mounts in."

The excitement in her eye told him she was convinced the plan would work. He wasn't. "We'll have to gather a great deal of power to create a chasm large enough to take them all down. I don't know what affect a summoning this large will have on the Hell Gate or the Barren. We could open up something terrible, Rachael."

"Or we can just ride out and give ourselves up."

He winced.

She didn't give him time for a rebuttal. "They've dug in well and good. They're not going anywhere. We've barely got enough supplies to make it through the week, and it could take several weeks before John sends anyone after us." She brushed her fingers against the back of his hand. "Lucian, I can't do this without you."

Lost in her gaze, he touched her chin and she didn't withdraw from him. "Can you trust me?" he whispered.

She said nothing, but he saw the doubt in her eye. Eventually, she said, "I have to."

He took her wrist and leaned forward. Her pulse throbbed beneath his fingers. He bowed his head and whispered against her ear, "I still love you."

"You love a memory," she said, her breath warm against the hollow of his throat. "You don't know me anymore."

His heart sank into his stomach, but he chided himself. What had he expected? That she would throw herself in his arms in gratitude when he'd been the cause of her suffering? He was no better than his sister, who had imprisoned him and expected his gratitude when she'd released him. His shame warmed his cheeks.

Rachael withdrew her hand from his grip and stepped back. "We shouldn't leave Lindsay alone for too long."

Lucian lowered his head. "Of course." Regardless of the love he'd seen in her soul when he'd healed her, he knew he should expect no sentimentality from her. If her heart lay behind a wall of stone, well, it was he who had provided the mortar.

†

Lucian sat with his back against the wall and watched Rachael show Lindsay how to tie the horses to the wagon. The girl only gave him an occasional glance as Rachael explained what would happen when they left the relative safety of Ierusal tonight. Lindsay didn't seem alarmed, but Lucian knew it was because she didn't understand the ramifications of Rachael's plan.

It was just as well her ignorance protected her. He wasn't sure how much comfort he would be able to give her tonight. She hugged her gym bag throughout Rachael's talk, and when Rachael finished, Lindsay drifted to sit beside him. She rested against him as she had when they were on the road and dozed fitfully.

Rachael brought the flask and sat on the opposite side of Lindsay. She passed the water to him and he drank. Silence drifted between them as they waited for Woerld to slip deeper into night. They had never needed words to fill the empty spaces between them. Often they'd sat reading or watching the fire, silent as a couple who'd spent their lives together.

When he had lived with Catarina, he would conjure those quiet times he and Rachael once shared, replaying them in his mind to soothe his anxiety. A slow ache of regret spread across his chest. Before he could stop himself, he said, "I missed you. Everyday."

She said nothing, but he knew she wasn't asleep by her sharp intake of breath.

"When I was in prison, and I didn't think I would last another hour without going mad, I thought of you. Of us." He tasted the salt of his tears but made no move to wipe his face.

"Stop," she whispered.

He looked up where a few stars blinked against the silken sky. A falling star arced through the air before the scattered clouds swallowed it.

"Make a wish," she said.

"Anything?"

"Make a wish."

Lucian closed his eyes and wished for another opportunity. *Lord, give me the time to win her back.*

"Well?" she asked.

"I did."

"I did too." Her words were as soft as a kiss.

Lucian relaxed against the wall. He could mend a broken body with his God-given talents, but it took patience to heal a broken heart. Five years ago, he wouldn't have had the empathy to understand her pain, but he was different now. He just needed time.

His thoughts drifted and with Lindsay's warmth against him, he dozed. The moon had risen behind tattered clouds when he felt Rachael's hand on his shoulder.

"Now," she whispered.

CHAPTER EIGHTEEN

defend us in battle

Rachael mounted the mare and watched Lucian seat Lindsay on Ignatius. "Stay alert, Lindsay," Rachael said. "When I give the signal, we'll stop fast. I don't want you thrown."

The girl nodded and took Lucian's cane so he could pull himself into the saddle behind her. He whispered, "Remember to shield your mind. Stay calm so you can think. And don't step into our soul-lights or we might accidentally draw from your power. St. Peter's Cross is not for an inexperienced Katharos."

"Just the desperate," Rachael muttered and ignored Lucian's dark look.

Lindsay nodded and twisted the cane in her hands. "I can do this."

"I know you can." Rachael met Lindsay's gaze.

The child sat straighter in the saddle and placed one hand on the pommel. "I'm ready."

No she wasn't. No amount of talk could prime Lindsay's mind for what was about to happen. Rachael bit down on her misgivings. Lindsay wasn't as frail as she first appeared. She'd survived the exorcism and Caleb's death; perhaps she'd weather this last storm too.

Rachael's horse pranced sideways; unlike Ignatius, the mare was high-strung and prone to bolt. She kept the horse on a tight rein and took the gelding's lead-rope. When she glanced back, Lucian had settled into the saddle behind Lindsay. The shadows rendered his features haggard and grim. He nodded and Rachael guided the mare onto the street. The entrance emerged ahead, a great, black void yielding to the moon's pale sheen on the other side.

Rachael examined the details of her plan and tried to quash her doubts. Too much lay outside her realm of control, and she chafed at the uncertainties before them. Then the wall was before her.

The darkness slid over them as they rode into the entrance tunnel. The cobblestones magnified the echo of their mounts' hooves. To Rachael's over-sensitive ears, they sounded like an army marching through the gate. Surely Speight's men would be waiting for them just on the other side.

Moonlight pearled on the meadow ahead. At the corner of the wall, a white rose wavered into view only to withdraw serendipitously. Rachael leaned over to release the lead-rope from the gelding's halter.

Her finger touched the metal clasp. Out of the corner of her eye, she glimpsed Lucian's face, marred by shadows. Last night, he'd promised not to leave her. Tonight she would know if he meant to keep his oath. If he chose to take Lindsay and ride away, Rachael was a dead woman.

And if he chose to stay by her side? Then what? Did she give him another chance and hope his loyalties wouldn't be divided between her and Catarina again? The mare shuffled beneath her. Rachael brought herself to the task at hand and snapped the rope off the gelding's halter. She could only handle one catastrophe at a time. First they had to survive tonight.

She drew her blade and slapped the gelding's hindquarters with the flat of her sword. The animal shot out of the gate and kept to the road, running for the tree line ahead. A distant shout told her Speight's men saw the horse. From the volume of the yell, she knew they hadn't moved from their position.

Rachael gave the nervous mare some slack and the horse pranced out of the gate, straining against the bit. She forced the animal to hold a walk and aimed her toward the hillock. They'd only have one chance at this.

Beyond the hill, a man shouted, directing the soldiers to their mounts. She guessed it was Speight. She sensed movement on her right and turned to find Lucian riding beside her. His sword was in his left hand, and Lindsay clutched his cane with one hand, the pommel with the other.

The mare tossed her head. Speight's men were mounted and moving to meet them. Rachael veered her horse to the left, and Lucian smoothly followed suit with Ignatius. *I will not leave you.*

She swallowed past the heat in her throat and concentrated on the enemy. Speight's men fell into formation and rode at a gallop to meet them.

The wind dried her lips as she began her prayer. "Saint Michael Archangel, defend us in battle."

Lucian echoed her words.

Rachael eased the mare into a gallop to match the soldiers' pace. "Be our protection against the wickedness and snares of the Fallen."

Lucian's voice rumbled beside her. "May God rebuke them, we humbly pray."

The hillock rose about thirty yards away and Speight's men were fast closing the distance.

Rachael raised her sword. "On my word."

Lucian gave no indication he'd heard, but she knew he was ready. She allowed them to close the distance by ten yards then shouted, "Now!" She yanked hard on the reins, and the mare reared. Rachael threw her weight forward and the mare's front hooves splashed in a puddle. Rachael leapt to the ground and turned the horse back toward Ierusal.

Free of his riders, Ignatius followed the mare. Lucian was with her. Rachael whirled in time to see Lindsay pass Lucian his cane. The girl stood back as Rachael dropped to her knees.

Killing magic, Rachael thought. John had taught her killing magic, and she never flinched from using it. *One shot, no second chances.* She raised her sword high over head, pointing the tip of the blade toward the sky. She was barely conscious of water from the wet ground soaking into the knees of her pants.

Lucian slipped, and Rachael held her breath until he righted himself. She hated making him a part of this slaughter. He abhorred bloodshed, but when she looked into his eyes, she saw his determination to see the plan through.

Lucian's blade touched hers and a shower of sparks passed before her face. She closed her eye and sought the quiet in her soul where the Spirit dwelled. The first words of her prayer passed through her lips, and Lucian's power flowed into her body.

Pure light surrounded her, filled her. Rachael focused on the area before the hillock, willing it to part. She channeled Lucian's energy into her spell. He opened his heart to her and gave her his soul. He shielded nothing of himself from her. If she wanted, he would give her his life.

She prayed their sacrifice wouldn't be that great. Rachael concentrated on her enchantment. With the skill of a master weaver, she intertwined their energy. Rachael conjured the image of the gully in her mind and visualized the earth moving. "O God, let my enemies feel your power."

†

Conscious of Lucian's earlier warning, Lindsay stood as close to them as she dared without stepping inside their light. Lucian's head was thrown back, his eyes shut. Rachael bowed her head, her hair obscuring her features.

The energy emanating from Rachael and Lucian drowned the painful buzzing Lindsay felt from the nearby Barren. She pressed her knuckles to her lips. "Hurry, you guys," she whispered.

Speight's men whipped their mounts. Not knowing how she could help, she began the first verse of the prayer Rachael had started earlier. She whispered through numb lips, "Saint Michael Archangel, defend us in battle."

As the first of Speight's men crested the small hill, the ground shuddered beneath Lindsay's feet. She kept her balance by stepping backward. "Be our protection... our protection..."

Just in front of the hillock, the sodden ground pulled apart with a sucking noise. Chunks of mud fell into the chasm that split toward the hill. The first four soldiers rode over the mound and fell into the hole. They didn't have time to scream before another pair of men came thundering over the hill to fall on top of them. The last soldier hesitated at the rise, and Lindsay recognized Speight.

A wail of terror tore through the night. The horses screamed. Another man cried out a name. Lindsay closed her eyes. Someone moaned, a long, low sound that rolled beneath the groans of the earth.

The back of Lindsay's neck prickled. She pressed her hands over her ears, but the men's cries seeped past her fingers and into her brain. *These men are not nice. They wanted to kill Lucian at the bridge. They're with the Fallen and the Fallen killed Pete—remember Pete.* Lindsay's grief opened like a wound. "They want to kill us. They want to kill us. Be our protection because they want to kill us." In the cacophony of noise, Lindsay didn't hear her own sob.

Someone cursed Lucian and the bitch with him. The man's hate escalated with his helplessness, and his oaths became more vehement. Another man's sobs rose over the other voices. He spoke no words, made no curses. He just cried.

Tears burned behind her eyelids, and Lindsay opened her eyes to release her sorrow. Speight wheeled his mount toward the Hell Gate. Neither Lucian nor Rachael looked, but Lindsay noticed a shift in the pattern of their prayers. Rachael's voice rose over Lucian's and the light surrounding them pulsed brighter. The earth opened and the crevice widened, chasing Speight toward the Hell Gate.

Lindsay felt Rachael's spell surge before it started to recede. The light surrounding her and Lucian dimmed.

The pitch of Rachael's prayer changed again, and the earth moved. This time clods of mud fell into the gap as it closed. The voices of the soldiers and horses rose in wild pandemonium as the moving ground crushed their bones. Their eldritch cries echoed through the night, reverberating through Lindsay's head.

The fissure closed, and Speight shouted, a bestial sound full of rage. He wheeled his mount and rode toward them. Lucian's blade broke contact with Rachael's and the light disappeared. Lucian's arms trembled, and Rachael pitched forward on her hands and knees.

"Speight's coming!" Lindsay pointed. "Lucian!"

"Run!" he shouted at her before he turned to face Speight's charge.

Lindsay froze, but not from fear this time. She'd been forced to leave Peter and he died; she wouldn't leave Lucian. She felt for the knife at her hip and pulled it free from its sheath. The sound of her pulse pounded in time to the hoof beats.

The captain's horse closed the distance between them, and Lindsay saw Speight draw his sword. Lucian was moving too slow. Rachael pushed herself to her feet and took three staggering steps before she picked up speed on the wet ground to run toward Speight.

Speight leaned forward in his saddle. Rachael shrieked like a demon and just before Speight's horse could run her down, she dropped to her knees. She slid on the wet ground and brought her sword level with the horse's legs.

Rachael's blade bit deep, and the animal screamed. The forward motion of the horse dragged Rachael for several feet, then Speight's mount went down. Rachael disappeared in the tall weeds.

Speight threw himself from his falling mount and hit the earth with a grunt. The horse nickered pitifully when it crashed to the ground. Lucian moved toward Speight, but Lindsay could tell he was having trouble keeping his balance.

The captain gained his feet and rose just before Lucian reached him. Lindsay looked for Rachael, but the woman had disappeared. Where was she? Lucian couldn't do this alone.

Speight charged Lucian with a howl of rage, and Lucian raised his sword. He didn't step away from Speight's maneuver. Instead he parried the blow with his blade and allowed Speight's forward motion to carry them both to the muddy weeds. Speight landed on top of Lucian and drove his fist into Lucian's face.

Lucian's fist shot upward and clipped Speight's chin. Lindsay wasn't sure if the crunch came from Speight's jaw or Lucian's knuckles, but the captain's head rocked backward. Speight was stunned but not for long.

Lindsay's heart felt like it would explode. Her magic was useless here, so she tried to remember everything Lucian and Pete had taught her about fighting. Pete taught her how to hurt somebody bigger than her, and his advice had worked with Caleb, but this wasn't like hitting Caleb with the cane. Caleb had been standing still and taking aim had been easy; she didn't know if she could hit a moving target.

"Rachael?" Lindsay edged toward the men and glanced over the field. If Rachael was out there, she was unconscious or couldn't hear Lindsay over the cries of the wounded horse. Maybe the horse kicked her. *Maybe she's dead*, an insidious part of her mind offered.

Lindsay couldn't wait for Rachael. She had to do something. Her palm sweated on the hilt of her knife. Her arm shook and she gripped her right hand with her left.

Lucian cried out in pain. Speight's hand was on Lucian's leg; his forearm was across Lucian's throat. Lucian managed to get his hands around the captain's neck; Lindsay could tell by Speight's smug glare that the captain was winning.

Focus. Lucian was always on her to focus. She remembered his instructions. Look for a break in the armor: knees, shoulders, elbows, neck. Lindsay tried not to think about pushing the knife into Speight as she circled the men. The tip of her blade wavered unsteadily.

She took a deep breath then ran at Speight's back. She brought her blade up to strike and suddenly found herself face-to-face with the captain's grin.

†

Speight's weight left Lucian's chest, and he glimpsed Lindsay's slight form. *Oh, God, no.* Lucian grabbed Speight's hauberk, but the captain easily pulled away. Speight caught Lindsay's wrists and twisted the knife out of her hands. He wound his thick fingers in her hair and Lucian almost cried out with the girl.

Tears came to her eyes when Speight jerked her head up. He put the blade to her throat and leaned over. "Be still!"

"Lindsay, stop!" Lucian held his hand out to her and she stopped struggling.

"First smart thing you've said." Speight yanked Lindsay close and wrapped his arm around her chest. "On your knees and get both your hands where I can see them, Lucian."

Lucian knelt and raised his hands. He still had Caleb's knife in his belt. Speight's position during the fight had prevented him from reaching for the blade, but he didn't dare draw it now. Speight would cut Lindsay's throat before he could get his hand on it. He clenched his jaw and waited.

"Hands on top of your head!" Speight barked.

Lucian glanced back toward the horse. Where was Rachael? Was she hurt?

Lindsay squealed and Lucian turned to see blood flowing from a cut on her cheek. The slash didn't appear to be deep, but tears streamed down her face.

Lucian's rage almost strangled his words. "Don't hurt her—"

"I'll cut her pretty face to fucking ribbons if you don't pay attention. Now do like you're told."

Lucian laced his fingers on top of his head. He couldn't see either his cane or his sword in the dark. All that remained before his eyes was Lindsay's frightened features.

"Think you're so goddamned high and mighty. I'm getting you chained, then I'm taking a chunk out of your ass for every tooth you've cost me tonight. You're going to crawl every fucking step of the way back to Hadra, you piece of shit!" Speight dragged Lindsay with him as he moved toward his downed mount. "We're going over to my horse, sweetheart, and you're going to get my manacles for me. Blink at me wrong, Lucian, and I'll put her eyes out."

Lucian said nothing and remained perfectly still; he had no doubt Speight would carry out his threat.

"Did you hear me, Lucian?"

"I heard you."

"I don't think you answered me properly." Speight's blade flashed in the moonlight, and Lindsay gasped when Speight pressed the tip to the sensitive skin beneath her left eye.

Lucian gritted his teeth; he knew what Speight wanted. "I heard you, *my lord.*"

"I'm sorry, Lucian, that didn't sound quite penitent enough." A drop of blood cascaded down Lindsay's cheek and she went rigid in Speight's arms. "Try again."

"I'm begging you, my lord. Please. Don't hurt her." He hated the pleading whine he heard in his voice. Yet he kept his hands on his head and his gaze on the ground. Lucian didn't have to fake his subservience. He would crawl through glass if it kept Lindsay safe. "Please. Don't hurt her."

The tension left Speight's stance, and he seemed mollified. For now. "That's better. I like that. Sounds like you mean it. See?" The knife went back to Lindsay's throat. "A little respect goes a long way." He pinched Lindsay and she whimpered. "You'll do well to remember that, sweetheart."

The knife at Lucian's belt taunted him, but he could do nothing unless Speight came close. If Lindsay could break away from him, Lucian would put an end to Speight. Five seconds was all he needed. Lucian tried to catch her eye, but Lindsay was mesmerized by the horse.

Speight reached his mount and scanned the field. "I don't know where that cunt went, but when I find her, I'm going to rip her tits off. That was a damn fine horse." He held tight to Lindsay's wrist and bent to cut the horse's throat.

His blade severed the horse's jugular and the animal's screams stopped. A hand shot out of the weeds and grabbed Speight's beard. Rachael rose like a spirit to drag his head down and plunge her knife into his throat. The captain tried to put Lindsay between them, but the girl jerked her arm free and ran to Lucian.

Speight slashed wildly at Rachael with his blade. She let go of his beard and caught his hand. Her lip curled and she twisted her knife in his windpipe.

Lucian almost fell backwards when Lindsay flung herself in his arms. He pushed her face against his shoulder and rocked her gently through Speight's death.

Speight lurched to the left, his mouth opening and closing like a fish. He grabbed his neck, his hands wet and black in the moonlight. Air whistled through his torn windpipe and he fell into the weeds.

Rachael wiped the blade of her knife off on her pants and limped toward them. She favored her left side, and Lucian saw her shirt clung to her skin. The wound from last night had reopened. "Are you all right?" Rachael asked.

Lucian was glad the darkness covered his humiliation, and he bent his head so he didn't have to meet her gaze. "We're fine."

Rachael located his sword and cane, then she knelt beside them. She put her hand on Lindsay's back. "Lindsay?"

The girl pulled away from Lucian and touched her torn cheek. "I'm okay, I think." She shuddered and looked back toward the Barren.

Rachael followed her gaze. Lucian observed their profiles and thought of lionesses on the hunt.

A faint noise penetrated the night's quiet.

Lindsay whispered, "Listen."

CHAPTER NINETEEN

whom shall i fear?

A low, steady hum penetrated the silence. Lucian released Lindsay and gripped his cane. Rachael was beside him, her hand around his arm to help him rise. Just as he gained his feet, the sound rose in pitch to become the whine of the Barren's flies. Lucian felt Catarina's tainted essence seep around him. "No more," he whispered.

They turned to face the Hell Gate.

The gibbous moon illuminated two figures cresting the rise of the hillock. Catarina perched on Cerberus' back, riding the hound like a steed. The demon sniffed the ground and picked his path around the lingering resonance of Rachael's enchantment.

They must have come through the Hell Gate, or perhaps his twin's power had grown and she'd ridden the moon. How she'd reached them didn't matter. Lucian tried to staunch his rising despair. She was here.

Rachael switched her knife to her left hand and drew her sword. She moved in front of Lindsay. "Get behind me. Give me room to move."

"Lucian?" Lindsay stepped away from Rachael.

"Do as she says."

Lindsay nodded and ran back several paces then stopped.

Lucian drew his sword and glanced at Rachael. "Stay behind me."

"No."

"Rachael."

"I will not leave you."

His desperation receded. She had her blind side to him, and he couldn't read her expression. Her words were enough. He wouldn't have to face his sister and her demon alone. Perhaps this time, he stood a chance; he returned his attention to his twin.

Catarina's clear, beautiful voice sang a wordless lullaby Lucian remembered from their youth. She had hummed the same tune when she closed the door to his cell. A song of sleep; a song of death.

The wind carried the earthy-sweet smell of the grave as she neared. Her gown barely covered her nakedness. She wore her long dark hair like a veil to obscure her features. The pendant with her emblem swung between her breasts; the ravens' obsidian eyes reflected the moonlight. Cerberus halted, his head swinging back and forth to view Rachael and Lindsay. Less than ten feet separated them.

"Have you missed me, Lucian?" Catarina asked.

Lucian placed himself between his sister and Rachael. "Go home, Cate."

Catarina tossed her wild mane out of her face. For one terrifying instant, Lucian saw a thousand eyes sparkle across her features. The flies whined in a maddening crescendo. Lucian blinked. It had to be an illusion. The multiple eyes disappeared, and the chorus of flies waned.

Catarina slithered off the demon's back; her bare feet sank in the mud. "You've led me on a splendid chase."

He hefted his blade and took a step forward. "You could have stayed home."

She smiled, her eyes glittering like shards of glass. "I think I'll make you my fool."

His next step faltered, and while he tried to convince himself his bad knee betrayed him, he knew the truth. She meant what she said and her power to terrify him had not diminished. No corruption was beneath her. She would make him her fool, paint his face, and force him into the streets to beg if it pleased her. To keep Lindsay safe, he'd do whatever his twin wanted, and she knew it.

Catarina's smile broadened.

Lucian swallowed past the dry click in his throat and whispered, "I'm not going back."

"Of course you are." She touched her pendant. "I will dress you in motley colors and you will perform your crippled dance for my guests." She capered in a tight circle, lifting her right leg awkwardly to mimic him. Tottering to a silent rhythm, she hunched forward, mocking his lumbering gait.

His face burned with shame. He resisted the urge to fling the despised cane aside. Unable to bear the thought of Rachael's pity, he kept his gaze on his twin.

"Good God," Rachael whispered, "she's gone mad."

Catarina stopped her dance and folded her hands demurely in front of her. "Rachael. Sister of my heart. Mastema sends his greetings."

Rachael said nothing, but Lucian could see her face now, and her eye narrowed to grow frigid with hate. She wouldn't trade taunts with Catarina. Rachael's weapon was silence, so he didn't wait for her to retort. "Go home, Cate," he said.

"And the foundling." Catarina looked at Lindsay, who shuddered beneath the older woman's glare. "Little Lindsay Richardson, pale as glass. I shall break you."

Ice plunged through his chest. "Leave her alone, Cate."

Catarina pushed Cerberus away from her. "Disarm Rachael. I want the girl."

Lucian tried to block Cerberus' path, but the demon trotted around him, heading for Rachael. The hum of flies rose in the night. Rachael summoned her soul-light into her blade. The resonance of her magic stirred within Lucian's soul as she whispered, "'The Lord is my light and my salvation; whom shall I fear?'"

"Fear me," Catarina said as she advanced, "you one-eyed whore."

Cerberus circled Rachael, growling low, but he didn't attack.

Rachael glared at Catarina and her voice grew stronger. "'The Lord is the stronghold of my life; of whom shall I be afraid?'"

The light in her sword grew to a blaze, and Cerberus backed away. It was a magnificent display, but Lucian knew she couldn't keep it up. As quick as his thought, Rachael's light dimmed to a bare glow. She was exhausted.

Catarina turned to Lucian. "You have forsworn yourself." She pointed to his hand where he still wore his father's ring.

Lucian clenched his jaw. Whenever she felt threatened, she began a trajectory of arguments that circled around him. She never changed her tactics, yet he wasn't prepared for the strength of the recollection.

He recalled his mother pressing the bloodied ring to his lips, forcing him to swear an oath that would be impossible to keep. He'd been a terrified child, and his mother had been half-mad with grief. The memory was so strong he tasted his father's blood on his tongue.

Catarina's power had grown, and she charged his memories with her own. Lucian remembered the smell of the herbs burning in the fire to sweeten the winter rooms, the odor of fresh thrushes on the floor. He saw his mother's dark eyes, red with tears; could almost feel her face next to his.

He shook his head to rid himself of the remembrance, struggling out of Catarina's spell. *God help me, please.* He saw a light in his soul and ran from the past toward the truth. He'd thought himself noble for always watching over his sister. All his life he'd taken the blame for her crimes, eased her emotional pain, healed her wounds, but she was never satisfied. She was a bottomless pit of need and he had nothing left to give. He'd been a fool.

When he looked up again, she had moved closer to him. She held something dark in her hand. "You swore, Lucian. You swore to watch over me all of my days."

"And you descended into madness despite my vigilance!" He flung his cane aside and yanked his father's ring from his hand. He threw it at her. "I am forsworn."

The ring smacked her shoulder and disappeared into the mud at her feet. He no longer cared.

"She's turned you against me." Catarina jabbed her finger in Rachael's direction. "Like Mircea turned everyone against father!"

"Stop it, Cate."

"She used you to drive us apart at the Citadel. You allowed it to happen. She was always jealous of us. This is your fault, Lucian. If you had left her alone, I never would have given myself to the Fallen!"

"No." That wasn't true. Catarina had been drawn to the Fallen's allure of power from the beginning. All she'd ever needed was an excuse.

"She's bewitched you!"

"No!" His roar stunned her to silence. "It is you, Cate. It is your selfishness, your hate, your incessant demands! If anyone bewitched and drove me away, it is you!"

Catarina's head rocked as if he'd struck her. Lucian shut his mouth. He'd gone too far. He saw it in her eyes. Fear stole his breath.

Behind him, Rachael continued her chant, and he heard Lindsay too. He attempted to concentrate on their voices, to enfold them in his heart, but their prayers faded. His twin held him locked within her murderous gaze. She would not let him go.

A fly brushed against his face and he waved it aside. He felt the flush of the Fallen's power wash over him, a red wave of Catarina's fury sent terror into his soul. The sound of flies thrummed through the air. Lucian summoned his soul-light and channeled it into Matthew's blade. He looked toward the Barren where a great, black cloud rose into the sky. The cloud began to move toward them.

"I warned you." Catarina's pallid features swam out of the blackness. "Remember that, Lucian. I warned you not to estrange yourself from me." She raised her arms as the cloud surged overhead. A clap like thunder tore through the air. The flies descended.

†

Lindsay saw the cloud fall toward them. Lucian's panic filtered into her mind, then he shut her out. She remembered to shield her mind as he taught her. Catarina wouldn't find her such an easy target again.

Flies landed on Lindsay's hands and face and pain shot across her skin, especially where Speight had cut her. The flies bit her like they were trying to eat her alive. Their bodies quickly grew heavy with her blood. The familiar panic washed over her, but this time, she pushed it down.

Lucian cried out, and by the light of his sword, she saw tears of blood streak his face. The insects engulfed him. He dropped his weapon and fell, trying to scrape the flies off his face. Horror seeped into her. The flies were in his nose, crawling into his mouth; he couldn't breathe.

Catarina laughed and kicked him in the stomach.

Lindsay shouted, but Catarina ignored her. She waved more of the flies away and tried to think. Her knife was gone, but maybe she just needed to stay out of the way. Rachael was here now.

Rachael moved toward Lucian. Cerberus darted between them, driving her back. She swung her sword at the demon. Cerberus easily pranced out of reach. Rachael favored her left side, and in the moonlight, Lindsay saw the woman was bleeding again.

Her sword no longer glowed and by her weak resonance, Lindsay knew Rachael couldn't summon even the faintest magic. Lucian said the Katharoi had to rest between enchantments. The Fallen's disciples used amulets to channel their power and didn't need to stop.

Catarina kicked Lucian again, her necklace swung between her breasts. Lindsay's anger raced through her veins and she focused on the amulet. The pendant glowed now as it had when Catarina attacked her and Lucian in the woods. That had to be where Catarina got her power.

At a command from Catarina, the flies rose into the sky and hovered over them. She stroked Lucian's hair and whispered to him. Lindsay didn't need to hear the words. Lucian coughed and retched, then shook his head. He wasn't going back. Catarina's lips were tight with rage; she straightened and brought her hand down. The flies descended again.

Out of the corner of her eye, Lindsay saw Cerberus' pallid form flash by on her right; the demon was only a few feet away. Rachael doubled over and gasped for air. Cerberus whirled and charged her again. She straightened and barely deflected the demon's attack. Lindsay stumbled away from the pair and returned her attention to Catarina and Lucian.

Catarina picked up Lucian's cane and swung it hard into his side. The mantle absorbed some of the blow, but Lindsay heard his ribs crack. *Oh, God, she's going to kill him.* The same terror and rage Lindsay felt at the Melasur Bridge rushed through her veins. She focused on Catarina's necklace and edged around the pair until she was behind Catarina. She'd messed up with Speight by hesitating. She wouldn't screw up again. Lindsay ran toward the woman.

Catarina swung the cane for another blow, and Lindsay launched herself at Catarina's back. She hooked one arm around Catarina's throat, then reached around and twined her fingers into the pendant's chain. It was like grabbing a chunk of ice. The cold was so intense, Lindsay almost released the links, but Lucian gagged, and she knew she couldn't let go now. Catarina would kill them all. Lindsay held on. Overhead, the stars wheeled as Catarina howled and whirled, trying to throw Lindsay off her back.

They crashed to the ground together, and Lindsay felt her arm slip. The bandages tore through her blisters and she cried out. She kept her arm around Catarina's throat and her fingers intertwined in the chain. Catarina reached backward and her fingernails found Lindsay's face. She dragged her nails through the open wound on Lindsay's cheek, and Lindsay didn't recognize her own voice. The sound that poured through her lips lay somewhere between a shriek of rage and the cry of a wounded animal. Tears gushed from her eyes, but she didn't lose her focus.

She ignored the burning cold that seared her hand and wound her fingers in the chain until she held the pendant. Two ravens locked together. The pendant seemed the weakest where the beaks joined. The amulet glowed, and Lindsay concentrated on the necklace. She visualized the pendant breaking. Nothing happened. Some kind of spell fused the metal tight. Lindsay reached into her rage; she poured her grief and hate into her spell. Sweat drenched her hair.

Catarina's elbow jabbed Lindsay's side and pain flooded her chest. Lindsay directed all of her fury into her magic and envisioned the pendant snapping in half. She felt the metal give and the glow seemed dimmer. *Come on, God. If I never do anything right again, let me do this. Please.*

Catarina's next blow caught the side of Lindsay's head. Blackness edged Lindsay's vision. *No! I'm not done!* She struggled to hold on to consciousness. Catarina grabbed the pendant and tried to wrest it from Lindsay's grasp. They both held a raven's body, and Lindsay gripped her half until her knuckles were white. She pulled and felt the metal give. The obsidian eye from Catarina's raven fell into the mud. Lindsay grunted and yanked with every ounce of her energy.

The pendant broke.

The flies died, falling to the ground like thick black raindrops. Catarina shrieked and threw Lindsay off her back. This time Lindsay let go and closed her eyes, wincing against her anticipated impact. Water and mud splashed around her, but the pain was nothing like holding that burning pendant. She opened her hand and her half of the raven pendant fell into the mud.

Lindsay felt Lucian's consciousness flicker in the back of her mind, guttering like a candle. He wasn't dead; she knew he wasn't dead. His thoughts were confused, and he didn't try to shield his mind from her. He struggled to his knees and vomited flies. Lindsay swallowed her own bile and looked away.

Rachael turned to see what happened. Cerberus' eyes glowed in the night. With a snarl, he launched himself at her. The demon feinted right, but when she turned to meet his attack, he dodged left with uncanny speed. She couldn't reverse her turn. The demon's talons caught her shoulder and they went down together.

The pair landed a few feet from Lindsay. Rachael fell on her back and released her sword. The blade landed a hand's span out of her reach. Cerberus snapped at her face. Lindsay screamed Rachael's name, and the woman whipped her head to the side in time to keep her nose.

Lindsay forced herself to her knees and saw Catarina stand beside Lucian. Her coal black eyes glittered in the night and her glare pinned Lindsay to the ground. Never had the girl seen such hate roil off another human, and she realized too late that Catarina's power went deeper than an amulet. She was once Katharos too. Lindsay's mouth went dry. She may have hurt Catarina, but she hadn't stopped her.

"Cerberus! Stop!" Catarina approached Lindsay. "You foolish girl."

✝

Lucian felt his sister's skirts brush his cheek. She reeked of ashes and death. Lindsay's fear joined his, and he shielded his mind from her. His head ached and his throat was on fire. He glimpsed the pale outline of Catarina's leg and reached out to snag her ankle. Catarina tripped and fell to the muddy ground. She kicked backwards and Lucian barely dodged her blow, but he didn't let her go.

"Release me or Rachael is dead!"

He saw Rachael sprawled beneath the demon, her sword out of reach, and his heart withered. He released Catarina.

"Come home, Lucian." She stood and looked down at him. "I'll let them go."

She wouldn't. She had no intention of allowing any of them to leave. Not now. Not ever.

His twin opened her hand and he saw his scarred prism. "Do you remember when you showed me the colors? Do you remember the garden, Lucian?"

He looked into the glass and recalled laughing with her when the prism's light had danced on the wall. Her hair had smelled of sunshine, and he'd thought of Rachael. "I remember." Hoarseness distorted his voice.

"You said it wasn't magic, but surely it must be." An eerie calm settled over her, and a tear flowed down Lucian's cheek.

His twin stepped closer. "I can't bring forth the light without you, Lucian. Come home."

He slouched forward and put his hand over his eyes. Only one thing would make her stop. He couldn't stand to see the hurt in Rachael's eye again. "Forgive me."

"What?" Catarina bent down. "Did you say something, Lucian?"

"Lucian," Lindsay said, "don't."

He screwed his eyes shut and extended his hand to his sister. God help him, he was the worst kind of coward. If he intended to do this, he should at least have the courage to look her in the eye. Lucian met his twin's stony gaze. "Cate, please." The words were gravel in his throat. "Forgive me."

Catarina smiled and took his hand. He drew Caleb's knife and yanked her down. With one quick thrust, he drove the blade into her chest. She fell against him with a small gasp. He wrapped his arms around her. "I'm so sorry, Cate," he whispered against her hair. "So sorry."

Lucian rocked her gently. When she struggled against him, he held her tighter. He had promised to take care of her and he failed. He couldn't save her from herself. A sharp pain spread through his chest as he took her agony for his own, but he didn't heal her. This time he would not heal her.

Her breath tickled his ear. "We are never the same," she said as she slid her bloodied thumb across his forehead, "without you at my side." Her dark eyes were afire with moonlight and madness. "I will come back for you, brother."

✝

Rachael turned her face away from the stench of Cerberus' breath. The demon pinned her arm so she couldn't move her knife. Water splashed her face and Cerberus twisted. The hilt of her sword bumped against her hand.

Cerberus growled and his tail lashed out. Rachael heard Lindsay yell in surprise and pain. Rachael grasped her weapon. Before she could lift it, Cerberus leapt away. She slashed wildly with her knife, hoping to hit the demon. Cerberus howled when the blade flayed open a length of his hide.

From her knees, she stabbed at the demon a second time with her sword and her weapon glanced off his ribs. He turned on her. She stood and her next blow took him across the jaw. Cerberus shrieked and ran for the Hell Gate.

Rachael let him go; she'd never catch him, not in her condition. He wouldn't be back. Not tonight. The Hell Gate crackled and the demon disappeared.

Lindsay sat on the wet ground and cradled her arm.

"What happened?" Rachael went to her and examined the long welt that went from Lindsay's elbow to her wrist.

"He was so occupied with you, I was able to get close enough to push your sword to you. He whacked me with his tail."

The burn didn't look serious, although Rachael knew from experience how painful a demon wound could be. She examined the girl's palm and frowned.

"It's okay. It hurts, but I'm okay." Lindsay pulled her hand away and looked toward Lucian.

"Yes," Rachael whispered. "Yes, you are. You did well. Lucian will be proud."

Lindsay didn't answer, but went to Lucian. Silence pealed across the meadow, and the girl stood beside him, rubbing his back. She looked up when Rachael neared. "He promised me he wouldn't kill anybody unless he had to." Lindsay's glare dared Rachael to contradict her. "He said God wouldn't be mad if we defended our lives and that's all he did. He defended us."

Rachael struggled to make her thoughts work but exhaustion

numbed her mind. Her tongue felt thick and useless. "Lindsay."

"I can't feel him anymore," she said as she brushed dead flies off his shoulders. "He's shut me out and won't let me see his thoughts." Lindsay looked up at Rachael, her gaze no longer defiant. "He'll listen to you. Just tell him he's not going to be in trouble so he doesn't feel bad anymore."

Rachael rested her hand on the girl's shoulder to stop her words. "All right." She knelt in front of Lucian, and Lindsay remained beside him, a ragged and dirty angel. When Rachael saw Lucian's grief, she forgot the girl was there. She wiped his face tenderly. "Lucian?"

"It was the only way," he whispered and stroked his sister's cheek.

"I know. Let her rest." She helped him ease Catarina's body to the ground. "Let her go." *Let her go.* She'd said it enough times when they were young, but tonight he finally listened to her. He released his twin and folded Catarina's hands over her chest.

She didn't look peaceful. Even in death, hate scarred her features; she'd harbored no emotion but rage. Rachael had known when Catarina rode up on the demon's back that she'd paid the ultimate price for her power. Dry as a husk, she had no love left in her. Even now, Lucian couldn't see his twin's faults.

He smoothed her hair and gasped, jerking his hand out of her tangled locks. A diamond hairpin fell into the mud, one stone winking in the moonlight.

"It's all right." Rachael turned his hand to better see the wound. The cut was small, a pinprick.

A drop of his blood seeped from his thumb to trickle between Catarina's parted lips. A pall passed over Rachael, but in her fatigue, she shrugged it off. Catarina was dead and the dead don't come back.

Lucian didn't notice. He removed his cloak and wrapped it around Catarina's corpse. "She was always cold."

Lindsay stood back, her face ghostly in the moonlight. Rachael glanced up at her; the girl didn't need to see this. "Can you find his cane?"

Lindsay nodded and left them to their task.

To keep her hands busy, Rachael helped him secure the mantle as a makeshift shroud. "We'll build a cairn for her in the morning. When we get to the Citadel, I'll send some Katharoi back for her body." Not for Catarina. Rachael didn't care if Catarina went back to Hell, but Lucian would never forgive himself for leaving his sister here. "We'll bring her home." For Lucian's sake.

He met her gaze with a look so lost her heart broke for him. No words could give comfort to his grief. She wrapped her arms around him so she wouldn't have to see his eyes. He took a low shuddering breath.

"There's nothing wrong with mourning her," Rachael whispered into his hair. Several minutes passed and he remained tense, locked tight in his memories; Rachael knew she'd never touch him. Just when she thought she should release him, a sob racked his body. She could only stroke his neck and speak the magic words John had once said to her. "It's all right. They have no power over you now. It's all right."

A flicker of movement caught her eye as Lindsay edged close. She held Lucian's cane tight against her chest and watched them, obviously unsettled by the intensity of Lucian's sorrow. Rachael drew the girl into their embrace.

Lindsay put her arm around Rachael's neck. "Is it over?" she whispered.

The tin box holding the sigil thrummed with a pulse all its own against Rachael's breast. She wasn't done. Not yet.

PART III

I have wandered home...

—Edgar Allan Poe
"Dream-Land"

CHAPTER TWENTY

cross creek

The deer trail branched before them, and Rachael guided the mare down the left track. Lindsay followed on the gelding, and Lucian guarded their rear, his countenance grim. As they neared the Citadel, he'd made no secret of his displeasure with her plans. Rachael wouldn't be swayed.

She had to have Catarina's Psalter. When the complicit saw Lucian, they would scatter to the four winds, but with the Psalter, Rachael could find them. There was power in a name, and a name written in blood was doubly potent. With the Psalter, she could chase them through their dreams and bring them to justice.

Lucian thought Reynard kept the book at the Citadel. That made no sense; the Psalter would carry its own taint from the Fallen. Reynard was no fool; he wouldn't keep such a damning piece of evidence at the Citadel. No, it was at Cross Creek—at her house. All so Reynard could implicate her if his plot was discovered.

Rachael stifled her need for revenge and surveyed the land before her. The pale afternoon sunlight drifted behind a mist that seemed to have followed them from the Wasteland. Through the foliage, she glimpsed a boulder; flecks of moss marred the dark gray stone jutting out of the ground between two oaks. The rock marked one of Cross

Creek's boundaries. She reined the mare to a halt.

Lindsay stopped the gelding and rubbed the horse's neck, probably more to calm herself than the animal. The slash on her cheek was healing nicely, but the same couldn't be said for the burns on her arm and palm. Lindsay didn't complain of any pain, but Rachael could already see she would carry the scars for life.

In spite of Rachael's efforts to keep Lucian and Lindsay apart, the girl had drawn closer to Lucian, sharing his grief for a lost sibling. The dark circles beneath Lindsay's eyes bore mute testimony to the nightmares she endured after her encounter with Speight and Catarina.

"Why are we stopping?" she asked.

Rachael gestured at the stone. "We're at Cross Creek."

Lindsay glanced at the boundary marker and twisted the reins in her fingers. "Is your house near here?"

"Half a league that way," Rachael said as she pointed through the trees.

Lucian navigated Ignatius around Lindsay's gelding. The new homespun shirt and brown cloak he wore were nowhere near as fine as his old woolen shirt and ermine-lined mantle. Yet Catarina's blood had covered his old shirt, and Rachael couldn't bear the way he'd kept wiping his hands over the stains. He'd buried her in the mantle and Caleb's coat had barely fit him, but the jacket had kept him warm until they'd reached a border town.

Unsure whether she could trust the Katharoi at the Eilat outpost, she'd avoided all contact with other people. Her only foray into town was to secure more provisions and purchase the clothes for Lucian. She'd been surprised at his gratitude and rather than complain of the quality, he'd treated the gifts with reverence.

"I don't like this, Rachael," he said. "We should stay together."

"I have to go on foot. That automatically rules you out." She hated how pitiless the words sounded. "Lindsay needs to be with someone who can protect her. That's you." She dismounted and handed him the mare's reins.

"You should go to John. He will order Cross Creek searched."

Frustration laced her tone. "And they will have plenty of time to destroy the evidence. Reynard keeps the book away from the Citadel for a reason. He'll be the first to know if John orders a search. Then it's just a matter of his messenger beating the constables to Cross Creek." She rested her hand on his thigh. "It's my house, Lucian. I know every pitch and angle. I'll be fine. Do you remember where we used to meet at Bear Creek?" He nodded and opened his mouth, but she didn't give him time to speak. "Take Lindsay and meet me there."

His frown deepened. "They will have wards to protect the Psalter. Don't move anything without checking for traps."

"I will be on my guard." She reached in her pocket and placed the box holding the sigil into his hand. "I've done this before, you know."

"I know." A whisper of smile touched his lips.

Nothing she said would ease his apprehension. He wanted to be beside her, and she wanted someone to watch her blind side, but he couldn't be with her and Lindsay both. Rachael licked her lips and continued. "If I haven't joined you by morning, take Lindsay and go to the Rabbinate. Ask for Adam Zimmer. He's a good friend. He'll give you shelter and will know what to do."

Lucian bent sideways and touched her cheek. His hand looked naked without his father's ring, but neither she nor Lindsay had been able to find it. Lucian hadn't cared, and even now, she didn't believe he missed the burden the signet represented; he seemed lighter without it.

"If you're not back by dawn," he said, "I'm coming for you." Before she could answer, he straightened and tucked the box containing the sigil into his breast pocket. "Lindsay, let's go."

Rachael moved aside as he nudged Ignatius to a slow walk.

Lindsay didn't immediately follow him. She looked down at Rachael with a worried gaze. "Be careful, okay?" She made a fist.

"I will." Rachael touched knuckles with her. The girl smiled and her weariness momentarily dissipated to reveal the child beneath the sorrow. She must have been a joy to her parents on Earth. Rachael wished she could leave Lindsay with a reassurance. Instead, she said, "Protect him like you did in the Wasteland. We're not safe yet."

The child faded to reveal the young woman Lindsay would become. Her fragility was a guise; Lindsay Richardson would one day make a fierce Katharos. No fear laced her words. "I will." She brought her heels against the gelding's sides and the horse ambled after Ignatius.

Rachael waited until they were out of sight before she turned to walk toward the farmhouse at Cross Creek. She didn't hurry; she didn't want to arrive before dusk. The path she took went down a small hill and she recognized the place where she and Caleb had found Peter's cell phone. There she had seen Lucian for the first time in sixteen years.

No, that wasn't true. She had first seen him in her dream. The Hell Gate hadn't been the only thing he'd opened that dawn. He'd resurrected her memories and had drawn her back into the vortex of his days with a sorcerer's skill.

During their journey back, every word he'd uttered, each familiar gesture had triggered a remembrance, a conversation, a touch. Yet the poised man she remembered was gone, buried beneath this new Lucian, who now seemed so unsure of his place in the world.

In the distance, a cow lowed, and the sound jarred her from her thoughts. Long expanses of meadowland were visible through the trees. She was at the edge of the farm.

Shades of dusk feathered the gray air, and a mild breeze rattled the autumn leaves. Stephan would be finishing the chores while Sara prepared their dinner. Rachael stopped beneath a gnarled oak on the border of the field. A row of apple trees stretched halfway between the woods and the house. About a hundred yards behind the house, the horse barn rose out of the gloom.

The pungent odor of horseflesh drifted beneath the tart smell of ripe apples. A simple longing rose in Rachael as she inhaled the scents of home, a place where she had once belonged. Before her possession, she'd loved visiting Cross Creek, taking her coffee on the porch while the world awakened around her. She hadn't been alone then; friends sometimes joined her, and Lucian often came to visit.

Rachael rubbed the patch over her missing eye. Everything circled back to Lucian. All those years, she'd lived with her fury directed at him when his sister and Reynard had played them both for fools. Catarina had devised the perfect scheme to drive Rachael away from Lucian because Rachael would never forgive a lie.

Except Lucian never lied. Rachael had analyzed the transcripts of his trial like some Katharoi studied Revelation, and he had never lied. He accepted his culpability in the plot and begged for a chance to redeem himself.

Darkness nestled around the house and lights from inside shed a warm glow. A shadow passed before one of the windows. A man's figure paused and he moved the curtain to look into the yard. Rachael drew behind the tree although she was sure she couldn't be seen. She had no idea if Stephan and Sara were complicit with the others; she would take no chances.

The man turned away from the window, disappearing into the house. She imagined them there, eating her food, staining her sheets with their sex, laughing at her, at the monster she had become. Rage flushed her cheeks.

An image surfaced in her mind: Caleb embracing her, mashing his lips against hers as she struggled against the Wyrm. She squashed the memory and closed her heart against the self-loathing rising in her breast. She wasn't ready to deal with those dark reminiscences, not yet, so she shoved them deep in the caldron of her heart.

The hours passed until a sliver of the moon rose high in the sky. All the interior lights had been extinguished for at least two hours. In her mind, she saw her home, trying to imagine where they held their rites. She would have noticed anything amiss inside the story and a half home.

The one place she seldom ventured was the cellar. Ever since her time in Hell, she couldn't stand to be underground. Whenever she needed something from the basement, she'd either send one of her hired men or fetch it herself during the daylight hours when she could leave the trapdoor open. She made no secret of her dislike for the space, and they would choose a place on her property that she shunned. She was certain that was where they held their rites.

Rachael left her hiding spot and crept toward the house. She crossed the distance and soon experienced the first echoes of the Wyrm's resonance. The demon's presence lingered around her home, a bitter odor that hid another spell. An unpleasant humming sensation vibrated into her arms and upper torso, and she discerned the sour magic of the Fallen. Had she not known to sift past the Wyrm's malevolent resonance, she would have assumed the evil surrounding Cross Creek originated with the demon.

Rachael circled to the back of the house to the root cellar's trap door. She held her fingers over the supple leather handle, trying to feel any wards that might protect the entrance. Nothing. She tugged on the door and the snap of wood against metal caused her to catch her breath.

The noise was explosive in the night. *What the hell?* She froze and glanced at the bedroom, but no light shone through the window.

She ran her hand up the door until she felt the cold metal of a lock. Lucian had her so concerned over wards and spells, it never occurred to her to look for something as simple as a lock. She felt like an idiot. Rachael fingered the simple padlock and checked for wards. She'd never kept a lock on the door, so why should they bolt it in her absence? Rachael clenched her jaw. Either Reynard didn't trust Sara and Stephan, or no one had expected her to return.

For all Reynard knew, she wandered the Wasteland beneath the thrall of the Wyrm. Let him think what he would. She was coming for him, and the less warning he had, the better.

Rachael found her tools and within seconds picked the padlock open. Before she tried opening the door again, she checked for more bolts and found none. The well-oiled hinges didn't make a sound. Rachael slipped the lock into her pocket and went down three steps, then eased the door shut behind her.

Her pulse thudded loud in her ears and sweat broke across her upper lip. She took a deep breath and inhaled the cider smell of apples and damp earth. Beneath the apples lay a rancid odor like vomit.

Rachael closed her eye and opened it but couldn't tell a difference. The darkness was complete, enveloping her in a cocoon of black. She gritted her teeth. She wasn't a child wailing in the valleys of Hell. She was a woman, and she had faced her demon. *I've spit in Mastema's face. This is nothing.*

She forced herself to go down one step. The wood creaked beneath her boot. Rachael froze and listened for footsteps overhead. She counted to twenty, then to fifty, ready to pivot and run for the exit. No one moved in the house. She lowered her weight to the next step and silence greeted her.

There should be a lamp hanging from a peg at the foot of the stairs. Her fingers groped along the wooden rafter, searching for the lantern. She touched something wet and sticky. Rachael jerked her hand back and wiped her trembling fingers on her pants. *God, what had they been doing down here?*

She debated using her soul-light. If she called forth a pinprick of light, she could see to get the lantern. Too much magic and she'd awaken Sara or Stephan. It was a chance she'd have to take. Rachael summoned her illumination and her eye settled on the lamp hanging from a nail below her. She grabbed the cold metal handle and flicked her soul-light to flame the wick.

Again she listened for movement from above while she waited for her sight to adjust. Shadows crawled along the walls. She shuddered and looked around the room, wondering where to begin.

Several wooden tables and shelves lined the three walls. Jars of varying sizes, all full of Cross Creek's fruits and vegetables stored for the winter, rested on the shelves and tables. Skid marks indicated one of the tables had been dragged to the center of the cellar. At the rear wall, directly across from the stairs, the marks stopped in front of a table. Baskets of apples were stored in neat rows between the legs. In the center of the tabletop, a five-gallon jar rested. A large mass floated in the dark liquid.

Rachael kept the lantern close to the floor. She was on top of evil; she felt it vibrate through her flesh and into her bones. With Lucian's warning singing through her head, she didn't disturb the jar. Whatever lay inside was dormant, and she wanted it to stay that way.

She touched the edge of the wood, feeling the echoes of dark spells, nothing more than old resonations. She gripped the edge of the table. Whatever ward they used to protect the Psalter would be similar to the low-level spell that protected the sigil in Caleb's coat. The complicit wouldn't use a spell that was too powerful or other Katharoi would feel the reverberation. She set the lantern down and ran her fingers beneath the table's ledge.

Still nothing. She moved two baskets of apples and knelt on the floor to look up. Nothing underneath, either. The wound in her side seeped a trickle of blood into the dressing Lucian had fashioned for her. She ignored the pain and moved the lantern close to the wall where the foundation stones were neatly fitted together. She ran her hands over the stones. One rock wiggled when she touched it. A tingle of magic whispered into her arms and she found the ward. It was similar to the one Caleb had worn on his coat.

Rachael summoned her prayer and cancelled the ward. A dark oily substance oozed into the hard-packed dirt at her feet. She pried the brick out of the wall. Overhead, she heard liquid slosh. Rachael glanced upward. Sweat leaked into her eye. The splash quieted.

Hurry, hurry, hurry. She withdrew the book from the niche. It was Catarina's. The first five pages were unchanged, as were the last five, but everything in between had been torn out. New pages had been sewn into the binding with the names of the complicit written in dark brownish-red ink.

The essence of each individual resided in his or her signature and here she had their name written with the power of a Katharos's blood. None of them could escape justice now. Oh, God, she had them. She tucked the Psalter into the pouch at her belt.

Another splash distracted her. Something bumped against the tabletop. Her hands shook as she replaced the brick and the baskets. She grasped the lantern's handle and stood. The jar on the table rocked. The lump inside flung itself forward and pressed its wizened face against the glass. It was a fetus. The child was large enough to have been taken late in the second or early third trimester, probably from one of the river town's whores. Whatever its parentage, it wasn't human anymore.

Rachael's limbs froze and she almost dropped the lantern. The fetus' milk-white eyes squinted with hate and the pinched lips opened in a silent scream. Needle-sharp teeth glinted in the light. It pushed against the inside of the jar, tiny, clawed feet kicking to thrust its body from one side to the other. The jar rocked precariously close to the table's edge.

Rachael set the lantern on the floor. A crate full of rags was in the corner. She ran and scooped up as many as she could carry. Dust motes flew into the air and she sneezed. The jar thudded against the table.

Too much noise, the damn thing was making too much noise. The floor overhead groaned. Someone stood. Rachael's heart drowned everything as she rushed back to the table. The fetus slapped the glass and grinned at her.

She covered her hands with several rags. Even with the cloth covering her fingers, she was loath to touch the jar, but she wrapped her hands around it. The fetus raked one claw against her palm, and Rachael flinched.

Voices murmured overhead.

Rachael swallowed and shoved the jar back against the wall, wincing as it scraped on the tabletop. She swathed the glass in the rags, then snatched the crate and up-ended it over the jar to hold the rags in place. If the fetus succeeded in knocking its prison over, the glass wouldn't break.

Heavy footfalls hurried across the floor overhead. She snatched up the lantern and reached the stairs in four quick strides. She extinguished the flame and left the lamp on the bottom stair as she ran. Her palm shot upward to shove the door open. She took in a great lungful of the night air. On her left, a light shone from a window.

Rachael let the trapdoor down and searched for the padlock with shaking fingers. On the second try, she shot the lock through the bolt and slammed it home. She ran for the woods.

The cloudy sky obliterated the moon, but she knew her yard like she knew her body. She reached the trees and plunged into the underbrush. A branch snagged her hair; she slowed her pace to look back. Light from the bedroom window shined onto the yard. A lone figure carrying a lantern emerged around the corner. She recognized the man's silhouette as the one she'd seen in the window earlier. He stopped by the cellar door and leaned forward to listen. Rachael held her breath.

He tested the lock and pulled on the door, then lingered as if unsure of what to do. A cricket ticked the seconds with a song. Stephan turned and held the lantern high to search the darkness, then returned his attention to the cellar door. He shifted his weight from one leg to the other. He turned and stalked back into the house. A door slammed and within minutes, the light in the bedroom went out.

Were they complicit? Caleb had been worried the stewards might find something like the burned account book. He wouldn't have been concerned if he had confidence they were complicit. She recalled the fear oozing from Caleb's pores like sweat; he must have been terrified of being discovered.

Stephan and Sara were there by John's command, not Reynard's, so it was possible they weren't involved in the Inquisitor's scheme. Rachael touched the Psalter. Soon she'd know for sure.

She forced her weak limbs to move and stumbled through the forest until she felt safe enough to stop beneath a pine tree. She withdrew the book and summoned her soul-light.

The first part of the book was the pact, and it was followed by a list of those who had taken their final vows. Neither Sara nor Stephan's names were there.

Yet Lucian hadn't led her wrong. Reynard's name was there in addition to the names of four other Council members.

"Merciful God." She remembered Reynard kissing her face, the Wyrm rising to meet its master. Each exorcism he'd performed had brought the demon closer to manifestation. Reynard, who didn't want to lose the Citadel's symbolic heir, who smiled with his face and spread lies with his mouth. Rage seared her chest. When she was done, they'd all know the wrath of days had come.

CHAPTER TWENTY-ONE

miserere

Asliver of moonlight trickled through the clouds as Lucian stood beside the boulder overlooking Bear Creek. Curled up near his feet, Lindsay slept. She murmured through her dreams, and he prepared to wake her if she suffered another nightmare. Her hair pulled from her braid to fall in drifts around her face. Even in sleep, her loss of innocence was apparent in the creases around her frown. He mourned her lost childhood almost as much as he mourned his twin.

Lucian rubbed his eyes and walked around the camp to stay awake. He shouldn't have allowed Rachael to go alone. Although she wasn't as reckless as when she was young, she didn't understand the Fallen's traps. Anything could have happened—could be happening—and here he stood as helpless as when he'd lived with his sister.

His forehead burned where Catarina marked him with her blood. No matter how he tried, he couldn't summon a clear image of her face. Her features distorted from the sibling he'd loved into the monster he'd killed. He couldn't resurrect her, not even in memory.

He didn't think he would feel her absence so keenly.

But he did.

The horses shuffled in the darkness, and Ignatius lifted his head, ears pricked forward. Lucian limped toward the animals; a shadow emerged from the trees to his right.

"It's me," Rachael said.

He exhaled in relief and went to her, not stopping until they were close enough to embrace. He summoned his soul-light and examined her eye where rage burned her iris dark. "What happened?"

"I found the Psalter. You were right. Every name was as you said it would be."

"What will you do?"

She didn't flinch. "I will accuse them. I will judge them and I will advocate for their deaths."

"And me?" He marveled his words didn't belie his thundering heart. "Will you judge me?"

Her anger receded and her words stilled his soul. "I already have." A smile trembled on her lips. "I will not leave you."

It took him a second to realize Rachael didn't use his words to mock him. She meant what she said—she would not leave him.

Whether it was his gratitude or his exhaustion, Lucian didn't stop to think of the consequences. He leaned forward and kissed her, his lips brushing against hers with the barest of touches. The taste of her filled him, and he kissed her again, slipping his arm around her waist to draw her close. She put her palms against his chest, and he felt her lean into him, her mouth seeking his, or perhaps he imagined it, mistaking his desire for hers. She withdrew from him to end the kiss, yet she didn't step out of his embrace.

He released her and she looked away, but not before he saw the color rising to her cheeks. He feared he'd overstepped the invisible barrier that stood between them. "Rachael, I'm sorry."

"You're not in the least."

"What?"

"You're not sorry at all." He could have sworn a spark of mischief flickered in her eye before she became grim once more. She handed him the Psalter. "We've got to go." She walked to the saddles. "I want to get there before morning Mass ends."

He fingered the worn cover of Catarina's prayer book as Rachael gathered the packs. While she was busy, he opened the Psalter to the first page. The resurgence of his sorrow took him off guard. The inscription from his mother to Catarina had not been disturbed, and for some reason this grieved Lucian worse than if they removed the page from the book. He creased the paper with his finger and tore it from the Psalter.

The Citadel could have Catarina and her lies, but his life with his sister had been different on Earth. No evil had stalked them there, and a mother's words of love to her daughter had no place in the Fallen's roster of the complicit. Lucian tucked the page into his breast pocket and closed the book.

He limped over and nudged Lindsay with his cane. "Wake up, child. We've one more duty before we're done."

She rolled over and looked up at him with sleep-crusted eyes. "Is Rachael back?"

"I am." Rachael lifted the mare's saddle and went to the black horse. "Go wash your face."

Lucian looked up where dawn pinked the sky and shook off his melancholy. If he intended to become part of the Citadel again, he'd have to leave the past behind. He went to help Rachael saddle the horses. Lindsay disappeared behind the boulder for a few minutes to wash her face and braid her hair, then she returned to help gather their things.

Once they were all mounted, Lucian gave Rachael the Psalter and the tin that held the sigil. She secreted the items in her pockets.

Lucian said to Lindsay, "Stay close to me and let Rachael do the talking. Remember everything I told you in the Wasteland and follow my lead in all things."

Lindsay twisted the reins in her fingers, and he was reminded of the way she flipped her hair through the purple band when she'd first come through the Veil. "Are you happy to be going back?"

He was scared to death. "Yes, I am."

Rachael reined the mare's head toward the Citadel and led the way. "Everything's going to be all right," she said.

The road was barely a path through the woods. The sun burned the clouds away and within a half hour they were at the Citadel. In spite of his trepidation, Lucian felt his heart soar with the sight of home.

"It's huge!" Lindsay whispered.

"It is indeed." Lucian maneuvered Ignatius until Lindsay rode between him and Rachael. The four guards at the outer gate snapped to attention as they neared, and the oldest Katharos stepped forward. "State your business."

Rachael didn't slow her mount. "Stand down, soldier. It's Rachael Boucher on the Seraph's business."

The man squinted at her, an expression of shock distorting his features. "Jesus Christ."

Rachael jerked the reins and the mare lifted her front hooves off the ground. She addressed the Katharos with a voice as brittle as ice. "What did you say?"

"I'm sorry, ma'am, Judge Boucher, it's just—"

Rachael cocked her head at the man. "What's your name, soldier?"

He recovered himself. "Kevin Brust, ma'am."

Rachael measured him with her eye. Lucian noted a trickle of sweat flow down the man's seamed cheek. "Carry on," she said.

He shouted his order to the other Katharoi. "Stand down for Judge Boucher!"

The other guards moved out of the road and to their posts. Rachael nudged the mare into motion again. The soldier was visibly relieved when they passed under the portcullis and into the middle ward.

The guards at the inner gate immediately stepped aside to allow them to pass, but the men's stares followed them. As they rode between the summer kitchen and the bake-house, Lucian looked up at the cathedral and crossed himself.

The courtyard was empty. A small herd of goats bleated from within the confines of their fence. No staff member came to take their horses.

Lucian glanced at Rachael. She fingered the hilt of her sword, her unease apparent as she reined the mare to a halt at the western door. She helped Lindsay down from the gelding. Lucian took his cane and dismounted.

"Is everybody at church?" Lindsay asked. She looked up at the relief over the cathedral doors that portrayed the archangel Michael standing over the subjugated Satan. She craned her neck and stared at the motif, her eyes wide with wonder.

Rachael fingered the pouch at her belt. "Can you feel it, Lucian?"

He calmed his mind and shut out the sights and sounds around him so he could listen with his soul. The dark resonance he recalled from

Catarina's house seeped through the stones. "One of the complicit is weaving an enchantment."

Lindsay's gaze snapped to Lucian. "In a church?"

Lucian nodded. "Catarina's priests took over several churches in Hadra. They find double meanings in the scripture and wrap their spells in the words. The sermons are manipulated, and the congregations succumb over a long period of time. It's like slow death by arsenic." He turned to Rachael. "When was the last time you attended Mass?"

Rachael blushed and looked away. "Years."

"Be grateful. If you'd been here, the Wyrm would have taken you long ago."

Lindsay frowned at the doors. "Have they won?"

"No," Lucian said, "it's not so easy. Those who have a strong will can resist the spells; only the weak succumb. I can feel John's presence. So long as the Seraph lives, there's hope."

Rachael ascended the stairs.

Lucian kneaded the head of his cane. He had not come all this way to live in the Fallen's shadow again. "Listen carefully: I don't believe Reynard will attack me or Lindsay. His goal will be to make you sound like a liar. Lindsay and I are more valuable to them alive than dead."

Rachael nodded and Lucian was glad to see a hint of fear in her eye. Good. If she was afraid, she'd be careful.

"The key, Rachael, is not to argue. Reynard will strive to be the most reasonable person in the room. If you become angry and lash out at him, he will use your anger against you. You will look like lunatic and he will sway their judgment."

"And the Seraph."

"Precisely."

"The magic's getting stronger." Lindsay took his hand.

"Of course." Still, he hesitated.

Lindsay squeezed his fingers. "Come on, Lucian. We can do this."

"She's right," Rachael said and gestured for him to join her.

Lucian nodded. He couldn't wait any longer. It was time to face them. He climbed the stairs with Lindsay at his side, his cane clacked against the stone.

"Into the abyss," Rachael whispered as she pulled the heavy door open.

The smell of incense drifted on the air. Rather than the pleasant scent Lucian remembered, the odor was cloying. He wrinkled his nose. The atrium was dark in spite of the sun shining through the arched windows. He tried to see around the colonnades, but shadows obscured the arcades.

They moved past the atrium and into the nave where statues of the saints leaned from their alcoves, their blind eyes sinister in the murky light. Rachael kept a fast pace as she led them toward the service, and Lucian matched her stride.

The chamber's acoustics amplified Reynard Bartell's voice and covered the sound of their footsteps on the polished floor. As they reached the wooden screen, Reynard's words thundered through the cathedral. "'They have as a king over them the angel of the bottomless pit.'"

Rachael held her hand up and they stopped. Lindsay shuddered, but her mouth was set in a determined line and her left eye narrowed as she evaluated the scene. He drew her near and peered through the lattice of the screen.

Tendrils of smoke coiled in the aisles. Several rows of pews were placed along the south aisle for those too lame or ill to stand, and these were filled. The younger Katharoi stood along the north aisle. On the right side of the quire was the lectern where Reynard raised his arms. "'His name in Hebrew is Abaddon, and in Greek he is called Appollyon.'"

John stood to the left in the pulpit, flanked by Xavier and Charles Dubois.

Sadness entombed Lucian's heart as his gaze swept over John. His Elder had aged so much. Though he appeared brittle with his years, one glance at the steel blue eyes warned Lucian that John didn't suffer frailty of either the mind or the soul.

Beside John, Xavier's scowl focused on Reynard. Dubois scanned the room with a hunter's eye. John's posture was similar to Xavier's tense form, and like Dubois, the Seraph examined the room.

He suspects something is amiss. Lucian recognized the glower shading John's features. He'd seen that look as a youth. *He intends to let them hang themselves with their actions.*

Behind the altar stood a resurrection cross, empty to symbolize the risen Christ, and it dominated the room. An urn of wine and a loaf of bread awaited the blessing for the Eucharist.

Many of the Katharoi focused on Reynard as if entranced. Lucian tried to gauge how many were in the room, but the people were pressed too close together. To his dismay, he noted staff members mixed into the crowd. They would have no defense against Reynard's spells.

Rachael became very still beside him, and the first resonance of the Spirit tinged the atmosphere. He didn't risk a glance in her direction, but he knew she reached deep into her soul to draw on the power of God. As she drew her spell around her, peace radiated from the essence of her being.

"'The first woe has passed.'" Reynard must have sensed it too. He surveyed the room with a frown and lost the rhythm of his spell.

Rachael's voice rang clear, startling the congregation. "'There are still two woes to come.'" She stepped away from the screen and into the aisle.

Lucian followed her; Lindsay's fingers clenched his hand.

"Revelation. How apropos." Rachael slowed her pace. "Let's talk of Hell, Reynard."

The Inquisitor blinked at her, then pointed at Lucian. "How dare you bring that traitor into God's house, Rachael Boucher!"

Xavier positioned himself in front of John, and Lucian avoided his old friend's gaze. A rustle of movement radiated through the room as other Katharoi awoke from Reynard's spell. They turned to look at the trio approaching the altar.

John stepped around Xavier. He glared at Rachael as if she was the enemy. Lucian's mouth went dry with fear. He'd thought himself resolved to his fate but lost his certainty in the face of John's enmity.

Reynard gripped the edges of the podium and leaned forward. "I asked you a question, Judge Boucher. Why have you brought that traitor into God's house?"

"The traitor is in the pulpit," Rachael said.

John's face flushed scarlet. "Tell me, Judge Boucher, what is the punishment for bearing false witness?"

"If one member falsely accuses another of being complicit, the false witness will have his tongue cut out and suffer banishment or death at the Council's finding."

Lindsay stiffened.

John nodded. "Do you wish to recant your statement?"

"I accuse Reynard Bartell of being complicit with the Fallen."

The crowd shuffled and a murmur fluttered through the dim room like a breeze before the storm.

Reynard relaxed his stance and shook his head sadly. "I beg you, your Eminence, have mercy on her. It's the Wyrm. The demon has taken her and causes her to sow discord amongst us."

Rachael stepped into a shaft of sunlight. No one could look at her and believe she was possessed. The sun's rays caught the red in her hair, and for a moment a fiery halo burst over her head.

Murmurs turned to a hum as the Katharoi whispered amongst themselves. Lucian halted at Rachael's side; they kept Lindsay between them.

John's eyes momentarily widened at the sight of Rachael then he drew his mask of indifference over his face again. He acknowledged Lucian's presence before his gaze settled on Lindsay. The girl shivered like a colt but made no move to break eye contact with John. Lucian realized the Seraph had slipped past her frail mental shield and was busy examining her thoughts.

John held out his hand and descended from the dais. "Come here, child."

Lindsay glanced up at Lucian and he nodded, reluctantly letting her go. A piece of his heart went with her. Rachael moved closer to fill the gap where Lindsay had stood.

John drew Lindsay near and smiled down at her. Her expression remained solemn, and Lucian noticed she turned so she could see him.

"What is your name?"

"Lindsay Richardson, sir." Her voice quavered, her confidence gone with the eyes of the congregation on her.

John's features softened with the same look he'd worn when Lucian and Catarina had emerged from the Veil. "Peter Richardson's sister?"

"Yes, sir."

"And who is your Elder? Rachael?"

"Lucian," she whispered.

Reynard left the podium. "Do not be seduced by the child's innocence, your Eminence. Look to the creature she was drawn to—a traitor, a liar. Can she be anything but a mirror of his soul?"

Rachael walked to John and passed him the Psalter. She placed her hand on Lindsay's shoulder, and the girl relaxed. Only Lucian noticed the slight tremor to Rachael's hand. John snatched the book and opened it.

Rachael said, "Only those with the highest integrity have the ability to draw a child through the Crimson Veil. The Veil will open for neither the Fallen nor the complicit. To say this child is corrupt is to say God has failed us. I will speak for her. And for Lucian."

Lindsay's head whipped around until she looked up at Rachael. Rachael didn't acknowledge the girl's stare. Without a word, Lindsay linked her fingers with Rachael's, then turned and glared triumphantly at Reynard.

Lucian's heart skipped an entire beat. *Oh God, what has she done?* By tying her fate to his, she'd shifted the battlefield beneath him. He would have to forsake his passive role or take Rachael down with him. Again.

Reynard left the pulpit, craning his neck to see what Rachael had given John. "Your passions blind you into seeing love where there's only lust, Judge Boucher. You'll let that traitor lead you to ruin once more."

"Like Catarina led you?" Lucian asked.

"You will be silent!" The Inquisitor pointed at Lucian.

"I will not!" Lucian's fury swam upward and choked him. He rapped his cane against the floor and the sound of wood meeting stone jarred his words loose from his mouth. "I've been silent for sixteen years and I'll not be silent another day. Catarina never loved you, Reynard."

The Inquisitor froze.

Every Katharos stilled until not even a robe rustled. John glared at Lucian but made no move to prevent him from speaking.

Lucian gripped his cane. "She used to mock you. She bragged how easily you'd fallen for her whispers of love."

"Shut." Reynard's face blanched white. "Up."

"Cate used you like she used me." *Like she used anyone who loved her.* "She's dead, Reynard." *Dead by my hand.* As much as Lucian wanted to confess his sin before them all, he couldn't make himself say it.

Reynard stiffened and just for an instant, Lucian saw the older man's grief before Reynard extinguished his sorrow. "You've gone mad if you think I care about that renegade."

Yet Lucian knew different. He'd seen Reynard's letters to his twin. "You can repent, Reynard."

The Inquisitor regained control. "I have nothing to repent."

"Is that so?" John asked. He returned his attention to the book. "I have your signature in a pact with Mastema. Right beside Catarina's."

"That is a lie, your Eminence!" The Inquisitor stepped forward. Dubois frowned and tried to see, but Xavier was faster, blocking the Commissioner's line of vision. Several of the seated Katharoi rose and the younger members strained to glimpse the book John held.

"And where was this pact found, Judge Boucher?" Reynard asked.

"Cross Creek."

"Your holding?" Reynard smiled as if he'd proven his point. "Admit it, Boucher, you've been jealous of my advancement from the beginning. This is your effort to destroy me. That could be anyone's signature. And wasn't it convenient the book was at your house."

Rachael smiled back at him. "I never would have thought to look there if I hadn't found this." She produced the sigil she had taken from Caleb's coat and gave it to John.

A few in the crowd jostled forward, but Lucian noticed the congregation had thinned. Many of the complicit members saw the handwriting on the wall and fled. They wouldn't fight; they were still far outnumbered by the faithful. To remain at the Citadel was suicide, so they made their escape while the parishioners remained enthralled by the tableau at the dais.

Lucian held his silence. The corrupted high-ranking members were trapped by their importance. Dubois sidled toward the edge of the pulpit with measured movements to avoid attention. With the appearance of the sigil, Reynard's ability to shift the blame to Rachael died. John held the cloth up for Reynard to see, and the Inquisitor paled.

Rachael said, "It was hidden in Constable Aldridge's coat."

John's lips were tight with rage. "And where is Constable Aldridge?"

"The Rosa took him."

Someone cried out, an inarticulate sound of grief and horror, but in the large room, Lucian couldn't see who it was.

Rachael started to say something else, but John raised his hand. "I've heard enough. Xavier!"

"Yes, your Eminence." The General stepped forward.

John handed him the book. "Arrest these people."

A door slammed from somewhere within the cathedral. Several people broke for the arcades where they could lose themselves in the winding corridors. Xavier shouted for his guards to seal the gates. More Katharoi left their seats to obey his command. Lucian wondered how many would use the opportunity to escape.

"These are lies, your Eminence!" Reynard's voice crawled an octave higher. "Lies designed to disrupt our unity and create another schism."

"Then you have nothing to worry about, Reynard." John turned and nodded to Xavier. "If you are innocent, the truth shall set you free."

Xavier grabbed Reynard and shoved him forward as he shouted orders at his soldiers. The General took Dubois by the arm, handing the struggling Commissioner over to one of his own constables.

Lucian was dimly aware of John ordering the Katharoi to their chambers where they would await word as to their impending arrest or freedom. He declared martial law and promised a directive within the hour to disband the Council until the members could be exonerated or condemned.

Members hurried from the cathedral, whether to burn damning evidence or to speculate on possible signs of corruption, Lucian could care less. He felt Lindsay's confusion and wished either Rachael or John would comfort the girl. She looked to him for guidance, and he motioned for her to be patient.

In the disorder, two girls about Lindsay's age paused for a better look at the new foundling. Lindsay released Rachael's hand to brush her fingers across her stained shirt. She brought the end of her braid to her lips as she studied the other girls and their neat cassocks. John dismissed the girls with a wave, and they joined their brethren in leaving the cathedral.

Tanith remained behind. Lucian realized how much he'd missed her and her dark eyes that glittered with love. She went to Lindsay, and though Lucian couldn't hear what she said, he knew she reassured the girl. Lindsay released her braid and took Tanith's hand.

John gestured to a side arcade, but Tanith ignored him and led Lindsay to Lucian. Tanith stood on her toes and Lucian had to bend down so she could kiss his cheeks. "I'm grateful the Goddess brought you home safe," she whispered in his ear.

He closed his eyes and, unsure of his voice, he said nothing.

Lindsay put her arms around him and whispered, "It's going to be okay."

He wished they could have a last moment alone, but one look at John's frown told Lucian he needed to be careful for Lindsay's sake. "Of course it is. Go with Tanith."

"Will you come soon?"

"Perhaps." Lucian had no idea what John intended. He wouldn't lie to her. "The Seraph will speak to me, and I'll have to do as he says." He tucked an errant strand of her hair behind her ear and tried to smile. "You're a good child, Lindsay Richardson."

Tanith took her hand, yet Lindsay hung back. "We're a team, you know. Nobody can change that. You're my Elder." She held her fist up and he gently bumped his knuckles against hers. "I know what that means now."

He leaned down, kissed her cheeks. "Now go with my blessing." Lucian released her, and she allowed Tanith to lead her out of sight. "Remember me," he whispered as she disappeared into the shadows of the Citadel. Gone, but never gone from him; she remained entrenched in his heart. Lucian kneaded the head of his cane and lowered his head.

John secreted the tin with the sigil beneath his robes and spoke to Rachael. "You've killed my Inquisitor, Rachael Boucher. I need a new one so you're moving back into the Citadel. Get someone to manage your holdings. I need you here."

Rachael bowed her head to him.

Lucian felt the weight of John's gaze settle on his face. He unbuckled Matthew's sword and knelt.

"Is Catarina really dead?" John asked.

"She is, your Eminence."

"May God have mercy on her soul." John crossed himself and shook his head. "Lord knows, we tried to guide her on the right path." He sighed and rubbed his eyes. "Now what do I do with you?"

Lucian offered the blade to John, who took the sword and ran his fingers over the sheath. "How did you come by this?"

Unable to look his Elder in the eye, Lucian spoke to the floor. "Matthew Kellogg gave it to me when he helped me escape Hadra. He said I should bring it you and tell you that in the end, he did what was right."

"Bloody fool got himself killed, didn't he?"

Lucian crossed himself. "He died so I could get out of Hadra. He said he dreamed."

"Best spy I had, Matthew Kellogg. And a good friend." Tears glistened in John's eyes, and he turned his head for a moment. "Damn." John returned his attention to Lucian. "That was a high price for your life."

Lucian studied his hands and didn't dare raise his head.

"What says my new Inquisitor?" John snapped at Rachael.

"*Miserere*," she whispered. *Have mercy.*

Lucian's heart broke. She, who he had hurt the most, wanted mercy for him. He would never know what he'd done to deserve her and Lindsay.

Rachael cleared her throat and began more formally. "*Miserere*, your Eminence, for Matthew dreamed and a vision sent by God cannot be denied. In spite of your better judgment, you sent me into the Wasteland based on a dream, and I returned free of the Wyrm. Know that if God sent Lucian back to us, it must be for a reason. This we take in faith."

"He violated his covenant not to open the Hell Gates." John tapped the hilt of Matthew's sword against the palm of his hand.

"It's not forgotten, but he only violated that covenant to bring a foundling out of Hell. Lindsay has extraordinary talents, and Lucian guided her through her first days in Woerld with great care. He encouraged her to pray and taught her to avoid the complicit by teaching her their signs. He watched over her as a true Elder. I find no complaint with his actions."

"There's my girl," John whispered. Louder, he said, "Get up, Lucian."

Lucian struggled to rise and felt a hand under his arm. Rachael helped him to his feet and didn't move from his side.

John raised his finger, his glare boring into them. "Your trial will be at dawn. Rachael, you'll present your arguments. I will not challenge you." He turned to Lucian. "Based on Matthew's actions and the child you drew through the Veil, I'm willing to revoke your exile."

Lucian leaned heavily on his cane. He needed to sit, not from pain but from relief. Rachael's fingers squeezed his arm, and he drew comfort from her strength.

"Don't go singing hosannas yet, son," John warned. "You'll be on probation for the next five years. You will not step outside these walls without written permission or you will be shot. Your movements will be accounted for and if you give me the slightest reason to doubt your loyalty to the Citadel, I will put the noose around your neck with my own hands. Do you understand, Lucian Negru?"

Lucian whispered, "I do, your Eminence."

John said, "You and Lindsay are going to have to spend some time apart. You have grown so close to that child, I can't tell where her soul begins and yours ends, so I am sending her away with Tanith for a while. When she returns, Rachael will act as Lindsay's guardian in all formal occasions until your probation is over. But God sent that child to you, so you will remain her Elder." John leaned close and whispered to them, "And may she never bring you the grief you two have brought to me."

Lucian opened his mouth, but John silenced him. "Don't say a word." He made the sign of the cross over them. "God forgives you, Lucian. He absolves you through me, but you've got a long way to go before you've earned my trust again." He handed Lucian the sword. "Matthew gave it you. A Katharos's soul remains close to their weapon, so you've got a guardian angel. Take care of his blade and cherish his spirit. He was a good man."

"Thank you." Lucian accepted the weapon.

"Thank God, son." John turned on Rachael. "Since you're so willing to tie your fate to his, you're responsible for him for next five years. Find accommodations for him. You're the Inquisitor, so he'll report to you. Get cleaned up and be in my office by noon. We've got work to do. I'm ordering a Purge."

A Purge dictated no mercy for the condemned. Exile wouldn't be an option; they would be hanged. *He'll take their blood on his hands,* Lucian thought. He locked the heaviness of his guilt for Catarina's murder deep in his heart. Better she die by his hand than be hanged as a traitor. Perhaps, in the end, he'd saved her after all.

John stared at the floor, his face sad. "We've a hard road ahead of us, Rachael."

"I know."

He shook his head and kissed her cheeks. "Don't keep me waiting."

"I won't." Her hand slipped down Lucian's arm as John left them. When he had gone, she moved to one of the pews and sank down to stare at the altar. Lucian sat beside her and put his hand on hers. She didn't pull away from him but remained so still, she could have been made of stone.

"Thank you," he said.

"I only told the truth. This doesn't fix what happened between us, Lucian."

"I know." He could never undo the past. In his youth and arrogance, he'd thought repairing the damage would erase the misdeed. Now he realized it was merely the first step on a long road to healing. "I wanted to make you well, take your pain. I loved you then." He whispered, "I love you now."

"Love doesn't cure everything." She sighed and rubbed the patch over her missing eye. "We can't go back to the way we were before all this happened."

"We could go forward."

"Forward?" She looked at him and he seized the opportunity.

"From here. We can't pretend nothing ever happened, but we can acknowledge the past. Move beyond it. Give me a chance, Rachael."

"A chance for what?"

"To earn your love again."

She turned her head, showing him only the blind patch covering her eye. The silence lengthened between them. He held his breath and tried to still his pulse.

"I can't promise you anything," she whispered.

He cupped her chin and turned her face to him; he was surprised to see tears glittering on her lashes. She was beautiful. "No promises," he said. "No more promises. All I ask is for an opportunity."

"Nothing more." Her voice carried a hint of warning, and he couldn't help but smile. She searched his heart and judged his words. Time slowed until she eventually said, "All right. We'll see. We'll see how it goes. A day at a time."

He understood this was as close to a commitment as she could come. He had no right to ask for more. "Today then." He kissed her hand and didn't press her. They sat together and watched dust motes dance in the sunlight, and Lucian recalled a star falling across the Wasteland's sky.

And a wish.

Soft as a kiss.

Lucian smiled.

He had an opportunity.

Nothing more.

But for now, that was enough.

†

ACKNOWLEDGEMENTS

First, foremost, and always to my husband Dick who spent many an evening consoling me through this project, because he believed in me. He forever has my heart. To my beautiful daughter, Rhiannon Reeder, my co-conspirator and constant companion throughout all the plot twists and character developments. We spent many an evening hashing out *Miserere*'s details after our long days at work. She is an inspiration to me.

I want to thank my vibrant agent Weronika Janczuk for her enthusiasm and for loving not just *Miserere* but all my writing. She challenged me to make *Miserere* better and I believe it was through her steady guidance that we brought Lucian's story to publication. She marvels me with her energy and beauty. I love working with her.

To Jeremy Lassen for taking a chance on *Miserere* and giving me excellent editorial advice to make *Miserere* the novel it is today. And a big thanks to Ross Lockhart who suffered through numerous emails and answered each patiently while editing *Miserere*.

My constant (and I do mean constant) readers: Kelly Kennedy Bryson, Liz Colter, Peter Cooper, J. R. Hochman, Valerie Jones, and Terri Trimble. All of you worked with me through multiple drafts of chapters and scenes until I got it right. You are all amazing writers in your own rights and I love and look forward to celebrating your successes with you. Thank you.

To Mary Gomez, my final reader: I knew the manuscript was ready when it received the BookLove seal of approval. To Kim Shireman for being there when I needed sage advice and clear sight; you have always been a power of example to me. To Sylvia Thagard for a thousand good mornings and the wisdom you bring to my life.

Thanks to David Felker for pointing me to some wonderful resources on Eastern Orthodox Christianity and exorcism. His advice and reading list helped me immensely.

For Kathryn Magendie: you and your novels will always have a special place in my heart. Thank you for cheering me on and giving me the benefit of your experience through the publication process but mostly for just being yourself. Kathryn introduced me to Lisa Mannetti, a wonderful author who has, in turn, introduced me to so many great horror writers and their works. Thank you, Lisa, for giving me so much wonderful advice and taking such time with me. And to Alex Bledsoe for his Eddie LaCrosse series, which resurrected my love of fantasy. He proved to me that you can do something different and do it successfully.

My most special thanks goes to the original God's Squad: a group of writers represented by James Allen of the Virginia Kidd Literary Agency back in the 1980s: Lisa W. Cantrell, Theresa Gladden, and M. Scott Gilliam. You ladies will always and forever be a part of my personal story, and I will never forget the laughter we shared. And yes, I still have that damn t-shirt.

Most of all, I would like to thank you, the people who read *Miserere*. Without you, the reader, none of this would be possible.

Night Shade Books Is an Independent Publisher of Quality Science-Fiction, Fantasy and Horror

www.nightshadebooks.com

$14.99

ISBN 978-1-59780-199-7

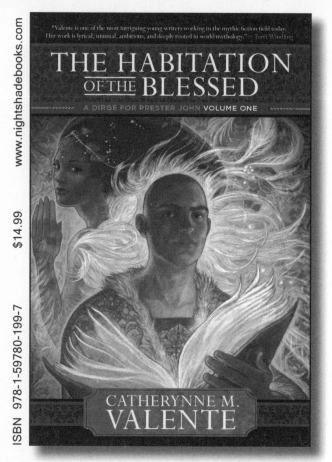

This is the story of a place that never was: the kingdom of Prester John, the utopia described by an anonymous, twelfth-century document which captured the imagination of the medieval world and drove hundreds of lost souls to seek out its secrets, inspiring explorers, missionaries, and kings for centuries. But what if it were all true? What if there was such a place, and a poor, broken priest once stumbled past its borders, discovering, not a Christian paradise, but a country where everything is possible, immortality is easily had, and the Western world is nothing but a dim and distant dream?

Brother Hiob of Luzerne, on missionary work in the Himalayan wilderness on the eve of the eighteenth century, discovers a village guarding a miraculous tree whose branches sprout books instead of fruit. These strange books chronicle the history of the kingdom of Prester John, and Hiob becomes obsessed with the tales they tell. The Habitation of the Blessed recounts the fragmented narratives found within these living volumes, revealing the life of a priest named John, and his rise to power in this country of impossible richness. John's tale weaves together with the confessions of his wife Hagia, a blemmye--a headless creature who carried her face on her chest--as well as the tender, jeweled nursery stories of Imtithal, nanny to the royal family. Hugo and World Fantasy award nominee Catherynne M. Valente reimagines the legends of Prester John in this stunning tour de force.

Night Shade Books Is an Independent Publisher of Quality Science-Fiction, Fantasy and Horror

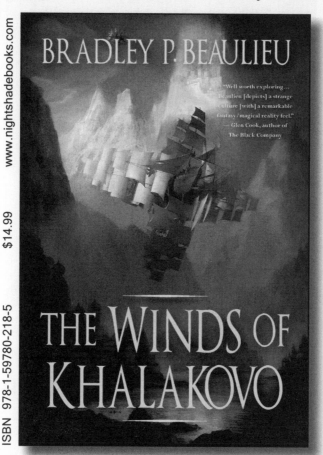

BRADLEY P. BEAULIEU

"Well worth exploring...
Beaulieu [depicts] a strange
culture [with] a remarkable
fantasy/magical reality feel."
—Glen Cook, author of
The Black Company

THE WINDS OF KHALAKOVO

Among inhospitable and unforgiving seas stands Khalakovo, a mountainous archipelago of seven islands, its prominent eyrie stretching a thousand feet into the sky. Serviced by windships bearing goods and dignitaries, Khalakovo's eyrie stands at the crossroads of world trade. But all is not well in Khalakovo. Conflict has erupted between the ruling Landed, the indigenous Aramahn, and the fanatical Maharraht, and a wasting disease has grown rampant over the past decade. Now, Khalakovo is to play host to the Nine Dukes, a meeting which will weigh heavily upon Khalakovo's future.

When an elemental spirit attacks an incoming windship, murdering the Grand Duke and his retinue, Prince Nikandr, heir to the scepter of Khalakovo, is tasked with finding the child prodigy believed to be behind the summoning. However, Nikandr discovers that the boy is an autistic savant who may hold the key to lifting the blight that has been sweeping the islands. Can the Dukes, thirsty for revenge, be held at bay? Can Khalakovo be saved? The elusive answer drifts upon the Winds of Khalakovo...

ABOUT THE AUTHOR

Raised in a small town, Teresa Frohock learned to escape to other worlds through the fiction collection of her local library. She eventually moved away from Reidsville and lived in Virginia and South Carolina before returning to North Carolina, where she currently resides with her husband and daughter.

Teresa has long been accused of telling stories, which is a southern colloquialism for lying. *Miserere: An Autumn Tale* is her debut novel.